Anthony Conway has been a Gurkha officer and has travelled extensively in the east. He has been a bestselling thriller writer under a pseudonym. *The Viceroy's Captain* is his first novel featuring Captain John Caspasian.

THE GENERAL'S ENVOY

Seconded to China by a vengeful Indian Army high command, Captain John Caspasian finds Shanghai a cesspit of despair and corruption. He is glad to escape on a solo mission to contact a general whom the British see as a bulwark against the revolutionary leader Chiang Kai-shek. Once he has left the International Settlement for a gunboat on the Yangtze, though, Caspasian smells danger. The supposedly friendly General Mok turns out to be a bloodthirsty sadist. And Caspasian has made two implacable enemies. One is a Chinese criminal. The other is a former British officer . . .

ANTHONY CONWAY

THE GENERAL'S ENVOY

Complete and Unabridged

ULVERSCROFT
Leicester

First published in Great Britain in 2001 by
Hodder and Stoughton
London

First Large Print Edition
published 2004
by arrangement with
Hodder and Stoughton
a division of Hodder Headline

The moral right of the author has been asserted

British Library CIP Data

Conway, Anthony
    The General's envoy.—Large print ed.—
Ulverscroft large print series: adventure & suspense
1. China—History—Warlord period, *1916 – 1928*
—Fiction 2. Adventure stories
3. Large type books
I. Title
823.9'14 [F]

ISBN 1–84395–249–1

Published by
F. A. Thorpe (Publishing)
Anstey, Leicestershire

Set by Words & Graphics Ltd.
Anstey, Leicestershire
Printed and bound in Great Britain by
T. J. International Ltd., Padstow, Cornwall

This book is printed on acid-free paper

To the memory of
Sister Frances Clare
1888 – 1976

Kindness exists outside of Time

Prologue

Dawn was the time for stand-to. Every soldier knew that. Dawn and dusk, two prime moments of vulnerability. So why had the officers let the men sleep on? Li knew the answer. They were useless. Useless and drunk. As he peered into the thinning darkness, every sense taut, he cursed the day his unit had switched sides. He had known it was a mistake for the Captain to entrust the company to men such as these, but as a simple foot soldier Li was not expected to have an opinion. He had to obey orders. Either that, or desert and become a bandit, joining one of the numerous gangs of opium-addicted thugs that aimlessly wandered the shattered landscape of China's fragmented provinces.

The officers were useless because their leader was useless. The one begot the other as surely as dog spawned dog. It was true that Colonel Lam had done well to establish control over such a large area, but Li knew that he had only succeeded because such opponents as had dared to face him had been even more incompetent than Lam himself.

1

Now Li and the rest of his sleeping comrades were about to pay for Lam's unprofessionalism. The Dragon was coming.

The moment he had heard it, Li had woken the youth sleeping curled in a ball at his side. The two of them had been on sentry duty all night. No reliefs had been arranged. They had simply been told to watch the southern approach to the town where the railway snaked out of the hills. Left to their own devices, Li had sorted out a rota of their own whereby they each stood guard for two hours and then slept for two, turn and turn about. Any more than two hours awake would risk fatigue and the chance of dozing off. Any less than two asleep, and the sleep would not be worth having.

The youth had stared into the darkness, his eyes instantly wide with terror as Li told him to run for help. The sound had come twice, each time the same, a distant subterranean growl, followed by the sigh of the waking beast. Stumbling towards the town, the youth had almost tripped over his loose puttees, but the thought of the Dragon was enough to spur him on his way. They had all heard the rumours. No one had supposed it to be this far north, yet here it was, come to sate its appetite for human flesh and quench its thirst for blood.

Left alone, Li tightened his grip on his rifle. With only five rounds in the magazine and his ammunition pouches empty, save for some corn and steamed bread, he felt the hopelessness of his position like a lead weight in the gut.

The sound came again, closer this time. The Dragon was making its way through the valleys, dragging its scaly belly ever closer to the scent of people. For a moment Li considered running for his life, tossing aside his rifle and simply bolting into the weed-choked fields. With chill understanding he realised that flight was impossible. He had seen what had been done to the six deserters who had been caught the previous week. Two of them had been beheaded and two had been beaten to death with staves, pummelled until their flesh had swollen and split like over-ripe melons. The last two had been identified as the instigators of the flight. They had been wrapped and bound in hessian sacking and then burned alive in the town square in front of the assembled soldiers and the few starving civilians who had failed to get out of town before it had been captured the week before by Colonel Lam on his self-imposed mission of expansion.

Li glanced over his shoulder to see if help was yet on the way. Behind him the silhouette of the town was sharpening into focus. A dog ambled out of the shadows, arched its back like a quivering hairpin and defecated. Relieved, it trotted away jauntily, sneezing. Two figures came round the side of a house, one, the youth, jogging towards Li, the other, the officer of the watch, dragging his feet. He ran one hand tiredly through his hair and Li could imagine the tirade and the beating he would get if he was wrong about the Dragon.

He was not. The next moment night ended. Dawn came, bringing death with it. A deafening roar and a tongue of flame leaped through the sky and engulfed the two approaching figures. They tottered and shrieked, hands flapping uselessly at their burning clothes. Li threw himself flat on the ground. Terrified, he peered round the edge of the sandbag emplacement where he had spent the night, and saw the Dragon heading straight for him. Swathed in the steam emanating from its lungs, it lurched out of the gloom, spitting fire. Li's rifle lay forgotten at his side as he huddled behind his precarious shelter and watched the monster swell in size.

Its giant head turned this way and that, seeking out fresh targets. Awakened by the noise, soldiers tumbled out into the streets. Most were still drunk from the night before.

A hidden wine cellar had been discovered in one of the houses and the officers had led the way into oblivion. Li knew that they were now about to pay for it with their lives.

As each group of men came into view, fierce jets of flame shot out of the Dragon's mouth. Li scrabbled tighter against the sandbag wall, wriggling in an effort to keep himself hidden from the monster that was rolling steadily into the very heart of the town. It gave one ear-splitting blast and then, from the full length of its dull green and black flanks, a hail of lead erupted as more than a dozen Vickers machine-guns opened fire from their mounts inside the Iron Dragon, the armoured train of General Mok.

★ ★ ★

Struggling into his uniform in his sleeping quarters, Colonel Lam shook himself free from the woman who clung to him. He hunted for his pistol, shouting for his aide as he did so. There was no one there. The man had fled. Out in the street Colonel Lam was met by a scene of complete panic. Soldiers in various states of undress ran in every direction. Here and there sergeants attempted to rally the men to form a defence. The officers were nowhere to be seen.

Colonel Lam gazed up in horror as a jet of flame arched across the sky and torched his one and only machine-gun post on top of the town's old prison tower. The air was filled with the nauseating stench of the flame-thrower's fuel, powered by compressed nitrogen, and of the charred flesh of the Colonel's men. The gun's ignited ammunition began to cook off, exploding from the flaming tower like mad firecrackers on a lunar new year's eve.

Incensed, the Colonel screamed to rally his fleeing men. Some of them grouped around him, rifles trembling in their hands. Across the square, the Iron Dragon pulled slowly into view, squealing along the rusty rails. Its vast bulk sat squat and ugly in the early morning light, the machine-guns still maniacally chattering at everything in sight. The bullets chewed their way through plaster and masonry as effortlessly as through flesh and bone. From the top of the armoured train, behind the turret housing the flamethrower, another iron cupola shielded the barrel of a French 75mm field gun. Turning this way and that, it fired its shells randomly throughout the town, the high explosive rounds shattering into steel splinters that wrought further deadly mayhem in the panic-stricken ranks of the Colonel's men.

Fleeing from the northern edge of the town, one terrified party broke from the outskirts to find themselves in a field of rotting maize. Unharvested for three years, the crop was choked with weeds and the remnants of decayed corn from the previous seasons. Dropping their cumbersome rifles, they stripped off their webbing to enable them to run even faster from the fight. No sooner had they done so than they heard the shrill sound of bugles and looked up in bewildered consternation to find themselves facing rank upon rank of charging cavalry. Outflanked, they were at the mercy of the elite arm of General Mok's forces. The strengthening sunlight glinted on the blades of their raised sabres as they streaked into the field. Before them, the hapless infantry of Colonel Lam could only cower and await their end. Some were cut down, others were trampled by the hooves of the cavalry's mounts. Most were rounded up and taken prisoner to face whatever retribution the General wished to visit upon them.

When the armoured train was in the very heart of the town, the machine-guns fell silent. There was an unearthly pause during which the survivors amongst the defending garrison wondered whether they might be spared after all. Then, with a sickening crash, the iron sides of the train's troop-carrying trucks slammed down, disgorging the General's infantry who poured into the attack. Following on the shock effect of the Dragon's initial assault there was little for them to do except mop up what few pockets of resistance remained. They worked their way methodically through the town, searching the houses, delving into cellars, seeking out every last survivor of Colonel Lam's unfortunate command. Standing close beside the Dragon, one of the general's staff officers spoke quietly into a field telephone handset, sending his reports into the bowels of the iron beast and receiving his instructions from its command centre.

It was a full two hours before the staff officer judged the situation sufficiently secure to report the town as captured. By then, the Colonel's surviving men had been assembled at the side of the tracks. Colonel Lam's officers had been discovered hiding in a cellar. Dragged protesting into daylight, they now stood in a frightened huddle. The Colonel himself was held slightly apart, his arms gripped tightly by two members of General Mok's personal bodyguard, tall swarthy northerners.

The staff officer spoke rapidly into his handset, listened intently to the reply, smiled ruefully, and then barked out instructions to his men. Colonel Lam and his officers were roughly manhandled to the front of the train, beaten to the ground and then forced to lie down on the rail tracks. Dazed and terrified, none of them resisted as they were fastened with ropes to the iron rails, knees protruding over one rail, necks aligned on the other. Some of them shouted, pleading to be heard, offering their services to General Mok. The staff officer chuckled in contempt, checking the bonds to ensure that none of them could escape.

When the last one had been fastened in place, the mighty engine bellowed and, with a squeal of iron, lurched slowly forward. As one, the Colonel's officers screamed, each scream rising to frenzied pitch as the foremost wheels of the train reached and then severed neck after neck. Bodies writhed in a futile effort to escape, but one by one the officers were decapitated. To one side of the rails a line of severed legs twitched, while on the opposite side, a row of heads stared blankly up at the passing locomotive. Last of all was Colonel Lam himself. Deliberately placed at the end of the row, he had been forced to bear witness to the summary execution of his entire officer corps. By the time the blood-soaked wheels reached him, he was mad with fear. Without faltering, the train rolled across his shuddering frame, nipping his head from his shoulders as effortlessly as a malevolent boy pinching the head from a fly.

Its task complete, the train halted in a cloud of steam. The Colonel's captive soldiers were arrayed in a long line down the length of the train, several ranks deep. Facing them were the silent black muzzles of the Vickers machine-guns. At the far end of the line near the rear of the mighty armoured train, stood Li. He had watched the whole spectacle in mute wonder, beyond horror, beyond fear. For several minutes there was a lull. Some of the captives tried to sit down, only to be prodded to their feet with bayonets. It seemed to Li that the General's men were preparing for some new display of savagery and Li secretly braced himself to run. A glance to his side however dissuaded him. The General's soldiers had closed to block off every avenue of escape. Like it or not, he was going to be forced to accept whatever fate General Mok had in store for them. Usually in a situation like this, the defeated foe would be invited to join their conqueror. With their officers slaughtered, the rank and file would be considered free to join whichever side they chose. Somehow Li felt in his bones that this was to be different, and again he cursed the day he had fallen in with Colonel Lam's incompetent army.

Further down the train, Li could see the staff officer receiving fresh instructions from the handset held clasped to his ear. Whoever was issuing them from inside the train was watching them at that very moment. Li studied the train carefully. Machine-guns and rifles protruded from a myriad of slits in the iron skin of the awesome monster. From the turrets on top, flamethrowers and field guns were capable of sweeping every conceivable arc of fire. The troop-carrying carriages, emptied of their infantry, occupied the middle section of the train, but even these were covered with armour plating. In addition there appeared to be dining carriages, magazine carriages and, in the very centre, sandwiched between two powerful steam engines, a command carriage.

Li sighed miserably. If only he had had the good fortune to serve such a commander as this. Who could say where he might have ended up? Certainly not like this, standing forlornly at the side of the railway, awaiting his captor's pleasure.

The next second, he knew. From the full length of the train, at a given signal, the machine-guns opened fire. In a torrent of lead, his comrades were mown down. Li braced himself for the inevitable. At any moment now he knew that he would be killed. With a strange detachment he found himself wondering what it would feel like. Would it be a hammer blow? Or perhaps like the red hot blade of a knife? Would he know what was happening to him, or would it be a sudden and painless introduction to oblivion and whatever might await him beyond?

All of a sudden the guns fell silent. Li stood, eyes clenched shut, knees slightly bent, every muscle taut in readiness for pain. None came. Uncertainly he opened his eyes. It was full daylight now. The long flank of the iron-clad train was wreathed in gunsmoke. To Li's right, it seemed that acres of ground were littered with the dead bodies of his comrades. Against all logic, he was frightened now more than ever before. He looked all around him. Not a living soul stood to keep him company. He was completely alone. A single being in a sea of corpses.

As the deafening sound of the machine-guns cleared from his ringing ears he was suddenly aware of another sound. Laughter. Beyond the wreathes of gunsmoke the General's men swam into view. All of them were watching him from the sidelines and laughing uncontrollably. Many pointed at him. Some of them slapped their sides, helpless in their enjoyment of the spectacle.

Li felt a warmth between his thighs and looked down to see that his crotch was soaked with urine. He felt the tears welling in his eyes. His cheeks bulged and he could feel his gorge rising, though whether to weep or to vomit he could not tell. With every remaining fragment of his will he fought against both.

From the turret immediately above the staff officer with the telephone handset, there was a squeal of rusty hinges and a hatch flipped open heavily, slamming down on to the iron roof of the train. To Li's amazement, a westerner emerged. A foreigner. He pushed a pair of goggles back on his head and looked around at the handiwork, nodding with professional appreciation. His eyes swept the thick ranks of the dead and finally alighted upon Li. He smiled, not unkindly, and spoke in a tongue that Li could not understand, although it was ugly beyond imagining.

From the ground beneath the foreigner, the staff officer listened carefully and took a step forward before translating so that Li might understand. He spoke deliberately, stressing each syllable as if he wanted to ensure that Li might remember everything that his European officer had said.

'You have been chosen to live,' he said. 'You are to go north and tell everyone you meet that the Iron Dragon of General Mok, whom I serve, is coming. Remember what you have seen here today and tell people of it.'

There was a pause while the white man took a sip from a flask. When he had quenched his thirst, he continued, his speech as ugly as before.

'Tell them,' the staff officer translated, 'that it is pointless to oppose us. Tell them that they may join us, but that if they fight against us, they will meet the same fate as your comrades here today. Tell them that I, General Mok's military advisor, guarantee this. I, Captain Smith, guarantee this.'

1

In the bar of the Cathay Hotel, Captain John Caspasian relaxed in an armchair with a copy of the *North China Daily News* and a bottle of Chefoo beer. He had spent the afternoon on consulate business in Avenue Joffre in Shanghai's French Concession but had finished up walking along the Bund, watching the steamers and barges, sampans, junks and gunboats meandering this way and that on the broad muddy green waters of the Whangpoo river. Deciding it was too early for dinner but late enough for a cold beer, he had made his way to the hotel. He had considered dropping into the Shanghai Club with its bar, supposedly the longest in the world, but the thought of encountering its mostly British members steered him away from its imposing canopied entrance. At this hour it would have been full of bankers, traders and other men of commerce, stopping on their way home from work to pick up the latest pieces of social tittle-tattle for which their wives, idly waiting in their mock-Tudor mansions elsewhere in the International Settlement, would be voraciously hungry.

Caspasian had little time for any of them. The spoilt young bloods of the various banking corporations with their overly loud braying voices and their equally vapid wives, Caspasian had seen more than enough of their kind. This evening he intended to spend with interesting company, someone who could talk about something besides the latest touring show, the latest fashion, the latest merger. He was due to meet Jack Swinton, correspondent for the San Francisco-based *Pacific Chronicle*.

As usual Jack was late. Caspasian glanced at his watch and smiled to himself. Tall and casually athletic, with slate-blue eyes, he had an unruly shock of sandy-coloured hair which was out of keeping with his profession as a soldier. His bearing was military, but buccaneer rather than drill sergeant. Less parade ground than no-man's-land.

An infantry officer for more than a dozen years, he missed his regimental home in the Indian Army, even though he had always been an uncomfortable fit in the officers' mess. Unlike their counterparts in the regiments of the British Army, officers of an Indian Army regiment were relatively few in number, the posts that in a British regiment would be filled by keen young subalterns fresh from the seed bed of an English public school and

Sandhurst being ably occupied instead by native officers holding a Viceroy's commission as opposed to the King's commission of Caspasian and his comrades.

Of all the diverse regiments of the Indian Army, Caspasian considered his own, the Gurkhas, to be the finest. And when he thought about it, which was often, he realised that it was the comradeship of the soldiers themselves that he missed rather than the life of the mess which he found strained and artificial. Of course he knew that his background had much to do with it. Having been born and brought up in Asia, his experience of England had only begun when he had arrived there as a boy on the brink of adolescence, sent by his grandfather to endure the unpredictable fortunes of a boarding school. In themselves, his eastern birth and upbringing would not have marked him out as unusual. Boarding schools were full of youngsters sent home for education by parents who were serving the Empire overseas in one guise or another. Caspasian's origins, on the other hand, were rooted well outside the Empire, and not simply in terms of geography. His upbringing had taken place in his grandfather's household in the port city of Yokohama, and while still a youngster he had travelled the seas and ports of the Far

East in the vessels served by his grandfather's ships' chandlery company. His mother had lamented on more than one occasion that the young John Caspasian was in danger of turning into a pirate. The boy had laughed, and borne the label away with him with pride. Only later, when in contact with his insensitive peers at school on the other side of the world in a very foreign and unfamiliar England, had it turned to stigma.

He folded his paper and tossed it on to the low table beside him, stretching out his long legs and flicking a thread from his stone-coloured suit. He picked up his beer and ran a finger down the sides of the glass, watching the condensation tumble in slender rivulets to the base, then fall in heavy drops on to the well-worn carpet. He glanced down, studying the pattern, faded from years of wear. Ornate Chinese dragons wreathed about each other, tongues of fire issuing from their snarling mouths, the drops of condensation seeming as if they were trying to quench them.

Out of nowhere, the words of an old Chinese poem came to him.

At departure they have no words for
   each other;
They only stand with backs to the light
   deep in thought;

She does not raise her head for a long
  time,
But her silk blouse is wet with tears.

Caspasian frowned, suddenly sombre.
Remembering. With an effort of will he
quickly tried to think of something else. He
tried to recall the name of the poet but it
evaded him. Irritated, the more he worried at
it, the further it scurried out of reach. He
knew it was eighteenth-century, but beyond
that his memory failed him. He shook his
head crossly and stared hard at the carpet as
if he thought he might spy the name written
in the worn threads. Intellect, cool and
rational, was once again taking charge, like a
hero in a disaster. Standing fast in the rout.
Wounded but reimposing order upon chaos.
Emotion was back in its box. But as
Caspasian well knew, it was a magician's
box, and the lock guarded only one of many
exits.

'John! God, my man, forgive me.'

Caspasian looked round, startled out of his
reverie. A smile of genuine warmth softened
his irritation. A large paw slapped down on
his shoulder as the other sought out his hand
and shook it exaggeratedly.

'What time did we say?' Jack Swinton
peered earnestly into his friend's face.

Caspasian laughed. 'Forget it. You're here.'

'I know, but I just hate being late for an appointment.'

'Sure you do.' Caspasian watched as Swinton pulled up an armchair and collapsed into it. For a second the big American froze before an immense sigh broke over him like a wave. 'God, what a day!'

Anticipating a tale, Caspasian nodded at the hovering waiter, indicating a beer for the new arrival and a replacement for his own empty bottle. The words of the Chinese poem lingered in the forefront of his mind, but resolutely withdrew like actors at the conclusion of their scene, making way for others.

Swinton rolled his eyes dramatically. 'Those goddamned union leaders. Man, they can talk! On and on and on.' His beer arrived and Swinton paused as the waiter poured it into the chilled glass, taking longer than was really necessary in the hope of picking up some gossip. Swinton knew better, keeping his peace until the man had withdrawn with a barely suppressed scowl.

Swinton picked up his beer, studied the golden liquid thirstily, and clinked glasses with Caspasian. 'Down the hatch, old bean,' he said in a mock English accent.

Caspasian smiled. 'King and Country.' He

knew the routine. With Jack it was always the same. Somehow it never bothered him though.

They drank in silence, Caspasian patiently waiting for his friend to continue. Instead Swinton sat back and looked around the room contentedly, sensing his companion's hunger for information. At last his eyes settled on Caspasian and he grinned innocently.

'What?' he said.

Caspasian smiled, enjoying the game. 'You were talking about the meeting you attended.'

'Meeting?'

'The unions,' Caspasian prompted tiredly.

Swinton widened his eyes. 'Oh, the meeting.' He relented. 'You know the trouble with you, John? You're in the wrong business. What's a guy like you doing pushing a pen at the British Consulate, for God's sake? With your brain you could have been one hell of a reporter.'

Now it was Caspasian's turn to stare wide-eyed. 'And that's a compliment?'

Swinton shrugged. 'Best I can do.' His expression suddenly became serious. He leaned forward, elbows on knees, rotating his glass in his hands. 'They're up to something.'

'The unions?' Caspasian asked. 'They always are. Intrigue's the other name for this city.'

'Not just the unions. Chiang's Commie allies too.'

Caspasian nodded thoughtfully. 'Are you so sure Chiang Kai-shek's a Communist?'

Swinton grinned. 'No, and neither are you. That's just bullshit, despite what everyone here says. I don't care if he is being bank-rolled by Moscow, he's no more Communist than you are.' He eyed Caspasian carefully. 'You're never going to tell me what you really do at the consulate, are you?'

'A pen-pusher. You said so yourself.'

Swinton smiled sadly. 'Yeah, OK.' He thrust himself back in his chair. 'I get the message. Back off, Swinton.'

Caspasian leaned forward and topped up Swinton's glass. 'Come on, Jack. You know how it is.'

'Yeah, I do.' He took a sip of his beer. 'OK, this is how I see it. Chiang Kai-shek's Northern Expedition out of Canton has been held up along the line of the Yangtze river. He wants to move on Shanghai but the coalition of warlords is too strong for him. What he needs is a Trojan Horse.'

'How do you mean?'

'A Trojan Horse. A rising from within. He

needs men inside the city to open the gates to him.'

'And you think that's what the unions are up to?'

'I know they are. I've never been more sure of anything in my life. Call it a reporter's intuition if you like.'

Caspasian thought about it. It made sense. Since arriving in Shanghai the previous year on posting away from his regiment as a Military Intelligence Officer assigned to His Britannic Majesty's Chinese Consular Service, he had learned a great deal about General Chiang Kai-shek and his Kuomintang party. Some in the service were calling Chiang the man of tomorrow, the future ruler of China, if he could only unite it and end the disastrous fragmentation that had followed the end of the last imperial dynasty. Others dismissed him as a dangerous Communist, a threat to western business interests. After all, what else could he be with Bolsheviks as his paymaster?

Then, as anticipated, shortly after Caspasian had taken up his post in mid-1926, it was announced that the general's long awaited Northern Expedition had begun. With the aim of ridding China once and for all of the warlords who had seized power after the fall of the Manchus, ruling their fiefdoms with complete freedom, Chiang had initially made good progress. However, the further he moved from his stronghold in the southern city of Canton, the more extended his lines of communication became. Furthermore, recognising the threat to their very existence, most of the northern warlords had drawn together to form a ramshackle coalition, fighting to preserve the independence of their provinces. But not all. Some had allied themselves to Chiang, seduced by his promises of continued autonomy. Others, more remote from the areas affected by the fighting, remained aloof from the shifting pattern of alliance and betrayal, continuing to expand their own areas of influence, warring with each other with little thought for the future and no concern for the people over whom they exercised their command.

'Sun Chuanfang's hardly going to sit back and let them get on with it,' Caspasian offered.

'The guy's a jackass,' Swinton said dismissively of the warlord whose area included the city of Shanghai. 'Like every other goddamned warlord. Like the rest of his kind he hasn't got the vision. Chiang has. In any case, Sun's too busy right now somewhere up the Yangtze, locking horns with Chiang's KMT and his so-called

National Revolutionary Army.'

Caspasian had heard from other sources of the union's work behind the scenes, and of the Communists' steady expansion of their organisation. The party had only been formed some five years ago but it was already insinuating itself into every aspect of working life in the city.

'Any idea when such a rising might take place?' Caspasian asked. His interest in the answer was genuine, so he was all the more surprised to find his inner struggle continuing for the identity of the poet whose lines had sprung unbidden to shatter his previous calm. It was worrying at him, dog at bone. That, and the conjured image of a love spurned. A love rejected. Regardless of the justification, be it vanity, duty, whatever. He knew from experience that a love avoided would always be a wound uncauterised, waiting to reopen.

'Not until Chiang's a lot closer, I'd say. If they stage it too soon, Sun's garrison will wipe them out. The troops have all the heavy weapons.' Swinton shook his head doubtfully. 'No, timing will be vital. Once Chiang's no more than a day's march away. I reckon that's when the Communists and the workers will rise.' He looked at Caspasian. 'Are you listening to me? You guys had better keep your heads down when it blows.'

'Oh, the westerners will be all right,' Caspasian said quickly. 'Even Chiang wouldn't dare enter the International Settlement or the French Concession. They'll shelter under the barrels of the gunboats as they always have done.'

Swinton smiled ruefully. 'They?' he jibed. 'Don't you count yourself as one of them?'

Caspasian felt his cheeks redden. He shrugged uneasily. 'Sure I do,' he answered, resenting being caught off guard, and cursing his preoccupation with a stupid poem, of all things.

Enjoying the game, Swinton persisted. 'You were born into the wrong race, John. You should have been an American. We're all hybrids. It's our national characteristic.'

'Dear me,' Caspasian said, seeking to cut the line the conversation had taken. 'Wrong job, wrong country. It seems I'm really up the creek.'

Swinton reached out and patted him on the arm. 'Just kidding.' He suddenly looked at his watch. 'Look, why don't we go and eat? I don't know about you but I'm starving. We can continue this over dinner.'

'All right,' Caspasian said quickly. 'Any preferences?'

'Yeah, as a matter of fact I do. I feel like some music. How's about the Ambassador?'

He grinned. 'Prettiest dance hostesses in all Shanghai.'

Caspasian felt his stomach lurch. 'Too formal. I'm not really dressed for a full cabaret.' The last thing he felt like right now was an evening of noise and excitement. Above all else he wanted to be quiet. Peaceful. He realised that with Jack there was little chance of achieving that.

'Oh,' Swinton said, disappointed. 'I suppose it would never occur to you to go home, climb into your tuxedo and meet me there?'

'It's too bad Del Monte's been taken over by the British Army.'

Swinton shook his head in disgust. 'What's it now? A convalescent home, for God's sake. All those gorgeous White Russian hostesses put out to graze.'

'Either that or earn their living down the alleys across Soochow Creek,' Caspasian said, his sympathy real.

'God help them then. What a waste.'

'What about the Regent, off Nanking Road?' Caspasian suggested eagerly, fixing on a compromise likely to be acceptable to both parties.

Swinton screwed up his face. 'Gee, you really are an outcast, aren't you? You'll be suggesting Blood Alley next, and a full-scale punch-up with the fleet!' He sighed. 'OK.

The Regent it is.' Then, brightening, 'I hear they've got a new bandmaster. Some guy from Chicago.'

Caspasian drained his glass. 'There you are, you see. I'm not quite such a no-hoper after all.'

'The jury's still out on that one.'

They left the hotel and hailed a taxi. The streets were coming alive with the usual evening traffic, cars and carriages of all shapes and sizes vying with rickshaws and trams. Across the Bund, Caspasian could see a string of barges moving laboriously up the Whangpoo river heading for Pootung, the area of reclaimed marsh land opposite the city where a number of factories had sprouted. Standing grimly to one side, a gunboat at anchor was despatching its motor launch laden with sailors out to enjoy a run ashore. Swinton's caution was justified. Blood Alley would be best avoided this evening.

It was a short journey to the Regent. The two men were shown to a table that gave a good view of the band, while being sufficiently sheltered to allow conversation to take place. They ordered quickly, after only a cursory study of the menu, and throughout the ensuing meal Caspasian learned all he could from his companion about the day he had spent attending a union rally and, afterwards, interviewing the speakers who had been only too happy to share their zeal with a member of the press corps. While masking whatever plans they might be hatching, they revelled in the thought that their cause might be broadcast to the world at large and Swinton had confessed to Caspasian that he could not help feeling a certain sympathy with their cause.

'After all,' he said towards the end of the meal, 'we Americans have been a subject people ourselves.'

Caspasian caught the amused glint in his eye and smiled. 'Sure. The poor oppressed Yankee. You haven't done too badly out of it.'

'No, not since we threw you Brits out.' He caught himself and grinned mischievously. 'Oh I'm sorry. You're only part Brit, aren't you? What's the rest? I mean, what kind of a name is Caspasian, for God's sake? I bet you're another of those White Russians.'

Caspasian smiled uncomfortably. 'I was born in Yokohama as you well know, Jack.'

Swinton grimaced theatrically. 'Gee, a goodamned Jap!'

'Hardly,' Caspasian said softly.

'What then? The steppes of central Asia, I suppose? I can just see you at the head of a mounted horde. A silver torque around your neck, goatskin jacket and wild hair.' Swinton chuckled and shook his head. But even through the fug of beer numbing his senses, he detected his friend's sudden unease and reined himself in. Caspasian was not a man he wanted to anger. Though the two of them had never spoken of it, Swinton had heard from others the rumours surrounding Caspasian's birth. That his father had been British and titled, and that his mother had been beautiful and vivacious. That the two had encountered one another and had enjoyed a brief but passionate relationship. That they had never married and that Sir David Edward had returned to his family and children on the other side of the world, deserting his lover as she was about to bear his child.

'In fact,' Caspasian said, going on to the attack, 'while we're on the subject of the Japanese, if you want to talk about oppression, let's not forget your very own Commodore Perry levelling his cannons at them and forcing them to open their ports to American shipping against their will.'

Swinton grinned sheepishly. 'That was different. We didn't want to rule them, just to trade with them. You Europeans have to completely overrun a place though. Plant your little flags all over them like dogs pissing out their territory.'

'OK, so what are you all doing here? You're being selective with your history, Jack. The International Settlement used to be two separate ones. Before they combined, one was British and the other was . . . now let me see?' Caspasian rubbed his chin thoughtfully, watching his friend. 'Was it by any chance American?'

Swinton laughed. 'Once again, John, you've got it all wrong. It was just trade.' He leaned across the table and jabbed a finger at Caspasian, the beer finally starting to go to his head. 'We're not trying to rule anything here.'

'Neither are we.'

'What?' Swinton exclaimed, aghast. 'With your gunboats hundreds of miles up the fucking Yangtze?'

'I beg your pardon?' Caspasian said, cupping one hand to his ear as if hard of hearing. 'Our gunboats?'

'Oh, all right, there might be the occasional American gunboat somewhere around there too, but they're just protecting the missionaries from that red bastard, Chiang.'

'Aha! So you do think he's a Communist,' Caspasian said with triumphant glee. He hunted around until he caught the eye of a waiter and summoned two more beers. To his surprise the waiter remained where he was, his eyes stone cold, boring into the two westerners.

Swinton caught the look. 'Oops. Looks like someone doesn't approve of our language.'

'Your language, Jack. Either that or it's your opinions that he finds distasteful.'

Swinton shifted in his seat, his eyes focusing on the waiter with difficulty. 'Let's explore this a bit further,' he said, his speech becoming slurred.

Suddenly aware that they were entering on dangerous ground, Caspasian laid a restraining hand on the American's arm. 'Leave it, Jack.'

Swinton tugged his arm away and chuckled. 'Hell, no. I want to hear what the little guy has to say.' He waved for the waiter to come across to them. In response the waiter looked suddenly scared. He glanced to left and right to see if his boss had noticed. He broke into an artificial grin and nodded his head vigorously, indicating that he would fetch the beers at once. Before Swinton could repeat his summons the man had gone.

'Well, there go our beers. I bet we don't see him again,' Swinton said sombrely. 'That's Shanghai these days, I suppose. Full of goddamned spies.'

'You think that's what he was?' Caspasian said, knowing the answer.

'Who gives a fuck?' Swinton sank back in his chair. He yawned. 'Damn. This always happens to me. I just start to get merry and I feel I'm about to fall asleep.' He yawned again.

Caspasian hunted around until he saw the head waiter and signalled for the bill. Swinton was suddenly galvanised into action and dug one hand into his jacket. 'Here, let me get this.'

'No. It's my turn,' Caspasian said.

'I was hoping you'd say that,' Swinton grinned, relaxing. 'I didn't have my wallet with me anyway.'

They made their way to the exit but just as they were about to leave, Swinton excused himself for a moment and veered in the direction of the toilets. Caspasian stood to one side, hands deep in his pockets, leaning against the wall and watching the dance floor where couples were swaying in time to the music. In the very centre, one Chinese couple in particular caught his attention. For a moment he wondered why, but then as they turned and the woman's face was presented to him he remembered. She had caught his eye earlier that evening. Several times in fact. Wearing a long, slim-fitting, sleeveless cheong-sam of pale blue silk with a slit up the side of the leg, and high Chinese collar, she was beautiful in a classical Chinese way. Unusually, her hair was long, and not styled in the more fashionable bob cut. It shone under the lights of the dance floor.

But the other reason she had attracted his attention was for the company she was keeping. It seemed somehow out of character. While she looked almost frail, a slender wand of a girl, her partner was broad and thickly set. As her face was gentle, his was harsh with the characteristics of a bull. If there was anything thoughtful in his eyes, it was cruelty. Caspasian had seen his type before, mostly in the Chinese Bund area which westerners were wise to avoid after dark. It was the sort of face he had seen in the bars of Blood Alley or the opium dens of Nantao and the Chinese City, on the sort of man who would sort out the drunken sailors when they had exhausted their punches on each other. That was when his sort would move in, cutting them down with short sharp business-like blows and slinging them out into the streets to be picked up by the shore patrols, or robbed and dumped in a creek with throat slit. But what such a man was doing in the Regent and in the company of such a beautiful companion Caspasian could not imagine.

At that moment the girl looked up and stared straight into Caspasian's eyes. As she did so, the words of the elusive poem stung him again. Incongruous but striking home, nonetheless.

She does not raise her head for a long
    time,
But her silk blouse is wet with tears.

He was not certain, but it seemed as if she smiled at him, so slight and fleeting that it was hardly there. But it must have been, for something of it had transmitted itself through her body to her partner who whirled to spy out what she had been looking at. His gaze fell instantly upon Caspasian and again Caspasian was reminded of a malevolent bull. The Chinaman froze where he stood, the adjacent couple almost crashing into him.

The girl, realising what had happened and, more likely, imagining what was about to happen, flushed a deep red and gently tried to coax him back into the dance. But it was now a matter of honour. Face. The bull had decided to make it one.

Pulling the girl roughly after him by the wrist, he thrust his way across the floor through the dancers, heading for Caspasian. Caspasian sighed.

'Shit,' he muttered under his breath, pulling himself away from the wall. He had eaten well and had allowed Swinton to encourage more beers into him than was his habit. The last thing he needed at this point in the evening was a showdown with an affronted barn door.

The bull halted two paces away from Caspasian, out of reach. Just. Clever, Caspasian reflected. Caspasian tried a smile. He had taken his hands out of his pockets and held them loosely at his sides.

'Good evening,' Caspasian said pleasantly. 'Enjoying the dance? The band's good, don't you agree?'

The bull stared at him, face blank, all the expression focused into the twin points of loathing emanating from his narrowed eyes.

'I'm told the band master's from . . . '

'You like my woman?' The bull's voice was strangely high-pitched, reedy. Caspasian judged he had probably taken one too many punches in the throat. There was no waist to his body. His vast chest simply expanded downwards. He was wearing a black dinner jacket, wing collar and bow tie. His short black hair was oiled tight against his square skull.

Caspasian smiled again. 'Look, why don't you continue with your dance, and I'll leave. Ah! . . . ' he said, noticing with the deepest regret the return of Jack Swinton who was frowning at the confrontation he could see by the exit. 'Here's my friend now.'

'Hi there, old buddy,' Jack said cheerily, joining the little party. 'Having a spot of trouble from fatso?'

Caspasian groaned. The bull swung.

Caspasian had guessed correctly. The bull knew how to handle himself. Swinton never had a chance. Even if his head had not been befuddled with alcohol Swinton would not have been fast enough to move out of the way. The roundhouse punch struck him just in front of the left ear where the jaw hinged on the skull. As Swinton's legs buckled and he started to go down Caspasian grabbed his arm and yanked him out of the exit door into the broad hall outside the ballroom. To his dismay the bull followed, shoving the girl before him. It quickly became clear to Caspasian that the bull had decided the girl would benefit from a display of his combative talents, and who better to exercise them on than a couple of western revellers.

To Caspasian's surprise the girl moved herself in front of the bull and tried to speak calmly to him. He blinked, the savagery in his eyes deepening, aghast that she should try to stand up for the very men who had caused him the affront. He slapped her hard across the face with the flat of his hand, sending her reeling against the wall.

Caspasian felt his blood rise but fought to control his temper. With his senses already blurred by drink he knew that he would need every bit of concentration if he was going to deal with the bull and avoid a severe beating.

With some fragment of residual concern for his female companion the bull's attention had remained on her just long enough to ensure that she was not hurt more than he had intended. Besides, as far as he was concerned the two westerners were not going to go anywhere. They were at his mercy and he would deal with them as he thought fit in his own good time. When he turned back to Caspasian therefore he was surprised to find himself staring at empty space. At that very moment, Caspasian's foot slammed into the bull's right kidney.

He let out a squeal of pain and spun round to find himself facing a very different Caspasian to the one who just a moment ago had seemed so ineffectual and weak. The man facing him now was in a well-balanced stance, feet a little more than shoulder width apart, fists in a mid-level guard. But it was the eyes that most surprised the bull. They were completely calm. As far as the bull could see, there was no fear in them at all. For the first time in a long while he felt unsettled. He was used to being in control, to being on the giving end of beatings. Now, he was not so sure.

Before anything akin to fear could surface in his mind, the bull gave vent to his aggression, launching into an attack. His action was poorly judged. Over the years he had sacrificed speed to power. His muscles were as hard as stone, but not as supple as they had been when he was a good few pounds lighter. His fist shot out and met thin air. His target, the westerner's face, had moved. Once again he felt the impact of Caspasian's foot in his kidney, this time the left one. Again he squealed.

Caspasian watched, getting the measure of the bull. He knew that he had probably now reaped all the benefit that surprise was going to yield him. From now on the fight was going to get harder. The bull was no fool. Caspasian could see it in his eyes. They had not survived to grow that dangerous without a good ration of cunning behind them.

Sure enough, when the bull came at him again his movements were faster than previously. He had laid aside his easy confidence. This was business. He fired two punches rapidly at Caspasian's face but Caspasian could tell they were feints, however good. The real attack was coming from the bull's right foot, a lightning kick aimed at Caspasian's groin.

Caspasian palmed it aside, trying for a foot sweep on the bull's balancing leg. He almost connected but, with surprising agility for a man of his weight and size, the bull hopped nimbly out of the way. For the first time Caspasian saw the flicker of a smile on the bull's face, mirthless and harsh.

Behind him, Caspasian could hear Swinton staggering to his feet and groaning. 'Get out of here,' Caspasian called over his shoulder.

'No way . . . '

'Do as I say. I'll be right behind you!' Caspasian yelled.

Scared faces were poking from the ballroom as the head waiter and his entourage peered anxiously at the brawl, jabbering whether or not to summon the police. Suddenly, a gang of four burly Chinese shouldered through the little throng. One look at them told Caspasian that the bull had just received reinforcements.

'Better hang on a minute, Jack,' he called. Through the answering silence came the sound of the front door slamming shut behind his friend. Typical, Caspasian thought bitterly. The first time Jack obeys an order I give him, and I need to countermand it.

With help at hand, the bull lowered his

guard and grinned. 'You sort him out,' he said dismissively to his companions. 'I'll play with him when he's been softened up a bit.'

Similarly attired in black dinner jackets, the men rushed at Caspasian. Here goes, he thought. Playtime's over.

The men came at him as they had exited the ballroom, like battleships in line astern. As the first one closed on him, Caspasian steadied his breathing and fired out a mae-geri middle kick, the ball of his right foot, the chusoku, driving hard into the man's solar plexus. Caspasian had focused the blow, not on the point of contact, but on the spine beyond, so the foot drove in hard. Every fragment of air was pounded from the man's lungs in a second and as the shock from the blow cascaded through his nervous system, his eyes rolled and he crumpled.

Behind him, his companions were unable to stop and piled into the body now blocking their path. Like ninepins they started to go down. As they fell, Caspasian closed in, lashing out with a punch here and an open-hand blow there, aiming for any vulnerable point he could reach. Robbed of any coherent approach to their enemy, the men thrashed about blindly, throwing punches and kicking thin air. The bull screamed in frustration, and to his horror

41

Caspasian saw him reach a hand inside his jacket. There was the black glint of gun metal and Caspasian braced himself for the bullet.

The next instant there was a shrill cry and everyone froze. Caspasian glanced round to see where the cry had come from. Standing in the doorway was a short slender Chinese man. With shaven head, he was dressed in the traditional long silk gown. Caspasian noticed that beneath the gown, the man incongruously wore an expensive-looking pair of western shoes. Brown brogues. His face was a sheet of anger, so perfectly set it was as if he had donned a mask. Under its ferocious gaze the bull melted, becoming a far more docile creature, obedient and suddenly tame. He slipped the gun away and moved back towards the ballroom, his companions recovering themselves, dragging back with them the unconscious form of their comrade who had run headlong into Caspasian's kick.

The new arrival barked out fresh orders and, shamefaced, the bull and his men slunk back into the ballroom from where the sound of the band had never ceased. Before he disappeared from view the bull cast one long look of pure hatred at Caspasian, transmitting with the greatest clarity the silent message that should they ever meet again he would take the greatest pleasure in having Caspasian dismembered piece by piece. The look was only interrupted when the bull tried to seek out the girl who was nowhere to be seen.

Reading his thoughts, the small Chinese man answered his unspoken question. 'The sing-song girl's gone, you idiot. Never mind her. There are plenty more whores where that one came from.'

As the bull disappeared back into the ballroom, the man stared hard at Caspasian. For a moment Caspasian thought he was going to speak. Instead the man said nothing. He simply stared. Then, nodding his head slowly, registering Caspasian's face for future reference, he turned and walked briskly away, closing the ballroom door behind him.

Caspasian felt the energy drain from him, sapped by the effort of concentration and the physical strain of the fight. He knew he had been lucky.

He turned and made his way out of the building. In the street life was continuing busier than before as Shanghai settled into another frantic night. The smells of the street assaulted his nostrils and he clamped a hand over his nose as a so-called honey cart was pushed past by four straining men, its cargo of human excrement bound for the fields outside the city confines. There was a shout from across the street and Caspasian looked across to see Jack Swinton waving from a taxi window.

'Over here. I've got a cab,' he called unnecessarily.

Caspasian waved him away and started to walk.

A moment later the cab drew alongside him, the driver keeping abreast of the walking man. Swinton leaned from the window.

'What's up, buddy?'

'You're up.'

'What do you mean?'

'Of all the stupid fucking things to say. Fatso.' He shook his head in stupefied wonder.

'Hey, I was only joking. I didn't know the guy was going to take offence.'

Caspasian turned on him. 'I almost got myself killed in there thanks to you.'

'Not thanks to me,' Swinton said, his tone hardening. 'Don't think I didn't see you sneaking looks at the guy's woman throughout the meal. That's fine by me. She was pretty good-looking. But don't blame it on me, OK?'

Caspasian was about to respond when he suddenly felt tired of the whole business. He waved his friend away and ducked down a side street before the taxi could follow. Swinton called after him twice, then swore, and ordered the taxi to drive on.

It was a good way back to his apartment but Caspasian decided to walk. However tired his body was physically, his mind was about as far from sleep as it could be. Overhead the night sky was an opaque sheet, any stars blotted from view by the lights, dust, smoke and filth of the city. He had only gone a short distance when he became aware of footsteps shadowing his own. Away from the bustle of Nanking and Bubbling Well Roads, he had entered a quieter part of the city. Here, instead of the busy thoroughfares and the night revellers, there were only the usual hawkers, beggars and still silent bundles lying amongst the rubbish that might equally be an arrangement of rags or a corpse. To Caspasian's experienced ear, the sound of following steps was unmistakable.

Pretending he had not heard, he continued on his way while altering his intended course, leading his pursuer away from his apartment and into an area where he might be able to turn the tables and discover who was following him. He stopped momentarily as if to inspect a shoe, and the following steps halted as well. Caspasian started to regret turning down Swinton's offer of a taxi ride.

Ahead of him, his path entered a patch of deep shadow before reaching a corner and light once again. The moment he entered the shadow he risked a glance over his shoulder. He could still hear the steps but see no one. All right, he thought. I'll take you at the corner.

Emerging once again into the light, Caspasian rounded the corner as casually as he could, but once around it, he turned and prepared to tackle his pursuer when they came round after him.

He waited for thirty seconds, then a minute. No one came. After a second minute he cursed under his breath and edged back along the wall to the street from which he had just emerged. Readying himself for action, he swung around the corner and peered down the dark street. There was no one there. Then, at the far end he heard the footsteps of someone running away.

'Damn you,' he muttered, and sprinted as fast as he could after them. When he reached the far end, he found himself in a broad well-lit street. He looked to right and left but there was no one to be seen. He strained his ears to listen but the only sounds were the sounds of the city.

Next time, he thought. Next time.

As he resumed his homewards walk, alert now, he was unable to shake off the feeling that the footsteps had been those of a woman.

But then how could a person be sure of anything in a place like this? As Swinton had said, that was Shanghai these days. Full of goddamned spies. Perhaps his mind was simply playing tricks on him, Caspasian reluctantly conceded, more affected by the girl at the Regent than he had cared to admit.

2

The next morning, Caspasian awoke with a foul taste in his mouth and a resolution in his head that in future he would avoid all locally brewed beer. It was more formaldehyde than anything else. If it really was made under the supervision of German experts, as the advertisement smugly assured, then they were veterans of the trenches avenging themselves on their former British, French and American enemies.

His accommodation had been found for him on arrival in Shanghai and was a well-apportioned, comfortable suite of rooms in Cherry Tree Apartments, a block of recently constructed flats standing on Rue Lafayette in the French Concession. He had declined the offer of somewhere closer to work in the adjacent International Settlement, preferring the broad tree-lined boulevards and the nearby French Park. When the air quality permitted, he would start the day early with some exercise in the park. This morning when he drew the bedroom curtains and peered blearily out, he squinted uncomfortably at the grey sky wreathed with plumes of black and yellow smoke and shook his head with disgust, realising that, once again, any exercise would have to be taken indoors if he was to avoid a morning spent coughing at his desk like an aged, opium-addicted hag.

As he made his way to his improvised gymnasium, throwing open the curtains of each room through which he passed, he thought with longing of India and of his regiment which he had unwillingly left behind there. The Twelfth Gurkha Rifles. Indian Army. The best.

He pondered sadly, once again wondering how he had ended up in the cesspit that he had found Shanghai to be. It truly lived up to its reputation as the whore of the Orient. He had been shocked to find even more dirt and disease than in Calcutta. Raw sewage leaked from the ground into the water supply making tap water virtually deadly, even for brushing the teeth. The streets abounded with every sort of beggar from White Russian whores in the final stages of disintegration, riddled with venereal disease, to Chinese lepers with rotting limbs.

Violence was so much a part of everyday life that members of the Chicago police force, on six-month secondment to the Shanghai Municipal Police, invariably asked to be sent home after the first month. The Shanghai police fired more rounds in a month than their Chicago colleagues did in a year. For the mostly British and Russian police officers from Shanghai who had been sent the other way, Chicago was treated as a holiday. They taught the Americans ju-jitsu and how to fire from the hip, and were fêted everywhere they went as eccentric but highly dangerous oddities.

This was in stark contrast to their treatment in Shanghai itself where, while they were expected to put their lives daily on the line to protect western business interests and to maintain the rule of law, they were nevertheless excluded from such institutions as the prestigious Shanghai Club and all the higher echelons of society. For many members of the British business and political elite, a daughter becoming romantically involved with a policeman was akin to her selling her body on the streets.

It was much the same as in India, Caspasian reflected, as he stripped out of his pyjamas and slipped into a pair of shorts. Only here it was even worse. The same colonial exaggerations, magnifying the social differences of the home country out of all proportion, as if, in being sequestered abroad, people felt obliged to cling to whatever status they possessed, or else risk dissolution in the poverty and filth that was so much of Asia.

Having been born and raised in an oriental port city, Caspasian had been accustomed from the start to the extremities that life could reach, in all its manifest forms. For others, unaccustomed to such awful variety, he could nevertheless imagine that the spectacles awaiting them in the Orient would be sufficient to drive them into tight little huddles, turning their backs resolutely on the strangeness around them, lest they awake one morning to find themselves part of it and unable to return, severed from the comforts to which they had so fortunately been born. This, Caspasian had come to believe, was the nightmare that sustained the invisible walls around the colonial westerner and his jealously guarded, rigidly structured institutions.

The room to which Caspasian had come was large, high ceilinged and completely bare. The floor was of stripped wood, smoothly polished. Light flooded the room from four tall curtainless windows that lined one wall. The other walls were whitewashed and unadorned. As he passed through the door, he halted momentarily, pulled his bare feet together, and bowed crisply from the waist.

51

He was entering his dojo, the place of training. It was a mark of respect which he had learnt many years before in Japan when, as a boy, he had come under the tutelage of his sensei, his master.

He began his daily training session with a series of warm-up exercises that loosened his sleep-tightened limbs. Now that he was the wrong side of thirty, he found he had to spend longer on this part of the routine. Either that or risk a pulled muscle and the consequent abstinence from exercise which would be necessary. He feared it was a pattern that would only get worse as the years went on. He took heart from the increase in experience which was more than compensation for any loss of suppleness. As he eased down into a squatting position, working on the hamstrings of his left leg he smiled sardonically. Who the hell was he kidding?

When he was sufficiently loose, he adopted a strong, low stance in the middle of the room, and started into a sequence of punching exercises, firing blows at low, middle and high target areas, gedan, chudan and jodan. His midriff was tightened into a sheet of muscle, while his legs rooted him to the ground, toes gripping the smooth cool wood of the floor. Sticky feet, his sensei had called it, using the best translation he had been able to muster.

As Caspasian worked, so his mind cleared, focusing ever more on the movements being executed with deadly precision. Having practised a broad series of hand blows, Caspasian went through a sequence of kicks. When he was satisfied with these, he started on the katas, the pre-arranged forms, each a set sequence of moves and blows in which the exponent took on imaginary foes.

It was a good hour later that Caspasian concluded his exercise routine. He knelt in the centre of the room, hands in his lap, closed his eyes, steadied his breathing and emptied his mind. When he stood, bowed and exited the dojo it was a different world. Or rather, while the world itself was the same grubby, extraordinary place, Caspasian himself now experienced it differently. Every sense was alert. Every colour more sharply perceived and every sound more keenly heard. Unfortunately, every smell was also more pungently unpleasant.

After bathing, he dressed in a lightweight suit, white shirt, regimental tie and brown brogues, picked up his battered dark brown trilby and left the apartment. In the entrance hall below he nodded good morning to the tall Sikh doorman, an ex-policeman with whom Caspasian had enjoyed many a reminiscence about India. He checked his watch and saw that he was early, so, scanning the street, he hailed a rickshaw, climbed in and set off for the consulate.

Turning north along Avenue Dubail, the rickshaw paralleled the park before entering Avenue Joffre. From there it was a long haul eastwards until they skirted the walls of the Chinese City at Boulevard des Deux Republiques and hit the river at the Quai de France. Heading north again in the direction of the International Settlement, Caspasian settled back and gazed at the broad sweep of the Whangpoo river. The river traffic seemed especially busy and he could identify at least three warships that had not been there the previous day, one Japanese, one Italian, and one British.

His mind drifted and he started to hum a dance tune that had annoyingly stuck in his head ever since he and Jack Swinton had visited a night club the week before, one that boasted the best Russian band in town. Russians were everywhere, the largest single group of non-Chinese in the city. They were bodyguards, musicians, prostitutes, chorus girls, mercenaries, and every other job in between. Following the Bolshevik Revolution they had flocked to the city in droves. Some were ex-soldiers or sailors, others were members of the middle or upper classes. Virtually all of them had now fallen on hard times.

The rickshaw had halted at an intersection in the middle of which a large Sikh policeman stood on top of a raised island controlling the traffic. He glared imperiously at all around him, his brilliant red turban giving a welcome dash of colour to the drabness of the morning. Caspasian watched him, smiling, and almost failed to notice the car that drew slowly alongside his rickshaw, similarly awaiting permission to go. When he did look however, he felt his blood chill. Glaring at him from inside was the shaven-headed Chinaman of the night before at the Regent. On the far side of the rear seat, craning past him, was the bull. His hand went inside his coat and he glowered menacingly as he withdrew a pistol.

Caspasian felt reasonably certain that they would not attempt anything in broad daylight, particularly against a westerner. Nevertheless, he deeply regretted his own lack of any sort of firearm and made a mental note to rectify it at the first opportunity. He glanced over the back of the rickshaw and to his consternation saw not one, but two cars, each full of men who could only have been bodyguards, for in each car he recognised at least one face of the men who had confronted him at the Regent.

He smiled sweetly and doffed his trilby at the shaven-headed Chinaman who was clearly a person of some importance. He also noticed something that had escaped him at the Regent. The man's skin had the sickly yellow pallor of an opium addict. To Caspasian's surprise, the man returned the smile, but chilled to pure ice. His lips parted to reveal large teeth, similarly yellowed by opium, and giving the impression of an oversized sewer rat.

There was a whistle blast and with a lurch Caspasian's rickshaw leapt forward. In front Caspasian could see the Hong Kong and Shanghai Bank building. He had now entered the International Settlement and was making his way along the Bund. With one final glare, the Chinaman and his armed escort peeled away and turned left down Canton Road. Caspasian sank back in his seat and heaved an immense sigh of relief. A few moments later the rickshaw trotted past the Cathay Hotel and the Jardine Matheson Building until finally the British Consulate hove into view standing beside Garden Bridge on the edge of Soochow Creek, the sluggish, foul-smelling stretch of water that emptied into the Whangpoo.

Caspasian was one of several MIOs on the staff of the consulate, their number having been increased to cater for the growing tension since the start of General Chiang Kai-shek's Northern Expedition.

'Ah, Caspasian, there you are.'

Caspasian turned at the sound of his boss's voice.

'Colonel, good morning,' he responded.

'Don't look so bloody surprised to see me.' Colonel Dick Preston was a short plump Royal Artillery officer. He had been heading the military intelligence operation at the consulate for almost two years and was shortly due for posting. He took no pains to hide his immense relief at the prospect of a quiet staff job in the more sweetly scented surroundings of Woolwich or Larkhill.

'I might not normally be in this early but there's a show brewing and you're going to be part of it.' He eyed Caspasian shrewdly and added, 'Something just up the street of a young trouble-causer like you, I shouldn't wonder.'

Caspasian blanched. 'I beg your pardon?'

'Don't think I haven't heard about the little fracas at the Regent last night. You and that big slob of an American. What's his name? Swinford?'

'Swinton, sir.'

'Whatever. I would have thought you'd have known better. There's no such thing as a secret in this damned place. Especially not when a white man's involved.'

'We didn't exactly go looking for trouble,' Caspasian said, affronted but trying to keep his temper. He had seen too many of the Colonel's sort in the war. Staff officers wedged firm as oysters in their luxurious commandeered chateaux, far behind the lines, planning one show — as they called it — after another, each as disastrous as the next. He was still amazed that he had made it through intact. Physically, at least.

The Colonel waved aside Caspasian's excuse. 'Not now. Personally I don't give a hoot. If you want to tangle with local criminals that's your affair.' He turned and fixed a stern eye on him. 'But next time, I suggest you pick someone other than Du Yuesheng.'

It was not often that Caspasian was caught off guard, but at the mention of the name he felt as if his mouth should be dropping open. Instead he set his jaw in a firm line and ground his teeth to hide his shock.

'Yes,' the Colonel said meaningfully, a sarcastic smile spreading from ear to ear as he saw recognition dawn in the young Captain's eyes. 'Du Yuesheng of the Green Gang. Its leader in fact. The most notorious and ruthless of all of Shanghai's criminal secret societies.' He was enjoying Caspasian's severe discomfort. Suddenly he spun on his heel and marched down the corridor towards his office. 'Follow me,' he commanded.

With head reeling, Caspasian walked meekly in the Colonel's wake. How could he have been so stupid, he asked himself. He had even seen photographs of Du, albeit poor quality ones. The man was known to be involved in virtually every criminal activity throughout the city. Furthermore, he had connections reaching up through all strata of society. Had he tried, Caspasian could hardly have crossed a more dangerous man. His only solace was that he had had little choice. Once the bull had singled him out the cards had clearly been on the table.

When they reached the Colonel's office, Preston rudely directed Caspasian to a chair and fumbled for a large map which he proceeded to unroll on the desk between them. 'What your little escapade has done, however, is help me resolve a puzzle.'

'Oh?'

'Yes,' the Colonel said, poring over the map to orientate himself. When he found what he was searching for he looked up. 'I've got to send someone up country.'

Caspasian felt as if a shard of brilliant sunlight had suddenly burst into the room.

'The question was, who to send.' He scowled. 'Until yesterday evening, that is. Major Logan is the most experienced in the China theatre. He's senior to you, speaks the language almost as well, and . . . ' he said, pausing for emphasis, 'he knows how to obey bloody orders.'

'Yes, sir,' Caspasian said quietly.

The Colonel slammed his hands on the table. 'When your old boss in Delhi, Colonel Readman, wrote to me and said you were a packet of trouble, I didn't believe him.' He shook his head. 'I bloody well should have done.'

'Yes, sir,' Caspasian repeated, wishing the old fool would get on with it.

'He warned me that the Viceroy himself keeps an eye out for you.' Preston stared at Caspasian. 'Well, seeing as we're in Shanghai not Delhi, and seeing as I'm British not Indian Army, I couldn't care less. Viceroy's man or not, so long as you're under my command you'll do what I bloody well tell you, do you understand?'

Caspasian gritted his teeth but kept silent, not trusting himself to speak. Behind his anger he could feel himself almost wriggling in his seat with anticipation. The thought of getting out of the city into open country was like a breath of fresh air in both literal and metaphorical senses.

'Now, thanks to your foolhardiness, it seems that a spell of absence from Shanghai might be in order for you.' He drew Caspasian's attention to a series of red arrows marked on the map. Caspasian instantly recognised them as indicating the main thrust of Chiang Kai-shek's Northern Expedition.

'Chiang is a direct threat to western interests in China, particularly here in Shanghai. We've done very nicely under Sun Chuanfang and it is our policy — mine at least — that we should support him and the coalition of northern warlords in every way possible. Chiang is nothing but trouble. His KMT is just another bunch of Communists taking instructions from their paymasters in Moscow. They're causing trouble here in the city and the Special Branch have got their hands full keeping the lid on the pot.'

Caspasian thought back to his conversation with Swinton but decided it was best to keep silent. The Colonel had already stated his intention to send Caspasian out of Shanghai. Why rock the boat and risk upsetting him?

The Colonel pointed to a small blue arrow on the map, north of the Yangtze in the

61

province of Hupeh. 'What do you know about General Mok?'

Caspasian shrugged. 'A minor regional warlord. One of hundreds. Nothing special.' He frowned at the Colonel, embarrassed at his lack of detailed knowledge. 'I don't think any of us knows much about him, do we, sir?'

'Exactly,' the Colonel said with a smile of mild triumph. 'But now we need to, and that's where you come in.' He was speaking very deliberately, as if to a simpleton, knowing how much it irritated Caspasian. 'Latest reports seem to indicate that the dear General's having a run of good luck. He's spreading his sphere of influence throughout the region,' he said, circling an impressively large patch of territory with one thick finger. 'He is using the Changsha, Hankow, Peking rail line as his main direction of thrust, that and all the branch lines leading off it. Apparently he's got hold of an armoured train from the Russians.'

Caspasian whistled his admiration. A number of the warlords used armoured trains. They had been a key feature of the Russian civil war and many White Russian soldiers and officers had fled south into China after the Bolshevik victory, taking their expertise with them. 'I suppose he's using Russian mercenaries?'

The Colonel flicked through some notes. 'Some, but actually, there's also a Briton involved. Infantry Captain in Flanders.'

Caspasian sat up. 'Oh, who?'

'Chap named Smith. D. Smith . . . where the devil is it?'

'Daniel Smith?' Caspasian ventured.

Colonel Preston looked up. 'Why, yes. How did you know that?'

Caspasian heaved a deep sigh. 'Just a hunch,' he said heavily. All joy at the prospect of getting out of Shanghai had evaporated instantly at the mention of the name.

The Colonel's eyes narrowed. 'You know the man?'

'Yes.'

'That's excellent,' he said, breaking into the first genuine smile of the day. 'An old acquaintance from Flanders?'

'You could say that.'

The Colonel shrugged. 'Well, you don't exactly sound pleased.' His smile clouded over and he wagged a finger at Caspasian. 'Listen, he'd better not be yet another bloody enemy of yours or I'll have your guts for garters.'

'No, he's not that, sir,' Caspasian said, becoming more miserable by the second.

'Well, what is it then?' the Colonel persisted, puzzled. 'I'd better know before I let you cock up something else.'

Caspasian shifted uneasily in his chair. 'He . . . ' he began, but faltered.

'He what?'

Caspasian ground his teeth. 'He saved my life once,' he finally blurted out.

The Colonel beamed. 'But that's splendid! The two of you will have an instant connection.' He rubbed his hands together with glee. 'You'll be accepted straight into the heart of Mok's organisation and be able to produce a full report on the man and his objectives. We should be able to establish contact with him and form an alliance immediately.' He looked back at Caspasian, detecting the obvious concern on his face.

'What the bloody hell's the matter with you now?' he barked furiously.

'It wasn't quite as simple as that, Colonel.'

'Why not? It sounds it to me. Bloke saves your life. What more to it can there be?' He stared at Caspasian and then sneered. 'Oh, I see. You don't like the idea of being in thrall to someone, is that it? Being in another man's debt doesn't sit easily with the great and proud Captain John Caspasian, Viceroy's favourite?'

Caspasian pushed himself to his feet, feeling himself turn scarlet. His fingers tightened upon themselves, digging into the flesh of his palms as he clenched his fists at his sides. 'No, sir,' he said through clenched teeth. 'It's nothing like that at all. There are many people, alive and dead, to whom I owe all kinds of debt. I honour them all, every one.'

The Colonel felt the heat of Caspasian's anger and relented. 'All right, all right. Calm down. Tell me then, what's the problem?'

'It was very complicated, sir. There was another man involved. A private. As a result of the action he was tried by court-martial for cowardice and shot.'

'Oh, I see. But what's that got to do with Smith?'

'Smith was the main officer pressing for the man's execution. I disagreed. I knew the man a little and . . . ' he faltered. 'I just couldn't believe it.'

'Then why didn't you say so at the hearing?'

'Because I wasn't there. I had been wounded in the attack. Smith saved my life. I was unconscious throughout the rest of the action. It was touch and go whether we could hold the position or not. By all accounts Smith was every inch the hero. Private . . . ' Caspasian struggled to say the name as the pain of that time flooded back to him. 'Private Dobson apparently broke and ran.

Smith said that his cowardice affected the rest of the survivors holding the redoubt and he had trouble keeping them in place.' He stared out of the window, reluctantly taken back to the mud and terror of the battlefield. 'Dobson was an old poacher, a simple country fellow. He didn't deserve the firing squad.'

'It sounds to me as though he did.'

Caspasian bit back the rebuke that was dying to spring out and cut the Colonel to the floor, the rebuke that was longing to point out that men like Dobson had at least faced the inner struggle between bravery and cowardice, while others, more fortunate, like the Colonel, had lain safely behind the lines in bed, ignorant of real, naked terror.

'I was convalescing in Kent. From the home, we could even hear the rumble of the guns in France.' He grinned bitterly. 'It affected some of the lads so badly they had to be moved to homes further north where they were out of earshot. When I heard about the trial and the execution I was . . . ' Caspasian held out his hands and let them fall against his legs, helpless.

The Colonel laid a consoling hand on his shoulder. 'All right, but the fact remains that Smith did his duty. More, in fact.' He brightened. 'And he saved your life, so the two of you should get on like a house on fire.'

'Yes,' Caspasian said with lead in his voice. 'Like a house on fire.'

* * *

As the train sped through the rolling desolate countryside, Captain Daniel Smith sat in the foremost gun turret, head and shoulders out of the open hatch, enjoying the rush of air in his face. He breathed deeply. It was cold but he felt exhilarated by the feel and bite of it in his throat and lungs. It was a welcome relief after the cramped confines of the train's dark interior, reeking of the Russians' inedible black bread and cabbage soup. They insisted on having their own bakery on board as they could not abide the Chinese diet of rice. For now Smith needed them, so he let them have their way. He had to concede, however reluctantly, that man for man they were far superior to any Chinese troops. The Chinese by comparison were little better than malevolent children, scared or cruel by turn.

It was true that General Mok's were better than most, but that was not saying much. And what little ability and battle discipline they possessed, they owed to Smith.

Someone tapped him on the leg and he peered down into the gloom. It was Markov. The sergeant grinned up at him.

'Mok wants you.'

'You mean General Mok,' Smith said sternly.

The big Russian shrugged unconcerned. 'If you say so.'

Smith wriggled down off his perch and dropped to the iron floor, the plates bolted in place to give protection against mines buried in the track.

'Where is he?'

The Russian stabbed a thumb casually over his shoulder. 'Back in the command car. Said it's urgent.'

It was always urgent with the General, Smith thought with irritation, though he kept the observation to himself.

To reach the command car in the centre of the train he had to negotiate a number of other carriages. As he ducked and stooped and dodged around every manner of weapon and obstacle, he took in his surroundings with a professional eye. The weapons were plentiful, but they were too broad a mix for his liking, having been obtained from diverse sources. There were at least six different types of rifle alone. Russian Moison-Nagants, German Mannlicher-Schonauers, Mauser Model 88s and their Chinese copy, the Hanyang 88. There were also Japanese Arisaka 98s and some British Lee-Enfields.

Smith desperately wished they were all Lee-Enfields. The rifle had proved its worth time and time again in Flanders, refusing to jam in even the worst conditions. With such a jumbled array in the inventory, ammunition supply was a nightmare.

With machine-guns and field artillery pieces, the problem was the same. Smith himself carried a Mauser pistol and an MP18/20 sub-machine-gun, a copy of the German MP 18 that had so impressed him during the war that he and a number of his comrades had used captured ones.

Working his way further back, he passed through the troop-carrying carriages. Most of the men were making good use of the spare time to sleep. Those that were not, played cards or otherwise indulged the Chinese passion for gambling.

When he finally reached the command carriage, Smith passed by the two Russian bodyguards. He found it ironic that the General trusted these foreigners more than the men of his own race.

'General's waiting in there,' one of the guards said, jerking his chin to the back of the carriage.

The carriage was split in two. The front half into which Smith had just entered was used for planning and controlling operations. The rear half was used by the General as his living quarters when on the move. Smith made his way past the maps, tables, canvas-backed folding chairs, field telephones and other paraphernalia of a standard operations room, and knocked on the door at the far side. There was a moment's pause before the door opened.

'Smith. Come in,' the General said simply. He smiled, exposing an array of gold teeth of which he was very proud. 'Where's my main force at the present?'

You should bloody well know the answer for yourself, Smith thought, while answering instead, 'At Cho-an, sir.'

'Is it really? Excellent.' He frowned, puzzled. 'And when is it we're attacking General Yuan?'

Smith bit his lip and then said, 'In a few weeks time, sir.' He folded his arms across his chest. 'You'll remember that we discussed this at yesterday's planning meeting, General.'

'Yes, yes, I know all that,' the General said defensively.

Instantly Smith was on his guard. Careful, he thought. Don't let the old bugger lose face. 'I recall though that the train was going particularly fast at the time. I could hardly hear myself speak,' he added quickly.

'Quite so, quite so,' the General chided

gently, gratefully seizing the excuse Smith had offered him. 'You really must choose your briefing times to coincide with our halts.'

'I will do so in future, General. An excellent suggestion.'

The General beamed delightedly. 'Not a suggestion,' he said merrily. 'An order!' He paused and then burst into a peal of laughter, as if he had cracked the funniest joke in the world, slapping Smith boisterously several times on the back.

Smith grimaced into a smile. He hated the whole damned charade, the whole pathetic oriental game of face. What about his bloody face? That never seemed to matter. In truth he could not care less, but the Chinese certainly did, as he well knew. It was one of the first things he had learnt. Just keep the simpletons smiling. Convince them they are doing the right thing, and fleece them stupid behind their backs. That was his philosophy. You could stick your bloody concept of face. He had seen it time and again. He and the Russians had a jolly good laugh about it most evenings when the General and his officers had retired, all convinced that they were the most efficient fighting force the world had ever beheld. Smith and the Russians understood the sad truth that the General and his men were only successful because their

71

opponents were even bigger cretins. That, and the fact that Mok let Smith do everything for him except wipe his arse. Smith sometimes wondered if Mok had his Russian bodyguards do even that for him.

The General droned on for a while until Smith began to wonder what he had been summoned for. He was about to raise the question when the General came to the point.

'This Yuan. I am worried about him.'

'Why is that, sir? He's not even a real general.' The instant he had said it and seen the General flinch Smith realised his mistake. General Mok had been a minor civil servant in the closing years of Manchu rule. He had only adopted the title when he had murdered his way to the top in his home province.

'What I mean is, Yuan has no military infrastructure like us, General,' Smith added rapidly. 'You have earned your reputation as the most feared warlord in all Hupeh through feat of arms. And soon, your influence will spread even further beyond.'

Like a cockerel's, the General's chest expanded. 'That's right, Smith. Yuan will be no match for me. I hear that he has barely one battalion of poorly armed troops, and no artillery.'

'That's right, sir,' Smith said. He himself had told the General this only yesterday.

'A few weeks,' the General mused. He stooped and gazed out of the window. 'Who can say where it will all end for me?' he said proudly.

Smith looked at the General's back and fought the impulse to shove him clean through the glass pane.

'Who indeed?'

3

The day after his briefing with Colonel Preston, Caspasian made his way to the waterfront opposite the Rue du Consulat. The motor launch that was to convey him to the British gunboat for his journey upriver was waiting at the quayside. By the time he arrived it was already half full with sailors returning from a run ashore, others weaving uncertainly towards it with visible efforts to remain upright. The master at arms, Chief Petty Officer Braggins, stood resolutely on the wharf scrutinising each man as he filed past and stepped down into the bobbing launch. As each one came beneath his piercing gaze, they felt themselves stripped and appraised. All knew that they had been found wanting.

'You sorry bunch of whore-fodder.' Braggins said it quietly, a lethal intensity compensating for lack of volume. His fist shot out and grabbed one young seaman by the dishevelled scruff of his neck. 'Watts,' he whispered, yet loud enough for Caspasian and others about them to hear. 'What's this?' he asked maliciously, twisting the man's name as if it was his neck. From the wry smiles on the faces of the sailor's comrades, Caspasian guessed it was a road well trodden.

Stupidly the sailor grinned. 'Nuffing, Mr Braggins, sir.' His accent was docklands, Shoreditch and Bow Bells.

Braggins hauled him closer, as if he was about to swallow the youngster's head. 'Nuffing?' he mimicked heavily. 'Nuffing? I'll give you nuffing, you miserable sing-song shagger. Straighten your collar and don't you ever dare turn up like that again!'

Releasing his grip, he took out a handkerchief and wiped his hands as if cleansing himself of some gross defilement. He looked up and glared at the next in line, shaking his head in dismay. 'Jones, Jones, Jones.' Carefully he leaned closer to the sailor and sniffed. 'Who've you been screwing this time? Smells like Shanghai Sally.' His face contorted in disgust. 'What heathen bloody perfume's she taken to covering her syphilitic corpse with now?'

'Eau de Whangpoo, Chief,' Jones retorted grinning.

Braggins broke into the sweetest of smiles. 'Funny man today, are we, Jones?' His face darkened. 'Report to the sick bay! Let's see if you're still smiling after the Doc's doused your bollocks with mercury!'

Next in line was Caspasian. The chief petty officer eyed him warily and consulted his clip board before straightening up and saluting. 'Captain Caspasian, is it, sir?'

'Permission to come aboard, Chief?'

Braggins smiled. 'Permission granted, sir. Pardon the language, if you will.' He glanced down into the launch with disgust. 'China sailors are all the same. Scum o' the earth. Hope you don't mind sharing the launch with them?' He glared at the giggling sailors who were obviously used to the Chief's banter. 'I'd as soon turf them all overboard and have them swim out.'

Caspasian handed down his holdall and stepped into the launch. Watts and Jones shifted sideways to make room for him. Jones leaned across. 'The Chief ain't as bad as he seems, sir. His bark's worse than . . . '

'Shut it, Jones!' Braggins growled over his shoulder, as he scanned the quayside to see if the shore party was complete. 'I promise you my bark is the gentlest thing about me.'

'Yes, Chief,' Jones called back with a conspiratorial wink at Caspasian.

An hour later the gunboat was under way. Caspasian stood at the rail and watched the Bund and its impressive colonial buildings slip further and further out of sight. With every mile he felt as if he was showering himself clean. Junks with maroon-coloured bat-winged sails rocked like cradles in the wake of the passing gunboat. Their Chinese crews stood and gaped, clinging to ropes, some of them waving and grinning.

They passed a Japanese warship and Caspasian studied it with keen interest. The death of the Japanese Emperor at Christmas and the succession of his son, the regent, had ushered in a promising new era. The young Emperor had taken as the title of his reign, 'Showa', two characters meaning 'enlightened peace'. Foreign affairs had been entrusted to Kijuro Shidehara who was conscientiously pursuing his 'good neighbour' policy. With the triumph of civilian, liberal elements in the government, it seemed that the ultra-nationalist forces in the Japanese military had been successfully countered. Knowing that extraordinary island nation as he did, Caspasian felt an immense relief. And yet, as he surveyed the looming warship, its sailors similarly staring back, their faces blank, an inexplicable shiver of apprehension disturbed his peace of mind.

Fourteen miles from Shanghai, at Woosung, the Whangpoo emptied into the immensity of the Yangtze. From there vessels either sailed the remaining forty miles to the

China Sea, or turned upriver and headed into the vastness of China itself, as the gunboat now did. Caspasian felt utterly dwarfed as he gazed out over the huge sweep of water, dark yellow with silt. The waves grew in size and the gunboat started to rise up, its prow cutting the foam.

'Captain Caspasian?'

Caspasian turned. Standing before him was the ship's Captain who introduced himself as Commander Hewson and shook Caspasian warmly by the hand. 'Welcome aboard.'

'Thank you, sir.'

'I believe you're going upcountry as far as Hankow?'

'That's correct, sir. I have to connect there with the Peking railway.'

'General Mok, isn't it?'

'Yes, sir.' Caspasian grimaced. 'He's to be my host.'

The Commander raised an eyebrow. 'I was up that way last month. From what I hear he's somewhat lacking in . . . how shall I put it? . . . neighbourliness.'

'Oh?'

'We boarded a junk that we suspected of smuggling and instead came across a scruffy band of ruffians who claimed they had once been soldiers. They told us horrific tales of Mok's local conquests. If their account's correct, he's little better than a mass murderer.'

Caspasian smiled bitterly. 'Then you might be surprised to hear that His Majesty's government views him as a potential ally.'

The Commander shook his head. 'Sadly, I am not surprised.'

'Apparently he's the lesser of two evils.'

'The other being Chiang Kai-shek, I suppose?'

'Yes, sir.'

'Well, you know what they say; when you sup with the devil, use a long spoon.'

'Thank you, sir. I'll bear that in mind.' As the Commander turned to go Caspasian quickly added, 'Did you hear anything about an Englishman?'

'Mok's advisor?'

'That's him.'

'Not much. It's well known that Mok's got a team of Russians working for him, like lots of the warlords. And, yes, I've heard it said that there's a British ex-army officer helping him too.'

'Those soldiers though, the ones in the junk, did they mention him?'

'In a way. One of them kept repeating a name over and over. He seemed quite terrorised by it.'

'What name was that, sir?'

'I can't remember really. I don't speak the language. But it was something like Tai Hang Shuang, or Tai Hang Shin. Something like that.'

Caspasian's expression darkened.

'I see it means something to you,' the Commander said.

Caspasian nodded. 'It would have been Tai Shang Huang.'

'Perhaps. I really can't remember.'

In his cabin that evening after dinner, Caspasian flopped down on his bunk, punched a couple of pillows into place and lay back. Legs crossed at the ankles, hands behind his head, he stared up at the cream-coloured bulkhead and let his mind drift back the ten years to his last encounter with Smith. Daniel Smith. Captain Daniel Smith whom the Chinese were now calling Tai Shang Huang. The God of War.

★　★　★

No one had been able to discover who had the bright idea for the redoubts. Defence in depth was the cry of the moment. The latest fashion in the succession of disasters and bungles that had been the sorry story of the Western Front since it had coagulated into place back in 1914 like a string of dried blood stretching all the way from the Belgian coast to the Swiss border.

Until then, the British and French had relied upon a continuous line of trenches. A forward trench would be backed up by a second and even a third, in roughly parallel lines. They would be linked, front to rear by communication trenches up which reinforcements and supplies could be fed into the battle.

Then, in 1917, the Bolshevik Revolution had knocked Russia out of the war and the Germans had been able to transfer vast numbers of troops from the Eastern Front to the Western. Faced with this massive increase in pressure, the Allied commanders had decided their defensive line needed greater depth if it was not to buckle and break.

The answer was the redoubt. A series of strongpoints would be constructed forward of the first trench line. Each one would be a self-contained island, protected by wire and mines, and mutually supporting, able to bring fire to bear on any Germans attacking the neighbouring redoubts to left and right, and similarly able to receive such support itself. Penetrating this network of defended islands, German attacks would be broken up before they reached the main trench line. Or so the theory went. What had become quickly

81

apparent to Caspasian and the other young infantry officers like him who were expected to hold these porcupines, as they were unaffectionately nicknamed, was that a very special kind of soldier was needed to man them.

It took a lot of guts to stand fast while the Germans swept by, heading for the rear. The theory held that the redoubt would be able to survive in isolation, having been prepared for all-round defence, and well stocked with arms, ammunition and even — in the case of the larger ones — with its own artillery. But what of the young soldier peering terrified over the crest of the sandbag wall? How would he feel knowing that for the first time there was no direct link back to base? What if he were to be wounded? How would he get back to the field hospital? Would he take comfort from the thought that his position was helping to break up the greater German attack? Or would he instead anticipate with mounting alarm the approach of the German following echelons who had been assigned to mop him up with bomb, bayonet and flamethrower?

It was particularly disconcerting to the young Caspasian therefore to discover that Redoubt Isis, in which he found himself, was manned by a hotch-potch unit hurriedly assembled from returning casualties like Caspasian himself, men sufficiently recovered from wounds to be thrust once again to the fore, just in time to face a fresh German onslaught. Without any regimental identity and no unit loyalties to bind them together, most of the men comprising the little garrison faced the prospect of combat with lonely terror. Most but not all. Private Nathaniel Dobson was one who did not.

The divisional commander had fancied himself as something of an Egyptologist and had named each of the redoubts in his sector after the various gods in the Egyptian pantheon. Close by Isis stood Osiris. Then there was Shu, Tefnut, Seth, Nephtys, Geb and Nut. Far to the rear, and the only redoubt with a communication trench linking it securely to the main British trench line, was the heavily fortified divisional command post, Atum Ra, named after the god who had given birth to all the others.

Caspasian had been in the redoubt for barely a week when he first came across Nathaniel Dobson. It was shortly after midnight and Caspasian was touring the redoubt during his two-hour stint as duty officer. He had just been checking on one of the Vickers machine-gun positions, when he came across a sentry leaning far out over the sandbag wall. Caspasian raced up to him, grabbed his webbing straps from behind and yanked him roughly back into cover.

'For God's sake man, don't you know there are snipers out there?'

The sentry looked calmly back at him, a mischievous twinkle in his eyes. Caspasian was surprised to see that the man was in his late forties. The hair at his temples was grey and he had a large bushy moustache.

'Easy there, laddie,' he said cheerfully. Then, catching first sight of Caspasian's badges of rank in the starlight, he corrected himself. 'Sorry, Captain. I was just . . . erm . . . just busy, like.'

There was a scuffle behind the man's back where his hands were stuffed out of sight.

'What have you got there?'

'Nothing Captain. Nothing at all.'

Caspasian had to struggle to stop himself from smiling. 'Let's have a look. Come on.'

Without any sign of embarrassment, the sentry plucked a rabbit from behind his back like a magician. He beamed in mock surprise. 'Well will you look at that now! How did that get there?'

Caspasian reached towards the animal and fingered the thin leather cord around its neck. 'I would think your bootlace snare probably had something to do with it.'

The man eyed Caspasian in a new light. 'Know something about snares do you Captain?'

Caspasian smiled. 'Don't change the subject. You're supposed to be looking for Germans, not rabbits.'

'Ah well, they're all vermin, aren't they, Captain,' and with as little effort as if he had been dusting the soil from his hands he snapped the rabbit's neck. With a barely perceptible wink at Caspasian he said, 'A little something for the pot, don't you see. A supplement to bully beef and biscuit.'

Caspasian peered out into the darkness. 'How did you find the rabbit run?'

'Standing here night after night, a man's got to have something to study. Otherwise he'd go madder than the buggers up at Div. HQ.'

'That's enough of that kind of talk. What's your name?' Caspasian asked. He tried to inject severity into his voice but instead felt very much the green youth before the bemused scrutiny of the sentry.

'Private Nathaniel Dobson, Captain.'

'Of?'

'Of Ethelstone in Dorset.'

'Of which regiment, you blithering idiot!'

The man gave a great burst of laughter at his own stupidity. From further along the trench there came a hissed warning to be quiet, followed immediately by the crack of a bullet snapping overhead. The two men ducked instinctively.

'Oh, dearie me,' Dobson scolded, clicking his tongue. 'Now look what's happened.'

'Exactly,' Caspasian snapped.

The man blinked at him. 'No, I mean look at my rabbit. I've dropped it in the mud.'

Given Private Dobson's independence of mind, it was no surprise to Caspasian that Smith took an instant dislike to the man. Captain Daniel Smith was the last to arrive in the redoubt before the German assault completed its isolation. One day they had been able to receive supplies, brought in escorted by strong fighting patrols, the next, they had found themselves cut off.

The discovery was made when a small party attempted to evacuate a wounded man back to the dressing station. He had been shot in the head by a sniper, but although a segment of his skull had been shot away to expose the brain inside, he remained conscious and surprisingly cheerful in spite of it. His companions speculated that he was happy because he had just got his ticket back home. Ten minutes later, both the wounded man and his carrying detail lay shot to ribbons in what had suddenly become no-man's-land, drilled full of holes by a German machine-gun that had materialised in the rear of the redoubt.

Major Dennis Cartwright summoned together his officers. 'That's that then,' he said, aping a confidence that Caspasian could tell he did not feel. 'Now we'll see if this whole redoubt malarky works.'

Deep in the Major's command bunker, seated next to Caspasian in the pale yellow light cast by the hurricane lamp, Smith swallowed audibly. 'What do we do, sir?'

The Major stared at him blankly. 'We hold.'

Later, as they emerged into the night air and made their way back to their own bunker which, as the only two captains in the ramshackle unit, they were obliged to share, Caspasian and Smith introduced themselves. He could not put his finger on it, but there was something about Smith that left Caspasian uneasy. Over the next few days, when the two of them found themselves off duty in the bunker together, Caspasian would catch Smith watching him. His expression was always the same, halfway between puzzled and suspicious. When their eyes met, Smith would beam brightly and seek to open some conversation or other, always bent, it seemed, on learning more of Caspasian's past.

For his part, Caspasian took to spending

more of his off-duty hours roaming the redoubt, even sometimes curling up in one of the fire positions to sleep, preferring the stars and fresh air to the stifling claustrophobia of the bunker and Smith's dark scrutiny.

Caspasian first became aware of Smith's antagonism to Dobson one evening immediately after stand-to, when he came upon Smith barking out some reprimand two inches from Dobson's face. He had made Dobson stand rigidly to attention and now, in front of the man's comrades, he was tearing into him for the untidy state of his dress and for his slapdash manners.

'Something the matter?' Caspasian enquired as casually as he could.

Smith whirled at the sound of his voice. His face was scarlet, partly with the residue of his anger and partly, it seemed to Caspasian, with embarrassment. Caspasian could not help thinking of the Gurkha soldiers of his own regiment for whom such a display of temper would have incurred an immense loss of face. Anger was a force to be controlled and channelled. It was, quite simply, unseemly. He longed to be back with his own men, and deeply regretted the wound which had now landed him in this redoubt with such a rabble.

'Thank you, Caspasian. Nothing I can't

handle,' Smith said coldly.

'All right then.'

Caspasian smiled, but moved only a couple of paces away and turned to survey no-man's-land through a trench periscope, whistling nonchalantly to himself.

Smith was silent for a moment, and then, with a final bark of, 'So just watch it in future!' spun on his heel and stalked away. Caspasian waited until the sound of footsteps clipping briskly along the duckboards had gone, and then he glanced across at Dobson.

The old soldier had his helmet off, the offence which had sparked Smith's verbal assault. Caspasian looked him up and down. Dobson's comrades had all disappeared the moment Smith had gone.

'You have to admit, you are a bit of a scarecrow,' Caspasian said pleasantly.

Dobson's shoulders slumped as he exhaled. It was as if he had been holding his breath throughout the dressing down.

'That young'un will see me dead,' he said simply.

Caspasian felt as if a cold hand had suddenly gripped him. He tried to shake it off. 'Don't talk daft, man! Look at you. It's hardly surprising, is it?'

Dobson sat down heavily on the parapet firing step. He smiled sadly across at

Caspasian. A moment later, the twinkle was back in his eye. He glanced to left and right before asking quietly, 'D'you get that rabbit leg I sent you?'

Caspasian nodded. 'Private Thornton dropped it by on his way past. Thank you.'

'All being well, I'll have another by morning. I've found another rabbit run. Across by the gunner party's observation post. I reckon there's a whole warren of them thereabouts.'

'Dobson, for God's sake forget about your blasted rabbits. Besides, how the devil could a whole rabbit warren have survived the last three years of artillery bombardments?'

'Why, like us of course! By digging.'

Caspasian laughed. 'You're as mad as a hatter. It's a rat run more likely.'

Dobson shrugged, his face thoughtful. 'It's all meat. The good Lord's creatures are all put on earth to sustain the righteous. It won't be the first time I've eaten rat.'

'Me neither,' Caspasian said easily, turning again to his periscope.

Dobson eyed him carefully. After a moment he said, 'You're not joking, are you, Captain?'

'Would I lie to you, Private Dobson?'

Dobson shook his head in disbelief. 'You're an odd sort of officer, Captain, if you'll permit me to say so.'

'I'm not sure I will.'

To his surprise, Caspasian found himself suddenly talking. There, as the redoubt slipped into its night routine and the men went fearfully about their business, Caspasian found himself talking to the old soldier with an ease he had not felt for a long, long time. It was only two hours later, when he returned to his bunker and slipped into his cot, looking across with distaste at the softly snoring form of Daniel Smith, that he recalled Dobson's words. 'That young'un will see me dead.'

As he did so, he felt again the same inexplicable sense of dread, and acknowledged for the first time his intuition that Dobson would be proved correct.

★ ★ ★

Two days out of Shanghai the gunboat came upon pirates. As the crew sprinted to battle stations, Caspasian made his way to the bridge, invited by Commander Hewson to view the encounter from the best vantage point.

'Make ready a boarding party, Mr Braggins,' the Commander shouted down at the chief petty officer who jogged grimly past, a cutlass in one fist and a revolver in the other.

'Aye, sir.' Braggins barked out the reply, a glint of pure joy in his eyes.

One of the sailors handed Caspasian a steel helmet. 'Best put this on, sir.'

Caspasian looked longingly at the sidearms worn by the naval officers around him. Commander Hewson smiled.

'Matheson, give Captain Caspasian a revolver.'

The sailor hesitated. Dressed in canvas shoes, loose cotton trousers and shirt, sleeves rolled up to the elbows, Caspasian looked more like a bureaucrat than a soldier.

'It's all right, Matheson,' the Commander grinned. 'I think we can trust Captain Caspasian here to handle the weapon safely.'

'Yes, sir,' the sailor snapped, abashed.

Caspasian drew the weapon from its holster and felt the reassuring press of the butt in his palm. He flicked open the cylinder and checked the load. Putting the gun back in the holster, he buckled on the belt, checking the pouch for spare ammunition. It was full.

The lookout had spotted the junk which had failed to respond to his signals. Instead, on seeing the gunboat turn in its direction, the junk had sped away, heading downriver.

Confronted with the British gunboat, the junk never had a chance of escape. Eventually, seeing the British warship bearing down upon it, guns fully manned and boarding party lining the decks, the junk dropped its sail and hove to.

The gunboat was pulling alongside, armed sailors levelling their weapons at the Chinese crew as grappling hooks were thrown across, when there was a shout from the junk. Commander Hewson stared in surprise through his binoculars and then broke into a broad grin.

'Well, I never!'

'What is it?' Caspasian asked.

The Commander chuckled. 'It's that mad bloody Scotsman. Ewan Cameron.'

Caspasian went across and peered cautiously over the side. Standing on the deck of the junk he saw a man in the uniform of the Shanghai Municipal Police waving at the gunboat. In one hand he held a revolver. With the other he clutched a rope, to the end of which was fastened a handcuffed Chinaman. The Chinaman appeared to be struggling. The big Scotsman scowled at his prisoner, leaned across, and clubbed him senseless with the barrel of his gun.

'Spot of bother?' Commander Hewson shouted through cupped hands as the two vessels came side by side. The grappling hooks were thrown across and the junk fastened securely to the gunboat.

'Nothing I can't handle,' Cameron shouted back, clearly enjoying himself. 'Sorry we didn't come about when you signalled. Thought you were damned Frenchies. I'm buggered if I'm going to surrender my haul to them.'

As the naval boarding party went aboard to see if there was anything they could do to help, Hewson and Caspasian made their way down from the bridge. Cameron stalked across to the gunwale and hauled himself up on to the gunboat's deck. He holstered his revolver and glanced suspiciously at Caspasian. Commander Hewson introduced them.

'Pleased to meet you,' Cameron said.

As the Scotsman exchanged pleasantries with Commander Hewson, explaining that he had intercepted the junk himself, two other policemen emerged from the junk, also shepherding prisoners.

'Did you not see my launch? I stayed aboard the junk myself with two of my constables while I sent my launch downriver to fetch help. I'm surprised you didn't encounter it.'

'Not surprising really,' Commander Hewson said. 'We probably passed it in the night. 'Damned brave of you to stay on board amongst those cut-throats with only two men as escort though, Ewan.'

The Scotsman snorted derisively. 'Foolhardy's what you mean.' He winked at Caspasian. 'The Commander's a polite Englishman, you see,' he said in a theatrical aside.

While the two men talked Caspasian decided to have a look for himself. He hopped nimbly over the side and clambered aboard the junk. Canvas tarpaulins covered the deck. He stooped and grasped the corner of one and hauled it back. Underneath was a large pile of tightly bound cloth parcels. He reached down and prodded one. Soft like putty. He sniffed his fingers and frowned.

Taking out his revolver, he held it by the barrel and whacked one of the parcels with the butt. Under the force of the blow it split open. Like flesh sprouting from a wound, a dark brown substance oozed from inside. Caspasian put away his revolver and took a pinch of the substance, rolling it in his palm to inspect. Raw opium.

'Watch out!'

At the shouted warning, Caspasian ducked and turned in the same movement. A Chinese broadsword whistled close overhead, the blade lodging in the pile of opium sacks with a thud.

He struggled to get his revolver free, his eyes picking out the man who had appeared

95

out of nowhere. Coming at him, the Chinese sailor glared hatred through his one eye. The other was a shrivelled empty socket.

There was the crack of a gun as Braggins fired off a shot, but the bullet went wide of its mark. Out of the corner of his eye Caspasian saw that Cameron had knocked aside the Chief's aim.

'I need him alive!'

As the man closed with Caspasian a knife appeared in his fist. Caspasian saw it only at the last moment, just managing to turn aside the upwards thrust with a palm heel deflection. With his other hand he clubbed his assailant behind the ear with a tettsui hammer blow. To his surprise the man simply blinked, shook his head and came on.

Caspasian backed away, fists in a guard position while his legs sought space for a solid stance amongst the sacks and other paraphernalia strewn about the deck. He was just about to counterattack when there was a blur on the periphery of his vision and a blunt dark object struck the Chinaman on the head, dropping him unconscious to the deck. It was Cameron's revolver, flung with surprising accuracy.

As the big Scotsman strode across and retrieved his weapon, he kicked the prone Chinaman savagely in the gut.

'Tie him up,' he shouted to one of his constables. He scowled at Caspasian. 'You want to be more careful.' He scanned Caspasian's clothes with ill-concealed disdain. 'An opium junk's no place for sight-seeing.'

Caspasian stared levelly back at him. 'Thank you for the warning.'

Commander Hewson offered to provide Cameron with an escort, but the policeman declined.

'That's kind of you, Commander, but where you're headed you can ill afford to lose a single man.'

'Oh?'

'Things upriver are getting hotter by the day. Chiang Kai-shek's getting closer every minute and he's stirred up the warlords like a hornets' nest.'

'Do you know anything of General Mok?' Caspasian asked.

Cameron shrugged. 'No more than anyone else. He hates Chiang Kai-shek, but that doesn't necessarily mean he's any friend of ours. Personally I'd hang the whole blasted lot of them.'

'Amen to that,' Hewson chimed, as his men withdrew from the junk and prepared to cast it loose. 'You're sure you'll be all right, Ewan?'

'I'll be just grand.' Cameron waved his hand vaguely upriver. 'You should be worrying more about yourselves. At least I'm headed in the right direction. Shanghai. You lot are headed straight into hell.' He gave a great bellow of laughter. The two vessels drifted apart and a few moments later the gunboat was continuing on its way. Caspasian walked back to the stern and watched the junk grow ever smaller. Standing at the helm, the big Scotsman glared fiercely downriver, sailing resolutely for Shanghai with his cargo of seized opium and his beaten and cowed prisoners.

4

For the first part of the passage upriver Caspasian was unable to note anything that might alert a casual observer to the great armed upheaval taking place in the land. The gunboat steamed past Nanking and then through the province of Anhui. However, as the days went on and the gunboat penetrated ever further into the interior, the telltale signs appeared, gradually magnifying until the evidence that they were in the middle of a ferocious civil war was plain to see on both the banks of the Yangtze as well as on the river's powerful and turbulent surface.

The first corpses wheeled past in the current, rotating like giant star fish, limbs spread-eagled, face down, bloated and green or black, depending on the length of time since death. Most were the bodies of men, still raggedly dressed in the disintegrating scraps of uniform that had marked them out as belonging to the army of one warlord or another.

The sailors would lean over the railings and fend them off with long poles to prevent them snarling the propellers. If that were to happen, it would necessitate sending some-one overboard to cut loose the rotting flesh. The water of the Yangtze was foul enough itself before the addition of human entrails. As the sailors were, to a man, unwilling to volunteer for such a loathsome venture over the side, and terrified of being detailed for it by Chief Petty Officer Braggins, they handled their poles diligently and with the greatest of skill.

From the river banks, wisps of black smoke arose into the pallid sky, slowly dissipating with altitude into dark smudges that over-hung the torched dwellings beneath. Fields had been untended for several seasons, the usual march of the farmer's year terminally interrupted. Packs of dogs could be seen wandering aimlessly at the water's edge, bereft of humans to give them direction. The boldest of them, on spying the gunboat and the men on board, would rush chest deep into the scum and flotsam, barking furiously, while those more timid yapped from greater distance, running to and fro until the vessel had steamed out of range.

'Cameron wasn't joking,' Commander Hewson said grimly as he and Caspasian stood reviewing the desolation.

Caspasian was busy scanning the landscape through his binoculars. Oddly, he found it comforting to travel through the war-scorched terrain aboard the gunboat, steaming safely out in midstream, and the thought of leaving its sanctuary was disquieting. It was like transiting a raging battlefield as the spirit of someone who has already fallen. There was nothing further to be suffered. Bullet, shell splinter, gas and steel, nothing could do Caspasian harm. He had gone through and had passed beyond. Now, secure in his ethereal form, he was free to survey the horrors which others must yet endure.

In the wardroom below, tea could be summoned, and later, after dark, there would be supper with Hewson, followed, after a last turn around the decks under the night sky, by an untroubled sleep in white sheets. The concurrent torments taking place less than half a mile away on either side were as remote as any battle from history.

Caspasian lowered his binoculars. He was surprised at the mental effort required to rid himself of the comfortable illusion, but his experience was too great to be so easily overwhelmed. He had seen and done too much to be beguiled by fantasy. He knew that in no time at all he would find himself ashore, and then it would be this brief, pleasant river jaunt that would take on the aspect of illusion. It would become the stuff of memory and he would have to shake it off smartly. Best do it now, he thought.

'Commander, do you think I might persuade your Master at Arms to let me sign out a couple of guns from his armoury?'

Hewson grinned. 'I wouldn't have let you go naked among the heathen, dear fellow. No fear.'

For Caspasian, stepping into the armoury was like stumbling into Aladdin's cave. Wooden weapons racks were bolted on every side and in them, a vast array of pistols, revolvers, rifles, and light machine-guns was stored. There was a rack of cutlasses, their blades finely honed and glinting, and, hanging behind each, its scabbard. There were cases of ammunition, drum magazines, chests of hand grenades, boxes of explosives. Stored in a glass-fronted cabinet, he saw prismatic compasses, Verey pistols and signal flares. Caspasian whistled softly in admiration.

'You should see the magazine for the main guns,' Braggins said proudly.

'Too bad I can't fit some wheels to the hull and take the whole lot with me.'

'You can have what you can carry, sir.'

Caspasian stared at Braggins in amazement. 'There's many a quartermaster I'd dearly love to hear that from. Most of them believe stores are for sitting on shelves. It's only the best among them that know otherwise.'

That evening over dinner, Commander Hewson voiced his concern. 'I don't like the idea of simply dropping you off in Hankow, you know.' He shook his head at the prospect.

'It won't be a problem, believe me,' Caspasian tried to reassure him, unconvinced himself.

'Are you sure I can't leave a small landing party with you? At least to accompany you until you make contact with this General Mok?'

'We'd only be putting more lives at risk. In any case, by all accounts General Mok is as keen as we are to establish contact. He needs arms and the western powers are his best chance, Britain foremost among them.'

The Commander leaned across and recharged Caspasian's glass. He had conjured a bottle of Chateau Margaux from his cabin, a particularly fine vintage that was wasted on the leathery steaks produced by the Chinese cook, but much appreciated by Caspasian nonetheless.

They chatted on for a further hour before Caspasian retired to his bunk. What with the wine, the steady thrum of the engines, and the motion of the river, he was soon fast asleep.

When he awoke the following morning, the Commander was already on the bridge. They were nearing Hankow where Caspasian was due to pick up the Peking Express which would take him north into Mok's territory.

As he said his goodbyes, Caspasian felt a gnawing in his gut, almost as when, in his schooldays, he had been forced to return to the horrors of an English boarding school after the peace of the holidays. In the absence of a father, his grandfather had made himself responsible for the boy's upbringing and, although he had meant well by sending him away to England, fearing lest the strong-willed and independent youngster ran wild in the ports of the Far East, Caspasian had found it hard to forgive the old man. At least, until he was old enough to understand.

With the same fortitude from those far-off days, Caspasian jumped down into the launch and let it take him to the quayside. He sat in the prow, his baggage at his feet, staring ahead, not looking back, but fixing his eyes instead on the wharf and the future.

The city was alive with rumour. The arrival of the gunboat had stirred a great deal of interest and as Caspasian slung his holdall over his shoulder, gripped a canvas haversack tightly in his other fist and struck out into the gaping crowd, he tried to ignore the hostile murmurs and the jostling that accompanied them. He was dressed unobtrusively in a pair of grey-green trousers, tucked into calf-length lace-up boots. Over a loose white cotton shirt he wore an open tweed jacket, sufficiently bulky to conceal the .455 inch Smith & Wesson revolver deep in one pocket, and the box of spare bullets in the other. He had secreted a few other acquisitions from the gunboat's armoury in his hand luggage, but he had felt it best to keep at least one weapon within easy reach. To complete his dress, he had brought his battered old trilby.

The staff of the British Consulate had long since been evacuated, first to Nanking and then to Shanghai. So, with nothing to delay him, Caspasian selected a rickshaw out of the many that noisily offered him their services, and ordered it to take him to the station. He expected to be able to contact General Mok's forces somewhere north of the town. His plan was hardly subtle. Get on the next train to Peking and keep going until it entered Mok's territory, whereupon it would be stopped to enable the passengers to pay Mok's 'toll'. At that point Caspasian would introduce himself and be duly conveyed to the General himself. Such was his plan. Unfortunately it foundered the moment he arrived at the station and discovered that the line was closed. The last train for the north had left the day before and fighting had severed the connection. No one was able to tell him when the line might be re-opened.

Having paid the rickshaw driver and watched him depart cackling, as if he had just delivered another damned soul to the gates of hell, Caspasian took in his surroundings properly for the first time. The town was in a mess, but then which place in China was not? He did not fancy the idea of staying there one moment longer than he had to, but with the railway system shut down to civilian traffic, and with an apparent absence of motor vehicles, he felt at a loss as to what to do.

He had no sooner slumped despondent on to a bench when he heard a sound that caused him to prick up his ears. It was the unmistakable throb of a motorcycle. He was on his feet in a second and, sure enough, a moment later the machine came into view, weaving its way through the carts and rickshaws. To Caspasian's amazement it was a Model H Triumph, a 550cc machine capable, when running to the best of its ability, of a top speed of 45mph.

Leaving his bags by the bench, he darted

across the street and clutched the rider who had stopped to allow a cart laden with an assortment of rotten fruit to pass. The man looked round, startled, his eyes filling with terror at the sight of a westerner. He glanced quickly to right and left to see who else had noticed the two of them together.

'Your motorcycle,' Caspasian shouted above the deep tone of the engine. 'How much?'

The man stared at him aghast, not seeming to understand a word he had said. Caspasian cursed and tried again, speaking in his clearest Mandarin. When that too failed he thrust a hand inside his jacket, pulled out his wallet and waved a fistful of bank notes in the rider's face.

'How much?' He tapped the machine's tank and waited. At last light dawned in the man's eyes, and with it, a glint of avarice. His fear suddenly vanished, he closed his eyes and shook his head firmly. A second later he peeped surreptitiously at the slightly fatter wad of notes in Caspasian's fist. The man sighed heavily, casting a loving gaze at the machine, as if it was his mother, wife and daughter rolled into one.

Caspasian scowled but increased his offer. Finally the man beamed and swung himself off the saddle. He snatched at the money and counted it as Caspasian retrieved his bags and tied them on as securely as he could. The tank was three-quarters full. It would have to do. With unexpected good grace, the previous owner handed Caspasian his goggles and then leaned across and started to explain the controls. Caspasian nodded impatiently, eager to be on his way.

'Thank you, I know.' Gunning the throttle to keep the engine alive, Caspasian buttoned his jacket one-handed, stuffed his trilby down the front, settled himself on the saddle, let out the clutch and veered away unsteadily. Finding his way out of town was easy enough. The road simply paralleled the rail tracks. Behind him was the river and in front lay the north. After a few minutes, the buildings fell away, he left the outskirts of the town, and the next moment he was out on the open road.

After all the time spent in the foul-smelling confines of Shanghai, and then the continuing vision of war and pestilence alongside the river during his voyage aboard the gunboat, Caspasian was seized by a wonderful feeling of release as he opened the throttle wide and let the motorcycle carry him into the wilderness. His earlier trepidation at leaving behind the gunboat and his fellow countrymen evaporated and he gave himself over to the exhilarating liberation that swiftly replaced it.

It was only when the first flood of boyish excitement had spent itself that he realised the true nature of his situation and sobered accordingly. He was in the middle of country torn apart by civil war, ravaged by competing warlords. His armaments were pitifully few and he was completely on his own. To his surprise, Caspasian found that he was smiling. He reached down to his jacket and felt the comforting weight of gun metal. Commander Hewson had ensured that he had rations sufficient for three days, and in addition, as Caspasian had been climbing down into the launch, had handed him a flask of brandy.

'For the nights,' Hewson had said with a wink.

Caspasian knew that he would be needing it. It was still early in the year and the nights were capable of a bitter cold.

By early afternoon Caspasian was riding along the top of a broad-backed earthen bund dividing two enormous paddy fields. The water had largely been allowed to drain from them, leaving a marsh overgrown with a dense tangle of something looking like mangrove. The road, now far north of Hankow, had dwindled to become a beaten track and he had been obliged to slow his machine accordingly. In fact, the slower speed made sense as it would help conserve his fuel supply. Unlike before, the nature of the track forced him to keep his eyes fixed on the ground immediately before him, gauging distances to the next pothole, selecting the best route around it, and then manoeuvring the big motorcycle. From occasional glances to either side, he had a rough picture of the rolling hills that had appeared flanking the valley. Their sides were thickly wooded, and from behind them he could make out the summits of even higher features in the background.

He was just negotiating a particularly hazardous stretch of the bund, revving the motor and only partially releasing the clutch to give the machine maximum purchase on the difficult ground, when he suddenly looked up to find himself staring at three Chinese soldiers, all equally as startled as him. They had unslung their rifles and levelled them at this strange apparition, and in the same instant Caspasian noted their youth, the fear in their eyes, and their fingers on the triggers.

As they straddled the track, allowing no way around, Caspasian drew to a halt, let the motor idle, and waved a gloved hand in as friendly a manner as possible.

'Hello!' he called out cheerily.

The largest of the three walked slowly towards him, his eyes mesmerised by the motorcycle so that Caspasian wondered if the youth had seen one before. He looked up at Caspasian with fascination, reversed his rifle, and swung the wooden butt at Caspasian's head with all his might.

Caught off guard, it was all Caspasian could do to duck in time, but in doing so he toppled from the saddle into the dust, the motorcycle fell onto its side with a crash, and the engine spluttered and died. With the fallen machine now between himself and the young soldier, Caspasian saw that he had one chance to draw his revolver. But as his hand moved to his jacket, the soldier's two companions quickly brought their rifle butts into the shoulder and aimed straight at him, eyes squinting down the sights.

'Wait!' Caspasian called out. 'I've come to . . . '

Before he could complete his sentence, the rifle butt of his assailant was swinging at his head a second time. Caspasian rolled aside.

'This is fucking stupid,' he mumbled to himself.

He was about to make one last attempt at communication, when the soldier stepped over the prone motorcycle, and drew back his rifle for a third assault. This time he held the weapon by the stock, obviously intending to bring the brass butt plate crashing down on Caspasian's skull.

'Fuck this,' Caspasian said. He waited until the soldier had put all his weight behind the blow and the rifle was swinging down, and then rolled out of the way. But instead of moving out of range as the soldier might have expected, Caspasian rolled in close. As he did so, he shot out his right foot using the sokuto, the outside edge, driving it up between the soldier's straddled legs. The youngster's eyes bulged out of their sockets and the wind left him with an audible sigh.

Instantly Caspasian dug in his jacket pocket, pulled out his Smith & Wesson, and, coming up on his knees into an aiming position, levelled it at the other two soldiers ready to fire. To his surprise they had lowered their rifles and were doubled over with laughter, falling against each other for support as they pointed at their stricken comrade and gabbled in a dialect that Caspasian found completely unintelligible.

Slowly he got to his feet. Keeping the revolver pointed at them, he stooped and picked up the rifle at his feet and tossed it out into the paddy field at the foot of the bund, and then moved across to the others. To his amazement they offered no resistance as he slowly reached towards their rifles and plucked them, one at a time, from their laughter-weakened grasp and similarly threw them safely out of reach.

'What the hell have we got here?' he said aloud, stupefied.

The soldier he had kicked was writhing on the ground, hands clutching his testicles, gasps and moans escaping from between his clenched teeth. As his two comrades gradually sobered, surveying Caspasian with bemused interest, they seemed to notice the revolver in his fist for the first time. The smiles fell from their faces to be replaced with an almost pantomime expression of fear.

Caspasian leaned closer to them, sniffed the sickly sweet smell, and understood. Their brains were completely drugged with opium.

'Well, you're a sorry bunch, aren't you?' he said. He heaved a great sigh of relief, the tension of the encounter dissipating, leaving him empty. Disarmed, the three youths were as much a threat to him as a sackful of kittens.

He pushed them roughly face down on to the track and then hauled over their comrade and flattened him, still groaning, beside them. Methodically he went through their web equipment and their pockets. All he produced was a meagre jumble of spare bullets, tobacco, cooked rice, some herbal medicines wrapped in oiled paper, and a scattering of worthless coins. The last thing he found confirmed his suspicions. It was a soft ball of dark brown raw opium, the size of a prune and the texture of putty.

One of them saw him studying it. They called across, indicating that he was welcome to share it with them if he wanted. Instead, Caspasian drew back his arm and tossed the ball far out into the field. The soldier shouted something and made to get to his feet, but Caspasian hefted the revolver at him and he quickly shut up.

Using their own belts, Caspasian tied their wrists securely behind their backs. When he was happy they were secure, he lifted the motorcycle upright and checked it for damage. It looked unharmed, but then he noticed a dark patch on the track where it had been lying. With a sickening lurch in his stomach he wrenched open the fuel tank and confirmed his fears. While lying on its side the petrol had leaked from the tank which was now virtually dry.

'Well, that's that then, isn't it?' he said heavily.

He was just wondering what to do when he

heard the sound of horses approaching. He judged there to be quite a number of them and they were coming at the canter. For a moment he considered grabbing his holdall and heading out into the paddy field on foot. One look at the tangled mass of weed and the marshy bed beneath it dissuaded him. Behind him, the track disappeared along the bund in a straight line for at least five hundred yards. There was nowhere for him to go. The next moment the issue was decided for him as a troop of cavalry came into view, powering down the bund in his direction.

One of his captives smirked, but Caspasian noticed that the other two looked less confident. In fact, to Caspasian they appeared terrified.

The cavalry troop rode in twos. In the lead, the officer stared fixedly ahead. He was crisply dressed in a light grey uniform with high collar and brown leather knee-length riding boots. A sword hung at his side, an ornate gold tassel on the pommel of the hilt. He wore a pair of binoculars around his neck and his shoulder-boards indicated a rank that Caspasian guessed to be either major or colonel. Behind him, each of the mounted soldiers carried a rifle slung across his back. Their chests were criss-crossed with canvas ammunition bandoliers and each of them also carried a large cavalry sabre in a scabbard strapped to the saddle. By their turnout and bearing Caspasian reckoned they were the elite arm of whichever warlord they served.

They drew up in a cloud of dust and the officer surveyed the scene before him with interest.

'Who are you and what are you doing here?' he barked at Caspasian in Mandarin.

By now, Caspasian felt certain he must already have entered the territory controlled by General Mok's forces so he swallowed hard and answered, feeling insufficiently reassured by the weight of the revolver in his hand.

'I am looking for General Mok.'

The officer smiled ruefully. 'Too bad if you were to fall into the hands of General Chiang Kai-shek's forces. They would execute you out of hand for such a statement.'

'Then it's lucky for me that I haven't met any of Chiang's men.'

The officer raised his eyebrows. 'How do you know we are not his?'

'Because you're not wearing the uniform of the Kuomintang Nationalist Army,' Caspasian replied tiredly, trying not to let his impatience with the officer's game show.

'Maybe I should shoot you myself,' the officer said. 'Only a spy could know so much.'

'If you did you would find yourself answerable to the anger of General Mok. He would be most upset with you when he discovered you had killed a man who could do him a great service.'

The officer scowled. 'We already have one of those,' he said bitterly.

Caspasian was about to press him for more information, when the officer's gaze fell upon the pinioned bodies of the three soldiers. He barked a command over his shoulder and four of his men dismounted and raced to retrieve the prisoners. To Caspasian's surprise, instead of untying them, they simply yanked them to their feet.

'Bring them with us,' the officer said curtly. He looked back at Caspasian. 'Follow me. If you try to leave the track I will have you shot.'

'What about my motorcycle?' Caspasian asked. He had grown attached to the machine and had an idea that it might come in handy later on. The officer was less impressed.

'It's hardly much use out here. Leave it and I'll have someone fetch it later.'

'But someone might steal it,' Caspasian protested.

Several of the cavalrymen sniggered. 'No one would dare,' the officer said, pulling his horse around and leading the way back along the bund.

Relieved of his revolver and luggage, Caspasian fell into step behind the mounted officer who never looked at him or addressed a single word to him thereafter.

The little column walked for the rest of the day, and it was not until the sky was darkening and night was almost upon them that they arrived on the outskirts of a small town. Although the houses had clearly taken a battering at some point in the recent past, an attempt had been made to patch them up. All of them seemed to be occupied by soldiers, the flickering lights of hurricane lamps and cooking fires appearing through open windows and doors. As far as he could tell, Caspasian also noticed that sentries had been posted to cover every route out of the town. They were similarly dressed to the three soldiers he had captured, but more alert. Indeed, he noticed how they glanced warily at the three unfortunate youngsters that the horsemen had now herded to the front of the column, as if to publicise their shame and make an example of them.

Rounding a corner towards the centre of the town, Caspasian was suddenly stopped dead in his tracks by the sight that loomed before him. There, sitting vast and squat on its tracks, stretched the threatening bulk of an armoured train. It was so long he could barely see either end of it in the late evening gloom. The officer saw his awe and grinned. 'The Dragon,' he said proudly.

Each carriage was fully armoured with iron plating, painted in the mottled colours of camouflage. Gun turrets, machine-gun ports and rifle slits covered every angle, making the whole terrible machine a hideous vehicle of death, bristling with weaponry. From inside Caspasian could hear the hammering of something being fixed and the shouted commands of those directing the operation. They were in Russian.

Suddenly there was a shout from behind him. 'Well, I never!'

Caspasian turned to see a familiar figure emerging swiftly from the shadows of a nearby house.

'Caspasian? Is that really you?'

The mounted officer reined back his horse to make way for Daniel Smith. Smith had aged well in the ten years since Caspasian had last seen him. He was still wiry and fit, and he plainly looked as though he took regular exercise. War obviously agreed with him. But as he drew closer and extended a hand which Caspasian reluctantly took, Caspasian noticed the same furtive look in the man's eyes, shifty and unsure. Added to it was something else. They were as cold as stone.

'What . . . I mean, how . . . ?' Smith held out his arms wide, gaping in astonishment at his old comrade. 'This is the middle of China, for God's sake! How the devil did you get here?'

The mounted officer answered for Caspasian. 'By motorcycle.'

'By . . . ' Smith burst into a peal of shrill laughter. 'Why, you old dog! Don't tell me you're looking for a job?' He cocked his head. 'Not after mine, I hope?' he enquired only half joking. 'I don't mind telling you that General Mok always has room for fine men of war. That's what's made him the best around.'

From the bowels of the armoured train came a burst of Russian invective. Smith grinned. 'See what I mean? A word of advice — don't cross the Russians. Nasty bunch, all of them.'

For the first time Smith noticed the three bound soldiers standing miserably in the shadows. He fired a question at the cavalry officer who replied in an offhand manner, briefly recounting the tale of their encounter with Caspasian. Smith said something rapidly under his breath and then, putting a hand on Caspasian's shoulder, turned him towards the house from which he himself had just come.

'Let's get you sorted out with some

accommodation and a meal. When did you last eat?' he asked pleasantly.

Caspasian hesitated. 'Just a second, Smith . . . '

'For God's sake man, call me Daniel,' Smith cut in.

Not to be deflected, Caspasian held back, gently but firmly. 'Did I just hear you correctly?'

'What do you mean?'

Caspasian smiled awkwardly, hardly believing what he thought he had just heard. 'What did you just say to the Colonel?'

'Major,' Smith corrected. 'Major Chiu.'

'Right. But what did you tell him to do?'

Smith chuckled. 'Nothing that need concern you, old man. Come on now, let's go . . . '

Caspasian dug his heels in, stiffening his voice while yet remaining as civil as he could. He was painfully aware that he was in the middle of a warlord's camp and in the presence of a man for whom his main feelings were suspicion and extreme dislike.

'Daniel, they're just youngsters. They didn't know what they were doing.'

The smile on Smith's face held, but whatever warmth it once possessed had gone. 'On the contrary. They knew exactly what they were doing. General Mok maintains the strictest discipline amongst the ranks. All the men know it.' Without looking at the miscreants he pointed in their direction. 'I know they've been using opium. I can smell it. Besides, they were reported this morning as having deserted. They deserve to be executed. In fact, they're lucky they're going to be shot. Sometimes when the General wants to set an example he uses other less instant methods. They're only going to be shot out of deference to you.'

'Me?' Caspasian stammered.

'Yes. I wouldn't want you to think of us as barbaric.'

'Then what do you call this?' Caspasian said, aware that his voice was rising in spite of the control he was struggling to maintain.

Smith stood away from him, smile now completely gone. 'Listen, Caspasian. I don't know what you're doing here. No doubt you'll tell us in the morning. But don't meddle in things that don't concern you. We're not in the British Army now.'

Caspasian could not help himself. 'No,' he replied coldly. 'And you had a taste for executing people by firing squad there as well, didn't you?'

'How dare you?' Smith said quietly, the words issuing from him in the form of both rebuke and threat. 'And after what I did for you.'

Only the sight, out of the corner of his eye, of the cavalry Major sliding his pistol from its holster in readiness to defend Smith, caused Caspasian to clench his teeth on the barrage of curses that threatened to escape him. He sucked in his breath. Careful. Careful, he thought. This is not the time or place for confrontation. Not yet. Not here.

He forced a smile and shook his head. 'You're right,' he said calmly, the very words burning in his throat. 'I'm sorry. I had no business . . .'

Instantly Smith jumped in, making excuses on Caspasian's behalf. He could well understand. Caspasian was tired. Caspasian was out of sorts. After all, this was China. Nothing made sense out here.

In an act of munificence, Smith turned to the Major and withdrew his previous command. On hearing this, the three young soldiers rushed forward and threw themselves at his feet, thanking him. He stared down at them like some potentate surveying his vassals. Caspasian's stomach churned at the spectacle.

Leaving the soldiers prostrate in the dirt, their hands still securely fastened behind their backs, Caspasian allowed himself to be led away by Smith. Chattering excitedly, Smith talked all the way to the building where he himself had his quarters. He showed Caspasian to a vacant room and summoned an orderly to fetch bedding for the new arrival. When at last he departed with promises to introduce Caspasian to General Mok in the morning, Caspasian was left alone in his bare room, wondering whether he was guest or prisoner.

5

It was only with difficulty that Caspasian fell asleep. When he did, it was shallow and troubled. Several times he awoke, fancying he could hear disturbances in the night. When he slept, it was usually to see the face of Private Dobson and to hear again his words: 'That young'un will see me dead.'

The German bombardment had begun almost as soon as the redoubt had been cut off. With the position isolated, the German advance continued deep into the British defences, carving a way through to the main trench lines. The task of mopping up the bypassed redoubts fell to the German second echelon. However, far from being second-rate troops, these had been specially selected and trained for the job. They were a new breed of soldier, with skills developed for trench warfare. The lessons of the past three years had been learned and taken to heart. An altogether new doctrine had grown out of the experience. Now it was time to use it to chilling effect. Nothing like them had been seen before. The Germans called them 'stosstruppen'. Stormtroopers.

Unlike the massed infantry attacks of the past, the stormtroopers attacked in small groups, using the tactics of fire and movement. They were equipped with automatic weapons and a wealth of grenades and other close-quarter weapons. And they only went into the attack when the objective had been thoroughly, meticulously and ruthlessly bombarded. Only then would they close with the survivors, advancing in short, tactical bounds, each group supporting the other with concentrated small-arms fire, as they worked their way ever closer, until finally they infiltrated the shattered remnants of the objective to hunt down and murder anyone left.

The biggest problem during the days of the preparatory bombardment had been keeping the men from going mad. Caspasian remembered huddling on the floor of the bunker as the earth around them heaved and shook. The air was choked with dust. They inhaled it, in spite of the handkerchiefs knotted around their faces. Caspasian recalled one young soldier, terrified beyond endurance, trying to rush up the shivering steps out into the open. As the bunker rocked like a ship at sea, the youth lurched towards the exit. Dobson was there before him. The old soldier clutched the youngster to his broad chest and quietened him. From the far side of the bunker Caspasian had watched, amazed by the older man's calm demeanour. In the snatches of lesser noise between the bombardment's peaks of fury, he could hear that Dobson was humming. It sounded like a ballad, the tune lilting. He rocked the youth like a mother with a child. The youth in turn clutched him, eyes tight shut, lips working soundlessly at some prayer or entreaty.

In that primeval setting, Caspasian discovered the deepest respect for the old poacher. The worst was yet to come. Of that he was certain. It would come a minute, perhaps two, after the ear-splitting silence that would follow the sudden cessation of the bombardment. That was the moment Caspasian was waiting for. That was the moment for which he was steeling himself. As an officer it would be up to him to lead the way up the steps and to see the machine-guns in position before the German stormtroopers could rush the last yards and jump down into the collapsed trenches. If he was too slow, there would be hand-to-hand fighting, as brutal and violent as Bosworth or any ancient battlefield slaughter.

But while the bombardment continued there was only insanity to fear. That and the instant obliteration of a direct hit. While he waited and endured, drawing on every scrap of past experience and every shred of will power to keep from screaming, Caspasian kept his eyes fixed on Dobson, and the small, terrified creature pressed against the rough damp wool of his khaki tunic. A single wreath of steam rose from the two of them like a spirit leaving.

★　★　★

The blast of a whistle tumbled Caspasian from sleep. He shot up in his bed, sitting bolt upright on the mattress that had been laid out for him on the bare floor. For a moment his mind was utterly confused. He scrabbled for the whistle about his neck. Not finding the cord, his fingers tore the blankets from him. How could he have let himself sleep? It was outrageous! Had he been hit? Had the bunker walls collapsed, suffocating them?

Gradually, as each slow second pushed aside the next, each one dragging him further from sleep, he blinked and rubbed his eyes, the unfamiliar surroundings coming into focus. The air was cold but crisp. It was silent. He was alone. Then the whistle blast came again. It was the Dragon. The armoured train of General Mok.

Caspasian sank back against the wall. His

heart was pounding, his forehead beaded with sweat. He swung his legs round and sat up again, running a hand through his damp hair. As his breathing steadied he pushed the memories from him and tried to take stock. There was a single chair in the room, its only item of furniture. Someone had placed a washing bowl and jug of water on the seat. Beside it, his holdall and the canvas bag. He scuttled across, ripped them open and rummaged through them. The cavalry Major had never returned his Smith & Wesson, but now Caspasian discovered that even the Webley that he had stuffed at the bottom of the canvas bag had gone. Likewise, his ammunition, compass and everything else of value had been confiscated.

He washed, shaved, dressed and went to the door. It was locked. He knocked on it, lightly at first, then harder, calling out. There were footsteps, the sound of a key in the lock, and the door opened on a soldier, a rifle slung across his shoulder. For a moment the man seemed in two minds as to whether or not he should allow Caspasian out. While he deliberated, Caspasian thrust past him, thanking him politely in Mandarin for his help. Clearly the sentry's orders had been less than precise and, before he could come to a decision unfavourable to Caspasian's immediate purpose, Caspasian was down the stairs and out into the sunshine.

A fierce cold light dazzled him and he blinked, one hand shading his eyes, squinting while they accustomed themselves fully to the day. As they did so, achieving focus, a vision of horror slapped him in the face. Across the street, suspended from an upstairs balcony, hung the dead bodies of the three young soldiers who had waylaid him the previous day. They turned slowly in the light wafting of air that scurried between the houses. The ropes creaked under the strain imposed by their burdens. Instinctively Caspasian took a couple of steps towards the dead men before he stopped himself. Their wrists were still secured by his own fastenings, but their mouths had been gagged. The next moment Caspasian saw why. Someone had put out their eyes.

'That bastard. That bloody, bloody bastard.' He murmured it quietly. He hunted around, yet not knowing what he would do when he located Smith. His fists clenched and unclenched. He fought to steady his breathing. Fought for self-control. At that moment he longed for the feel of a gun in his hand, but at the same time was thankful he was unarmed.

He was even more thankful for the lack of a

gun when he turned and saw Smith approaching.

'Why?' Caspasian called out. 'For God's sake, Smith! Why?'

There were two soldiers behind Smith. As they drew near, they moved forward to flank him.

'There was nothing I could do, John. Believe me. You heard me, didn't you? I stopped the execution.' He shrugged. 'When the General heard, he had a fit. It was all I could do to stop them being roasted alive.'

Caspasian pointed at the dead men's faces. 'And this is better?'

Smith looked surprised. 'Oh, yes. Believe me, John, it is.'

At first Caspasian was lost for words. Then he said, 'What happened to you?'

Smith smiled. 'China happened to me, John.' He eyed Caspasian cynically. 'Don't tell me you still believe all that rubbish about playing the game, honour and all that?'

'I never believed in playing the game, as you put it. But I also never believed in cold-blooded murder either.'

'That's rich coming from someone with your reputation. You forget, I saw you in the trenches. I saw you fight.'

'That was totally different.'

'Was it, John? Tell me how?'

'That was the heat of battle. This is execution. More. It's torture for God's sake!' He peered at Smith, standing boldly before him, hands on hips. 'My God, you enjoy it, too!'

Smith's face darkened. 'Steady, John.' He stabbed a finger at his own chest. 'This is my territory, not yours. You'd do well to remember that. This is a nasty, bloody civil war.'

To Caspasian it seemed as if Smith tried to gather himself, seeking some justification for his behaviour. Good, Caspasian thought. You're still afraid of me, you little shit. And so you should be.

'I'm a professional,' Smith continued. 'Oh, I know you never had any respect for me. I know you always thought you were so damned superior. Well that's OK. I don't hold that against you.' He waved his hand, banishing the past. Then, as an afterthought he smiled bashfully and added, 'After all, it was me who saved your life.' His smile broadened into a grin. 'Come on. We should be friends, the two of us.' He drew closer, lowering his voice as if speaking to a co-conspirator. 'We're the only two English-men here. Stuck amongst all these damned Chinks and Russians. We're allies, you and I.

We're on the same side.'

Caspasian bit back the denial that sprang to his lips. 'Where's Mok?' he asked coldly. 'I'd like to see him now.'

Smith bristled but decided to ignore the snub. 'Yes. Of course. This way.' He turned on his heel and led Caspasian through the town.

Now that he could see it in daylight, Caspasian was able to get a better idea of the size and organisation of Mok's forces. Before leaving Shanghai he had received the latest intelligence on Mok's army, but even that was scant. What the British did know was that they wanted him as an ally against the relentless advance of Chiang Kai-shek. Anyone opposed to Mok was going to be considered an enemy of Britain and the other western powers. That meant supporting him in whatever local expansion he was currently engaged. Mok was to receive cash and guns, if he needed them. From what he already knew of Chinese warlords, Caspasian could not imagine Mok or any other warlord turning down such an offer. It put Caspasian in a strong bargaining position and, to a certain extent, secured his own personal safety while in Mok's domain.

Of course, the presence of Smith should have been a further boon, but there was too much in their shared segment of the past that threatened to undo such a cosy arrangement. Caspasian knew that he would have to tread very carefully. The spectacle that morning of the three hanged men had struck him with the dark significance of a Tarot prediction. Somewhere a hidden truth lay awaiting discovery, a truth that would impact on both Smith and Caspasian, and perhaps on the wider mission on which they were both currently engaged.

They came again to the railway tracks. In full daylight, the armoured train was, if anything, even more impressive. For the first time Caspasian caught sight of one of the Russians. He was sitting, stripped to the waist, on top of one of the gun turrets, worrying at the cupola hinges with an enormous spanner. He looked down at them as Caspasian and Smith passed below. A deep horizontal scar cut clean across the centre of his face from left to right, starting under one ear and finishing beneath the other. Where it intersected the nose, the ridge was deeply grooved.

'Sabre cut,' Smith said quietly as he saw Caspasian nod in greeting to the Russian who ignored it. 'We call him Scarface.' He shrugged. 'Not very original, I know, but that's General Mok for you.'

'Can I have a look inside?' Caspasian asked.

'Ask Mok. I don't see why not.'

Caspasian smiled. 'You mean only he can give permission?'

He could feel Smith bridle. 'Of course not. Come on. We'll do it now.'

Smith strode briskly to the end of the nearest carriage and hauled himself inside. Caspasian was amazed at how easy it had been to manipulate him.

After the dazzling sunlight of the cold morning outside, the interior of the train was gloomy and claustrophobic. The rank smell of human sweat mingled with that of old cooking, rust and cordite to assault the nostrils. Caspasian felt himself gagging. Smith grinned maliciously.

'Not exactly the Sincere Department Store perfumery, is it?'

Caspasian grimaced. 'No.'

In most parts of the train it was impossible to stand full height. It was a bit like being on a submarine, except there were weapons and gun ports wherever you looked.

'This thing must drink ammunition,' Caspasian observed, noting the banks of Vickers machine-guns stretching away down either flank.

'That's where you're going to help, I

suppose?' Smith asked sarcastically.

'What makes you say that?'

'Call it an educated guess. You're not a mercenary, Caspasian. I can tell.'

'Oh?'

Smith smiled proudly. 'You won't like me saying so, but you haven't got what it takes.'

'Thank God for that.'

Smith laughed, not unpleasantly. 'I know what you think of me, John. I don't care. No, I'd say you're here to strike some kind of deal. That's what Mok reckons anyway.'

'Your prescience is truly amazing, Daniel. And spot on. His Majesty's government, terrified of what Chiang Kai-shek will do to western business interests if he takes Shanghai and the coastal ports, is prepared to ally itself with the devil. In this case, that means Mok.' He paused, inspecting the mechanism of a Vickers for cleanliness. 'And you.'

Smith laughed again. 'You don't approve, I take it?'

'Far be it from me to either approve or disapprove. I'm just a minor imperial functionary.'

'Yes,' Smith said firmly. 'Well, I'm not. And you'd best remember that. I work for Mok now. So long as our interests coincide, you and I can get along just fine. But stop pushing me, John. I don't like it. We're not in France now.'

'The only pushing there, Daniel, was your own ambition.'

Smith was silent. He turned away sharply and started off into the bowels of the Dragon. 'Do you want to see the fucking train or don't you?'

When they eventually arrived at Mok's quarters in the town, both men were hot and dusty. Smith introduced Caspasian curtly, then sat to one side sulking. Mok greeted Caspasian cordially and ordered refreshments for the three of them.

'So you're the man whose life Captain Smith saved?' Mok boomed.

Caspasian smiled. 'I'm the one, General.'

'He has told me all about it.'

'So it seems.'

'And of the redoubt, and of how he rallied the men, fought off the Germans and was awarded one of your DSO decorations.' He beamed at Smith like a prize pupil reciting his lesson. Smith stared out of the window, legs crossed, fingertips impatiently drumming on the dusty sill.

'I am lucky to have such a man in my service.' He turned his attention fully on Caspasian. 'But tell me, what are you doing here and how can I help you?'

'It is more a case of how I can help you, General. Or rather, how the British government can help you.'

General Mok chuckled like a spoilt child. 'Everyone wants to help me! Am I not a lucky man, Smith?'

'Yes, General,' Smith replied, barely concealing his boredom.

Caspasian kept his message brief. When he had finished, General Mok was silent for a moment. Caspasian could tell it was purely for effect. Whatever answer he was about to give had clearly been given to him earlier, no doubt by Smith.

'It will be an honour to assist your government and its allies, Captain Caspasian. I have sufficient supplies of ammunition for my next expedition, but after that I will gratefully receive whatever you can ship to me.'

'Your next expedition, General?' Caspasian asked, concerned.

'Yes. There is one more local bandit I must deal with before I can turn my attention to Chiang Kai-shek and his Kuomintang villains.'

Caspasian felt his impatience growing. 'General, if I may, my government feels that General Chiang is by far and away the greatest threat. Any delay or diversion is to be avoided.'

What he did not say was that the constant bickering and competitive slaughter between the myriad warlords was playing right into Chiang's hands. As they busily fought and annihilated one other, Chiang was steadily sweeping the board, from Canton north. Soon he would be at the outskirts of Shanghai and the warlord era would be over, and with it, western commercial interests in China. Chiang's stated aim was to rid China of foreign domination. Wherever his forces had been, westerners had been attacked and either killed or expelled. The warlords were certainly not Caspasian's idea of worthwhile allies but, as he had told Smith, he was simply the messenger and instrument of higher powers.

For the first time since the exchange had begun Smith intervened. 'John, this bandit to whom the General refers, General Yuan, is the biggest cut-throat and brigand in the whole of China.' He smirked. 'If you thought this morning's display was unsavoury, you should see what Yuan does to his prisoners.'

The General vigorously nodded agreement. 'Yuan is inhuman. His men desert in droves. They flock to me, begging to be accepted into my army.'

'Then he won't be much of a long-term problem,' Caspasian said in a last effort to dissuade the General from a wasteful expedition. 'Leave his forces to bleed themselves dry.' He glanced across at Smith. 'Any organisation ruled by terror will never last.'

The General shook his head. 'I know you mean well, Captain Caspasian. But in this instance you do not know the full story. Believe me, Yuan is evil.' A thought suddenly occurred to him. He turned to Smith. 'Captain Smith, there is a way we can demonstrate to Captain Caspasian that what we say is true. He should see for himself what Yuan does. How he rules the territory that he steals from the people.'

Smith looked across, eyes narrowed suspiciously. 'What?'

The General nodded, warming to the novelty of an original idea. 'Take him into the hills and let him see for himself the horrors of Yuan.'

In the brief silence that followed, Caspasian thought he could detect some unspoken communication pass between the General and Smith, but nothing in the facial expression or demeanour of either betrayed what it might be. Nevertheless, when Smith rose from his seat, agreeing to the suggested course of action, Caspasian could not help feeling that some new danger was about to unfold.

The next two days were spent in and around the town. Caspasian was allowed to see enough of General Mok's army to convince him that they were about as good as any other warlord's outfit, which was not saying much. The cavalry appeared to be the best trained and equipped unit in the force, and of course the armoured train which was Mok's prize possession. Its armaments were remarkable but there was the obvious limitation that they were confined to the railway tracks. Capable of dominating anything within reach of the Hankow to Peking railway, anything out of their range was comparatively safe. As an implement of terror however, and as a status weapon, it was unrivalled throughout the whole province.

At last the day dawned for the expedition that would introduce Caspasian to the horrors of Yuan, the next local bandit who was about to face the onslaught of the Dragon and its associated forces. Smith had laid on a single troop of cavalry as being all he judged necessary to escort himself and Caspasian into the border country where the General's territory marched with that of Yuan. This was where the proof of Yuan's brutality was to be exposed, justification, Mok felt, for his coming assault.

'Besides,' he had said, as Caspasian and Smith mounted up ready for departure, 'how can I turn to face Chiang Kai-shek, with Yuan's army at my back?'

Caspasian had to admit, though not to Mok, that acting to prevent a battle on two fronts did indeed make sense.

It felt good to be on horseback again, although Caspasian regretted the loss of the Triumph. In spite of Major Chiu's assurance, it had not been seen again. After much urging the Smith & Wesson had been returned to Caspasian, although the Webley had not. The one revolver was the only weapon he was to be allowed. The box of spare bullets was back in his pocket, together with his compass.

What struck Caspasian most during the course of the ride was the complete absence of civilians. Whoever had once worked the fields and managed the farmsteads that now lay in charred ruins had long since fled. He had seen many such refugees in Shanghai, mostly in the Chinese City. The Shanghai Municipal Police kept them out of the International Settlement and the French Concession. In the Chinese City on the other hand, they crowded the alleys and streets, selling whatever they possessed, then begging, and finally dying. The young women invariably turned to prostitution, contributing to Shanghai's reputation as the city with more brothels for its size and population than any other on earth.

There was a hopelessness about it that had struck Caspasian like a hammer blow. The whole grim spectacle had made him question his current mission. Was the Kuomintang so wrong in seeking to unify China? Had the British and other western powers not enjoyed the fruits of their forcibly seized concessionary territories for long enough? How much more did they want to bleed from the country?

He forced it all from his mind as best he could. Such thoughts had got him into plenty enough trouble in the past. Wherever he was sent, he seemed incapable of staying out of deep water. He gritted his teeth. Just do the blasted job you're given, he told himself. For once, obey orders.

They camped that evening by a stream which gave them water for the horses and for cooking. Smith had given up his attempts at being friendly and kept himself to himself. In so far as he spoke to anyone, it was only with Major Chiu, and that was little more than cursory. Caspasian noticed that the bare mechanics of soldiering were maintained.

Sentries were posted, mounts were groomed and fed, and a rough sort of stand-to was even held at dusk. However, he guessed from the smirks and giggles of the soldiers and the glances in his direction that much of it was being staged for his benefit.

More to the point, he noticed that no one stripped and cleaned their rifles. During stand-to, the soldiers simply flopped down beside their bedding and stared into the dark, irrespective of whether the position had a decent field of fire or not. And the sentries, though sited to cover all the best approaches into the camp, mostly focused their attention inwards, inquisitive as to his own activities, rather than facing outwards in the direction from which any potential assault might come. All of which suggested to Caspasian that they were confident that no such assault was imminent.

Resigning himself to the fact that he was completely in their power, Caspasian unrolled his bedding on the ground, curled up in his blanket and went to sleep.

The next day they eventually broke camp after a less than urgent breakfast. The soldiers appeared tired and disgruntled, all of which reinforced Caspasian's impression that they were unused to sentry duty. Furthermore, their hostile glances were all at him, as if he was the cause of the distress.

Throughout the day he became increasingly aware of a change in mood amongst the troop. Added to the fatigue, the soldiers grew noticeably wary. Finally, in the early afternoon they came upon a farmstead. Little more than a hovel, its destruction had clearly been recent. There was an unpleasant smell in the air which Caspasian, with a tightening of the stomach, recognised all too well. Smith disappeared around the far side of the building and its attendant shacks, to emerge a moment later, a look of triumph on his face.

'Here you are, John. Come and have a look at this.'

Warily, Caspasian dismounted, handing the reins of his horse to another, and followed Smith. There, at the rear of the hovel, was the dead body of an old Chinaman. Shot through the middle of the forehead, his corpse had been hauled upright and nailed to the wall of his dwelling with bayonets. An old cigarette stub had been wedged between the man's lips.

'That's Yuan's handiwork for you. Nice, eh?'

Caspasian had seen worse in his time. Far worse. Nevertheless, the apparent senselessness of the murder struck him anew with a deep sadness.

'OK,' he said eventually. 'Let's bury him and get back. You've shown me what you wanted.'

Smith mounted his horse. 'If we buried every corpse we found we'd be doing nothing else. The dogs and crows'll find him soon enough.'

Caspasian glanced around. It was strange, he thought, that they had not already done so.

The crack of the rifle shot came a second after the bullet smacked into the wall close beside Caspasian's ear. Smith's horse bucked.

'Ambush!' He wheeled it about, struggling to regain control of the panic-stricken beast.

A second shot rang out and another bullet cracked past Caspasian. He dropped to one knee and took out the revolver, hunting for the firer. A line of trees fringed a bund fifty yards from the farmstead and when the next shot cracked he saw the puff of smoke identifying the gunman. It was too far for his Smith & Wesson. Any shots of his would be wasted at that range.

He turned to see why no one else had returned fire. The cavalry troop was already some fifty yards away and going full pelt in the opposite direction, returning the way they had come. At their head rode Smith, whipping his horse in a frenzy, and behind him, in the firm control of the soldier to whom Caspasian had handed the reins, galloped Caspasian's horse.

Caspasian opened his mouth to shout but quickly decided against it. There was just a chance the ambushers did not know anyone had been left behind. The smack of a bullet into the dirt beside his knee slammed the door on that shred of hope.

For a second Caspasian wondered if the troop had withdrawn to dismount out of contact and were about to return from a flank, but a moment's thought clarified the situation for him.

'Straws, John. You're clutching at straws,' he muttered to himself as he flattened on to his stomach and hunted for a way out of his predicament.

A fresh hatred of Smith threatened to flood his mind and he had to fight it back in order to think clearly. The man had run. He had panicked and flown, and his useless troop of cavalry with him.

He crawled on his belly towards some scrub. From there he could see a fold in the earth which would conceal him from the firer. If he could just work his way along that he might be able to . . .

Another rifle fired from the flank, its shot cracking so close that Caspasian almost felt it in his hair.

Where the hell did you come from?

He rolled onto his side and saw the smudge of gunsmoke betraying the new firer's position. He had sited himself well, covering ground invisible to his partner. Only by hugging the ground as tightly as he could, flattening himself like a lizard, could Caspasian remain just below the immediate line of fire, though bullets continued to smack close overhead as the firers sought to winkle him out.

He tried to back towards the hovel and got as far as the back door before his opponents realised what he was up to and put down a savage fusillade. With bullets slamming into the wattle and plaster, Caspasian wriggled the last yards into the hovel, then rolled aside the second he was through the doorway and judged himself out of view. To his dismay, bullets proceeded to slam clean through the thin walls as his attackers continued to hunt him.

He slithered back down to the floor and quickly scanned the inside of the hut. It was pitifully furnished and equipped, the handful of possessions lying scattered on the floor. Through the front doorway, similarly open, he could see the road stretching into the distance. By now there was no sign of Smith and his men. They had made good their escape, leaving him at the mercy of whoever the firers were. If they were Yuan's men, then

Caspasian tried not to imagine the consequences of falling into their hands alive. On the other hand, he was not going to give up without a fight.

Like most of the roads, the one down which the troop had fled ran along the top of a bund. Once again, the fields on either side were choked with tall, dense weed. If he could make it into there, Caspasian thought, he would see how good Yuan's men were. If they followed him in, it would be a close-quarter fight. His revolver would come into its own.

Steeling himself to run, Caspasian gathered his legs beneath him and took several deep breaths. Then, in one great spurt, he shot out of the doorway in the direction of the nearest paddy field. The second he passed through the door frame, something moved at the corner of his vision. His attention fixed on his objective, he had missed something, but he never knew what, for the savage swing of the rifle butt took him full on the forehead. He felt himself halted in mid-stride, his legs knocked from under him. He fell to the ground, senses reeling, a rain of blows pounding him into oblivion, as he succumbed to the frenzied assault of the soldiers of Yuan.

6

Crossing Soochow Creek from Hongkew, Wu Yun left behind him one of the poorer areas of Shanghai and entered the more salubrious part of the International Settlement south of Garden Bridge. Squat, thickset and powerful, Wu Yun was proud of his physique. Caspasian had not been the first to notice the similarity to a bull. Wu Yun had been a member of the Green Gang since early adolescence. It had been a way out of poverty. All that had been required of him had been unswerving loyalty to whoever was boss at the time, and absolute ruthlessness. Wu had excelled at both. He was just bright enough to know that, while he would never have the brains to be leader himself, he was more than capable of acting as deputy and executive. Such had he duly become.

As deputy he had been briefed the previous evening for a task which was simply breathtaking in its audacity. All the way down the Bund, he could not stop thinking about it. Their time was coming. The Green Gang was soon to be one of the most powerful forces at work in the great city of Shanghai.

His city. City of his birth. City of his future, and city of China's future.

He looked at his watch. There was still plenty of time. He did not have to rendezvous with the others for another hour yet. Then they would go together to the quay in Nantao and wait. Wu smiled. He was good at waiting. It was an art. He knew when to wait, and for how long. He also knew when to act. Both had their place on the path to success. Waiting and action, the one inevitably preceding the other in an unending dance. Yin and Yang. Counterpoised. He was hardly a philosopher. In fact it bored the arse off him. But he was smart enough to recognise the truth of something that had played such a large role in his life. Things learnt through experience always had greater veracity than stuff gleaned from books, he felt.

He settled back into the comfortable rear seat of the car, ignoring the driver who, now and again, cast fearful glances at Wu in the rearview mirror. Yes, he felt good today. Powerful. He started to pick his nose, idly at first, and then with a will. Completing his task, he wiped his fingers on the seat cushion and stared lazily at the crowds surging along the waterfront.

The thought of power had stirred him. He shifted in his seat, restless. He checked his watch again. There was just time. He leaned across the driver's shoulder and ordered him to drive down Bubbling Well Road. The driver grinned, knowing where Wu was heading. He made a comment, trying for intimacy. Wu ignored him.

Several minutes later, the car drew up outside a restaurant, a large gaudily painted sign above the entrance announcing the Lotus Blossom. Ordering the driver to wait, Wu marched quickly in. Striding past the waiters who scuttled to his side with offers of the best table in the house, he went through the kitchens at the back, located the familiar stairway, and barged up to the first floor. At the top of the steps, an old woman sat at a table, idly playing with a dog-eared pack of cards. At the sound of Wu's footsteps she looked up, sullenly at first, then terror-stricken when she saw who it was.

'I didn't know you were coming,' she crooned. She had jumped to her feet and almost toppled over. Wu could not prevent himself from glancing down at them. They were bound. In the ways of the old China, the toes had been tightly curled beneath the sole of the foot in early childhood, probably when the woman had been about five years of age. Cloths had secured them in place, breaking and deforming the bones to achieve the so-called lily foot, highly prized by Wu's forbears. To Wu it was horrific. And the smell was simply putrid.

'Tell her I am here,' he commanded, raising his eyes to the old crone's wrinkled face, the creases of flesh etched with grime and yellow from opium.

Again the woman cackled nervously. 'You should have called ahead,' she persevered, glancing over her shoulder down the dimly lit corridor of the brothel.

Wu's brow furrowed as understanding dawned. His shoulders started to swell, growing in breadth as if he was being inflated by a pump. He pushed roughly past the old woman, knocking her to the floor. As she scrabbled for the banister, tottering to her crippled feet, she called out a warning.

It was too late. Wu burst through the door of the woman's room. His woman. Maisy. Since the disappearance of the slender girl he had picked up at the Regent on the night of his brawl with the despised westerners, he had consoled himself with an old flame.

The immediate view was of another man's buttocks. Wu stopped dead in his tracks, puzzled. Whoever it was, he was so taken with his furious activity that the arrival of Wu had gone completely unnoticed. But not by Maisy. From the far end of the bed, her earnest face craned round from underneath the glistening expanse of the man's back. Her skin was likewise covered in perspiration and Wu could see that they had been occupied for some considerable time. Pinioned to the bed like a specimen in a glass case, Maisy tried to rise, but the man at work on her mistook her wriggling for excitement and accelerated.

Wu's eyes scanned the room casually, taking in the discarded items of clothing. He shook his head sorrowfully, coming back to Maisy's face which was now terrified. She cried out as Wu advanced slowly towards the bed, her fists drumming on the man's back. In response the man covered her mouth with his own, holding her firmly in place. Unable to move or speak, her attempts at warning unrecognised, Maisy's eyes bulged from their sockets as she watched Wu unfold the blade of a lock-knife and search, almost scientifically, for the most desirable point of entry. Tilting his head on its side, he sighted between the man's industrious buttocks, reversed the knife in his grasp for a backhand thrust, drew back his fist and struck.

In the restaurant below, diners choked on their food as the scream tore through the building. At the top of the stairs, the old mamasan hobbled along the corridor towards the open doorway of Maisy's room where the girl's screams had now joined those of her customer. She peered surreptitiously round the door frame and saw the naked body of a man on the floor, Wu on top of him, a knife at his victim's throat. The man's hands were clenched around Wu's wrists, the blade edging closer to his flesh. From beneath him, the old woman saw blood pooling on the carpet. Maisy sat upright in bed, clutching the blood-stained sheets to her chin. There was a slight smile on Wu's face as he effortlessly bore down on the blade, cutting the scream dead. Only Maisy's continued.

Wu sighed, appeased. He wiped the blade on the dead man's skin, folded it away, got to his feet and put it in his pocket. He went to the door without looking back at Maisy. As he went out in to the corridor he spoke briefly to the mamasan.

He jerked his chin at Maisy. 'I want her out of here in five minutes. All her stuff as well.'

'Yes, of course,' the old crone answered, furiously nodding her assent, grateful that she herself had not been murdered.

'She is not to work in any establishment ever again. Nowhere in Shanghai, do you hear?'

He allowed himself one brief glance at the terrified woman on the bed. 'Let her earn her living down by the creek with the other living corpses if she wants. That's her business.'

Despite the hardening of the years, the mamasan felt a momentary bolt of sympathy for the inconsolable Maisy. She knew the reach of the Green Gang. She also knew the life of the alleys.

Wu marched briskly out of the restaurant, ignoring the terrified stares of the customers until he realised that he was covered with blood. Out in the street, he got quickly into the waiting car and told the driver to make his way to the rendezvous. Then, as an afterthought, he ordered him to stop briefly in Canton Road. He would pick up a change of clothes before meeting the others. It would not do to turn up in soiled shirt and trousers. Not for whom he was about to meet.

As the first flush of the murder left him, he felt regret for his decision over Maisy. Perhaps he had been hasty. Still, he had given the order. It would never do for him to rescind it. Someone might misconstrue it as weakness. No, Maisy had done wrong and would have to pay. So what if she was now sentenced to a living death? Wu pushed the unpleasant images from his mind. She should not have done it to him. It was all her own fault. She was only getting what she deserved.

If only that cursed westerner had not driven off the girl at the Regent. Now she had been a girl with promise! Looking out at the bustle of the streets, Wu wondered where she might be at that moment. He would dearly love to find her again. The thought of the westerner was like salt in an open wound. Still, the coming meeting would have a bearing on that. In fact, if it turned out as the boss hoped, it would change everything in Shanghai and China for good.

⋆　⋆　⋆

In subterranean darkness, Caspasian's head pounded with the non-stop bombardment. Shells rained down, feeling as if they were detonating inside his skull. The aftershocks of every burst reverberated through his brain, numbing thought, shuddering nerve and sinew, seeming to dislocate every joint of his skeleton. He felt as if his head was about to split asunder, cleaved down the middle like sliced fruit.

He moaned, and the sound brought him a fraction closer to consciousness. He could hear himself, a pitiful, guttural moan. But it clarified things for him, separating what was real and what was imagined. The moan was, in truth, the only sound. The pounding of the guns was internal, a chthonic upheaval taking place inside his own head.

He tried unsuccessfully to move. A second, more concerted attempt revealed that his limbs were bound, secured by fastenings to the frame of a bed on which he was lying. Unable to reach up and touch his eyes, he rolled his head to either side, fighting back the searing pain that movement produced, and established that he had been blindfolded.

Opening his eyes, for a moment he stared into total darkness. He blinked once, then twice, the tight cloth surprisingly soft against his eyelids. After a moment the palest of lights penetrated the binding. Although he could see nothing through the blindfold, by looking to left and right he found he was able at least to deduce that the light was natural and not the artificial glow of bulb or flame. So it was day, he thought with growing interest. Furthermore, by noting the intensity he thought he could identify the direction of the source. To his left was a window and to his right a wall.

He rested for a moment, horrified to find himself so easily tired by such a meagre physical effort, and it was then he remembered the surprise attack at the farmstead, and the sudden beating as he had tried to escape. Fear flooded through him as he realised he had been badly hurt. With the fear came accelerated breathing, shallow and rapid. He could feel his heart beating faster, and the panic starting to rise. The words of General Mok and of Smith repeated themselves in his head like gleeful taunts, recounting the reputation of Yuan into whose hands he had now fallen.

Provoked by these memories, and with his resistance weakened by physical injury, the fear started to run riot. He jerked at his bindings, each effort producing bolts of pain in his neck and head. He broke into a sweat and tried unsuccessfully to lift one shoulder high enough to rub his blindfold free. If he could only see, if he could only give some shape and form to his surroundings, if he could only identify where and how he lay . . .

With superhuman effort he fought for self-control. Concurrent with the panic, some other part of him began to counter the rising tide of terror. Against every inclination he forced himself to lie still. To conserve his pitiful strength. Though he could not immediately control the rate of his heartbeat, he knew that he could control his breathing, and this he now did. Working with the diaphragm, he forced his breathing to deepen. He started to suck in the air using the muscles of his lower stomach and abdomen, breathing with the whole of the lungs and not simply the highest part of the chest.

The mere business of focusing on the effort of deeper breathing distracted his thoughts from his capture. The fear began to subside, becoming more controllable, and the more controllable it became, the smaller it grew, each stage in the process feeding the other until Caspasian began to feel himself once again master of his thoughts and emotions, though not of his limbs.

With his breathing now deep and regular, he felt his heartbeat moderate. Only now could his mind start to operate, to see if there was some shred of consolation to be drawn from his seemingly desperate straits.

Despite the comfort yielded by the pitiful light seeping through his blindfold, Caspasian forced himself to close his eyes. He knew that for now they could yield him precious little in the way of useful information. But with eyes shut, he could expand his other senses, gather what information he could and then analyse it.

The bed beneath him was not uncomfortable. It had a mattress, firm and probably stuffed with horse hair. He was lying on some sort of cover, possibly linen, but too fine to be a woollen blanket. Next, his bindings. He was fastened to the bed by wrists and ankles, but

160

the bindings that had been used, though tight, were smooth like his blindfold. This was strange. Why had his captors not used rope, twine or even wire?

He worked with his fingers, trying to curl them back on to each wrist to see if he could contact whatever knot there might be. It was no use. Whoever had secured him had done their job well. Furthermore, and also cause for surprise, though the wrist bindings were fast enough to prevent his escape, they had not been tied so tight as to block the flow of blood to his hands.

Caspasian suddenly noticed that his shoes and socks had been removed. He wiggled his toes and again discovered that the bindings had not been fastened any tighter than absolutely necessary. In fact, he was astonished to find that, apart from the searing pain in his head and the aches in every limb, he was otherwise as comfortable as could be expected.

Next, smell. The air in the room was musty and dry, but not cold. Whatever windows there might be were shut, and although there was clearly no fire in the room, Caspasian deduced that the room was part of a reasonably well-heated building. He was certainly not in some barn or outhouse. He wondered if he were in some disused wing of a large house. This impression was reinforced by the nature of the faint sounds of which he now became aware.

He stilled his breathing as much as he could, opened his mouth and popped his ears, gently straining after the sounds. He frowned, puzzled. How on earth could he describe them? Bucolic rather than martial. He felt the corners of his mouth twitch with the crease of a smile. There they were again. No shouted commands or shrill injunctions, no curses and parade banter. The voices were more like peasants at work in a field. To his consternation Caspasian suddenly heard the faint laughter of children at play. There was the clang of metal, but it was of a farming implement. Swords into ploughshares, he mused smiling. The last thing he noticed was a smell of cooking, like boiled vegetables, but more interesting.

He opened his eyes again, now completely confused. With the return of the pale light came a fresh surge of pain. However bucolic his captors, they had subjected him to a rigorous beating. All the conflicting signals pouring into his brain produced a sensation of utter bewilderment.

'So you are awake.'

If he had not been so securely tied, Caspasian felt he would have jumped clean off the bed. With the shock of the voice his heart was pounding in an instant, as if he had been physically struck across the face.

'Who's there?' he barked, his own voice sounding oddly strained in his ears. How the devil had he completely missed the presence of another man in the room? There had been no indication. No opening door. Nothing. Whoever it was, he had been there, watching, all along.

Though there was no sound of laughter, Caspasian could almost feel his observer smiling. Yet, by the tone of the voice, he envisaged it as a smile of gentle bemusement rather than smug triumph.

Caspasian cleared his throat and spoke again. 'Who are you? Can you remove this blindfold, please?'

'I must apologise for my men.'

Again Caspasian jumped. The speaker was now standing over him, but on the opposite side from before. How the devil could he have moved so quietly? Caspasian wondered whether his hearing had suffered as a result of the blows, but there had been the sounds of children that he was certain had been in the distance. Whoever was now with him in the room seemed capable of moving like a disembodied spirit. Caspasian tried to concentrate on the voice and was shocked that it only now struck him that the man was speaking English. Although fluent, it was not his mother tongue. It had the pleasant musical lilt of a native Mandarin speaker who was slipping, albeit with ease, into the narrower tonal confines of the English language. Swinton had once likened it to a member of Diaghilev's Ballet Russe being obliged to participate in a Sandhurst drill parade.

'The blindfold?' Caspasian prompted.

Declining to respond to the request, the man was obviously surveying his captive's injuries. There was a sigh, regretful rather than tired. Caspasian felt the faintest touch of a fingertip on his temple. Instinctively he flinched away.

'I'm sorry. Did that hurt?'

'What do you think?'

'I am afraid that you are going to be bed-bound for some time.'

'Is that a pun?' Caspasian asked bitterly.

To his amazement there was a good-natured chuckle. The man had understood. His English was even better than Caspasian had thought.

'Who are you? Are you General Yuan?'

'More to the point, who are you?'

Caspasian tugged awkwardly at his bindings. 'Why the bed? Why the concern?'

Again there was the chuckle, pleasant as before. 'Did you expect to find yourself hung upside down or perhaps roasted over a spit?'

'Why the blindfold?' Caspasian persisted.

'Precautions,' came the reply.

'Against what?'

'You haven't yet told me who you are or what you're doing here.'

Caspasian shook his head. 'You go first.'

'I don't really think you're in much of a position to bargain.'

The reply was so reasonable and the tone so heavy with irony that Caspasian had to laugh, suddenly struck by the absurd image of himself spread-eagled to the bed, blindfolded and injured.

'That's better,' came the equally bemused response. 'Humour is the key to many a door.'

'Old Chinese proverb, I suppose?'

In the dark and silence Caspasian again felt his observer smiling. It was impossible to gauge the man's age. More old than young, but not distinctly either.

When the voice came again it was from some distance away. 'I will send someone to tend your wounds.'

There was the sound of a door opening and then closing, leaving Caspasian wondering whether, this time, he was really alone.

He must have fallen asleep, because the next thing he knew was the touch of a wet cloth against his cheeks. The light seeping through his blindfold was now different from before, having the yellowness of flame. The water was pleasantly warm and the touch of the hand was confident but light.

'Who's that?' Caspasian asked, turning towards the person. 'Is it you again?'

This time there was no reply, so he assumed it was someone else, presumably some menial or other. He recoiled as he felt hands unfastening the buttons of his shirt, but then remembered that among the wounds he had sensed on his body was a deep gash on the right side of his ribcage. He forced himself to relax. If his captors had intended to harm him they would hardly be dressing his wounds.

The gash had been tightly bandaged and as the hands now removed the old cloths to cleanse the wound and replace them with fresh, fingers accidentally brushed his skin and he realised with shock that he was being tended by a woman. Underneath the blindfold he could feel himself blush, and he was surprised at his prudery. After all, in the war he had been tended by nurses on many occasions, even if he had not been bound and blindfolded at the time. Furthermore, he sensed that the woman knew he had realised her gender and was similarly embarrassed, for when she touched him again she was hesitant, self-conscious.

'Come on then. Florence Nightingale, who are you?' He tried speaking in Mandarin, but still there was no reply. 'I don't suppose you'd care to remove the blindfold and untie me?'

Silence. The hands completed redressing his side and, slowly, began to refasten his shirt.

'Too bad I can't see your face,' Caspasian said. 'Mind you, it might be a blessing. I might find myself fantasising over some wizened hag. Some decrepit mamasan.'

There was the sound of articles being gathered for departure. Suddenly Caspasian dreaded the thought of being left alone again, especially as the removal of the lamp or candle would leave him in pitch darkness.

'Don't go,' he said, quickly repeating it in Mandarin.

He felt the other person pause.

'Please tell me your name.'

For a moment there was silence. Then the faintest sound of a single footstep. A shadow fell across the bed, and a hand brushed back his hair. He caught a smell of soap or flowers and then it was gone. The footsteps crossed

167

to the door, paused for longer than necessary to undo the lock, and left the room.

★ ★ ★

Jack Swinton had been in Shanghai long enough to know that everything was connected. Whereas in other great cities a coincidence would merely be the result of chance and nothing more, in Shanghai there was always more. Like a narrow dark alley connecting two bright thoroughfares, in Shanghai a coincidence always came from somewhere and led to somewhere, and somewhere meaningful to the moment. Call it a mystical oriental law if you wanted, to Swinton it had proved itself time and time again. Always.

So, when he jogged down the steps of the American Club at 209 Foochow Road and caught sight of a passing large black car heading for the Canton Road turning, and recognised Fatso from the Regent brawl, leaning over the front seat, he did not have to think twice before hailing a cab and following.

Like Caspasian, he had discovered that Fatso worked for Du Yuesheng, leader of the notorious Green Gang, Shanghai's most powerful criminal secret society. However, unlike his good friend Caspasian, he had also discovered that Fatso's real name was Wu Yun. Being a journalist, Swinton had delved deeper, exposing an unsavoury catalogue of Wu's past sins. While he now followed without hesitation, smelling a story, it was not also without some considerable trepidation, and from as great a distance as he could contrive.

When Wu's car pulled over outside a clothes shop and Wu got out, Swinton was puzzled to see the dishevelled nature of the man's dress. His jacket was off and he walked awkwardly, clasping it to his front. When he reached the shop door, he stood to one side to let someone past and Swinton was certain he caught a glimpse of some dark stain on the small part of Wu's white shirt that was visible. With a shudder down his spine he realised that it was blood.

'Oh, shit,' he murmured, ignoring the suspicious glances at him of his own driver.

It was barely ten minutes before Wu emerged a new man, changed into a brand new suit and accompanying accoutrements. He looked every inch the respectable man about town. A banker or stockbroker perhaps. Swinton smiled. Maybe not so respectable then.

Wu hopped back into his car with the same

169

nimbleness that had taken Swinton and Caspasian by surprise when they had seen him in action at the Regent. A second later the car was heading east in the direction of the Bund.

'Come on,' Swinton urged his driver, irritated.

The man muttered something and pulled out into the traffic. He was clearly unimpressed with his assignment and Swinton wondered whether he too had recognised Wu Yun. If so, Swinton could well imagine the terrors presently coursing through the poor man's brain.

Leaving the International Settlement, Wu's car entered the Quai de France in the French Concession and drove south. To his discomfort, it kept on going when it reached the intersection with Fong Pang Road, heading for the Chinese City and for Nantao.

Swinton began to wish that Caspasian was with him. The fellow was a useful companion to have with you in a spot of trouble. He was damned clever with his hands. And his feet, come to think of it, Swinton mused. He had been impressed on several occasions when he and Caspasian had been out on their various jaunts that Caspasian swore he did not enjoy, but that he nevertheless attended readily enough.

It was some time later that Swinton saw Wu's car pull over and stop. Swinton ordered his driver to do likewise, making sure he kept well concealed and out of Wu's direct line of sight.

Seeing Wu get out, Swinton stuffed a couple of bank notes into the angry palm that his driver waved under his nose, left the taxi and prepared to follow on foot. He could see Wu talking to some other men who had now joined him. They turned down an alley that led straight to the waterfront, right on the embankment of the Whangpoo river.

Cautiously Swinton approached. Fortunately there were plenty of people about. Here in Nantao, life adopted the concentrated freneticism which, even when severely diluted, only partly resembled existence in the International Settlement which, however insanely busy itself, was almost stately by comparison.

He came to the corner of the street and peered round. Wu and his companions were at the far end. They had reached the edge of the embankment and were standing, clearly waiting for someone or something. In front of them a narrow wharf protruded into the river. Although the water level was below Swinton's line of sight, he could tell from Wu and his men that a launch was approaching. It was as if they were soldiers on a parade ground, bracing to attention. Broad smiles of deference lit their faces and Wu moved forward to lend someone a helping hand. A small figure stepped into view, but he was shrouded in a vast overcoat and his face was hidden by the broad brim of an enormous hat.

Anticipating their return his way, Swinton ducked back around the corner and hurriedly sought out a new vantage point. Across the street, a row of foodstalls steamed and sizzled, flames shooting out of their woks as their vendors tossed and tumbled the uncertain contents, loudly shouting for customers.

Swinton jogged across to them, narrowly missing a rickshaw that swerved to avoid him, the man labouring between the poles too exhausted to shout the abuse that Swinton could see in his glance. A moment later, Wu and his party came once again into view. Their guest had his own entourage with him. While modest in numbers, the newly arrived guard party compensated with physical stature. Their eyes were everywhere and it was all Swinton could do to remain hidden yet capable of observing.

For the first time the extreme danger of the situation struck him. He felt his mouth go dry and his palms moisten. He glanced to right and left, wondering which way he would run if he was spotted and pursued. To his immense relief, when he looked back at the party, he saw three large cars drawing up beside them. Wu, the new arrival in the coat and hat, and two more of the guard party got into the middle car, the rest of the bodyguards dividing between the cars to front and rear. Then, with everyone secure, the convoy moved off and headed north in the direction of the French Concession.

Realising that if he was going to continue tailing them he would need wheels of his own, Swinton turned in search of a taxi. To his surprise he found himself looking at his old taxi driver who stood about twenty yards behind him. However, Swinton's initial relief turned swiftly to dismay when he noted the two burly thugs beside the man. He was speaking quickly to them and gesturing in both Swinton's direction and, of greater concern, in the direction of the departing cars.

Swinton took a step out into the middle of the street and was almost run down by the cars themselves. It seemed that they had decided to change their order of march and, while manoeuvring the central vehicle to the rear, thereby covering it more heavily with guards well to the fore, the central vehicle itself had drawn alongside Swinton. To his immense relief, Wu was looking out of the far window. The new arrival however was seated at Swinton's side. As Swinton jumped back out of the way, the man looked up, startled. His face emerged briefly from under the broad brim of the hat and Swinton felt as if he had been stabbed through the heart. Time stood still as their eyes met and, although to the small Chinese man Swinton was a complete stranger, to Swinton the other was instantly recognisable. He felt his mouth move, starting to form a question, more to his own incredulity than to anyone else, and he thought he detected the faintest trace of a smile on the man's lips.

The next instant the car had gone, powering away with its accompanying bodyguards to the north. Swinton paused for a second, but no more. One glance behind him brought him sharply back to his senses, and then he was running for his life.

7

'How are you feeling?'

Caspasian jumped. He had been dozing and had not heard anyone entering the room. Instinctively he tugged at his bindings but found them as secure as ever. He forced himself to relax, his arms and legs going limp as he sank back into the mattress. He drew in his breath and began.

'General Yuan — I assume that's who you are — my name is Captain John Caspasian. I am a British Army officer on the staff of the British Consulate in Shanghai. I am here on an official mission which is confidential. That is all I can tell you. Now if you would be kind enough to untie me, I'll . . . '

'You'll what? Return to your new ally General Mok and make him even stronger than he already is?'

Caspasian smiled. 'I'm afraid that whatever passes between General Mok and the British government is of their concern only.'

There was an answering chuckle. 'Hardly. Will it be only of their concern when Mok uses British arms to murder people who are under my protection?'

Caspasian was on the brink of responding with indignation, acting out his role as loyal instrument and mouthpiece of British governmental policy. He caught himself just in time. Even from his brief experience of Mok, he had seen enough to doubt the moral correctness of his mission. That, combined with the wholly unexpected sincerity that he heard in the disembodied voice of his captor, now stopped him in his tracks and set him upon an altogether new course.

'General Yuan,' he said with a new calmness, 'please remove the blindfold. Leave me tied up if you wish, but can I at least see who I'm talking to?'

For a moment Caspasian almost wondered whether the other man had left the room. Then, the next thing he felt was the touch of someone attending to the cloth binding his eyes. Caspasian tilted his head to one side to assist.

'It is quite bright in the room. You had better close your eyes for a moment,' the voice gently urged.

Caspasian did as he was told and, sure enough, as the cloth slid from his head, the sunlight streaming through the closed windows pummelled at his tightly clenched eyelids like miniature fists. He winced and turned his head away, the force of the light combining with the ache of his wounds into a continuous pounding throb.

His captor heard the groan. 'I am sorry. This has not been well done. Not at all.'

Caspasian was amazed to hear the tut-tutting. Slowly he turned in the direction of the voice and tried to look. Instinctively he moved to raise one hand to shield his eyes. His wrists and ankles remained securely fastened to the bed. Squinting as best he could, he focused on the figure slowly and painfully emerging out of the dazzling light. The man was standing with his back to the windows.

'Could you perhaps . . . ?' Caspasian said, jerking his head in the direction of the more shaded part of the room.

'Of course. Forgive me,' his captor said apologetically, stepping deftly to the far side of the room where the shards of light were brimful with jostling motes of dust.

Into Caspasian's painful vision stepped the figure, at first only his outline, the detail slowly accumulating, a feature at a time, until the man was at last revealed.

'Behold, the dreaded General Yuan,' he said.

Of medium height and slight build, General Yuan was surprisingly unremarkable.

He was dressed in a high-collared, loose-fitting grey cotton tunic and trousers, a pair of simple rope-soled canvas shoes on his small feet. His black hair, severely greying at the temples, bristled like a brush. Strangely, the small neat moustache he sported was entirely grey, giving the appearance of having been stuck on as an afterthought like a theatrical prop. It parted naturally in the middle, separating into two tidily cropped halves on either side of his upper lip. It reminded Caspasian of Douglas Fairbanks. He could not quite remember the title of the film but suspected it had been *The Thief of Baghdad*.

The epicanthic fold of his eyelids was pronounced, narrowing them into slits. Yet somehow Caspasian felt he could detect a twinkle of humour there.

As if in direct response to this thought, the General held out his arms and broke into a smile. 'You see? Not much to be frightened of here.'

Caspasian responded with a smile of his own. 'Nor here,' he replied, indicating his bonds.

'Yes, I really must apologise,' the General said, while doing nothing to remove them. 'Just as soon as we have uncovered the exact nature of your mission I will be

178

delighted to release you.'

'How exact do we have to get?' Caspasian asked. 'You must realise, General, that I am under orders.'

The General waved the comment aside, dismissing it. He turned and moved back to the other side of the bed where a plain wooden chair stood beneath the window. For a moment Caspasian thought he was going to sit down. Instead the General threw open the windows, letting a gush of cool fresh air into the room. Only then did it strike Caspasian how stifling it had been. His whole attention had been fixed on his captor.

'Why are the British so intent on making Mok their ally? Do they not see what kind of man he is?' General Yuan shook his head in dismay. 'He is a monster, not a man.' He turned to face Caspasian. 'You yourself saw what he did to the farmer.'

'At the place where your men captured me? But Mok's men said you had done that.'

The General smiled bitterly. 'Old Chen was just a simple farmer. He was under my protection.' He snorted in disgust. 'I didn't give him much protection, did I?' He stared at Caspasian. 'Why ever would I murder a simple farmer? A man I've known for years?'

'I don't know, General. But it seems that

most generals don't think they need a reason to murder.'

'I'm afraid you're right. I can imagine all the other rubbish Mok has told you about me. The British believe him, liar and murderer that he is, and as a consequence I will be destroyed. Me and all my followers. Isn't that what you have come here to engineer?'

Caspasian's head was spinning but the General continued. 'From what little I have observed of you, you do not strike me as a gullible man. Surely, if you have spent any time at all with Mok, you must realise that what I say is true?'

'Even if it is, General, my own thoughts on the subject are irrelevant. His Majesty's government has decided it needs Mok as an ally against Chiang Kai-shek. I am afraid that there is nothing I can do to change that.'

'Then you must convince them!' For the first time Caspasian felt he could detect an air of desperation in his captor. The next second it was gone. Yuan stared out of the window, clasping his hands behind his back. He breathed deeply, his shoulders rising and falling.

After a moment Caspasian said, 'What am I to convince them of?'

The General spun back, hope suddenly

alive. 'That Mok is evil. That he will take whatever the British give him, and betray them the next instant if it suits his best interest. That . . . ' he paused, uncertain whether to reveal more. 'That he is no good for the long-term interests of China.'

Caspasian smiled. 'And you are, I suppose?'

'That is not what I said. But I am not a murderer and tyrant like Mok.'

'Even if that is true, what makes you think the British or the other powers care a jot about the long-term interests of China? So long as their concessionary ports are left free to trade, why should they mind who governs in the interior?'

Now it was General Yuan's turn to smile. 'An interesting sentiment from one of His Britannic Majesty's captains,' he observed shrewdly. 'Refreshingly honest, if a little cynical.'

He eyed Caspasian carefully for a moment and then said, 'Captain, if I release you, do I have your word that you will not leave until I give my permission?'

Caspasian laughed. 'I'm hardly in any fit state to leave. But in any case, how do you know that my word is worth having?'

'That is a chance I am prepared to take.'

'All right. You have my word.'

The General leaned out of the window and shouted to someone below. There was the sound of feet running up the stairs, and the next moment two guards entered the room. While they stood with rifles levelled at Caspasian, General Yuan went across to him and started to unfasten the bindings securing his wrists and ankles to the bed.

When he had been freed, Caspasian tried to sit up. He was horrified to discover that he could not summon the strength.

'Here, let me help,' the General said, taking him by one elbow and easing him upright. As he sat up, Caspasian felt as if his head was about to explode. With a superhuman effort he swung his legs off the bed, but the moment he tried to put his weight on to them the effort overwhelmed him and he almost blacked out.

With more tut-tutting, General Yuan put his hand on Caspasian's shoulder and gently urged him to lie down again. 'It is too soon. I am afraid that you will need longer to rest.'

Caspasian sank back against the welcoming cushions that the General pushed behind his shoulders and head. 'Your men did a pretty good job on me.'

'They were frightened. When men are scared they will hit out. Aggression and terror always go hand in hand.'

'I'll have to remember to reassure them next time they ambush me.' Caspasian closed his eyes and the darkness was like a soothing balm. The pounding in his head abated and he felt a great peace wash over his aching limbs.

'I think it is best you sleep now,' the General said. 'Please excuse me if I leave a guard outside your door. It is as much for your own protection as for mine. Some of my men are justifiably suspicious of you and would not be sorry to see you dead.'

'A couple more blows with those rifle butts and they'd have had their wish.'

'I will send up some food in a couple of hours when you have had time to regain some strength. This talk has tired you. Sleep now.'

Caspasian was surprised to find that he trusted the General completely. He could detect no ulterior motive or hidden meaning in his words. There was the sound of his captors leaving the room. The door was closed and locked, and then there was peace. From outside he could hear again the same noises as before, only louder now that the windows were open.

In a strange way, Caspasian felt as he had when a boy at home, lying on the bed in his room on a holiday afternoon. There was the same pleasurable indolence, the same sense of overwhelming ease, seemingly unending at a time when it felt as if nothing would ever end. The same simple pleasures and the same reassuring securities would just roll on and on throughout life. Life itself appeared as a mere figment, a concept wholly without significance in the face of such contentment. A succession of equally carefree days would unfold and those whom he loved would always be there for him. On the other side of the door, in the rooms downstairs, in the meticulously tended garden beneath his open window.

The pain of the illusion seared through his contentment the moment it struck him as false. He fought to recapture the sense of peace but it had fled like a frightened animal into the depths of a wood. Such was the nature of illusion, and Caspasian marvelled at the remarkable dichotomy of fragility and power. Everyone from those days had gone, and here he was, alone and adrift in the wastelands of China, yet haunted as ever by ghosts.

True to Yuan's word, Caspasian estimated that it was two hours before he heard a quiet knock at the door. It struck him as comical that anyone should take the trouble to knock when the door was locked from the outside.

Nevertheless he called for the person to come in.

Caspasian was resting with his eyes shut. He had propped himself up on some cushions in an attempt to accustom himself gradually to a fully upright position. It was like acclimatising for altitude at the start of a difficult Himalayan climb. He had not slept, his thoughts occupied by memories of his boyhood. Being so completely at the mercy of a benevolent captor had an oddly restful quality that gently amused him. If he had nothing to fear and nothing to do, then why not surrender to contemplation?

As the door opened a wonderful smell of food entered the room. It was only then that Caspasian realised how hungry he was. In response his stomach rumbled noisily and he instinctively tightened the muscles of his abdomen to suppress it. He opened his eyes and was amazed to find himself looking at a young woman. She was beautiful. With the realisation of that came recognition.

'You!'

She smiled when she saw the penny drop. 'I am afraid the only bands around here are armed with rifles, not saxophones.'

'How … ? Why … ?' Caspasian stammered, feeling like a complete idiot. He stopped himself. 'Who are you and why are you here?'

'My name is Lilin and I am here to bring you some lunch.'

'That's not what I meant. I . . . '

'You have used up all the questions you are allowed for one day.' She was carrying a tray and as Caspasian backed into his cushions, pushing himself into an upright sitting position with difficulty, she lowered it onto his knees. In the middle of it was a large china bowl with a lid. Beside it, a small porcelain drinking cup and a tea pot.

'Jasmine,' she said, touching the pot delicately with the tip of one finger. 'I hope you like it.' She lifted the lid from the bowl and a cloud of steam erupted from underneath like a genie. It smelt wonderful and as it cleared Caspasian saw a generous mound of rice noodles with peppers, shredded pork and chicken. 'I am afraid these days you can't get hold of prawns this far from the coast, otherwise we could have done even better than the Regent or the Shanghai Club.'

'Of course you'd know all about that, wouldn't you?'

Lilin smiled innocently. 'I am sure I don't know what you're talking about.'

It was only then Caspasian noticed that the guards had left them alone. She noticed his glance at the closed door and read his thoughts. 'Don't bother taking me hostage. There are plenty more serving girls where I come from.'

Caspasian smiled. 'Apparently we're both expendable. I wonder what else we've got in common?'

'You, expendable? I hardly think so. A British Army captain.'

'Indian Army, if you don't mind.'

To Caspasian's amazement she smiled, understanding. 'How you British love your little pretensions.'

'That's a bit cruel,' Caspasian said. 'But I suppose it's true.' He picked up the chopsticks and started to eat. He stirred the noodles, meat and vegetables and lifted some to his mouth. It was steaming hot but tasted wonderful.

She stood beside the bed with arms folded, frowning. 'What kind of name is Caspasian anyway? It's hardly English.'

He almost choked. 'Who the devil are you?' he said when he had swallowed his mouthful. 'And don't give me any more of that serving girl nonsense. How the hell do you know what is and what isn't an English name?'

'Just because you're in the countryside, don't assume we're all peasants.'

'Oh, I see, you're the wild-living Shanghai

187

girl now, is that it?' Although he wanted to question her further, his hunger forced him to continue eating. Between mouthfuls he asked sarcastically, 'How's your boyfriend? Now there's a nice piece of work. Does General Yuan know who you spend your free time with?'

Lilin's face darkened. 'He was not my boyfriend.'

'It certainly looked like it to me.'

'Then perhaps you should learn how to look.' She turned abruptly and made to leave the room.

As she reached the door Caspasian called after her. 'Don't go. I'm sorry.' He slid the tray on to the mattress beside him and tried to stand up. He could not.

The door was open but the girl paused in front of it. She glared back at him, and the hurt in her eyes surprised him. 'You know nothing about me. You know nothing about what we are trying to do here.' Then, as she made up her mind and left, she shouted back at him, 'You are just like all the others.' And that stung Caspasian the most.

⋆　⋆　⋆

Pacing his office, General Mok was agitated. 'You should never have killed him. I know it.

You shouldn't have done it!'

'We didn't kill him, General, I told you. Yuan's men did.'

The General turned angrily on Daniel Smith. 'Don't play word games with me. You know what I mean. Deserting him like that is the same as putting the gun to his head and pulling the trigger.' He strode back and forth like a caged animal. 'This could jeopardise British support,' he muttered.

Smith sighed, exasperated. 'Look, General.' He paused while he wondered how best to tackle him. An appeal to his vanity usually worked. 'You've got this the wrong way round. You don't need the British. It's the British who need you.'

Mok's agitation had deafened him for the moment. 'You were only supposed to give the Captain a demonstration. Show him what Yuan's like.'

'And that's exactly what I did,' Smith said, struggling to keep his voice calm when he most wanted to grab the General by his gold-encrusted epaulettes and shake the life out of him. 'Some of the lads engineered the demonstration and we led Caspasian to see it.'

The General spun on his heel and pointed accusingly at Smith. 'Yes, and you left him there to die!'

'How was I to know Yuan's men would be there when we returned?'

The General faltered. 'Yuan . . . ' he said the name with difficulty, as if it stuck in his throat. 'Yuan likes to think he can look after his people. You should have known he would lay an ambush to catch you.'

Smith shook his head dismissively. 'It was no ambush. It was just a couple of soldiers probably checking on the silly old bugger we'd shot.'

'Then why desert Caspasian?' the General shouted. 'You had a whole troop of cavalry! If it was just a couple of soldiers, why run away?' A thought occurred to him. 'You saved Caspasian's life before. You told me so. I don't understand.' He frowned with the effort of the problem. 'I didn't want him killed. He was more useful alive. Now the British . . . '

'The British will be told the truth. That Yuan killed their envoy. If anything it will cement their support for you. Don't you see, General? I couldn't have planned it better myself.' He warmed to his subject. 'If anything we must play it up. Tell the British that we lost numerous men in the attack. Portray it as a battle. Caspasian stuck his nose in as usual and got his head blown off.' He burst out laughing. 'Why, it's perfect! Their own man died in your service.'

He fixed the General with a cold stare of triumph. 'Convinced of the justice of your cause against the evil Yuan, Caspasian took the field of battle on your behalf, as a representative of the British government itself. They'll be incensed when they hear about it. They'll rush a boatload of arms up the Yangtze quicker than you can say Chiang Kai-shek.'

The General stopped his pacing, his brain grasping the drift of Smith's argument. A smile spread slowly across his face. 'Yes,' he said cautiously, like a rat emerging from its hole. 'Perhaps you're right. Yuan has done us a service.' The smile suddenly froze in place.

Smith noticed it. 'What's the matter?'

'What if Caspasian didn't die?'

'Didn't die?' Smith asked incredulous. 'Of course he died General. I saw . . . '

'What did you see?'

Smith blushed. 'I was there.'

'When he died? The moment Caspasian was shot? Shot dead?'

'No,' Smith conceded. 'I had withdrawn the cavalry to a fallback position to regroup and counter-attack.' He coughed to clear his throat. 'When I realised that Caspasian must be dead, I decided to avoid further loss of life and retire back to camp.'

'You?' the General said grinning mischievously 'you, avoid loss of life?' He guffawed loudly, a sound that Smith found unbelievably ugly. 'And tell me, how do you know Caspasian died?'

'When he stopped shooting.'

'You could hear that?'

'Of course. I heard his revolver and then it went silent. He must have died.'

'Or been captured.'

Smith was appalled that the thought of Caspasian's survival had never occurred to him. 'Well, if he was captured, then God help him.'

'Be careful, Smith,' the General said with uncustomary insight. 'You are starting to believe your own stories of Yuan's cruelty.'

Smith felt himself go cold. Caspasian alive. The thought of it chilled him to the marrow, but the solution came almost in the same instant. 'Then we must advance the date of the attack on Yuan. That way, whether Caspasian is alive or dead, it will make no difference.'

The General grinned. 'And all of this for the friend whose life you once saved.' His eyes narrowed. 'Why do you hate him so much?'

'Me? Hate Caspasian? Don't be absurd. Why ever would I hate the man?'

'Why indeed? That is what puzzles me.'

Smith calmed himself. He took a deep breath and then broke into a pleasant smile. 'General, I am doing this for you and for you alone. Caspasian is completely irrelevant.'

For the moment the General seemed convinced. 'All right then, when shall I attack?'

Relieved to be off the subject of Caspasian, Smith threw himself into a discussion of the necessary preparations. He summoned his aides and together with the General they studied the maps of the ground across which they would have to move their forces.

'The Dragon must spearhead the attack,' the General said irrelevantly in the middle of a discussion about supply lines.

'In this instance, General, it might be best to hold the Dragon in reserve,' Smith cautioned. 'The ground is not well suited to it. The rail lines only have good fields of fire in a few places, and those are of little use. Look.' He bent over the map and traced the point of his pen along the thin black thread indicating the rail lines. 'See? They go round Yuan's heartland, not through it. The Dragon will have little bearing on the outcome of any battle. For a decisive victory we must engage the bulk of Yuan's forces on his key terrain. Here.'

He stabbed his pen aggressively into the map where he had earlier drawn a red crayon circle. 'This is Yuan's base area. He will defend it. He has to. If he loses it he loses control of all the surrounding province. Then he becomes little more than an itinerant bandit and we can hunt him down at our leisure.'

As if he had not been listening to a word Smith had just said, the General repeated, 'The Dragon must spearhead the attack.'

Smith glanced up at him across the map and noticed the telltale signs. The lower lip protruded slightly. The shoulders had been squared, the breath was coming through pinched nostrils. Like a petulant child insisting on having its way, the General was digging in. Smith sighed. 'General, please. You have hired me to give you the best military advice of which I am capable . . . '

'Exactly, Smith. Advice, not commands.'

Smith chuckled amicably, knowing that confrontation with the General never worked. 'Of course, General. I agree that the Dragon is a key weapon system, but like any weapon system, it has to be matched to the terrain to maximise its potential. You . . . '

The General drummed his fingers on the map. 'The Dragon will spearhead the attack, Smith. Just build that into the plan, all right?'

Smith swallowed hard, suppressing his hatred of Mok. In the background one of the aides sniggered and muttered something to a comrade. Smith noted the man's identity and filed it away in his memory for later. One day there would be a reckoning. There always was. He would see to it. The fellow was as good as dead.

'All right, General. As you wish.' He paused for a moment, surveying the map. It was stupid. Absolutely insane. The Dragon would be out on a limb, cut off from the main body of the force which would be committed to battle miles away attacking Yuan's base. Still, if that was what the General wanted, then that was the way it would have to be. Smith would far rather have used the Dragon to move up his reserves after the battle had been won. To sweep round the ground captured by the infantry and the cavalry. Instead it would have to sit out on a flank, firing at wildfowl and any passing peasant it came across.

'Perhaps we can place a small force on board. They can disembark here,' he said, indicating a point where the rail line interesected a road, 'and march in to attack Yuan from the flank. If nothing else it will provide a useful diversion.'

'It must be more than a diversion, Smith. I

thought I had made myself clear. The Dragon must . . . '

'Yes, I know. Spearhead the attack.' Smith almost slammed his pencil down on the table. 'All right then. The Dragon will move before the main force. It will disembark its infantry who will initiate the attack. The ground is far from ideal, but . . . '

'Excellent,' the General said, beaming with delight. 'And I shall go with it.'

'No, sir, please,' Smith pleaded. 'You must be with the main body of your army.' He saw that the General was about to protest, so before he could speak, Smith quickly added, 'It will be the safest place for you, sir. Once the infantry have left it, the Dragon will have little more than a token force on board.'

He saw that his point had struck home. The General weighed the advice for barely a second. 'Yes, you may be right,' he admitted grudgingly. 'My men must be able to see me as they go into battle.'

That is the last thing they need, Smith thought to himself. He would go with the Dragon himself. If the Dragon was to be given the unnecessary task of initiating the attack, then he could at least ensure that it was done properly. The General meanwhile could march with the main body where he could do least damage to the overall attack plan. Secure in the bosom of his army, all he would have to do would be to march stolidly forwards on a compass bearing. Surely, Smith reasoned, even General Mok could manage that?

'And what about my artillery?' the General asked.

Smith blinked. The General hardly had any. 'Well, sir, the guns are very low on ammunition, as you know. I think it might be best to hold them in reserve. What ammunition we have would best be used by the Dragon.'

'But I thought you said the Dragon won't have anything to shoot at?'

Smith laughed awkwardly. What he had meant to say was that he wanted to conserve their meagre ammunition stocks but he knew that such frugality and foresight would be lost on his employer.

'General, as you quite rightly pointed out, the Dragon should spearhead the attack. It cannot do so without an ample stock of ammunition for its howitzers.'

'Yes, I know all that,' the General said impatiently. 'But surely my infantry will need the reassurance of a preparatory bombardment by the guns before the main attack goes in?'

'Perhaps we can spare some then,' Smith

conceded. He actually did not think that their enemy Yuan would be able to muster sufficient troops to mount any sort of significant defence.

'There we are then,' the General announced proudly. 'I have given you the outline of a battle plan. You can now work out the minor details. I have done the hard part for you.'

With that, General Mok strode from the room leaving the aides staring resentfully at Smith, the foreigner from whom they were obliged to take orders.

Smith breathed a sigh of relief the moment he was left in sole command. He glared around at those left with him. 'Right you lot,' he said bitterly, 'let's get some work done here.' So saying, he barked out instructions while the aides scribbled feverishly. He ran through the myriad essential coordinating details automatically. It was second nature to him. Timings, movement plans, supplies, reinforcement, casualty procedures, battle drill rehearsals.

But all the while, his mind was elsewhere, and the one name echoing through his head was Caspasian. He had never heard Caspasian's revolver fall silent, because he had never heard it in the first place. His ears had been full of the sound of the horses' hooves and the panicked shouts of the General's cavalry all about him. The idea that Caspasian might have survived the encounter with Yuan's men sent a shiver of pure dread through his body and, as he continued to rattle out his orders for the forthcoming battle that would take place in a few days time, Smith pondered the likelihood of meeting again his old comrade in arms.

Mingled with his thoughts of the coming battle, he could now hear other guns and other shells. Screaming in with lunatic savagery, they shook the ground beneath his feet. He reached out to grip the edge of the table. His pencil rolled off the map and on to the floor. Some of the aides looked up, glancing uncertainly at one another. Smith seemed suddenly to be very far away. He was staring fixedly out through the window, though not at anything that any of them could see.

8

Lilin did not return to Caspasian's room for the next two days. Instead, his food was brought by an old peasant woman who grunted acknowledgement of his thanks, but otherwise did not appear to understand one word of his Mandarin. Caspasian was surprised to find himself disappointed at Lilin's absence. He had only seen her twice, yet whenever the meal time knock at the door sounded, he looked up in anticipation until the wrinkled old woman shuffled into the room and once again dashed Caspasian's hopes.

The food was wholesome even if lacking in variety. There were three meals a day. Shortly after first light the old woman would bring him a pot of jasmine tea, some cold rice and fish. At midday there would be thick white rice noodles with shredded meat and steamed green vegetables. At last light there would be an ample bowl of fried rice or beans sprouts with some fruit, usually an apple. Each meal was just sufficient to combat his mounting hunger while leaving him wanting more. As a result, he felt himself both losing weight and growing in strength at the same time.

One morning after he had finished his breakfast and the old woman had removed the tray, Caspasian decided it was high time he was up and about. The wound in his side had almost completely healed and he was now able to stand and walk.

He stood slowly, getting his balance, and walked carefully across to the window. It was open and a fresh, invigorating breeze swirled into the room and eddied around the furthest corners. The door rattled lightly, worrying at its loose hinges. Caspasian breathed deeply, filling his lungs and holding the air a long time before letting it go. He could feel his head clearing. The throbbing pain had decreased to the point where it was manageable and he knew that in a little while longer it would go altogether.

Gingerly, he took a step back and sank into the zenkutsu-dachi stance, his right leg back, locked into position. He twisted his hips into the stance and tried a very slow, gentle punch. When he had tried it only the previous day the effort had almost thrown him off balance. Today however he felt rock solid. His right fist glided forward with the smooth precision of a rifle bolt sliding into the breech. In the same instant, his left fist pulled back against the side of his chest. Action and reaction. The countermove by the left fist had the effect of accelerating the right punch, each fist slamming forward alternately, counter-balanced and focused by the opposite movement of the other.

He slid his rear foot forward and to the side, sinking lower into a kiba-dachi stance, as if straddling an imaginary horse. Again he tried a couple of punches. Finding them possible, he steadily increased the speed, and from the speed came greater power. He was careful not to overdo it. He had suffered enough injuries in his time to know how far he could push himself. There was no point in stretching too far too soon, only to find the advance undone by impatience. So, when he had performed a small variety of hand blows, executing each one barely a dozen times, he gently rose, shook his limbs loose, and continued with further breathing exercises. A slow smile spread across his face. He was back in business.

He was delighted at lunchtime therefore when the old woman was followed into the room by General Yuan himself.

The General took one look at Caspasian and beamed. 'Well, you're certainly looking much improved.'

Caspasian was sitting on the edge of the bed, his back straight, hands in his lap. He smiled and nodded at the old woman. 'It's the diet. It might not be the grill at the Cathay, but it's good food nonetheless.'

'Excellent. I am glad to hear you approve. Here in the valley we have been able to keep pace with the seasons. I have ensured that the farmers have been able to harvest their crops and so even if we have all lost a little weight, so far no one has starved.'

Caspasian was genuinely impressed. 'That's a rare achievement, General. You are to be congratulated.'

General Yuan shrugged. 'But not by the British I suspect.'

Deciding it was best to avoid the subject for the moment, Caspasian said, 'General, I would very much like to see the valley for myself.'

General Yuan seemed pleased by the request. 'Actually, that's the reason I'm here. I think it is something you should see. Then you can return to Shanghai and report the truth to your superiors.'

'I am afraid I am not the sort of person they generally listen to.'

'That may well be, but in the absence of any other envoy you will have to suffice. You're the only witness I've got.'

'True,' Caspasian smiled.

While Caspasian ate, General Yuan talked

about the circumstances that had brought him to power. He explained how his family had lived in the valley for several generations. The graves of his ancestors were grouped together in an auspicious location on a nearby hillside. 'From there they keep watch over us,' he said. 'I feel them judging me continually.'

'How disconcerting.'

The General smiled. 'Not at all. Their judgement is always beneficent. It is uncritical.'

Caspasian raised his eyebrows. 'Then you must have been doing an excellent job.'

The General tilted his head modestly. 'I do my best.'

'So do I,' Caspasian said. 'But I dread to think what sort of judgement my ancestors would make of my efforts.'

General Yuan eyed him carefully. 'Perhaps you demand too much of yourself? Maybe you try too hard.'

'Too hard to do what?'

'To be.'

Caspasian laughed, the sound ringing harshly in his ears. 'That sounds very oriental.'

'What do you expect from a Chinaman? But in any case, I suspect you are not someone to whom such sentiments are completely foreign.'

Caspasian was struck by the perspicacity of the General's observation. Before he could respond the General said, 'You see, I have heard all about you. I know more about you than you think.'

Suddenly Caspasian realised. 'Of course. The girl.'

The General smiled. 'Yes, Lilin. I can't think of any other Englishman who could handle the thugs of the Green Gang the way you did. Where did you learn to fight like that?'

'My family lived in Yokohama. I was brought up there and spent the first years of my life in Japan.'

General Yuan looked puzzled. 'That still doesn't explain how an Englishman comes to be proficient at an oriental art. All the Englishmen I have ever encountered have taken great pains to keep themselves as far removed from the local customs as possible. How is it that your family was so different?'

Caspasian was starting to feel ill at ease. 'They just were. That's all.'

The General noted the change of colour on Caspasian's cheeks and smiled pleasantly. 'Then you were fortunate indeed.'

'Was I?' Caspasian said with a bitterness more transparent than he had intended.

'Come,' the General said abruptly. He had

no wish to make Caspasian any more uncomfortable than he obviously already was. 'How about the guided tour?'

Caspasian took a final sip of jasmine tea, stood, and followed the General from the room.

The moment they exited the building the contrast between Yuan's camp and that of General Mok struck Caspasian. The first thing he noticed was the absence of fear in everyone he met. Yuan was greeted with respect, but no one showed any sign of the barely suppressed terror that had characterised General Mok's soldiers.

Next, there was an orderliness about the settlement that, while it differed from military discipline, nevertheless portrayed a sense of purpose, a belief that routine was guaranteed. People knew that under General Yuan they would not be subject to the vagaries of unpredictable changes of mood. The whole atmosphere was an expression of confidence in their leader.

Caspasian had come across the same thing countless times before. On arriving in a new unit, he could tell almost at once how its morale stood. It always stemmed from the individual at the top. People took their lead from him. Always. If he was incompetent, the loss of faith that inevitably followed would be transmitted by a gradual process of osmosis down through the ranks. It would start in the officers' mess with a remark critical of the leader, muttered under the breath but intended to be heard. The infection would spread like a virus to the warrant officers' and sergeants' mess, and from there down to the rank and file. With luck the incompetent leader would be removed in time. If not, disaster followed as surely as night followed day. In one instance, Caspasian had witnessed a mutiny. Needless to say, it was the common soldiers who had been punished. The Colonel responsible for starting the rot had already moved on to another posting in the natural course, leaving his hapless successor to face the music. Unfortunately the successor lacked both the insight and the concern to detect the root cause of the trouble, so although honour was eventually saved, justice was left to miscarry.

As they walked through the town, Caspasian asked the General where he had spent his military service. 'Presumably you were an officer in the imperial army before the fall of the last dynasty?'

To Caspasian's surprise the General threw back his head and laughed. 'My dear fellow, I have about as much military experience as the old woman who brought you your lunch today.'

Caspasian began to understand. It was hardly unusual for warlords to lack any real grounding in a genuine army. Many were little more than brigands. General Mok for example.

'You will remember I said that my family have been here for many years,' General Yuan continued. 'When the old empire broke up, fragmenting into warlord fiefdoms, we in this province found ourselves in something of a vacuum. Putting it simply, the nearest warlords were a long way away, and in those days all of them were too busy consolidating their power. We were left alone.

'Then the bandits came. They still do from time to time. Poverty creates them just as it creates lice. With the old system of law and order swept away, it became clear to me that, if we were to preserve our way of life, we needed to organise ourselves into some sort of armed force. Otherwise we would fall prey to lawlessness and every kind of vice.'

With his fingers he pinched his moustache into shape. 'So I became a general. It was as simple as that. We had a few rifles, and over the years we have added to our stock. It is surprising what can be achieved against bandits by even just a little discipline. Merely calling myself a general has a deterrent effect and keeps them away. Most of the time.'

'That may be, but I'm afraid General Mok is a far more serious threat than a gang of armed bandits.'

Yuan sighed. Caspasian felt he could almost see the burden on the man's shoulders. Looking about him, he wondered how long Yuan's men could withstand an assault by General Mok's army. Mok by himself would be bad enough, but with Daniel Smith to advise him, Caspasian knew that he would overrun whatever defences Yuan could organise. Yuan would succumb in the first serious engagement. Unless he had help and professional advice of his own.

He pushed the thought from his mind. This was not his fight. China was awash with injustice. So what if one more miscarriage was about to take place? Caspasian had all but wrecked his own career by going against the party line before. He was determined to put things right this time. His mission was clear. General Mok was the chosen ally. In truth, if a counter to Chiang Kai-shek was the aim, then militarily Mok had to be the better bet. Why complicate things now with original thought?

Lilin unexpectedly stepped out in front of them, running headlong into Caspasian. He caught her by the arms to stop her from falling. Startled, she stared at him.

'Don't worry,' Caspasian reassured her. 'I'm not escaping. The General's giving me a . . .'

Ignoring him, she spoke urgently. 'Father, there's been an attack on the farm at the willow bridge.'

'General Mok?'

'No. Bandits. The farm workers managed to get away unhurt. They think they know where the bandits have their camp.'

The General turned to Caspasian and noticed the look on his face. 'What's the matter?'

'This is your daughter?'

'Yes,' Yuan said proudly.

Caspasian looked from one to the other, feeling stupid.

'Lilin is not only my daughter. She is also my commander-in-chief.'

Lilin smiled at Caspasian triumphantly. 'Are you surprised that a woman can lead?'

'In China, yes, I'm stunned!'

'You forget the last Empress Tsu-hsi.'

'Yes, but she was an exception.'

Lilin looked nonplussed. 'Well so am I.'

General Yuan stepped in. 'Having no sons, Lilin is the only option I have.' He beamed at her. 'And she has never disappointed me. Not once.' He turned back to Caspasian. 'Captain, I am afraid I will have to complete our tour some other time. I will get someone to escort you back to your room. Lilin and I must take care of the bandits and drive them away before they can do any more harm.'

Before he could be dismissed, Caspasian said, 'General, I'd like to come too.'

General Yuan barely gave the suggestion a moment's consideration. 'That's out of the question. Willow bridge is at least an hour's horse ride away. You are far too weak.'

'Whose fault is that?'

General Yuan shook his head. 'No. I'm lucky you are still alive. The last thing I need now is for you to be killed while under my protection. That would play right into Mok's hands. He would tell the British I killed you myself.'

'General, I have no intention of getting myself killed.'

'People rarely do, but they still die.'

'I'm a professional soldier. I know the risks. Let me come. I can help you.'

Yuan was silent, pondering. He looked to Lilin for a steer but she was not going to help. 'It's nothing to me,' she said. 'So long as he doesn't get in the way.'

While preparations were being made, Caspasian did his best to appear in a fit state to undertake the ride. A force of platoon strength was assembled, and again he was impressed by the quiet confidence and self-discipline of the men. Although they lacked a proper uniform, an attempt had been made to dress as similarly as limitations allowed. Of greatest concern to Caspasian was the shortage of modern weapons. Only half the complement had rifles, and most of those were old models. Nevertheless he was impressed to note that they were spotlessly clean, well oiled and maintained. Ammunition bandoliers seemed to be mostly empty, but even the brass cases of the scarce bullets had been burnished to a shine.

Mounting his horse, General Yuan saw the expression on Caspasian's face and read his thoughts. 'I like to look on the positive side,' he said, swinging himself up into the saddle. 'Because we have only a few bullets, we have learnt to make every shot count. I suspect you won't find better marksmen than these in all of China. Every one is an expert.'

'They'll need to be when they meet General Mok,' Caspasian retorted grimly.

The ride was far harder than Caspasian had anticipated. He noticed General Yuan glancing at him after every difficult patch, and whenever their eyes met, Caspasian conscientiously forced a smile. Lilin, on the other hand, appeared to be ignoring him. Her eyes were everywhere except on him. She scanned the surrounding landscape and Caspasian was impressed to note that she rode as if she had been born in the saddle.

When they had been riding for over an hour, they took shelter in a glade beside a river.

'The willow bridge is about five hundred yards ahead,' General Yuan said quietly, drawing his horse alongside Caspasian's. 'We will go on foot from here.'

Before he could move away, Caspasian caught the General by the sleeve. 'General, can I have a gun?'

General Yuan eyed him suspiciously.

'I'm a soldier, for God's sake. Give me a gun and I can be of some use,' Caspasian persisted.

'You're not here to be of use.'

'Then why did you let me come?'

'Because you wanted to. In any case, we don't have any guns to spare.'

When they had dismounted, General Yuan left Lilin to detail a handful of men to remain with the horses, while he moved with the remainder silently through the trees in the direction of the bridge. A moment later, Caspasian looked round to see Lilin jogging up to join them. For armament she carried a rifle cut down to size. It looked like it had once been a Hanyang 88, but both the barrel and the butt had been sawn off to create a dangerous-looking implement little more than a foot in length. At long range it would be next to useless, but at close quarters Caspasian could imagine the devastating effect it would have.

She saw him studying it and smiled. 'It's a handy size for Shanghai as well.'

'Clearly,' he said, impressed.

They heard the bandits long before they saw them. General Yuan gestured for his men to fan out and with rifles at the ready they stealthily approached through the brush. Caspasian drew alongside the General as he sank down on to all fours and crawled through a clump of undergrowth to catch a glimpse of their prey.

Believing themselves secure, the bandits had stripped off their weapons and were taking their ease in the cool water. Caspasian counted a dozen of them. Five or six were splashing noisily in the middle of the shallow river, tossing water at each other and clearly enjoying the relaxation after the exertions of their raid.

A pile of sacks and bundles littered both banks of the river where they had been going through their loot, deciding what was worth taking with them and what could be discarded. Among the men behind him Caspasian could hear angry mutters. They themselves came from similar farms around the valley and each of them could imagine the destruction wrought in minutes on a homestead that had taken years of hard work to establish. General Yuan hissed at them to keep quiet.

Of the bandits on the river bank, all were lying back fast asleep in the grass, basking in the warm sunshine. Only one man was sitting upright. He did not appear to have been posted as a sentry however. Instead he sat disconsolately by himself, arms clasped around his knees, staring bleakly at the ground. He reached out suddenly and picked up a stone and tossed it into the river, watching the ripples it made spread out towards the banks.

General Yuan drew his men into a firing line. They brought their rifles into the aim and Caspasian waited for the command to open fire. If their shooting was as good as the General had said it was, it would take a single volley to account for the raiders.

To Caspasian's amazement however, instead of giving the order, General Yuan stood up and stepped through the last of the bushes out into the open. He had broken cover about fifty yards downriver from the bandits. Slowly, and with complete confidence, he strolled towards them, as if coming upon them quite by chance while out for a pleasant stroll. He was armed only with a revolver, and that remained buckled in its brown leather holster at his belt.

Caspasian looked questioningly at Lilin who had lain down beside him. She shrugged nonchalantly, as if this was an everyday occurrence, but he could see that underneath the show of bravado she was scared. Not for herself, but for her father.

'What the hell's he up to?' he whispered.

Without taking her eyes from her father she said, 'He believes there has already been too much killing in China. He always gives everyone the benefit of the doubt. He likes to give such men the option of joining us first.'

Caspasian stared at her dumbfounded. 'But these are bandits, for God's sake. They're probably high on opium and won't even understand his offer!'

Lilin kept her eyes fixed on her father. Caspasian could see the film of tears forming in them. 'You try telling him that.'

None of the bandits noticed the General's approach until he hailed them. He called out pleasantly, raising one hand as if encountering a group of old friends by chance. In the tense stillness of the treeline, his voice detonated like a hand grenade. On the bandits it had an altogether different effect. The ones in the river stood immobile, the playful expressions solidifying on their faces, to be gradually replaced by a dangerous suspicion. On the river banks, the sleepers awoke with a casual ease, pushing themselves into sitting positions like a pride of lions staring with pleased disbelief at a calf wandering innocently into their midst.

Caspasian noticed that only one of them reacted with any sense. The one who had been sitting alone, clasping his knees. At the sound of the General's voice he had rolled over into a firing position, taken up his rifle and brought it into the aim, albeit somewhat shakily.

'My friends,' Caspasian heard the General saying, continuing his steady advance towards the bandits, 'I am told you have some property that doesn't belong to you. If you hand it over, I am prepared to make you an offer.'

The bandits looked at one another in amazement. One of them laughed. Another took it up and soon all of them were chuckling merrily. One of them who seemed to be the leader stepped from the water, wiping himself dry with the shirt he had discarded on the river bank.

'Who are you to make us offers?'

'I am General Yuan.' He gestured around him. 'The people who farm this land are under my protection. They work for me.'

There was an exchange of excited chatter among the bandits. Caspasian leaned closer to Lilin. 'Why doesn't he tell them he's not alone? He's simply asking for trouble.'

Her sigh of exasperation was audible. 'Free will.'

'What?'

'Father says that anyone will agree to join us at the end of a gun barrel. Anyone who joins without the use of threats however will stay and can be trusted.'

Caspasian stared back at the General, astounded. 'How in God's name has he lived this long?'

To left and right of him, Caspasian noticed Yuan's men snuggling down behind their rifle sights, pulling the butt plates firmly into their shoulders, fingers on the triggers. Everyone was ready. They had obviously been through it before and Caspasian wondered how many times. Against his better judgement he found a powerful respect growing inside him for the General standing out in the open, confronting the bandits face to face.

For a moment there appeared to be a

stand-off. The bandits began to laugh again and Caspasian thought he could feel the mood change, but in the wrong direction. The laughter had become cruel. Those who had been sitting rose slowly to their feet, and again Caspasian was seized by the image of the lions sloping lazily towards the unsuspecting calf.

Suddenly a cry rang out. Caspasian looked across and saw that the man who had been sitting alone had jumped to his feet. He was shouting something and for a moment Caspasian thought that he had detected Yuan's men hiding in the treeline. But then he understood. The man had slung his rifle over his shoulder and was wading through the water. Caspasian could hardly believe it, but it seemed that he wanted to take up the General's offer and join forces.

As he passed through the other bandits, he plucked at the sleeve of a youngster, a friend. They spoke urgently together and he seemed to be on the point of persuading the other when the bandit leader let loose a tirade of abuse at the two of them.

Then everything happened at once. The bandit leader drew a handgun and levelled it at the two men who were about to desert him. One of Yuan's men, believing the leader was about to open fire on General Yuan, fired.

True to the General's boast, the bullet struck the bandit leader in the temple, blowing the front of his skull wide open and showering the two deserters with brains and fragments of bone.

However, because Yuan's men had not fired in a single volley, the coherence of the ambush was lost. What should have been a devastating and decisive attack became a ragged fusillade of rifle fire. The bandits had reacted quickly at the first shot and most of them made it into cover before the General's men could kill them.

'Where's the General?' Caspasian shouted above the noise. In the confusion, dust and gun smoke, the General had disappeared.

Lilin stretched forward, craning to see. A bullet snapped through the leaves close overhead, showering both her and Caspasian with green foliage and pieces of twig.

'There!' she shouted, pointing at the river bank.

Caspasian could just see him. He had thrown himself at the water's edge and was half in and half out, crouching behind a smooth, round boulder. Bullets were ricochetting off it as some of the bandits tried to winkle him out. Most of them were trying to pull back however. They were raiders, used to taking on isolated farmsteads manned by unarmed peasants. An encounter with a disciplined force was not to their liking.

Two of the General's men rose out of cover and dashed forward to help him. They were met by a burst of rifle fire from the bandits and both of them fell dead. The General shouted back that no one else should move.

Lilin cursed and swore, working the bolt of her swan-off rifle, sending random shots blazing uselessly over the bandits' heads. Most of them had tucked themselves down below the level of the river bank and were now impervious to the rifle fire of the General's men.

To Caspasian's horror, Lilin tried to stand up. His hand shot out and grasped her loose cotton shirt, dragging her to ground.

'Don't be so bloody stupid!'

'We can't just leave him there!' she bellowed back. Her voice was filled with terror and Caspasian could see the desperation in her eyes as she strained to catch sight of her father.

He swore under his breath. He had asked to come along. Well, this was where it had got him. What the devil had he expected?

'OK, if we're going to get him out of there we'll do it properly,' he shouted above the noise. 'Get the men to put down covering fire when I give the word.' He saw that she was about to question him. 'Just do it!' he snapped.

As Lilin turned away to pass the word, Caspasian reached out and snatched the sawn-off rifle from her grasp. She cried out in protest, but before she could react he had wriggled away down the treeline to the point where it came closest to the river. When he was in position he looked back and found Lilin glaring at him intently.

'Now!' he shouted.

Instead, Lilin shouted something at him.

Caspasian missed what she said and mouthed again, 'Now!'

He saw her about to speak again, but then she thought better of it and passed the word.

A second later a fusillade of rifle fire rang out. It had the desired effect. For a moment the bandit's guns fell silent. Caspasian launched himself out of the bushes and headed for the water. To his horror, his legs felt as if he was wading through knee-deep mud like a slow motion nightmare. The General had been right. He was in no fit state for action. But it was too late to bother about that now.

By the time he reached the water the bandits had woken up to his rescue attempt. He threw himself headlong into the river safely obscured from their line of sight by a sharp bend in the bank. Twenty yards ahead he could see the General, his back to Caspasian, returning the bandits fire with his revolver. The General glanced over his shoulder and grinned at Caspasian.

'They'll give up in a minute,' he called back confidently.

'That's terrific,' Caspasian shouted as bullets snapped in the air above his head.

Suddenly there was a change in the gunfire. The bullets being fired at the General and Caspasian stopped and instead there was a burst of firing further up the river. A few moments later everything went silent.

Caspasian crawled forward to join the General. There was a shout and the General turned to Caspasian and grinned. 'What did I tell you?'

The shout came again. The General listened intently, his smile broadening. 'It's that fellow who wanted to join us. He says the others are dead now.'

'Surely you don't believe him?'

'As a matter of fact I do. If you remember, he revealed his intentions before his comrades opened fire. It takes a brave man to do that.'

Before Caspasian could restrain him, General Yuan stood up and walked forward. Sure enough, when Caspasian himself followed he saw the same man who had been sitting alone, now advancing towards them. He held his rifle above his head. Behind him, his friend was following with considerably less confidence.

The man called out again. 'We shot them, my friend and me. No good bandits. Rubbish. Now we are free to join you.'

Caspasian jogged to the General's side. With his attention focused on the two surrendering bandits, he almost missed the flicker of movement from the water's edge in the periphery of his vision. Rising out of the water, one of the bandits loomed upright, a shotgun cradled in his hands. Barely more than ten paces distant there was no way he could miss. Time slowed as Caspasian swung to meet the attack. Grasping the sawn-off rifle in both fists he brought it up, pointing it at the centre of his target's chest, and squeezed the trigger. The sound of the firing pin clicking harmlessly onto the base of a spent round was more deafening than any gun shot.

Caspasian watched in horror as the bandit raised the shotgun. The split second before he could fire, the bandit's chest burst open and he was flung backwards into the water, dead. Caspasian turned. The surrendering bandit stood there as steady as a rock, his rifle barrel smoking.

Caspasian stared in disgust at the sawn-off

rifle in his hand. The disgust turned to anger, anger with himself for not having checked that it was loaded.

'That's what I was trying to tell you,' Lilin said coming towards him. 'I had run out of bullets.'

Caspasian went over to the two bandits who were talking to the General. He held out his hand in thanks. The bandit looked at it in puzzlement, then stared at Caspasian, fear in his eyes.

'What's your name?' Caspasian asked.

The man looked questioningly at the General who nodded reassurance.

'My name is Li,' the man said. 'This is my friend. His name is Ku. He deserted from General Mok last week.' He looked suspiciously from General Yuan to Caspasian and back again, his earlier confidence dissipated now that he had seen the Englishman.

'What's the matter?' General Yuan asked. 'Have you deserted from Mok as well?'

Li shook his head urgently. 'Never. He killed my comrades. The Dragon came. It killed all my friends, and now it is hungry again. Ku has told me so.'

Caspasian turned to the small frightened youth at Li's side. 'How do you know this?'

The youth blinked at him stupidly, unable to penetrate Caspasian's dialect.

Li answered for him. 'He says that the Dragon is on the move again.' He stared at Caspasian with renewed dread. 'And Tai Shang Huang is coming with it.'

9

Word spread quickly among General Yuan's troops that the Dragon was on the move again. Tales of the Dragon had circulated for months, to the extent that everyone knew stories of some gruesome episode or other, and all of these were now repeated, heavily embellished, so that fear increased with the telling, leaping from man to man with the tenacity of a forest fire whipping through the tops of tinder-dry trees. Although few if any of General Yuan's men had actually seen the armoured train, such was the awe in which they held it that in their fear-stricken minds it became more mythical beast than engine of war.

The dead comrades of the two surrendered bandits were gathered by General Yuan's party and Caspasian was interested to see that they were buried before the General gave the order to depart.

'It's not that my father has any particular feeling for such people,' Lilin said by way of explanation. 'It is simply a question of hygiene. If they were left where they fell, they would pollute the water supply for all the farms downriver from here.'

Nevertheless, Caspasian noticed General Yuan move apart from the others when the task of burial was complete, and stand alone for a few moments in silent contemplation. When he turned to walk back to where Caspasian stood with their horses, he smiled sadly. 'An unfortunate waste,' he said simply, accepting the reins of his mount from Caspasian with thanks and swinging himself up into the saddle with greater ease than Caspasian who found that his hands were shaking from the recent exertion of the fight.

'Are you sure you're all right?' the General asked, his brow furrowed with concern.

'Not really, no,' Caspasian answered as he settled himself uncomfortably in the small Chinese saddle. 'Give me a couple of days and I think I'll be fine.'

'If our new friend is telling the truth, we might not have even that much.' He paused before continuing, 'We must get you away from here. Back to the coast and Shanghai.'

Caspasian nodded and left it at that for the moment. His mind was in a turmoil but until he had sorted out his thoughts on the matter, he judged it best to keep his peace. His brief experience of General Mok had confirmed his suspicions that the man was, at best, corrupt. There was no particular surprise in that. Corruption was endemic to China, for the present at least. It was the bedfellow of greed, and together they were running rampant throughout the land, laying waste the work of centuries, dismembering the once noble empire, the land of Confucius and Lao Tzu turned into a combination of gambling den and abattoir.

Like many of his fellow warlords however, General Mok had passed beyond corruption. Caspasian had met evil men before, and in Mok he recognised it again. The blinding of the three hanged deserters had provided ample evidence. The apparently loyal service provided to Mok by Daniel Smith also cast Caspasian's old acquaintance in a new light. It did not come as a surprise to Caspasian to find his opinion of Smith confirmed, but it had the added effect of bringing Private Nathaniel Dobson back into his thoughts. During the ride back to General Yuan's camp, Caspasian let his mind drift back to the battle in the redoubt. He knew that, come what may, he would have to find out what had really happened. He owed it to Dobson.

But what really concerned Caspasian, was the notion of his own government allying itself to a man such as General Mok. While it was true that Mok had the largest armed force in the region, its reliability was highly questionable. Everything Caspasian had seen convinced him that its morale was low. The soldiers followed Mok out of terror, not loyalty. General Yuan's soldiers, on the other hand, possessed a morale rooted in a genuine respect for their leader. Yuan led by personal example. The incident at the river had just proved that. His personal courage was beyond question, even if it was a little reckless. The idea of being forced, not just to witness the destruction of such a man by Mok's murderous thugs, but even to assist in it, sickened Caspasian to his very core.

As Caspasian wrestled with the dilemma, trying to ignore the severe discomforts of the hard ride, he realised that in a strange way Daniel Smith might unwittingly have given him the way out that he was so desperately searching for. Even if Smith had not actually arranged the ambush at the farmstead, by deserting Caspasian and leaving him to die, Smith had blocked off any possibility of Caspasian returning to General Mok. Caspasian was certain that the intention had been for him to perish. If he were to return, then the image of the calf wandering towards the lions that had struck him when he had seen General Yuan's act of bravery would turn about and would apply to himself.

If he was going to try and convince his

government that Mok was unsuitable as an ally, he would have a better chance of succeeding if he were able simultaneously to provide them with a realistic alternative. Surely, General Yuan was such a candidate?

Caspasian felt as if a load was starting to lift from his shoulders. He straightened his back and, for the first time since his capture, felt a surge of energy through his aching limbs. He turned in the saddle and found that Lilin was watching him from her place further down the small column. He smiled at her but she looked away quickly.

As soon as they arrived back at the town, Caspasian sought out General Yuan and put his proposal before him. General Yuan watched him carefully while he spoke. Lilin had joined them and glanced from Caspasian to her father, gauging the effect that the Englishman was having. When Caspasian had finished there was a long silence while General Yuan considered Caspasian's plan.

At last he said, 'Captain Smith made a grave error the day he allowed you to fall into my hands.' He grinned. 'I do not think you will be surprised to learn that I have been hoping for exactly this.'

Caspasian shrugged. 'To me it is common sense. Whether my government agrees is another matter. Putting it simply, I'll propose

231

that we swap General Mok for you.'

'But we don't have even a fraction of his numbers,' Lilin cut in, 'whatever you say about their low morale.'

'And it might also turn out that by the time you get the agreement of your people in Shanghai I will already be dead. If General Mok is preparing to attack, there simply won't be enough time for you to travel to Shanghai, secure the cooperation of your government, and get arms and reinforcements to me here.' He shook his head. 'This should all have happened a month ago. As it is, our backs are already against the wall and the firing squad is trooping into the courtyard!'

'Then we will have to trip them up,' Caspasian said.

'And how on earth do you intend to do that?' Lilin asked mockingly.

General Yuan was kinder. He put one hand on Caspasian's shoulder and said, 'I know you mean well, and I greatly appreciate your assistance. Especially after the reception we gave you! Usually I am an optimist but I am also realistic in my expectations. In this case I can't see how we can resist long enough for help to arrive. In fact — and I do not mean this as a slight on you — knowing your government, I should think they would rather see which side wins before deciding who to back. That being the case, arms are unlikely to arrive in time to save me.'

For the first time, Caspasian had been shown into the General's private house. They were standing in a large three-sided room, the fourth side of which opened directly on to a patio paved with large slabs of pale grey stone. Worked into them Caspasian noticed a carving of two large fish, interwoven in the manner of the Yin and Yang symbols, one light, the other dark, the two eternally contesting forces of nature yet each perfectly balancing the other.

Lilin saw him studying them. 'My father comes here every morning to practise Tai Chi,' she said, and Caspasian smiled with sudden understanding, remembering how the General had so surprised him moving silently around the room when Caspasian had been blindfolded. Only a practitioner of that most peaceful of arts could have moved with such stealth.

An intricately carved trellis with an archway of dark rose-coloured cherry wood separated the two areas. Caspasian walked beneath it slowly as he thought about all they had said. Above him, the ceiling had been replaced by a lattice work covered in thick vines, the ends of which had been threaded back through the narrow beams to create an overhead carpet. It fragmented the sunshine into a thousand splinters.

'General, the history of warfare is full of examples of small forces taking on and defeating larger ones. That is what you have got to do.'

Lilin threw up her hands in the air. 'Great! So that's all! We fight and beat General Mok. Now why didn't I think of that? We fight and die in the hope that you will return with good news from Shanghai before we have all been butchered.'

Caspasian turned to face them. 'I never said anything about returning to Shanghai. I'll stay here and help you. When we've defeated Mok, that's when I'll go to Shanghai. Then, and only then. I'll present my people with a *fait accompli*.'

'They'll hardly thank you for that,' the General observed drily.

Caspasian smiled. 'They never thank me anyway, whatever I do. I might as well do what I believe to be right.'

General Yuan summoned a servant and sent him to fetch some tea. The man returned only minutes later and set out the pot and cups on a table in the shade of the vines.

'We have known for some time that we were in a desperate situation,' the General began, when the servant had withdrawn out of earshot. 'Short of evacuating the entire valley, the only alternatives we have are either to surrender to Mok or else to fight him. Evacuation is out of the question. Everyone here has farmed this land for generations. So too is surrender unacceptable. Mok is renowned for unpredictable brutality. I could never submit my people to a man like that.'

Lilin passed a cup of jasmine tea to her father, and then offered a second cup to Caspasian.

'That leaves the third option. To fight. I have feared it must come to this. My only hope is that, with the help of someone like you, we might just have a chance of saving ourselves from disaster.'

Caspasian noticed the General and Lilin swap glances. Lilin's nod of consent was almost imperceptible. But not quite.

'You must have wondered what my daughter was doing in Shanghai,' the General said, slowly rotating his cup on the table top.

'The question had crossed my mind,' Caspasian admitted, understating the burning desire to know that had consumed him since he had first seen Lilin here in the General's camp.

'Information can often mean the difference between life and death. No one knows better exactly what is going on throughout China than the Green Gang.' The General cocked his head on one side. 'I take it you know of them?'

Caspasian had gone as white as a sheet. He nodded.

'Their tentacles reach into every organisation. And I do mean every organisation,' he said, stressing his point. 'With Chiang Kai-shek and his Kuomintang troops advancing northwards, with the British and other western powers seeking out allies, with the fortunes of China's most powerful warlords waxing and waning almost daily, for the sake of my people I simply had to know what was happening if I was to have any chance of plotting a course through the minefield that my poor country has become.'

Caspasian stared at him astounded. 'You used your own daughter as a spy,' he stammered, 'letting her become involved with the most notorious and ruthless criminals in the country?'

Lilin cut in. 'My father didn't make me do anything. It was my idea!'

'You mean . . . ' Caspasian began.

'I would never have allowed her to do it if I had had any other choice. It was not for me, you understand. It was for all the people who depend on me. For them alone.'

'Did you ever consider, Lilin, what the Green Gang would do to you if they found out?'

She tossed back her hair defiantly but did not answer. Another thought occurred to Caspasian, shocking him more than the last. 'How far were you prepared to go? For God's sake, I saw you with the bull at the Regent. Had you . . . ?'

General Yuan said, 'The meeting you witnessed was my daughter's first encounter with him. Thanks to you, it went no further . . . '

'Thanks to Caspasian, Father, the meeting was ruined! Who knows what I might have learned?'

'I think you would have learned things you hadn't counted on,' Caspasian interrupted.

Again Lilin looked defiant. She started to reply but, with a glance at her father, fell silent.

The General smiled. 'My daughter wants to save her father's feelings.'

'I can imagine,' Caspasian said.

'You probably do not find us a very typical Chinese family?' the General said quietly, pouring them all some more tea.

'You're certainly not traditional,' Caspasian said.

The General acknowledged the comment.

'I will take that as a compliment. However, nor, I strongly suspect, are you traditionally British. Which is why, against all the odds, I find myself hopeful.'

'About?'

'Our chances with the fight against General Mok. Surely, in such a situation as ours, a traditional solution would never be enough. We need something revolutionary. Something he will not expect.' He raised his cup as if proposing a toast. Steam rose from the brim, breaking across his face as he inhaled the delicate perfume. He looked up, his eyes mysterious, searching, studying Caspasian through the veil of tea fumes. 'And so I put my trust in you, Captain Caspasian. My trust and the fortunes of my people. I am sure you will not disappoint us.'

★ ★ ★

Li was disconcerted on return to General Yuan's camp to discover that he and Ku were to be treated as prisoners, for the time being at least. He had hoped that, by switching sides, he might at one stroke amend his fortunes. He had been amazed when he had seen the confident figure of General Yuan marching fearlessly towards the bandits and his cry accepting the General's offer had issued from the depths of his soul unbidden, certainly before he had had time to give serious consideration to the man's proposal.

The fact was simply that Li had never before seen such an act of raw courage and leadership. In his experience, Chinese officers rarely participated in combat. If they were seen at all, it was after the fight was over. Then they would skulk from the shadows to claim the credit for victory, each vying with the other to achieve, by lies and fabrication, some degree of merit where none had, in truth, been earned. In the event of a defeat, then even the shadows would be empty, for the officers would have been the first to take to their heels.

The only time things had been different had been when the Dragon had caught them all unawares. Then there had been no time for flight. It still surprised Li that he had not felt more solace as he had watched the officers of Colonel Lam decapitated beneath the monstrous armoured train's iron wheels. But then he had been anticipating his own death, and Li had found that there was nothing like the threat of imminent extinction to blunt a man's capacity for gloating, while simultaneously sharpening his terror to an agonisingly fine point.

The prison cell into which he and Ku had

been shown was in fact just an ordinary cellar used for the storage of dried meat. For one terrified moment, his companion Ku had imagined that it must be human flesh and that they were about to be skinned alive and similarly prepared for future consumption by their captors. But a quick examination by Li had set Ku's mind at rest. Li had seen dried human flesh before and this had nothing of its vile, stomach-churning pungency.

It struck Li as strange that they should have been confined in such a cellar, and not in a proper guardroom, jail or dungeon. To Ku the answer was obvious. The dungeons were already full to overflowing. This was the only place the General's men had left in which to incarcerate them. However, Li was not so sure. He recognised that his companion was a little unhinged and overwrought following his experience of service under General Mok. When they had first met up in the bandit gang, Li had initially avoided Ku, feeling the same terror of him as he had of Ku's ex-commander's armoured train. He had soon discovered that the fellow was harmless, so much so in fact that the bandits considered slitting Ku's throat in order to save their meagre rations. But then they had arrived in General Yuan's territory, and none of them had ever before encountered such a land of plenty, not even those who could remember life before the revolution of Dr Sun Yat-sen.

Li walked slowly around the cellar. They had been left unbound, another cause for surprise. Even though the cellar was more than half full, the empty portion was nevertheless capacious. Barred windows set high in the wall, immediately below ceiling level, let in the light. Peering up through them they could see the legs of people walking past. Once or twice, a passer-by had stopped to peer curiously into the subterranean gloom, squinting at the two captive occupants as if they had been placed on display for the amusement of Yuan's men and their dependants. Again, Li was surprised when this happened to note that the observers were usually children, and, what was more, children in the care of an adult. They were not the strays or half-starved waifs that haunted all the other garrison towns with which he had had the misfortune to become acquainted during his years of service as a soldier. These children neither begged from him nor taunted him. They were simply curious. It was as if they had not encountered such beings as Li and Ku before, although Li knew that this was impossible. Nowhere in the whole of China had escaped the ruinous attention of one or another of the passing warlord armies. He could only assume that the children here were simple in the head. The valley folk had obviously been inbreeding for centuries, and these simpletons were the result.

It was early the following day when Li heard the cellar door being unlocked. Both he and Ku were asleep. When Ku woke up and saw the General's men marching into the cellar, he screamed and clutched at Li, begging him for help, convinced they were about to be taken out and burned alive in the town square. Li did his best to calm the fellow down, but he was still remonstrating when they were both securely bound and then frog-marched up the steps and out into the daylight.

With his hands tied behind his back, Li squinted furiously in the full glare of the street. The sunlight seemed to pound off the surrounding walls of the buildings with physical force. It was like trying to stand against a torrent of water and he doubled over with the effort. Because of this, he didn't notice where he and his companion were being taken until they were thrust once again into the shade of a room. This time however his surroundings were very different from the gloom of the cellar. The room was similarly cool, but there any similarity ended. Though sparsely furnished, the room was clearly in the quarters of a someone of note. A landlord, most likely. Li had been in one or two such places, and although on those occasions the households had been looted and the occupants put to the sword, they had had a similar air of refinement about them.

But here it had not been contaminated by violence and as Li straightened up he looked about him with keen interest, like a schoolboy entering his first ever museum, momentarily transfixed between curiosity and boredom.

The interval lasted no more than a handful of interesting seconds, for the sound of bold footsteps turned his head towards the door on the far side of the room and when the tall, blond-haired foreigner strode through the doorway, Li felt his bowels turn to water and his knees almost gave way. Only the supporting grip of his guards on either elbow kept him from sinking to the ground. Ku was even less composed. He let out a shriek and tried to swivel this way and that to escape. His guards cursed and shook him until he was still, small terrified whimpers slipping between his quivering lips every now and again.

The foreigner stood before them, his lean but powerfully muscled arms folded across his broad chest. He was a sight to behold and in spite of his fear, Li could not help staring at the man. He was taller than the other foreigner, the one in the service of General Mok, and there was something else that was different about him, although at first Li could not identify what it was. He had always prided himself on being a good judge of men however and eventually he settled upon the foreigner's eyes. Incredibly, they were a piercing blue colour. Quite extraordinary, though not, Li had been told, unusual among foreigners. But it was not their colour that marked the man out as different from General Mok's foreigner. Rather, it was a strange quality within them. It was a combination of threat, but with good humour there too. Mischievousness and sincerity. Intelligence and world-weariness.

At last Li settled upon it and was surprised to discover that here was a man he felt he might be able to trust. At that, he smiled, just a little.

'What are you grinning at?'

Again, Li was appalled at the ugliness of the foreigner's Mandarin, but at least this time he could understand it.

He took a step forward, the strength returning to his legs, but the guards yanked him back. The foreigner said something to them and, to Li's amazement, they not only let go of his arms, but actually untied him. The foreigner spoke again and they untied Ku as well. Li and Ku swapped stares, incredulous. Li was about to address the foreigner when the man spoke to him again.

'You said you had information about the Dragon and General Mok.'

This time when Li stepped forward his guards moved aside, though keeping a close eye on him in case he should make any aggressive move. Faced by the daunting spectacle of the tall, blue-eyed foreigner, an assault was the furthest thing from Li's mind.

He cleared his throat, summoning all his courage. 'Yes, General, that is so. It is on the move again, just as we said.'

There was the flicker of a smile on the foreigner's face and Li marvelled at such a display of contempt in the face of impending danger.

'I am not a general,' Caspasian said.

'Of course, Colonel. I understand. Please forgive me. I am only a simple soldier,' Li said quickly, blushing. He bowed deeply from the waist to abase himself. The foreigner was not wearing any identifying badges of rank, so how the devil was he supposed to have known better, he thought miserably?

'Nor am I a colonel,' Caspasian replied.

Then, seeing the consternation on Li's face, he said, 'I am a captain in His Britannic Majesty's Army. I am temporarily in the service of General Yuan, as, I believe, are you.' Noting Li's blank stare he added, 'General Yuan's the officer you decided to join at the river yesterday.'

This was extraordinary, Li thought. The foreigner had spoken as if the two of them were somehow similar. It had never happened to him before. In his experience, Chinese officers did everything they could to set themselves and their men apart. This man, on the other hand, was including him.

He beamed delightedly. 'Yes, I did, Captain.'

When he tired of Li's grinning, Caspasian prompted, 'The Dragon?'

'Yes, of course.' Li was ashamed to admit that the information the foreigner wanted was held by Ku, not him. So, deferring to his companion, as if ordering a subordinate to speak up, he imperiously nudged Ku and hissed at him to open his mouth.

'The Dragon is to move to Shankow. It will have only a small force of my comrades on board. I should have been with it, but I deserted just after we had been ordered to move. The General will march north with his main force a couple of days afterwards.' He stopped and glanced at Li who nodded reassurance and prompted him to continue. Ku blinked and looked back at the foreigner who was studying him with a ferocious expression that made Ku swallow. His throat was bone dry and he almost choked.

'That's all I know,' he concluded, fearing lest he had disappointed his small but terribly important audience.

Caspasian turned away. Shankow. That seemed fair enough to him. By a stroke of good fortune the rail lines followed a circuitous route around General Yuan's territory, thereby sparing them a confrontation with the armoured train. General Mok would doubtless be disappointed to be denied the use of such a powerful weapon. Quite apart from its immense firepower, it had a numbing shock effect on an opponent out of proportion to its real capability. And that was severe enough by itself. But together, the combination of shock effect and firepower was a battle winner.

It was only then that the idea struck Caspasian like a bolt from the blue. He stopped dead in his tracks, staring into empty space. His eyes narrowed as he rapidly calculated times and distances. He had been up most of the night with General Yuan and Lilin poring over the General's maps of the valley. They had been searching desperately for a way to defeat Mok, Smith and their army. The best that Caspasian had been able to come up with was for the use of guerilla tactics, such as the Boer farmers had used against the British Army in South Africa. There they had taken on and defeated time and again superior numbers and superior firepower. Caspasian had urged the use by General Yuan's men of similar tactics.

'Hit and run,' Caspasian had said finally, after hours of discussion. 'Inflict maximum casualties and then withdraw before Mok's men can deploy and get to grips with us.'

General Yuan had sighed, tired after the night's fruitless deliberations. 'That's all very well in somewhere as vast as South Africa, but how can I trade land for time when the land I'm trading is the farmland of my men? They will refuse to retire, and then they will be slaughtered.'

'Then you will have to convince them that any surrender of territory is only temporary. We will wear Mok down until his men lose heart and he withdraws. Then your men can return . . . '

'To what?' General Yuan said sharply. 'To a burnt-out wasteland. To torched houses and ruined crops.'

'But they can rebuild,' Caspasian pleaded.

248

He had to win the argument. He could see no other way.

'No,' the General said firmly. 'They will lose heart. I know them too well. For all this time I have managed to preserve their way of life. That is why they trust me. But they are not stupid. They know what is going on in the rest of China. If I let their homes be destroyed they will believe that the inevitable has finally caught up with them. Their morale will be broken and that will be the end.'

With a finality that shocked Caspasian, the General had turned away with arms folded, his stern posture admitting neither entreaty nor appeal.

But now, having heard what the two Chinese bandits had just said, Caspasian was struck by a new idea. In an instant he had seen what must be done.

He turned to Li and Ku smiling, thanking them for their help. They nodded uncertainly, wondering what fate awaited them now that they had served their purpose. They exchanged timid glances, waiting for the bark of an order that would see them hauled from the room to be shot out of hand. After all, what possible use could such a man as this foreigner have for them?

Li was thunder-struck therefore when Caspasian turned to one of the guards and ordered him to see that Li and Ku received a cooked meal and fresh clothes before being enrolled in the forces of General Yuan.

Li stared stupefied at his companion who had also heard the instructions. Slowly a smile broke across their faces. Against his will, Li could feel the tears welling in his eyes and he blinked severely to conceal such a sign of weakness. He had been right after all to speak out in front of the other bandits and to trust the man walking towards them with nothing more than an offer.

Suddenly he remembered his benefactor and turned to thank the tall foreigner who had just handed him back his life. But Caspasian had already left the room and was striding quickly in search of General Yuan and Lilin to tell them of his plan to attack and destroy the Dragon, the armoured train of General Mok.

10

Daniel Smith threw open the heavy iron cupola and pulled himself up from his seat in the turret on top of the Dragon's command carriage. As he wriggled his head and shoulders up through the tight circle and emerged into the onrush of air, he was met by a clammy blast of steam from the engine several carriages in front. He winced, rubbing his eyes until the wind had cleared the air, dissipating the steam into the colourless morning sky.

He reached down to the small fold-away table set immediately in front of his seat and picked up a pair of goggles. Setting them in place, he looked about him at the landscape rolling past on either side. He was passing through the bleak extended no-man's-land that stretched for mile after mile where the adjoining territories of the two generals marched, that of his current employer, General Mok, and that which had been until now under the authority of his adversary, General Yuan. Like all marches, it was a landscape of neglect, tended by no one because it belonged to no one. It was as if it had been deserted by the seasons themselves. Spring had bypassed it for several years now, denying it the crops and care of industrious farmers.

Where men had retreated, nature had stepped in. Deserted farmsteads were choked with weeds and creeper, gutted by fire and patrolled only by stray dogs that bayed and yapped at the passing train. From further along the Dragon, one of the Russians, Scarface, let rip with a long burst from a Vickers, test-firing the machine-gun. He was using a belt containing tracer rounds, the better to check his aim. Smith watched with only the mildest interest as the scarlet stream of bullets arched like water from a hose in the direction of the howling animals. When the bullets fell to earth, spitting up the dirt around the farmyard, the dogs danced away yelping, sprinting with tails between their legs.

Ignorant of the bullets' reach and lethality, the boldest of the dogs darted sideways, as if the surrender of a mere yard or two might be enough to remove it from harm's way. Smith knew what was about to follow, snatched up his binoculars and tightened the focus on to the creature just as Scarface tweaked the gun fractionally sideways and squeezed off a fresh burst. The livid jet spiralled through the air, perfectly mirroring the movement of Scarface's wrist, and fell with full and deadly effect around and upon the dog. It was as if the animal had been dropped of a sudden into an invisible mincing machine. Limbs and torso spun in the air, dismembering into their bloody constituent parts. Smith lowered his binoculars and grinned down the length of the train, giving the thumbs-up to Scarface who nodded his pleasure.

Both in front and behind, the long dark line of the armoured train bisected the land with the determined forwards flow of a giant centipede, matching itself to every contour and weave of the rails. Alien in a landscape of vegetation and earth, its writhing iron bulk claimed everything as its own, mile by mile, like a miser accumulating profit with the clicking beads of an abacus.

Tiring of the view, Smith dropped back down into the turret, wriggled off his seat and stepped down to the floor. After the bright daylight, he was momentarily blind in the gloom. All the windows were shut, their iron plates bolted in place ready for action. Here and there, narrow slits reluctantly admitted slashes of light. Wending his way down the body of the train, Smith went forwards, working through the other carriages.

He transited the troop-carrying compartments, ignoring the sullen stares of the infantry. They did not know how lucky they were, he mused bitterly to himself. Having been detailed to travel under the command of Smith, they were going to be spared the incompetent leadership of General Mok who was advancing at a snail's pace far to the south. With Mok there would be no knowing what might have happened to them. With Daniel Smith, on the other hand, they would benefit from his wide military experience and training. They would be thrown into the flanking attack in correct fashion. Unbeknown to Smith, it was exactly this prospect that so alarmed them.

He met Scarface and the other Russians in the forward-most carriage. They numbered half a dozen in all, big men, grown lean from years of professional soldiering. Scarface looked up as Smith approached.

'Nice shooting,' Smith said as he ducked into the carriage, weaving round one of the howitzers whose fat muzzle protruded through the side of the iron wall.

Scarface smiled, his sabre-torn features translating it fittingly into a vicious sneer. Like his comrades, he had little time for Mok's Englishman, as they called him behind his back.

Smith winced at the man's expression. The big Russian looked as though his face was the product of two different heads having been imperfectly stitched together, a jagged horizontal line separating the two halves. The mouth twisted, baring tobacco-blackened teeth, and above the broad livid scar, his unnaturally wide, staring eyes locked on Smith's, as coldly merciless as an enormous serpent.

'Too bad we couldn't stop to pick up the pieces,' he rasped. 'Dog meat is good when beaten until tender.'

'I dare say.' Smith stooped over the cooking pot that the Russians were gathered around. 'Well, what a surprise,' he said sarcastically. 'Cabbage bloody soup. Don't you lot eat anything else?'

'Sure we do,' Scarface intoned lazily, dredging his voice of anything that might have been mistaken for respect. 'Caviar, a little salmon, venison now and again. Washed down with a fine champagne.' He slapped his filthy pockets as if he had mislaid something. 'Now where did I put that bottle?'

Seated around the pot his comrades sniggered.

'All right, all right,' Smith conceded. 'You all think you're so bloody hard. Just do your job and we'll get along fine.'

'Sure we will,' Scarface enthused earnestly, raising his huge palms as if beseeching Smith's indulgence. 'We get along just fine. English, Russian. We're like brothers, you and me.'

He tried to place an arm around Smith's shoulders but Smith shrugged it off and walked quickly away before he lost his temper. He was beginning to hate the Russians with a passion. They took nothing seriously. True enough, they were ferocious in action. He had seen them on numerous occasions. It was their only saving grace, although he conceded that perhaps grace was the wrong word. They were murderous and he admired that. It was the reason he advised General Mok to keep them. One day however he wanted nothing more than to have the lot of them shot. He smiled to himself. He would beg General Mok to leave Scarface to him. He would do it personally, looking into the man's eyes as he pulled the trigger. Of course he would have him bound first. But the joy of it!

There was a whistle blast from the engine and Smith made his way without haste to see what the driver was up to. He judged that they were well inside territory under the authority of General Yuan by now. He stooped to peer through one of the slits and saw that the nature of the landscape had changed dramatically in only a comparatively short distance. It was rugged, hilly country, unsuitable for farming. Surprisingly green and verdant, the hills bore clumps of forest on their lower slopes that thickened the higher up the sides they extended, until on the summits they joined in one continuous thick mat of trees. Smith was surprised to find that it was pleasant to look at.

He moved to the other side of the carriage and saw a similar picture. Here however, the hillsides came much closer to the rail lines. In fact, he noticed how the country was closing in on both sides. Puzzled he undid the flap of his jacket pocket and pulled out his map. He squatted down, leaning back against the iron wall of the train, the vibrations of the wheels on the tracks pummelling his spine. With his finger he traced the course of the line northwards, noting the gradients of the hills and the steepening surrounding contours. Yes, it matched his observations. Squinting at the map in the gloom, he tried to read the tiny lettering, but the characters were Chinese and he cursed. Although he could speak the ungodly language, his command of the script was at best rudimentary.

Getting to his feet, he strode as fast as he could back towards the engine, searching for someone on the way who might be able to translate. The train was picking up speed, the driver taking advantage of a downhill gradient to save fuel. The train's massive weight was combining with gravity to build a momentum that caused the noise from the tracks to become deafening inside the iron hull.

The first person Smith came upon stared blankly at the map thrust under his nose. He shrugged, giggling to conceal his fright, explaining that he was unable to read. Smith pushed him roughly aside and went on to look for someone else, reaching out with one hand to steady himself against the increasingly violent swaying motion of the train.

After two more fruitless attempts at obtaining a translation of the Chinese characters, he shouted a curse at the last man to disappoint him, and spun away to head straight for the engine itself. As he went back through the troop-carrying carriages, he noticed that the rhythmic rocking of the Dragon had coaxed the infantry to sleep. He marvelled at their ability to doze off in the most unlikely of settings. He tripped over the outstretched feet of one soldier and lashed out at the man with his map case. As he did so, he recognised the face of someone he knew could both read and write Chinese.

Mumbling an apology, Smith ignored the

man's scowl and poked the map at him, jabbing the spot in question with one finger.

'What does this say?' he barked impatiently. 'Here, man, here!'

The soldier quickly sat up, jerked into wakefulness by the savagery in the Englishman's expression. He had seen Smith in a temper before and knew what the consequences could be.

He stared hard at the map and then nodded as he grasped the meaning. He looked up at Smith and spoke. At that moment the carriage rattled across some points, the noise swallowing his words. Smith fumed, and asked the man to repeat it.

'Cutting,' the man shouted above the din.

The word sent a shiver down Smith's spine. He turned away and hurried as fast as he could towards the engine. As he went, he tried to calm himself. Perhaps he was being stupid. What was unusual about a rail cutting, for goodness sake? Nothing. He slowed his pace. Steadied his breathing. Best not show the alarm he was feeling. It might start a panic and there was certainly no cause for that. Not yet, at any rate. It was just something niggling at the edge of Smith's instinct. Something that smelt wrong. Dangerous.

Again he calmed himself. He was over-wrought. That bastard Russian Scarface always had this effect on him, provoking him to the point of violence.

He reached the engine, stepped through the adjoining corridor, opened a hatch and pulled himself up and out of the carriage and on to the platform of the engine's cabin just as the driver reached for the overhead wire and gave it another sharp tug. The effect in the confined space was ear-shattering. Smith clasped his hands to his head as the whistle blasted, feeling as though his brains were about to burst from his skull.

'Shut that fucking thing up!' he screamed. Deaf to his entreaty and looking the other way, the driver had failed to notice Smith's arrival. In response, Smith grabbed him by the shoulders, swung him round and hit him hard across the cheek with the flat of his hand.

The man staggered back, eyes filled with terror as he saw the look on Smith's pinched, livid face.

'Why the hell are you going so fast?' Smith screamed.

The man shrugged. 'Why not?' he shouted back. 'This way we'll make better time. It's downhill now all the way to the open plain on the other side of Shankow cutting.'

'This is a tactical advance not a fucking race!' Smith blasted back, his face only inches from the driver's. 'And why are you sounding the whistle?'

The man jabbed a thumb over his shoulder towards the front of the train. 'To clear anyone off the track.'

Smith frowned, not understanding. The driver tried to smile pleasantly, hiding his loathing of the Englishman. He would have to explain to the ignorant, dog-faced barbarian.

'The smoke,' he shouted. 'There's obviously a forest fire or else someone's burning off crops.'

'Crops?' Smith shouted, his blood turning to ice. 'What fucking crops? And it was pissing rain on the trees all through the night!'

The driver leaned over to one side so that Smith could see past him, out through the cab's small round window. Sure enough, a short distance ahead the rails disappeared into a thick swirling blanket of smoke. Of even more concern to Smith was the spectacle of the hillsides now starting to rise sheer on either side as the Dragon powered at reckless speed into the Shankow cutting.

The train careered into the wall of smoke and the moment it struck Smith's lungs he gagged, recognising the smell. It was burning wood all right, but there was something else mixed in with it, thick and cloying. Oil.

'Brake!' he screamed at the driver. 'For pity's sake brake!'

The driver frowned, but reached for the brake lever. The train was already well into the cutting, weaving at breakneck speed through the narrow stone-sided defile.

'Brake, I say!' Smith screamed again, grabbing at the pistol holster on his belt. His hand was halfway there when, from the distant front end of the train, invisible in the dense smoke, there came the sickening roar of twisting metal. In the same instant, the shockwave of impact rippled through the length of the armoured train, buckling the carriages, exploding the magazines, and flinging Captain Daniel Smith into the air.

★   ★   ★

From his vantage point on the hillside overlooking the cutting, Caspasian watched in horrified fascination as the armoured train of General Mok piled headlong into the obstacle that it had taken his men half a day to prepare. The moment he had seen the cutting he had known that here was the place to tackle the Dragon. Catch it in the one place where it would be unable to bring its firepower to bear. What even he had not dared to count upon was the stupidity of the driver who had sent the train hurtling into the cutting at high speed. The result was devastating.

For the site of his obstacle, Caspasian had selected a place where the tracks rounded a bend. It was nothing particularly spectacular but, given the momentum of the iron hulk, it was all that was needed. The rails had been removed for no more than fifty yards, and a deep hole dug immediately in front of the sheer rockface of the bend, the intention being that not only would the train be derailed, but that it would also career into the cutting wall opposite the bend. To complete the obstacle, Caspasian had sought to disguise it until the last moment when braking would be impossible. Young saplings had been felled and, when doused with oil and set aflame, their green leaves belched out a thick impenetrable smoke. Confined by the stone walls, the smoke filled the cutting, issuing out of the mouth as if coming from the lungs of a real dragon.

Beside him, Lilin looked down mesmerised at the destruction below. General Yuan had remained behind with his main force to delay the advance of General Mok's army. He had approved Caspasian's plan the night before, but had only felt able to spare him a hundred men for the task of the Dragon's destruction. Deployed along the side of the defile, these men now marvelled at the ease with which the fearsome Dragon of General Mok had been dispatched. At the same time, their respect for the foreigner who had constructed the plan, soared. As one man they turned back to seek him out, grinning, waving and cheering.

But Caspasian's attention had already switched to the next phase of the ambush. A success did not become a victory until it had been consolidated. However impressive the initial blow that they had inflicted upon the Dragon, Caspasian knew that just as the smoke had concealed the obstacle from the train, so too did it now hide from his eyes the true extent of the damage caused. The opponent had been knocked to the floor of the ring with one punch. But had it been a knockout blow, or was the other fighter at this very moment recovering himself for a counter-attack? There was only one way to find out.

Caspasian had already selected a team composed of the best marksmen. These he now left under the command of Lilin on the high ground flanking the wrecked train. Each man had been given instructions to engage any pockets of resistance they spotted as the smoke began to clear. Meanwhile Caspasian himself led the main force down off the hillside and into the mouth of the cutting behind his obstacle. They would advance up the floor of the cutting, mopping up any of Mok's men who had survived the crash. General Yuan had insisted that as many of Mok's men as possible should be taken captive, as he was certain that he would be able to persuade them to join his own force.

Caspasian was not so sure, but in order to carry out the General's instructions, he had positioned men in the rear of his assault group to whom his fighters could pass back any prisoners. These would then be bound and held under guard until the battle was over and their fate could be properly decided.

As he led the way along the rail tracks, heading for the bend, Caspasian could hear the continuing explosions from the wrecked train. There was a huge eruption as one of the engines went up, bolts and iron plating cart-wheeling high into the air. General Yuan had returned to Caspasian the Smith & Wesson revolver taken from him when he had been captured. In addition, he allowed him to select any other weapon he chose from his own personal armoury. Caspasian had been shocked to see how pitiful the supply was, but after a moment's deliberation had selected an old naval cutlass. In the close-quarter fighting that he anticipated, they were the best combination he could think of, the cutlass clasped firmly in his right hand, and the revolver in his left.

Ahead of him the obstacle loomed. But it was no longer the neat, smooth-sided hole that he and his men had dug earlier. Heaped all around it was a vast mass of twisted iron, smoke and steam rising from the groaning mountain like the sulphurous fumes from a brooding volcano. The wreckage was barely recognisable as a train. Only here and there, a wheel or a buffer gave away the identity of what the beast had once been.

'Spread out,' Caspasian called to his men.

Their eyes were transfixed on the wreckage and none of them was alert to danger. So complete did the destruction appear to have been that Caspasian himself began to wonder whether anyone at all had survived. He got his answer the next second when a single shot rang out, the sound magnified by the rock walls on either side. Next to Caspasian a man stumbled and fell, shot through the chest.

There in front of them, rising out of the smoke and dust, a lone figure wobbled to its feet, a gun in its fist. Miraculously, it was one of the Russians who had been in the foremost carriage. A fusillade of shots rang out from Caspasian's men and the tall man rocked backwards and fell dead.

They reached the site of the crash where the front of the train had sailed across the hole and smashed into the rockface. Bodies littered the ground, but some of them were alive, and these were hauled away, being manhandled into captivity.

Caspasian climbed up on to a flattop. Once a troop-carrying carriage, the entire walls and roof had been torn off it. On either side, injured men groaned and lay mingled with the dead. The wreckage completely blocked the cutting at this point and Caspasian led the way, scrambling up and over the tangled iron mountain to see what lay on the farther side towards the rear of the train where the least damage would have occurred.

'Stockpile all serviceable weapons and ammunition!' he shouted. Protruding from one pile of iron, he saw the barrel of a howitzer. 'Take that, too,' he called.

Clearing the ruins of yet another carriage, Caspasian jumped down into an open space. The smoke was starting to clear now. His men had doused the flames and as the cutting became visible, more shots rang out from further down the train. He ducked into cover, searching for the firers. From the cliffs above there came the answering shots of Lilin's men, doing their job of providing fire support. Caspasian was relieved to see arms and ammunition littering the ground. There would be no more shortages for General Yuan's troops after this. First, they had to clear the cutting and either capture or drive off the survivors.

More men dropped down beside him and together they advanced towards the rear of the train. There was a further burst of firing and the slow, painstaking business of fighting through an enemy-held position began in earnest. Once again Caspasian was pleasantly surprised at the quality of Yuan's men. They might not have uniforms like General Mok's army, but they knew how to use fire and movement to cross ground. Running in short bursts, they slowly fought their way onward, but in only one place did they encounter stiff resistance. Mok's men, never resolute in defence, had been stunned by the train crash. Their morale had been broken and they only resisted where one of their more courageous comrades temporarily rallied them to the fight. In nearly every case, after only token resistance, they threw down their arms and either put up their hands in surrender or fled out of the cutting, running back in the direction they had come.

Caspasian himself had fired only two shots, and his cutlass seemed so out of place that he began to regret having brought it. Deciding to give his men their head, he let them sweep on without him. They seemed more than capable of operating without his leadership, apart from which, he had reached one of the intact but overturned carriages and wanted to have a look inside. So, while his men pressed on towards the rear of the train where the last pockets of resistance were starting to throw away their arms and run, pursued by the accurate sniping from Lilin's troops on the hills above, Caspasian took off his jacket, laid it aside with his cutlass, stuck his revolver in his belt, and hauled himself into the carriage through an open hatchway.

The interior was filled with smoke, thick and acrid. Caspasian clasped one hand over his nose and mouth and squinted into the gloom. It was just as he had hoped. It was the command carriage. With any luck he might find some worthwhile information about General Mok's broader intentions. If he had any broader intentions other than his self-serving greed, Caspasian thought.

Seeing nothing before him, Caspasian turned and almost took the full force of a man's fist that came flying at him. In the moment of turning, however, his foot had slipped in a pool of oil and he had started to go down. It saved him. The blow glanced off his temple, giving him just enough time to spin out of the way as his attacker raised his booted foot and tried to bring it crashing down on his ribcage.

Scuttling out of reach, Caspasian jumped to his feet but was forced to double over in the confined space of the overturned railway carriage. To his horror he found himself staring at the gruesomely distorted features of Scarface, the Russian mercenary he had seen once before but had not forgotten. The man grimaced in what Caspasian understood to be a cruel imitation of a smile.

'So, you live after all, English,' Scarface snarled. Blood streaked his face, though whether it was his own or another's Caspasian could not tell. He reached for his revolver but the gun had gone. The big Russian chuckled.

'It is over there. But you won't be needing it now. Nor ever again, you piece of filth.'

'That's rich coming from you,' Caspasian said evenly. 'Have you looked in a mirror recently?'

Again Scarface chuckled, the rumbling sound coming from deep in his chest and hinting at some form of internal damage. To Caspasian he nevertheless appeared more than capable of causing him harm.

'I think I will make your face a little more like mine. Would you like that, English?' And when he raised his hand from his side Caspasian saw that he was holding a long-bladed knife. 'With this I can slice flesh as easily as I slice cabbages,' he hissed.

He lashed out with the blade, the swipe far faster than Caspasian would have imagined possible for a man of the Russian's considerable size. He jumped backwards, but in the confined space there was almost nowhere for him to go. He felt the upturned table against his back. Steady, he thought to himself. Steady. He thinks he's got you. Well then, let him carry on believing that.

'Look, I have money,' Caspasian said quickly. 'Lots of it. And I know where there's more.'

At the mention of the magic word Scarface faltered. 'Where?' he asked suspiciously.

'In my jacket outside,' Caspasian said. 'You can see it from that window if you like. Have a look.'

The Russian eyed Caspasian carefully. 'If you are lying I will make your death long and painful.' He edged towards the side of the carriage and craned to see out. There below them was Caspasian's jacket and the cutlass lying neatly on the ground.

'Thank you, English,' Scarface said triumphantly, 'I will take it before I leave.' And with a backhand swipe he swung the lethal blade at Caspasian's face in a horizontal arc that would have cut him open exactly as the Russian himself had once been disfigured.

Caspasian was ready for it. As Scarface had been peering out of the window, Caspasian had grasped hold of a wooden map case he had spotted on the table top behind him. As the knife swung towards him, he darted sideways and met the knife with the wooden case in mid-air. The blade bit and lodged in it. Leaving Scarface to try and wrestle his knife free, Caspasian crouched down and, balancing on his left foot, shot out his right in a kansetsu-geri kick aimed at the Russian's knee. The blow connected, taking the knee side on. Caspasian drove it in hard, projecting the kick clean through to the other side. Scarface cried out in pain as the ligaments tore and he crumpled with the agony.

His head swivelled to face Caspasian, his eyes mad with a mixture of hatred and pain. He had freed the blade from the wooden map case and, tossing the case aside, he lurched unsteadily towards Caspasian, howling in defiance and rage. Once again Caspasian was ready for him. He let the blade come straight in, making it seem as though he was wide open to the attack. He backed a single step, luring the Russian off balance, and then with lightning speed enveloped the wrist holding the blade with both hands, twisted his body in a tae-sabaki side-step, reversed the direction of the Russian's own thrust, turning the blade upon its owner, and allowed Scarface's momentum to pull him on to his own knife.

The blade went in deep, driving into the solar plexus. Scarface gasped and doubled over. His face was only inches away from Caspasian's. He opened his mouth to speak but only blood came out. His eyes fixed upon Caspasian's and glazed over in death.

Caspasian let go of the body and it crumpled to the floor. He went quickly across to where his revolver lay and stooped to pick it up. At that moment there was a shout from the rear of the train and Caspasian froze on the spot. It had only been a word, and coming from some distance away, but he could recognise that voice anywhere. It was Daniel Smith.

Dropping out of the carriage, he snatched up his cutlass, and ran towards the rear of the ruined train where the sound of the fighting was ebbing away. Sporadic firing was continuing, combined with sniping from the hillsides. As he ran, Caspasian looked up to the sides of the cutting above, searching frantically for Lilin. At last he found her. She was standing out in the open, directing the fire of the soldiers.

'Lilin!' he screamed. She started at the sound of his voice, scanning the ground until she saw him. He could see a flood of relief in her face and she broke into a broad smile.

'We've won!' she shouted back. 'They're running away!'

'Daniel Smith!' Caspasian shouted urgently. 'He's here with them. Don't let him get away!'

In spite of the noise of battle, Lilin heard him and understood. She gathered a handful of those closest to her and ran away to see if they could spot General Mok's military advisor, for without him they knew that Mok would be lost.

Darting back past the wreckage of the train, Caspasian gathered his men as he went, urging them on to greater efforts in the pursuit of Smith. On every side now the surviving soldiers of General Mok were throwing down their arms and running. Those closest to Caspasian and his advancing troops threw up their arms and begged for mercy. But while his men seized them and herded them to the rear, Caspasian was after only one man. And at last he spotted him.

Caspasian had finally reached the end of the train, the mouth of the cutting barely a hundred yards beyond that. Bullets suddenly tore into the ground at Caspasian's feet and he threw himself to the ground.

When he looked up he saw the backs of General Mok's soldiers fleeing in the distance. But there, in the midst of them, was Captain Daniel Smith. A revolver in his fist, he was glancing behind him, loosing off rounds at random at those of Yuan's men rash enough or brave enough to continue the pursuit.

For one moment Smith looked directly at Caspasian and their eyes locked. He seemed to falter, stop dead in his tracks. His face was bloodied and his uniform in tatters. He glared at Caspasian, pouring more hatred and loathing into it than Caspasian thought possible. Though well out of effective handgun range, he aimed at Caspasian and fired off his last two rounds, but even after that Caspasian could see the hammer clicking on empty chambers. Smith was shouting something, but the words were drowned out by the noise of Lilin's marksmen who had spotted him. But they were out of ammunition. Confined to the hill top, they had been unable to seize fresh supplies of ammunition from the captured prisoners or the ruined train. They had done their job well and the survivors of General Mok's armoured train were fleeing as a result. But so too was Smith, and as Lilin and her men raged on the hillside, powerless to stop him, Captain Daniel Smith turned his back on Caspasian and the whole scene of carnage and jogged out of sight.

11

General Yuan lay still in the tall grass looking through his binoculars at the advancing column of Mok's army. They were marching in a long seemingly endless file that snaked away as far as he could see, disappearing into a cloud of dust that issued from the distant plain. He had resolved to meet the invaders while they were still in the area of no-man's-land that marched with his southernmost territory. That way he would demonstrate to his men that he was prepared to fight for every one of their farms, and was not just protecting his own lands further to the north. Now, reviewing the mass of the approaching invasion force, he doubted he could halt them, or prevent the capture of the province his ancestors had farmed for generations.

Just as Caspasian had predicted, General Mok had not seen fit to push any sort of vanguard or scout force forward of the main body. The leading troops were the front ranks of the marching army itself. Yuan knew that the word 'army' was a grand description for what, in European terms, would have amounted to little more than a division of some ten thousand men. But in Chinese terms, and in the context of local warlord armies, it was nevertheless a formidable force, and one to be reckoned with. To confront it Yuan himself had barely a tenth of that number, under one thousand fighters, and a hundred of those had been sent with Caspasian and Lilin to ambush the Dragon.

Although the site of the cutting was far to the west and out of both sight and earshot, Yuan glanced anxiously in that direction as if expecting to see his daughter and the British officer riding to the rescue, bearing tales of their success. He sighed heavily, his brow furrowed by the worry that had gnawed at him since they had parted. He trusted the Englishman. He had no doubts on that score. Yuan found that the man attracted trust as naturally as a magnet attracted iron filings. That said, there was something unsettling and dangerous about him, meticulously concealed, except to Yuan who had seen enough of life to recognise one of its walking wounded.

For a moment, lying in the grass and waiting for the arrival of the invading army, General Yuan doubted the wisdom of entrusting Lilin to Caspasian's care. Of course his headstrong daughter would not have seen it like that. He smiled ruefully. Of course not. As far as she was concerned, it was she who was keeping an eye on the foreigner. Nonetheless Yuan had not been able to stop himself worrying as Lilin had ridden away in the company of the stranger, even if, time and again, she had proved more than capable of looking after herself. The escapade in Shanghai had proved it.

He shook the feeling off and turned back to scan the advancing column. Caspasian and Lilin had their job to do. Yuan had his. General Yuan. Again he smiled. He was no more a general than Lilin was. No more than Mok or most of the other puffed-up pretenders to the myriad thrones that had sprung up around China following the decay and fall of the Manchu dynasty. Most of them were simply bandits and criminals, like the gangsters he had heard about from America's wild west. The only difference between himself and the others, Yuan conceded, was that he knew he was a fraud. Men like Mok had come to believe their own lies.

There was an inevitable dynamic at work, whereby power drowned truth. A man would start out as a small-time crook, fiddling the books. Slowly he would acquire followers and hangers-on, but still, for a time, they would feel free enough to speak their mind and to criticise. Then one day it would happen. An invisible line would be crossed. For the first ever time someone disagreeing with the leader's selected course of action would hesitate before speaking out. And that would be that. Like ants transmitting a silent message to one another by some unseen chemical transfer, all the other followers would understand and comply, probably without even realising the route they had just taken.

Like rain clouds gathering at night, power would accumulate invisibly. One day an unsuspecting newcomer would break the unspoken taboo and speak out. He would be murdered. From that point there was only one direction to follow. Mok had taken that road long ago, promoting himself through fictional ranks as the whim took him. His humble origins had been forgotten, the rank, the riches and the fawning had all worked their insidious poison, and a monster had been born. The hangers-on, feeling unable to resist but recognising the opportunities for self-interest, had clung to his coat tails and been dragged along in his slip-stream. Lacking the brute force and ability to set up in their own right, they had accepted the next best thing for criminals, and subjugated themselves to the rising star of their leader. It was a crude variation of the old Chinese saying: When a sage goes to heaven, he takes his dogs and his chickens with him.

Then Yuan spotted him. General Mok, sitting straight-backed on a white charger in the middle of his troops. He was hideously attired, as if he had borrowed a theatrical costume. The front of his high-necked tunic was adorned with medals, brightly coloured ribbons and with gold braid. He wore white gloves, as if attending the opera, and on his head was a French-style *képi*, with a tall plume of white horse hair issuing like a fountain from the front. In riding breeches and highly polished black boots, he was armed with a dress sword and a pearl-handled, chrome-plated pistol, the latter being more status symbol than practical instrument of war, for General Mok would have no intention of getting anywhere near the actual fighting if he could possibly avoid it.

Scanning the column as best he could through the dust that it was throwing up, Yuan was relieved to see no sign of the General's cavalry. Far to the rear he thought he spotted some horsemen and he hoped that Mok was keeping them safely out of harm's way, preserving his elite arm. Yuan's own men used horses purely for getting from one place to another. At best they were mounted infantry. They had neither the training nor the equipment to act as proper cavalry and, rightly or wrongly there was a mystique about cavalry that Yuan knew filled his men with terror. It was an instinctive fear that foot soldiers had felt towards cavalry since the very earliest days of warfare. The horse extended virtually every one of the opponent's faculties. Speed, range, endurance, reach and power. Quite simply, it elevated the rider from man into god. Since ancient times it had been the shock weapon of the battlefield. In spite of all Yuan had heard about the employment of tanks in the European battlefields of the Great War, he doubted they would ever replace cavalry.

Glancing to left and right, Yuan saw that his men were in position, watching him. He raised his hand and gave the signal. From the skirmish line that had been lying in wait along the shallow ridgeline since early morning, a series of shots rang out, purposely hesitant and ragged. Yuan did not want to telegraph his true strength to his enemy. He had few enough surprises as it was. He had to maximise every advantage he could engineer. Deception was to be his game.

Though few, the shots were remarkably accurate. Ammunition had to be conserved, at least until such time as Caspasian and Lilin could return with fresh supplies captured from the Dragon. Yuan studied the effect of the initial volleys through his binoculars and smiled with satisfaction. In the foremost ranks of General Mok's column, a number of men had been struck. In spite of the fact that they were firing at the maximum range of their old rifles, the marksmanship of his men had born fruit once again. Bodies littered the dirt track, while the wounded staggered like drunks. Such was the distance that their cries, muffled by a cross-wind, reached him only moments later.

For an instant, the able-bodied stared stupidly at their fallen comrades, awaiting an order before dispersing into what little cover was available. Yuan had chosen the spot well. For a hundred yards on either side of the track, there was only patchy scrub and a few shallow depressions in the ground where men could attempt to hide themselves.

He signalled again and a second fusillade rang out. This time, other firers discharged their weapons, while those who had fired first rested, taking their time to select their targets for when their turn came next. It also had the effect of making the enemy's task of locating the exact position of the snipers extremely difficult. Yuan knew that it would seem as if only a handful of men were engaging the column, moving rapidly between fire positions along the top of the ridge.

As he watched the confusion down below, Yuan wondered how long it would take General Mok to make up his mind what he was going to do next. He did not seem to have any prearranged battle drill and had obviously been expecting a clear march all the way into Yuan's heartland.

Finally, and much to Yuan's relief, General Mok gave orders for the column to deploy into attack formation. Splendid in equally ridiculous uniforms, officers on chargers cantered up and down the cowering column of soldiers, now all hugging the earth. Discordant bugles sounded, competing with each other in a meaningless cacophony and, with visible reluctance, the infantry were cajoled to their feet and assembled in extended lines, one in front of the other, facing up the long, gentle incline that led up towards the ridge. Surveying them through his binoculars, Yuan shook his head in disbelief. It was exactly as he had hoped, and as Caspasian had predicted, but he nevertheless deeply regretted the loss of life that was about to occur.

With the officers riding in the rear, pistols drawn in order to shoot down anyone who turned and ran, and with sergeants moving at either end of each line, trying to keep some sort of order in the ragged parade ground assembly, the deployed forward units of General Mok's army began to trudge stolidly upwards.

General Mok himself, secure in the middle of his mounted entourage, moved to a small hillock safely out of rifle range to observe the developing manoeuvre. Yuan studied him carefully, twisting his binocular eyepieces to sharpen the focus. General Mok was being presented with refreshments. Dismounted orderlies proffered silver trays, and Mok accepted a goblet and drank deeply to wash the dust of the march from his throat. In his greed he obviously spilt some wine down the front of his tunic because Yuan suddenly saw a flurry of urgent activity with much dabbing from the orderlies, and slapping and kicking from General Mok, driving them away with wild gestures that spoilt the decorum of the whole spectacle. General Mok's horse took fright and bucked, almost throwing the rider. Mok's *képi* fell over his eyes and when he eventually regained control of his mount, with the assistance of those about him, the horse hair plume had come loose and hung sideways at a drunken angle.

The timing of his distraction could not

have been better. Yuan raised his hand and gave the next signal. As one, the entire force that he had brought with him to this first engagement, fired. The volley was stupendous, the noise thundering, sending General Mok's charger into a second spasm of jitters. The effect was devastating, as Yuan had known it would be. The bullets tore through the front ranks of Mok's deployed infantry, wreaking havoc. In every part of the formation men broke and tried to flee the carnage. The officers and sergeants stood ready to stop them. Yuan watched as pistols cracked and sabres swung. Amazingly, none of Mok's fleeing infantry attempted to overpower those who sought to stop their retreat. Yuan sighed, disappointed. Defeat of his enemy was not to be so easily achieved. Mutiny, if it came at all, would have to wait for later.

Taking advantage of the disarray amongst General Mok's army, Yuan gave one more signal, and then crawled backwards until he was hidden from the enemy's line of sight behind the ridgeline. He then joined his men who had similarly wriggled out of their fire positions to execute a controlled disengagement. Yuan's study of tactics had largely been academic. Nevertheless, he had always been a diligent student and, aided by a long conversation with Caspasian the night before, he felt confident as he and his men now carried out the difficult manoeuvre. He even allowed himself a smile of satisfaction. Breaking clean was always most dangerous when in contact with the enemy, and yet his men had managed it. Yuan felt a surge of pride as he watched them. They sensed the success themselves, and as they jogged for the horses, which had been held by handlers to the rear of their first position throughout the engagement, they grinned at one another, confidence returning like a tonic.

'Come on,' Yuan urged sternly, reining in his optimism lest it run away with him and turn to complacency. 'We've barely started. Mount up and let's get moving.'

Sobered, his men swung into their saddles and spurred their horses away to the north. Everyone knew where they were headed. Yuan had given detailed instructions that morning at first light. Yuan himself left the position last. Before he rode after his withdrawing men, he glanced back at the ridgeline. It seemed a great shame to leave it without further fighting. The first engagement had gone so well. Surely it would not have hurt to wait until Mok's men had reformed and continued the advance. A further volley would have caused even more casualties and might, just might, have done the trick of pushing Mok's men over the edge, of breaking their already low morale.

As he wrestled with the temptation, Caspasian's words of caution came to him. Hit and run. Remember the Boers. Force the enemy to deploy, then withdraw before he can get to grips with you, leaving him to strike at thin air. Play for time. Trade ground for time. Time and casualties. Wear him down. Wear him out.

The problem was that he was not leaving General Mok to strike at thin air. This was his territory, Yuan's land. It was all very well for the English Captain to speak. It was not his country.

Yuan shook off his doubts and took hold of himself. Caspasian was right. He knew it. He could not possibly fight with Mok on any kind of equal footing. This was the only way. For now.

★ ★ ★

For his second position Yuan had chosen a spot where high ground overlooked a river. Cutting across the line of General Mok's advance, the river meandered from right to left. It was not broad nor deep nor particularly fast flowing, but it was still an obstacle. It would impede the advance of General Mok's troops and that was all that Yuan and his men would require.

Waiting for him at this second position was another segment of his force. Having given Caspasian and Lilin a hundred men for their own mission, Yuan had then divided his remaining men into three groups, each of three hundred. By using them in succession he could be confident that at every engagement his men would be rested and prepared. At each ambush site, he would be meeting General Mok's men with fresh troops, albeit in greatly fewer numbers. General Mok's men, on the other hand, would become increasingly exhausted as the battle wore on, marching into one surprise attack after another.

Yuan's initial plan had been to meet General Mok with his entire force of nine hundred at each engagement, making use of maximum firepower before withdrawing. It had been Caspasian's idea to divide his force into three. Under Caspasian's plan, two groups would be used to leapfrog backwards from position to position. The third group of three hundred would be held in reserve. Yuan had protested vehemently at this. It struck him as an appalling waste of manpower. He argued that he had precious little by way of arms and ammunition as it was.

Caspasian had listened patiently before speaking. 'General Yuan,' he had said finally, calmly, 'the essence of any force is balance. A force that is wholly committed to battle lacks balance. The commander has no flexibility. Nothing with which he can influence the battle. He has placed all his cards on the table, declared his hand. He has nothing with which he can confront the unexpected.'

Yuan had understood and conceded.

Caspasian had hammered home his point relentlessly. 'Your reserve will be the ace up your sleeve. Keep it out of sight. Guard it jealously, and commit it wisely. Handled correctly, it will have an effect out of all proportion to its numbers.'

As Yuan now rode into the second position to find his second group of men already there, waiting for him, he knew that Caspasian had been right. The men from the first engagement carried on through the position, heading ever northwards to the position where they would make the third ambush. As they rode past they called out words of encouragement to their comrades, shouting out tips, jokes and friendly taunts. Yuan watched them go and he smiled. It was indeed reassuring to know that, securely out of contact and far to the rear, he had yet another group in reserve. Things were going according to plan. Everything just might turn out all right after all.

★ ★ ★

General Mok was fuming. He had never been more furious in all his life. He was surrounded by incompetence and bungling. Fighting to maintain control of his horse, he cursed the wretched beast. It was always the problem with such fine animals. If you wanted a good one, it was invariably highly strung. The creature had been bucking and side-stepping since early in the day, but the volley sent it completely haywire.

When it finally quietened, General Mok looked up, knocking aside the plume that dangled askew from the crown of his *képi*. It flopped lower, the horse hair trailing into his eyes and mouth. Angrily he spat it out and then, in a fit of rage, snatched at the thing, tore it free and hurled it down into the dust. To his satisfaction his horse saw fit to trample it underfoot, the first useful thing it had done all day.

Of considerably less satisfaction was the latest development on the hillside before him. Mok raised his binoculars to his eyes and saw with dismay the state of his infantry.

Fortunately he had only so far committed a part of the entire force. Nevertheless, he could imagine the effect that the spectacle of slaughter was having on the rest of his men, sitting to the rear, watching like himself and awaiting their own turn at the front. He knew that it did not take much for fear to catch on. Once it did, even the pistols of his officers would be unable to halt a mass flight.

He was greatly relieved therefore when the firing from the ridgeline abruptly ceased. It was some time before his officers and sergeants had beaten the men back into formation and the extended lines wormed their way uncertainly onwards, but this time there was no further fire to greet them. A few minutes later they had done it. They had reached the summit and the first extended line wavered and then dropped down out of sight on the far side. General Mok waited impatiently for the sound of hand-to-hand fighting, but heard nothing. The aides about him shrugged uselessly and giggled like girls. Angrily General Mok spurred his horse into a canter and headed up the incline towards the front rank, secretly confident that it was perfectly safe to do so.

Sure enough, when he reached the top of the ridge, it was to find his men sitting and lying in the warm grass, congratulating themselves on a hard-won victory. An officer rode up to him.

'The enemy has fled, General. We have defeated them. The province is ours!'

General Mok beamed. If only that arrogant foreigner Smith had been there to witness such a great moment. Victory in battle. Could there be any pleasure as sweet?

Every inch the stern commander, General Mok berated his officers for allowing the men to idle about. 'We must press on,' he shouted grandly, illustrating the intended direction of travel with sharp decisive chopping motions of his gloved hand.

Officers and sergeants thrashed and kicked the worn infantry to their feet, forming them once again in column of route. An hour later they were ready to move off.

General Mok felt sufficiently confident this time to ride further forward in the column, positioning himself behind the first battalion. He sat straight-backed in the saddle, revelling in the excitement of the march, lost in daydreams of what he would do to General Yuan and his men when he caught them, and picturing how he would treat their women. He had heard tales about Yuan's daughter. Apparently she was remarkably beautiful. General Mok would save her for himself. What a time he would have!

The sight of the river reminded him that he had not quenched his thirst for some time. General Mok waited until the first elements of his men had waded across and then spurred his horse forward to the cool, sweet-smelling water. When he reached it, he dismounted, swinging one leg over the pommel of his saddle, slipping his buttocks out of the seat and letting gravity do the rest. The second his feet touched the ground all hell was let loose. At first General Mok did not know what had happened and wondered whether perhaps he had landed on a mine. Whatever the case, he found himself face down in the icy water with the dead body of an aide on top of him.

Cursing with all his might, he struggled free, wriggling from underneath the corpse, and noting with horror the filth of mud and blood streaking his already soaked uniform. The gold braid was encrusted with mire and several of his medals had been torn from his tunic leaving great ugly rents in the expensive cloth. All about him was utter confusion and carnage. Soldiers were running away in all directions except the direction of the enemy where Mok judged an assault would have been most useful. Bodies littered the river banks as if they had grown fatigued by the day's exertions and lain down for a nap.

General Mok knelt on all fours like a wet and shaggy dog. 'Rally!' he bellowed. 'To me! Rally to me!'

For the first time he felt the old pang of fear. It had become unfamiliar since he had grown too powerful for any of his neighbours to challenge, and the sudden and unexpected reacquaintance with it was highly unpleasant. Fortunately, sufficient of his officers remained in the vicinity to react to his cries which surprised General Mok. He made a mental note of their names, but then forgot them the next instant when a second terrifying volley rang out from the high ground beyond the river.

Fresh slaughter erupted all around him, the screams and moans of the dying and the wounded adding to the General's own mounting terror. Smith, he thought bitterly. He would have known what to do. It was his fault for not being there, the General thought, forgetting that it was he who had detailed Smith to accompany the train.

Eventually the General saw the comforting sight of fresh infantry advancing towards the river in extended lines, one behind the other. Once again the column had deployed into line of battle and struck out, albeit slowly, for the enemy defences. Reaching General Mok's crouching position, huddling behind the body of his aide which was now riddled with bullets, they advanced on past him and started up the incline in the direction of the firing. Except that the firing had ceased some time before. General Mok frowned in puzzlement, wondering what on earth was going on. What was that bastard Yuan playing at? Either he was running away or he was not. If he was, then why would he not bugger off, and if he was not, then why not stand and fight? The man clearly had absolutely no idea how to handle troops in combat.

Picking himself up, General Mok stood miserably on the bank of the river, trying to wring the blood and water from his uniform. He had lost his *képi*, his horse had bolted, and what had started out as an enjoyable expedition was starting to lose all appeal. He stooped to retrieve the glistening orb of a huge gaudy star-shaped decoration that had come off his tunic and now lay beneath the surface of the water. As his fingers closed about it, a thought occurred to him. It was something Smith had once said to him. Idly fixing the star back in place, he wrestled with the remembered words, wondering how, if at all, he might apply them to the present situation. He was a general, after all. Surely it could not be that difficult.

★ ★ ★

Riding back from the river ambush, Yuan's men were exuberant. For the second time they had given General Mok's army a severe mauling. The battle was going far better than any of them had anticipated. They had inflicted two successive defeats on their enemy and they were barely out of no-man's-land. Their treasured farmlands still lay safe and untouched behind them. Added to which, there had been reports of a faint plume of black smoke rising into the sky far to the west which could mean only one thing. The ambush on the train had succeeded. Why else would there be smoke? It was too much to issue from a single burning farmstead. None of them had seen it themselves, but the word had spread like wildfire amongst them.

Even Yuan was starting to feel his first tentative confidence growing into something more akin to certainty. They had done it. He really felt that they had. Instantly he shook himself free of the dangerous emotion. It was too early yet to be sure. Too early yet.

When he reached the third ambush position, the men from the first were there waiting for him. They had had plenty of time to rest and now looked eagerly to him to take the lead once again. He was becoming tired.

He himself had been on the go non-stop since the previous day, planning throughout the night, and then fighting two consecutive battles. Now he was expected to fight a third.

While the men who had just fought at the river waved jubilant farewells and sped back to take up yet another position to the rear, Yuan dismounted wearily, handed the reins of his horse to one of the handlers, and went to find a good vantage point from where he could observe the ground selected for the third ambush. He soon found the ideal spot, to the side of a knoll with a covered withdrawal route for after the ambush had been successfully sprung. He sank to the ground. If the last time was anything to go by, he could expect a long break before General Mok was able to marshal his forces and continue the advance. Surely they could not go on like this indefinitely? They must break soon. He eased back against the warm grass. He was so tired.

Yuan suddenly jumped. Someone was tugging at his sleeve. He was appalled to discover that he had fallen asleep.

'How long have I been sleeping?' he asked angrily.

The man smiled broadly. 'Only a couple of hours, General.'

'A couple of hours! Why the devil didn't you wake me?'

'There was no need,' the man replied. 'Everyone is in place. We have done it before. We can do it again now.'

Yuan rolled on to his stomach and looked through his binoculars, fighting to calm himself. The column was in sight, closer than he would have wished, but there was no cause for alarm. His breathing steadied. His men had probably done the right thing. It would not do to allow himself to become overly tired. He had to keep a clear head. Slowly his confidence returned.

As before, infantry were leading the column. It looked like a fresh battalion, and this time there was no sight of General Mok. Yuan was hardly surprised. His men had tried desperately to pick him off at the river but the wretched man had a charmed life. Still, Yuan's heart had soared to see the great General grovelling in the blood-soaked water.

He waited until the head of the column had entered rifle range and then gave the signal. Once more, selected men opened fire. Yuan shook his head in disbelief as General Yuan's troops reacted with the same absence of foresight as on the two previous occasions. There was the same blundering around, the same staggering casualties, the same painfully slow deployment into line of battle, and the same faltering advance into the teeth of the fire laid down by Yuan's men.

Time and again Yuan's men fired. In front of them, General Mok's men advanced. To their rear the officers and sergeants whipped them forward. Here and there men broke and ran, and were duly shot down. On they came, leaning into the rifle fire as into a stiff wind.

Yuan prepared to give the signal for his men to cease firing and withdraw to the next position. But in front of them something was happening. General Mok's men were breaking. Not just in ones and twos now. Whole segments of the line were throwing down their rifles and turning tail. Yuan stared in disbelief. They were overpowering their officers and sergeants. He thought he saw one of the officers cut down by his own men.

'This is it!' he shouted triumphantly. From further along his firing line, a small cheer started to go up.

With all thought of breaking contact and retiring now thrown to the wind, Yuan's men poured the last of their dwindling supply of bullets into the oncoming ranks. Every battle had its turning point, the pivot about which great events revolved. This was it. Yuan was certain. Caspasian's plan had done its job. It had worked as far as it went. Now was the time for decisive action. For original thought.

'Fire! Give them everything you've got!' Yuan shouted.

It was only after several minutes of intense firing that Yuan saw something to the rear of General Mok's lead battalion. He stared through his binoculars, waiting for the smoke and dust of battle to subside. To his horror he saw a second battalion deployed in extended lines, advancing through the chaos of the first. But this second unit was continuing up the slope without breaking. It was extraordinary. Previously the troops not engaged had remained to the rear in column. Now however they were advancing in succession like waves against the shore. General Mok had deployed his entire army. Yuan hunted for the hated General but in all the confusion there was still no sign of him.

'Fire!' Yuan roared. 'Engage the second echelons.'

The man next to him laughed nervously. 'I have no more bullets, General.'

Yuan looked down the line. Only a fraction of his men were now obeying his order. The fire they were putting down was barely enough to stop a bolting rabbit.

With mounting alarm, Yuan gave the signal to withdraw. Instantly his men obeyed, but Yuan felt something new and unpleasant in the atmosphere. It was panic. He had left it late. Maybe not too late, but late. He glanced over his shoulder as he pulled back from his vantage point. The fresh troops of General Mok were perilously close now. It was going to be a close run thing. But they could do it. They had to.

His men were running for their horses. One of them tripped and was stampeded by his comrades.

'Help him!' Yuan shouted angrily. 'Stay calm. There's plenty of time.' He forced a smile, slowing his pace to a walk. No one followed his lead. Some of the horses sensed the panic and broke free from their handlers. Their owners ran after them in fright, screaming and further terrifying the animals.

Yuan reached his horse and pulled himself tiredly into the saddle. He swung its head around to let his men see him. 'It's all right!' he bellowed. 'We've plenty of time.'

Some of them took heart from his example. It was working. They were going to be all right. They were going to break contact. They would make it. Just.

The bugle call from their rear split the air with a shivering intensity. All about him Yuan's men froze like statues. Yuan glanced over his shoulder in the direction of the call, as its last note echoed away. His blood turned to ice. Arrayed in rank upon rank, stretching to left and right and blocking his line of retreat, the proud mounts of General Mok's elite cavalry arm, cavorted hungrily, pawing the ground, begging to be unleashed. A seemingly endless line of drawn sabres shimmered with the dazzle of sun on water, and there, safely to the rear of the centre, was General Mok.

Yuan stared transfixed. While he slept, their position had been outflanked. Holding him in place with the staged display of mutiny, General Mok had manoeuvred his elite strike force into place and now held Yuan and his men as if in a nutcracker. Yuan's mounted infantry, out of ammunition, squared off against cavalry. And in his heart Yuan knew that there was no contest. No contest at all.

12

Having seen off Daniel Smith and the last stragglers who had fled from the wrecked train, Caspasian posted lookouts on the hillside and a strong guard force at the mouth of the cutting in case Smith decided to rally his men and counter-attack. Caspasian did not think for one moment that Smith would, but he had to be prepared. There was a great deal of work to do salvaging as much as they could from the Dragon, and they would need to be able to work unimpeded by the threat of surprise attack.

Lilin and her snipers came down from their positions along the top of the cutting and joined Caspasian at the side of the tracks. She stared at the ruins of the once mighty Dragon and shook back her hair.

'Where on earth do we start?'

Caspasian chuckled. 'Destroying it was the easy bit. Now the work really begins.'

First of all he organised a tally of the prisoners and the wounded. Miraculously his own wounded amounted to barely a dozen, and only two of those were serious casualties. A quick head count of the prisoners showed there to be sixty. Because most of those who had been able to run away had done so, a much larger proportion of the prisoners were wounded than might otherwise have been expected. Of the sixty prisoners, nearly two thirds were casualties to some degree or other, and half of those were unable to walk. It presented Caspasian with a problem. Eventually they would all have to be taken back to General Yuan's encampment in the town. The able-bodied prisoners could be used to construct stretchers and then to carry their wounded comrades. One benefit of the large number of wounded however was that Caspasian felt able to post only a handful of sentries to watch over them. This left the majority of his force free for the arduous task of stripping the train of everything that could be of later use.

Of prime importance were the guns, followed by the small arms and all their associated ammunition. Caspasian had come equipped for the task and handlers now led forward the mules and any spare mounts in order to carry the heavy loads on the journey back to camp. While Caspasian carried out an initial inspection of the train's less damaged carriages to estimate the likely size of the task they now faced, Lilin addressed the prisoners on behalf of her father. Most of them were still too shocked to be able to take in what she was saying to them. The ease with which the fearsome Dragon had been overpowered had stunned them all. Even so, several of them immediately volunteered for service with General Yuan.

Lilin eyed them suspiciously. 'Excellent,' she said. 'Then you can be the first to demonstrate your new loyalty by pulling the howitzers that cannot be broken down for the mules.'

From the command carriage, Caspasian took several pieces of chalk that had been used for marking up the report boards attached to the walls. Then, moving from carriage to carriage, he went right through the train from back to front, assessing everything that was re-usable and marking each of the items with a large and clearly visible white chalk cross. Behind him, the work parties set about their huge task. Howitzers and machine-guns were removed from their mounts and manhandled out on to the track. Loose small arms were scattered everywhere and all were now gathered up, checked to ensure they still worked, and then stacked by type, rifles of various makes, pistols, revolvers, swords and so on. There was even a handful of sub-machine-guns. Ammunition was similarly stockpiled and then sorted by calibre.

Someone came across several boxes of hand grenades and there was a jubilant cheer that brought Caspasian and Lilin running.

'They've never seen such an assortment of arms,' Lilin explained. 'With this we will at last stand a chance against General Mok.'

The closer Caspasian approached to the front of the train, the worse the damage became. All the carriages were overturned and twisted, and a number of them had been gutted by fires that still burned, belching out noxious clouds of smoke.

'Tell everyone to keep well clear of these,' Caspasian warned Lilin. 'There's likely to be ammunition in there and in that heat it could cook off at any moment.'

No sooner had he spoken than there was a burst of shots like firecrackers from inside the carriage beside them. Caspasian threw himself at Lilin shielding her with his body and taking them both flying to the ground. Bullets whipped and cracked close overhead, pinging off the metal rail tracks and ricochetting on the stone sides of the cutting as if confinement within the narrow space had driven them to a frenzy.

Caspasian covered Lilin, protecting her as best he could, and waited for the storm to pass. With a final flurry of explosions, the cases of ammunition that the fire had found expended the last of their fury, sputtering into silence. Gingerly, Caspasian raised his head. The air about him was heavy with cordite fumes. He eased himself off Lilin and sat up, brushing the dirt from his clothes.

'Are you all right?'

Lilin pushed herself up on one elbow. She smiled at him. 'Life with you is nothing if not exciting.'

'And that from the girl at the Regent!'

She laughed. It was a light, beautiful sound, the first time Caspasian had heard her laugh like that. He looked at her for a long time, watching her straighten her blouse and riding breeches, wondering what it must have been like for her, growing up as the only child of a warlord in the middle of China.

She looked up suddenly and grinned to find him so intent. 'What is it?' she asked

Caspasian shook his head. 'Nothing.' He smiled. 'Come on.' He stood up and held out his hand to help her to her feet. 'We've got a lot of work to do.'

The front two carriages were so badly twisted and damaged by fire that Caspasian did not even bother trying to look inside. With the exception of Scarface and the one who had fired the first shot, all the Russians had been killed in the crash and then cremated. Having been travelling in the foremost carriages they had never stood a chance.

It was a further two hours before the work of gutting the train had been completed. For a moment Caspasian considered torching the remaining hulk, but the few pieces that might possibly be serviceable again would require considerable repair work to make them so and he was sure that General Mok did not have the capability to undertake such a task. Nor, with the Russians dead, would he have had the expertise to handle whatever lesser armoured beast might be resurrected. So, leaving the once proud Dragon to burn itself out and smoulder in ruins, Caspasian detailed his men to load the mules and set about the long and difficult journey back to General Yuan's camp.

Of the heavier guns, they had managed to save four howitzers, with approximately fifty rounds apiece. There were two Stokes mortars with a similar amount of ammunition, but most useful of all, Caspasian had been able to identify no fewer than ten Vickers machine-guns. These now stood in a row beside the track, a large pile of wooden ammunition crates loaded with belted ball ammunition next to them. Caspasian and Lilin stared at them in wonder.

'The next time we encounter General Mok's army, the fight will be considerably less one-sided,' Caspasian said.

It was as if he had broken a spell. Lilin's smile froze. She shivered and folded her arms tightly. She looked up at the sky into which the wreathes of filthy smoke rising from the many separate fires aboard the wrecked train had spun together to form a single giant plume towering high into the otherwise clear morning air. She looked at Caspasian and the same thought struck them both. Her father, General Yuan. What had happened with the delaying action? They had been so intent on their own task that the possibility of the other part of the battle failing to go equally well had not occurred to them. Until now.

Hurriedly, they assembled their force, the number now considerably swollen by the addition of the prisoners. The captured arms and ammunition were strapped to the mules or, in the case of the howitzers, hauled on to makeshift limbers to be towed by horses, mules and men alike. Caspasian was worried by the amount of material they now had to get back to the security of their base area. There could be no question of abandoning any of it. Supplies were hard enough to come by as it was. With the armoury taken from the dragon, General Yuan's small force had been upgraded at a single stroke from a local militia to a well equipped pocket-size army. Though numbering little more than a British battalion, Caspasian had seen enough of their fighting spirit and discipline to recognise the potential. With the right training and leadership they could form the nucleus of an impressive force, capable of wielding power and influence over all the surrounding provinces. With General Yuan at the helm, Caspasian knew that the influence would be a positive one.

Before they set off, Caspasian told Lilin to select two dozen of the best men. No more than that could be spared. These he divided into four small patrols. One was pushed well out in front to act as a vanguard, and one was detailed to bring up the rear and ensure their column was not being shadowed. The other two groups he pushed out to guard either flank. All were mounted in the hope that speed would compensate for their lack of numbers. Caspasian himself with Lilin, moved at the head of the main body. He had nominated twenty mounted men to serve as a mobile reserve, able to react to any alarm that the four guard groups might suddenly raise. It was a pitifully weak reserve but it was the best he could do. Every other able-bodied man was being used to manhandle the mass of captured equipment, assist with the wounded or guard the prisoners.

Riding beside Lilin, Caspasian looked up at the sky, worried by the approach of night. There was no question of reaching the security of base before dark. They would be lucky to arrive back by noon the following day, bearing in mind the shockingly slow pace at which they were now having to travel.

An hour later they hardly seemed to have moved, yet the men were working as hard as they could, sweating like slaves, their fatigue exacerbated by the fact that the march had come on top of a battle and, before that, a full night's labour preparing the ambush site for the Dragon. Caspasian and Lilin rode up and down the struggling column, urging the men on.

'We're going to have to stop for the night,' Lilin said, drawing to a halt beside Caspasian.

He glanced at the country around them. Gently undulating, there was little in the way of good cover. The woodland had been left behind at the cutting and they found themselves now crossing more open terrain that made Caspasian feel uncomfortable.

'We've got to try and reach that forest,' he said, pointing ahead to a dark line that cut across their line of march a mile in front. 'If anyone caught us out here in the open they'd make mince meat of us in our present state.'

Lilin nodded. She was worried that the men were being pushed too hard, but Caspasian was right. 'I'll take half a dozen men and ride on ahead to mark out a night harbour position,' she said.

Caspasian did not like the idea of letting her ride off with so few men, and for a moment he considered going instead. On the other hand, he realised that the column was the priority and that his place was to remain with it. Indeed, if it was suddenly attacked it would be far more dangerous than a reconnaissance to the forest. Lilin gathered her men and, as she rode away, she turned briefly and waved. Caspasian smiled and felt, with a lurch in his gut, that she had become important to him. How it had happened he could not say but it was true. He cared about her, and the sight of her riding away into the gathering darkness filled him with trepidation.

To take his mind off it he occupied himself with work. Some of the wounded and the men with the heavier pieces of equipment had fallen behind. Caspasian rode back and set about urging them to join up with the main body. He organised the redistribution of the more difficult loads, and made sure that no one was avoiding their fair share of the labour. Eventually his efforts bore fruit and the column once again drew together, the men beginning to force the pace now that they were approaching a night harbour and rest.

The distance to the treeline seemed to retreat the harder the column tried to reach it. It was like a mirage, tauntingly withdrawing the greater their effort to close the gap. Darkness had almost fallen by the time the front of the column finally entered the deep gloom of the tree cover to find Lilin's men waiting for them. Acting as guides, the scouts led each section of the column to its assigned place, positioning the captured stores, heavy weapons, and the wounded in the centre of a large square. At each of the four corners, Caspasian sited a Vickers machine-gun, being particularly careful to ensure that their lines of fire covered the main approaches into the position. Anyone trying to advance upon them during the night would receive a very rude shock.

Lilin herself had taken two men and ridden through the forest to the far side, to scout the route they would have to take at first light. She had still not returned by the time the night harbour was secure and a meal had been cooked. Caspasian declined the offer of food, saying that he would wait for Lilin to return first. They would then eat together. In the meantime, and to keep his mind off what might have become of her, he toured the perimeter, ensuring that sentries had been posted and that they were awake and alert. After the day they had all had it was going to be difficult to keep them on their toes. The only solution was to relieve them at regular intervals, making sure that no one did more than his fair share, and that the names of every able-bodied man were included on the roster.

Finally, when Caspasian was on the verge of riding out himself to search for her, Lilin appeared. She was riding slowly with her guards, but as she came in through the perimeter, there was a cry from the sentry who had first spotted her, and Caspasian ran across to see a further group of men trailing behind Lilin. Some were mounted, but most were on foot, numbering no more than twenty in all.

'Who are they?' he asked. But one look at the expression on Lilin's face told the story.

Caspasian ran up to the man riding at the head of the newcomers. 'What happened?'

The man slid down from his horse. He was exhausted and covered in mud, sweat and blood. His clothes were in tatters and he was unarmed save for a knife tucked under an empty bandolier slung across his shoulder.

'General Mok's cavalry outflanked us. We were out of bullets and trying to pull back. Then there they were. They appeared out of nowhere. Scores of them. They charged and that was that. We never had a chance.'

'What happened to the rest?'

'All dead. Dead or prisoner, and I hope for their sakes that they all died in battle.'

Hardly daring to ask, Caspasian said, 'What about General Yuan?'

Lilin dismounted and came across to join him. 'I've already asked them. They don't know.'

The man looked at Caspasian pleadingly. 'We didn't want to run away. We fought for as long as we could, but what could we do against cavalry?'

Caspasian put his hand on the man's shoulder, wanting to console him but knowing that it was useless. He suddenly remembered. 'What about the rest of the force? Surely Mok's cavalry only caught one of our ambush groups?'

The man frowned as if thinking of it for the first time. 'Yes. It was just us.'

'Right, so that still leaves six hundred intact.'

The man looked confused. 'I suppose so, but so many died and General Yuan . . . '

'Did you see him fall?' Caspasian asked.

The man frowned, thinking.

'Well? Did you?'

'Not exactly.'

'Then there's every chance he's alive!'

Lilin looked up, hardly daring to believe that it might be true. Caspasian gripped her by the shoulders and stared hard at her. 'Lilin, you know your father. If anyone can survive, he can.'

Slowly she nodded her head, not really convinced but longing to believe. Caspasian could hardly believe it possible either, but he had to hold them all together. If the men lost heart now, that would be the end of it. General Mok would have won. The destruction of the Dragon would have been for nothing. He had to hold the force together.

* * *

Flat on his stomach, General Yuan slithered like a snake through the tall grass. His boots had gone and he was completely unarmed. But he was alive. He had to keep reminding himself of that one simple fact in order to hold despair at bay. He was alive and so, for the moment, was the majority of his force. The group who had been preparing a fresh ambush at the next fall-back position, the reserve, and of course the small force with Caspasian and Lilin. They were scattered and leaderless, but they were still free of General Mok for now. His greatest concern was that, thinking him dead, they might lose heart and surrender or flee without trying once more for the victory which he was certain they could yet wrest from the disaster that had just been suffered.

He had to fight to push from his mind the image of General Mok's cavalry breaking from that shimmering line into the furious gallop that had scythed through his disorganised infantry, scrambling for their horses in a terrified bid to escape. Few had done so. Very few. The engagement had been brief but intense, with a savagery he had never known before, nor wished to encounter again. His men had fought bravely but had never really recovered from the shock of seeing their withdrawal route severed, and by such an awe-inspiring sight as the cavalry.

General Mok had remained frustratingly out of reach, sitting on his mount surrounded by a bodyguard of mounted thugs, watching with relish the destruction of his foe. Yuan himself had tried to lead a counter-attack, going straight for General Mok. They had been decimated and pushed back before they had gone fifty yards.

Finally, seeing the wholesale slaughter of his men on all sides, Yuan had screamed for every man to break out and flee as best they could. Few had made it beyond the encircling ring of steel sabres. Fortunately, in their eagerness to kill, General Mok's cavalry had broken ranks and it was through those one or two gaps that an escape had been effected. Fleeing the battlefield was the hardest thing Yuan had ever had to do in his life, with the screams of his dying men ringing in his ears. His eyes had been blurred with tears of rage and shame as he had ridden helter-skelter from the carnage, a handful of his men about him.

Seeing themselves pursued, they had split up, each survivor going his separate way. Yuan's only consolation was that Lilin had not been there with him. He had to assume that the attack on the train had gone all right. To contemplate failure there too was more than he could bear. He had faith in Caspasian and somehow felt certain that Lilin was as safe with him as she could be with anyone in the terrible nightmare that was unfolding.

General Mok's cavalry had not given up their relentless pursuit. They were clearly under orders to hunt down every last man who had so humiliated Mok at the previous ambushes. He was going to have his revenge, come what may. Eventually Yuan's horse had dropped dead beneath him, throwing him clear but knocking him senseless. By the time he had regained full consciousness, Yuan had found Mok's cavalry almost upon him. Fortunately he had been within striking distance of woodland so, moments before discovery, he had managed to slip away on his belly into the cover of the trees, praying for the speedy arrival of darkness to shield him.

The cavalry had found his dead horse and, with no rider beside it, had continued to search for him. Yuan did not think it likely that they knew the identity of the rider. Had they done so he was sure they would have sent for reinforcements. As it was they had split into several small groups and had started a methodical sweep of the woods. Although they were unable to see him, they called out tauntingly, shouting descriptions of what they would do when they laid hands upon him. Yuan was not sure whether or not to be thankful that he was unarmed. Had he possessed a gun he would have felt less frightened, but then he might equally have been tempted to turn it upon himself to escape the torture he knew would come if they did indeed capture him, especially as his identity would quickly become apparent.

For a long while he had lain as still as a

corpse, burying himself in the heart of a thicket and pulling leaves and moss and earth on top of himself. At one point a horseman had brushed right up against his hiding place and Yuan had steeled himself for discovery and one last desperate struggle. But at that moment one of the horseman's comrades had cried out, believing he had found their quarry, and the horseman had spurred his mount quickly towards the scene.

After what seemed like an age, the cavalry had drifted away and Yuan had been able to crawl out of the thicket and get his bearings. By then it was almost dark and he knew that unless he sorted out his approximate location he would spend the night wandering aimlessly, perhaps even in the wrong direction back towards General Mok. If on the other hand he could use the night for covering ground, he estimated that by daybreak he should be back in friendly territory.

Now, several hours later, he was moving through country he had never seen before. He was starting to fear that he had gone wrong and somehow doubled back unwittingly. He had been moving at a snail's pace, crawling across every patch of open ground he came to, such as the piece of tall grassland he had just reached. In the darkness he could not see the edges of it to decide whether or not to go around it. For all he could tell it might be several miles wide. He had been able to get a glimpse at the stars and set his direction, and the only way was to move straight across it. On his belly.

The elbows and knees of his clothes had worn right through. The skin had quickly broken and now the cuts were encrusted with dirt. Every so often he was forced by exhaustion to stop for a rest. His breathing was so laboured he felt certain the sound of it must be deafening, sure to give away his position to anyone who might be listening.

He rolled over silently on to his back. He wiped the sweat from his eyes and stared up at the night sky. Huge clouds were scudding across the heavens, the wind that drove them less forceful at ground level where it moved through the tall grass with a gentler rhythm. It washed over him, drying the perspiration that beaded his brow but helpless against his sweat-soaked clothes that clung to him as if he had just swum a river.

He was just starting to relax, feeling his joints stiffen, when he heard the noise. He froze, then ever so slowly, eased himself back on to his front, drawing his legs up beneath him in case he was about to have to run. He listened intently until it came again. It was another man. He was sure of it. He racked his brains for a course of action. The noise was heading straight for him, but it seemed to be someone crawling like himself. It must be a fugitive therefore. Most probably one of his own men.

Yuan waited until the noise of crawling was almost upon him. For one moment he considered springing at whoever it was, but decided against it. If they were armed they might well kill him in the struggle before he could establish their identity. Instead, he mouthed a silent prayer and knelt upright, his hands ready to ward off an attack. He had only ever used his practice of Tai Chi as an aid to meditation. For the first time he wished with all his heart that he had studied a more combative art, like Caspasian.

'Identify yourself!'

There was a terrified shriek and a couple of paces away, a figure sprung out of the grass and streaked off in the opposite direction. Yuan shot after the fugitive and brought him down before he had run ten yards. The man was clearly out of his wits with fear and flayed at Yuan with his fists.

'Be still, damn you! It is me, General Yuan,' he hissed.

The man stopped struggling, peering up at Yuan.

'I know you,' Yuan said, staring down at the

face beneath him. 'You're the bandit.'

Li stared hard at the man on top of him and then fell back in the grass, weeping with relief. Yuan had not known that he had been in the group cut down by General Mok's cavalry and felt a sudden shame that the man who had trusted him had been brought so rapidly to this.

'What's going to happen to us, General?' Li whimpered. 'My friend, Ku, was killed.' He shook his head, inconsolable. 'The moment he saw the cavalry he knew what they would do to him if they took him alive. Before they could do so, he rushed straight upon their blades.' He stopped to wipe the tears and mucous from his face. 'His head was cut clean open, right down the centre like a melon. I saw it all. That was when I ran.'

Yuan longed for a handkerchief to hand to him but he was in as sorry a state himself. 'Well, you're alive. And we're going to get away from here. We'll rejoin the others tomorrow morning and then we'll sort out this whole mess.'

To his amazement, Li believed him. His shoulders stopped heaving with the sobs and he quietened. 'Will we really?' he asked.

Yuan forced a smile. 'Yes,' he said, and then, before he could stop himself, he added, 'I promise.'

He stood up and held out his hand to Li. 'Come on. Let's get moving.'

Li stood up with difficulty. Like Yuan, he had been crawling for so long that his joints were screaming for rest and every limb was covered in cuts and bruises. Like two ancient veterans, they hobbled away, looking fearfully about them. The moon had risen and, in spite of the intermittent cloud cover, the landscape was dangerously bright. Whenever the clouds parted to reveal the moon, the pair knelt down and were still, using the opportunity both to catch their breath and also to scan as far as they could see for the enemy.

The sound of the horses' hooves reached them only a moment before they saw the mounted patrol. Still in the open grassland, they looked about desperately for somewhere to hide. There was nothing. Not a ditch, depression, or bush.

'Down!' Yuan whispered unnecessarily, for Li was already flat on his stomach, burying his face in the grass as if he was trying to nose his way underground.

The grass was now little more than a foot high. There was just a chance that, if they lay perfectly still and the horsemen did not pass too close, they might remain undetected.

They could not tell whether the horsemen had spotted something, but all of a sudden the patrol veered directly towards them. Li looked at Yuan, his terrified eyes appealing for salvation. His whole body was shaking. In that instant Yuan knew exactly what he had to do. Suddenly a great calm came over him. All fear was gone and his breathing steadied. He smiled, a smile of the purest compassion. Then he stood up and started to run.

Leaving Li concealed in the grass, Yuan shot off as fast as his exhausted legs could carry him, heading away from their hiding place. He vaguely heard a shout from the leading rider, and then the snort of the horses as the patrol turned sharply and came after him.

He felt as if he was running faster than he had ever done in his life, picking his feet up high to clear the long grass lest he trip and fall. He had to lead the cavalry as far away from Li as he could. From the man who had placed his trust in him. In his exhaustion he saw stars. There was a fleeting image of Lilin. He could taste blood. His lungs were burning, fit to burst. The sound of a bridle, the creak of saddle leather, the pounding of hooves closed upon him from behind. Yuan was still sprinting as the cavalry Major drew his sabre, stood upright in his stirrups angling for a better cut, and swept his arm downwards in a perfect arc.

13

Cresting the rise, Caspasian slowed his horse to a trot and then halted. Lilin drew alongside, glancing at him expectantly.

'Here?' she asked.

Caspasian surveyed the landscape stretched out below, his narrowed eyes absorbing every depression and fold of the ground.

'Here,' he said at last.

Behind them, Yuan's commanders gathered uncertainly. Robbed of their leader, they were still unconvinced that this foreigner could save them from disaster. They knew of the successful ambush on the Dragon, but none of them had been present. The story had been related to them by others. As far as they were concerned Caspasian's reputation rested on hearsay alone, and since the disaster on the battlefield and the news of Yuan's disappearance, any confidence that had buoyed them after the destruction of the armoured train had now been considerably diluted with fear.

Caspasian reached into one of his saddle bags and took out a folder. Flipping it open, he plucked a pencil from his pocket, moistened the tip, and began to sketch the landscape before him. Yuan's commanders glanced at one another, craning to see what he was up to. One or two of them muttered. The foreigner's activity hardly seemed a suitable way of addressing their current dilemma. Aware of their impatience, Lilin coughed lightly to alert Caspasian. In answer he smiled.

'Won't be a moment,' he said, refusing to be coerced into an explanation before he was ready.

Confident, rapid strokes of lead on paper swiftly reproduced the undulations of the ground. A sudden blur of shading accurately placed the sporadic clumps of woodland. A stream cutting deeply through the plain became, under Caspasian's hand, a thick line, the multiple twists and turns of the original simplified into a couple of symbolic bends which he judged sufficient to serve his purpose.

When he had achieved all he could from his vantage point, he closed his folder, stuffed it securely back in its bag, and spurred his horse on. For a moment the commanders and Lilin were taken by surprise.

'Come on then,' she said to them gruffly, spurring to follow him.

Caspasian rode quickly down from the rise, heading directly for another vantage point.

When he was satisfied with his new position he again took out the pad and again set to work on his sketch, adding or adjusting the detail to complement the picture with the information offered from this new perspective. Moments later he rode on again, the commanders and Lilin tumbling after him as if linked by elastic.

At one halt, Caspasian slid from his saddle, jogged away from the skittering mounts of the commanders, and lay down on his stomach. He raised his head and scanned the ground, then got up, moved thirty yards to the left, lay prone again, and repeated the exercise. Brushing the grass from his trousers as he remounted his horse, he smiled up at Lilin.

'Just checking the fields of fire at ground level.' He pointed to the flattened grass where he had first lain. 'Can't see a thing from there. No more than twenty yards. Sitting on horseback it looks great for a machine-gun, but once you actually try it out, you see that it would be disastrous.'

One of the commanders overhearing this slowly smiled, nodding as he understood. He spoke rapidly to his comrades.

It was well over an hour before Caspasian led the group back to the first vantage point and dismounted. For a moment the others watched him suspiciously, expecting some new trick or display. Instead, Caspasian walked across to a small hillock and sat down. He opened his sketch pad, the drawing now complete, and glanced back over his shoulder at the horsemen.

'Come and join me.'

Lilin jumped down, tossing back her hair and pretending she had known his intentions all along. One by one the commanders followed. When they had assembled in a tight little clutch in front of him, each one peering curiously to glimpse the sketch, Caspasian turned his drawing to face them and spoke.

'Gentlemen, the battlefield.'

He rested the edge of the sketch pad on his knees, holding it upright so that everyone could see it clearly. Before he continued, he studied the men before him carefully, looking them one by one in the eye. Their future, and the future of everyone of General Yuan's followers, would depend on the next few minutes. If he could convince them of the worth of his plan, then they would convince the others, those beneath them. But if they themselves remained doubtful, then all was lost. Somehow Caspasian had to wrest back control of the situation. It was that simple. And this was the moment.

Lilin repositioned herself at his side, one hand resting lightly on his shoulder as if she sensed his intent and was lending him her own authority and, through her, that of her absent father. Caspasian felt the gentle touch and began.

'General Mok thinks he has retaken the initiative. He thinks he is winning. As far as he is concerned, from now on it will just be a matter of mopping up the remnants of us. He thinks it will be like a day's hunting.'

He paused for effect, his eyes narrowing into a dangerous smile in which he included the commanders, joining them all together as co-conspirators. One or two of them felt his infectious confidence and smiled back.

'But where Mok expects to find a wounded deer, he is going to walk into a waiting tiger, teeth bared, claws sharpened, belly empty.'

His smile broadened into a grin. He had them all now. The only sound was the soothing wash of the breeze. Even the horses were attentive, as if alert to the poignancy of the moment.

'This is the way he will come,' Caspasian continued, indicating a bold arrow that he had drawn on the sketch, then turning to point the direction on the ground behind him. Heads turned, then nodded, as under-standing deepened. One by one Yuan's commanders realised that the foreigner knew his trade.

'We will deploy a screen of lightly armed mounted troops forward of our main position. They will be the bait. It will be their job to act like the wounded deer. Faltering, seemingly disorganised, forever falling back. Mok will smell blood and follow. In his eagerness he will run ahead of himself. His lust for blood and revenge will get the better of whatever wise counsel he is given by others. He will come on, and we will be waiting for him.' With one bold stroke of the pencil Caspasian drew a line that described an arc, partially enveloping the plain. 'Here.'

He raised his eyes and pointed to the plain below them. The commanders and Lilin turned as one and stared at the ground. From the glint in their eyes Caspasian could tell that, like him, they were already seeing it littered with the corpses of their enemies. It was a battlefield in the making. A piece of ground that would never be the same again, for as long as men lived and remembered.

Caspasian turned to his sketch map, the commanders leaning towards it now that they grasped his purpose.

'This will be where we kill him.' His pencil encircled an empty white space on the paper, invigorating it with potential. Caspasian again raised his eyes and the commanders looked up to survey the ground itself. Eyes narrowed. Mouths creased into smiles.

'We will turn his own weapons against him, captured from the Dragon.' Caspasian marked the positions on the sketch. 'Machine-guns here and here, with overlapping fields of fire that sweep the entire plain.'

He marked a series of crosses behind the blur that signified woodland. 'Our artillery will be out of sight behind the trees.' He pointed. 'There.' Everyone checked. Nodded.

'We will put observers in the treeline to direct the fire. Ammunition is scarce so the guns will not open fire until his forces have bunched and lost cohesion. When the forward elements run headlong into the machine-gun fire they will halt. Those behind will keep on coming. Their officers will drive them forward. That is the only thing they know. As the rear elements push forward, that is when we will open fire with the guns.' He looked up from his sketch to find the eyes of all the commanders on him, mesmerised.

'When the destruction is at its height, we will advance.' He marked the direction with an arrow. 'Infantry will lead, while cavalry envelop, cut off, rout and destroy.' A final sweep of the pencil lead swept across the paper's last remaining corner of virgin white, indicating the conclusion of the slaughter to come.

'Any questions so far?'

Caspasian sat back and waited. Silence.

'Good. Then let's get down to the detail.' He glanced up at Lilin and said quietly, so that only she could hear, 'I need you to pay particular attention.'

She frowned, puzzled. 'Why?'

'Because you might have to direct the battle.'

Alarm registered on her face. 'Where are you going to be?'

Caspasian smiled. 'Someone's got to lure Mok into the trap. I'm going to lead the screen force.'

Lilin blanched. 'But that's ridiculous. Anyone can do that.'

'Not convincingly,' Caspasian replied levelly. 'It's got to look good. If it doesn't, we're finished. We've got to make him think he's got us on the run. Anything less will spell disaster. You either achieve surprise or you don't. There are no half measures.' He smiled, trying to dispel her fear while forcefully suppressing his own. 'Don't worry. If all goes well, I will be back in good time for the battle.'

'And what if you're not?'

'Then the fate of your father's followers will be in your hands, and yours alone.'

Daniel Smith sat with shoulders hunched, a mug of hot tea cupped in his hands, the steam billowing gently against his face, eyes closed, nose scenting the warmth.

'How?'

General Mok paced the large tent, hands clasped behind his back. Somehow the word was more accusation than question.

'It was Caspasian,' Smith answered, as if the name alone should be sufficient explanation.

Mok blinked, not understanding. He had met Caspasian and not been particularly impressed. He had seen a tall, darkly blond man, blue eyes hooded, strangely almost Asian. Incongruous. Apart from that there did not seem to be anything remarkable about the fellow. Watching the miserable Smith however, Mok realised that his advisor clearly felt some trepidation towards the other Englishman.

Realising that Mok expected him to expand, Smith took a sip from the mug, as if drawing strength from the three heaped spoonfuls of sugar dissolved within it, and continued. 'The ambush was textbook. Pure bloody textbook.'

Mok smiled uncertainly. 'But, perhaps you

335

can explain, Captain Smith. I pay you to be my expert. You are supposed to be the one who produces textbook solutions to my problems. How is it that you allow the Dragon to walk into such a textbook ambush?' He injected the phrase with as much venom as he dared. Sure enough, Smith was in his employ, but Mok was just sufficiently aware to realise that he was nonetheless a dangerous and unpredictable man.

Smith shrugged, aware that the gesture was more pathetic than he had intended. 'Your driver didn't help. Belting into that ravine like a bull in a china shop.' He shook his head. 'Stupid. Absolutely bloody stupid.'

Mok nodded. 'Then it is lucky for him that he died in the attack.'

'Too damned right it is,' Smith said bitterly.

A thought occurred to Mok. 'The Dragon had a great deal of weaponry aboard. Ammunition too.'

Smith read the signals and stiffened.

'What happened to it all?' Mok concluded solemnly.

Smith shook his head, his face a mask of concentration, as if straining to recall. 'It would have been destroyed. The crash and then the fire was catastrophic. Nothing could have survived.'

Mok smiled pleasantly. 'And yet you did,' he said simply.

'I saw it as my duty to get out of there alive. To return to you so we can seek vengeance on Caspasian, Yuan and the lot of them.'

'That's very noble of you,' Mok said. 'I am indeed lucky to have you in my service.'

Smith forced a smile.

'My only point in asking is that, should this Captain Caspasian have laid his hands on any of my weaponry . . . '

'Small chance of that, General,' Smith said, a little too quickly.

Mok raised his eyebrows. 'Oh? How so?'

Smith thought quickly. 'I saw it. There was a huge explosion. I was at the back of the train, you see. Everything was destroyed. There was nothing I could do. Nothing at all.'

'Everything was destroyed?'

'That's what I said,' Smith declared resolutely.

Mok surveyed him steadily for a second more, and then relented. He placed a hand on his shoulder in a gesture of consolation that made Smith's skin crawl. 'It's lucky that I turned the course of battle against Yuan myself, isn't it?'

Smith felt his bile rise but forced a crooked smile to hide his loathing and contempt.

Mok warmed to his subject. 'When Yuan ambushed me,' he said, not sparing Smith the emphasis, 'I saw through his petty stratagem and outflanked him. Though I say it myself, it was a stunning defeat.' He paced towards the open mouth of the tent, staring into the night. 'Tomorrow we will complete the destruction of his main force. And then we will lay waste his entire province.' Mok turned and grinned with pure evil. 'There will be women aplenty. Enough for all of my men.'

Smith glared angrily past him. 'All I want is Caspasian. I want his heart in my fist.'

Mok smiled at him, shaking his head gently. 'And this from the man who once held Caspasian's life in his hands.'

Smith was about to retort when there was a sudden commotion outside. He and Mok both looked towards the dark mouth of the tent as the hubbub of voices grew louder. Someone cheered. A horse whinnied, spooked by the crowd of soldiers who were now visible crowding around it. On its back, the outline of a cavalry officer became visible as he approached General Mok's tent. It was Major Chiu. In one hand he clutched the end of a rope. The other end was obscured by the press of excited men that teemed on all sides, eager to witness the reaction of their General

338

to the news the officer was bringing.

Smith stood up, putting his mug of tea to one side, and together with Mok went out to investigate. Major Chiu urged his horse on, pushing clear of the soldiers packed around him. Everyone was grinning and chattering.

Smith's face darkened. 'Quiet! Who the devil's in charge here? What's going on?'

Major Chiu ignored him, addressing Mok. 'General, I thought you would like to see what I have captured.'

General Mok stepped forward, frowning. 'Go on.'

The Major jerked savagely on the rope and a bent figure staggered forward. The other end of the rope had been fastened around his neck. He stood wavering, only half-conscious. His hair was matted with blood that had also soaked his jacket, crusting into a darkly shining morass. His face was caked with dirt and he looked as if he was about to expire at any moment.

Mok peered at him with little interest. The blood appeared to have flowed from a wound on the back of the prisoner's head. Like all skull wounds, it had bled profusely and was probably not quite as severe as it might at first seem.

'Why are you bothering me with another prisoner? Put him with the others. We'll execute them later.'

Major Chiu smiled proudly. He slid down from his saddle, stepped beside the prisoner, grasped a handful of the matted hair in his fist and yanked back the head so that everyone could see the face. When he saw that his General remained unimpressed, he said dramatically, 'It's Yuan.'

Mok stared, unbelieving. 'What did you say?'

'It is him, General. It's Yuan.' He grinned from ear to ear, his teeth bared, broken and filthy. 'I almost killed him,' he added chuckling. 'We were patrolling to the east. We had already cut down a score of the enemy, catching them as they fled and killing them on the spot. This one,' he said, jerking his chin in the direction of his prisoner, 'broke from cover and ran like all the others. I had almost ridden him down, and was about to cut off his head when he turned as he ran and looked back at me over his shoulder. It was only a glance but it was enough. I recognised him. I saw him once before, you see, and I never forget a face.' He smirked with self-satisfaction. 'I only just managed to turn my blade in time. Even so, I hit him full force with the flat of it.' He squared his shoulders and stood proudly before his commander. 'But there's no mistake. It is

General Yuan all right.'

For the first time the prisoner raised his head and showed some awareness of his surroundings. The eyes were clouded with pain, their focus imperfect.

General Mok peered closely into the prisoner's face, still doubting what he had been told. At first sight the man seemed just like any other filthy captive after a battle. Bloodied, bedraggled and dumbstruck. However, as he pulled back and looked the man up and down he noticed other things, small things that would be incongruous were he to be just another peasant. The clothes he wore were encrusted with mud and blood, but beneath the evil coating Mok could see that the quality was good. The edges of the man's jacket were trimmed with gold-coloured thread. It looked like silk, hardly the cloth of a common soldier.

Also, there was something about the fellow's bearing. Sure enough, he was beaten and bowed, his senses clearly still drunk with the shock of the sabre blow. But even Mok could see that fighting through the mist of confusion there was a man of character struggling to regain control. The eyes, though blurred, clenched and squinted for vision. In Mok's wide experience, any ordinary captive would have slumped to the ground, awaiting death. This man, on the other hand, was attempting to surface, like a swimmer emerging from the depths of the sea.

Mok smiled. The prisoner was obviously still badly concussed, for had he realised his position he would have tried to disguise himself as someone of no account. Instead, Yuan's natural resilience and force of personality were the very things that had betrayed him, revealing his identity to General Mok.

'Well, well, well,' General Mok crooned softly. He was like a man who has returned home unsuccessfully from a quest, only to find the very thing he sought, lying across the threshold of his house.

'Let me have him,' Smith interjected, thrusting forward and seizing the tottering figure of Yuan by the lapels of his filthy jacket. 'I'll get him talking for you, General. He'll soon be singing like a lark. I'll get him to tell us everything about his forces' deployment and the whereabouts of Caspasian.'

Mok frowned angrily. He seized Smith's wrist and prised it from Yuan's coat. 'I don't care about the Englishman. And you're not going to lay a finger on this man.' He smiled dangerously. 'In his present state he would not be able to tell you anything. Even a fool can see that.'

Smith released his grip, smarting at the public rebuke. One of Mok's soldiers chuckled. Major Chiu, who had ignored him so far, glared at him now for the first time, adding, 'You might be able to lecture us on modern weaponry but interrogation is our specialty.'

Mok nodded. 'When Yuan is rested, then we will ask him our questions. Right now, he is too close to death to be able to tell us anything of value.'

He turned to the Major and clapped a hand approvingly on his shoulder. 'You have done well. Very well. Your diligence will not go unrewarded.'

Major Chiu beamed, bowing stiffly from the waist.

'Have the prisoner's wound seen to. Feed him when he is able to take nourishment. Nurture him. Keep him alive and well.' Mok's eyes narrowed. 'Then we will start the interrogation, and learn everything we need to know before we continue the attack.'

★ ★ ★

Yuan's head was a mess of pain. He knew that he was hurt, and he knew that he was facing the greatest peril of his life. Beyond that, firm knowledge closed its book. Only

343

rumour and suspicion existed, hinting at his plight, speaking in riddles. To a man of his self-possession, used to being in command of all his faculties, it was infuriating. He imagined it was what it must be like to be old. Senility encroaching on the fringes of territory once strongly garrisoned by reason. It was not just infuriating. It was obscene.

He was aware of being alive. At least he thought he was. Existence had acquired the quality of a nightmare. The movements of his limbs were being directed by others, vague shapes that he took to be men, but in whom he could detect a gleeful menace. They might as well be ghouls. He had observed the outline of a face being thrust close to his, but it was studying him as if through an opaque screen that concealed every detail but the barest cluster of features. Nose, high cheek bones, forehead, chin and, somewhere in there, far behind the screen, a pair of eyes like two dark chasms. It filled him with fear. The primeval dread of childhood. The fear an animal feels when faced with death. Yuan shuddered. That was exactly what it had been like. A personification of death.

Shortly thereafter he had felt himself being moved on his way. He was aware that he fell. Hands seized him and at that point he must have passed out for the next thing he saw were crystal-clear images of himself and Lilin riding through acres of billowing rice. The tall green fronds waved this way and that, as if trying to shake off the briskly passing shadows of clouds scudding overhead. Lilin turned in the saddle and Yuan was surprised to note that she was a young girl again. She opened her mouth and spoke, but Yuan heard no sound. He was puzzled and urged his horse to move closer to his daughter's.

Suddenly lightning crashed through Yuan's head and he was back in his battered corporeal form. He was submerged in darkness, but this time it was different from before. This was a darkness outside himself. He was within it, and though it limited his vision, the things that he could see were no longer blurred. With the realisation that he was conscious once again, came the pain. It seared through him like flame leaping up a silk veil.

He was lying on his side and to his surprise he found that his hands were unfastened. The longer he was conscious, the more the dark retreated, his eyes becoming accustomed to it, albeit grudgingly, their every movement accompanied by bolts of pain stemming from the wound on the back of his head. Here and there light carved slender dust-flecked pathways through the darkness. Starting from the pools they cast on the earthen floor in front of him, Yuan traced each of them back to their origins. One came from beneath the door, another from a slit in the wattle forming one wall and still another from a small hole in the thatched roof overhead. He deduced that he was incarcerated in some sort of outhouse. He himself owned many such buildings on his land, using them for storing produce or farming implements.

He was about to try and move when he heard footsteps approaching. Instantly he froze. There was the sound of a chain being unfastened on the other side of the door. A bolt was slid to one side, and light from a campfire somewhere out in the night filled the doorway before being blotted out by the outlines of two large figures. They stopped, framed in the doorway, big and threatening. Yuan had closed his eyes at the first glimpse of them. He steadied his breathing, focusing all his energy on his hearing. To his relief this was sharp and clear.

'Look at him, the poor old sod,' one of them said. 'Sleeping like a baby.'

'He wouldn't if he knew what the General's planning for him,' the man's comrade replied, his voice lowered, although Yuan was sure it was not out of respect for his supposed slumber. More likely the speaker was

346

attempting to conceal the horrors of their captive's fate. Yuan could guess what this might be.

One of the men moved towards him and crouched down for a closer examination. Yuan could hear his breath. He could smell it, too.

'He looks dead if you ask me.'

The other man approached. Yuan realised what was coming and did his best to roll his eyes up as far as he could, just in time as one of the men prised open one eyelid.

'No,' he said. 'But he's out cold.'

'Should we move him? Try to bring him round?'

There was the sound of a smirk. Cruel. 'What the hell for? Mok's gone to sleep now.'

Yuan heard the man's knees crack as he pushed himself upright again.

'What about this? Shall we leave it?'

Yuan smelt food.

'Do you do anything except ask fucking questions? I don't know. What is it anyway?'

'Some crap left over from supper.'

'Give it here.'

Through his pain Yuan realised that he was starving.

'You're not going to eat it, are you?'

'Why not? He's got no use for it. Here, have some.'

As Yuan listened, the two men ate his meal, bolting it down in seconds like dogs with a scrap.

'This is shit,' one of them mumbled, his mouth crammed.

'Hasn't stopped you wolfing it though, has it?'

The two men chuckled. One of them belched. 'Come on. Let's go. Tell the officer he's still out and then get some shut-eye ourselves. I'm knackered.'

They left the hut. Yuan resisted the temptation to peep until he heard the door slam shut. The men chatted as they walked away, their voices trailing into silence.

Yuan opened his eyes and exhaled. The pain returned but this time he fought it. Slowly, he shifted on to his back. Straightening his neck was like setting a broken bone. He struggled to steady his breathing. He had to regain control of his body if he was going to stand any chance of survival. On the face of it there seemed little hope of that. He was sure that what the men had said was true. He was only being kept alive in order to face even greater torment when Mok saw fit to inflict the interrogation. Somehow he had to escape.

The very thought of it made him smile. Surely it must be hopeless? He was in the middle of the enemy camp and in a desperately weakened state.

Out of the blue, something occurred to him. Deprived of vision, his hearing had become more acute. When the men had left, sure enough, they had closed and fastened the door. Yuan had heard the bolt sliding back into place, but there had been no further sound of the chain that they had unfastened in order to enter.

Summoning his strength, he attempted to sit up. As he did so his head swam and he nearly passed out. A wave of nausea engulfed him and he vomited. Forcing himself to continue, he eventually managed to get himself upright, then turned slowly and knelt. On hands and knees he shuffled towards the door. His forehead contacted the wood before he saw it. It was insubstantial and moved easily on its hinges. It had been constructed as a storeroom, not a prison.

Feeling his way upwards, the palms of his hands moving across the coarse surface of the door, Yuan found the latch and tried it. The outside bolt held the door firmly shut. But Yuan could see the bolt through the crack where the door fitted badly in its frame. To his amazement, the crack was wide enough for him to slip the tips of his fingers through. He edged them towards the bolt and felt the touch of cold metal. Pinching it tightly, he tried to rotate it so as to manoeuvre the bolt's handle upwards and slide it back and open.

It was rusty and his first attempt failed, his fingers sliding free. The effort of the task combined with the pain shooting through him to bring on a sweat. His hands moistened, making the task all the more difficult. The temptation to sink back, give up and rest was almost overwhelming. He struggled against it, knowing that if he submitted he would be accepting his death. He remembered his brief vision of the young Lilin and ground his teeth to suppress the pain and the weakness swimming through his limbs.

He rubbed his palms dry on his trousers and went again for the bolt. Once more he coaxed the bolt's handle upwards before attempting to slide it to the rear. Piece by tiny piece, it moved in the direction he wanted. Then all of a sudden, long before he expected it, the tip of the bolt slid free of its loop on the doorframe and the door started to creak open of its own accord.

Yuan clutched at it, holding it shut. He could barely believe his success. Peering through the crack, he saw that he had been right about the chain. It hung uselessly down one side of the doorframe. For a moment

Yuan was unsure what to do. He glanced back into the room, not knowing what he was looking for. There was nothing to take with him. As the men had said, he was like a baby, possessing nothing. But he was free. It was impossible to know how long his freedom would last. Perhaps only a couple of paces beyond the shed door. But any hope that existed lay on the outside. Inside was only the prospect of death. Yuan eased open the door and, still on his hands and knees, slid through it.

The coolness of the night air was like a refreshing tonic after the fetid atmosphere of the outhouse. It even lent him strength to combat the pain that shivered from his head down the length of his spine. He crawled away from the building, heading for a cart that stood some five yards distant. Sacks were piled beside it and Yuan slid between the wheels, concealing himself in the deep shadows beneath it.

He blinked to clear his vision and surveyed his surroundings. To his surprise he found that there were several similar outbuildings surrounding his own. Beyond them, on one side, the light of campfires and the noise of voices indicated the direction of General Mok's encampment. On the other side, an impenetrable darkness beckoned to Yuan, offering to cloak him within it and spirit him away from immediate danger. Before he set off, he returned to the shed in which he had been imprisoned and refastened the door, securing it properly this time using both chain and bolt. He was going to need every minute he could buy.

As he crawled away, weaving like a snake between the buildings, he marvelled at the absence of sentries. General Mok must be confident indeed, he reflected.

It was impossible to guess at the hour. The sky was blanketed with cloud and neither moon nor stars were visible. Moments later, Yuan felt himself entering the night, leaving captivity behind him. He realised that his freedom might be shortlived, but for the moment he felt a great surge of hope. The darkness that had been his enemy had changed sides, switching its allegiance with the fickleness of a deserter. Yuan powered himself forwards, forcing himself to ignore the pain in every part of his body. This is good, he thought. This is very good.

The sound of a man coughing shook Yuan down to his soul. Panic rose out of nowhere and seized control. He spun round and saw, back in the area of the farm buildings, a lone figure approaching the shed in which he had

352

been imprisoned. The man was still some way off and for a moment Yuan hoped that he might be headed elsewhere. But in his hands the soldier carried two lengths of rope, the sort that might be used to bind wrists and ankles, and Yuan understood that the man was going for him. It would be only seconds before his escape was discovered. In his present state there was no question of running. The best thing he could do would be to lie up somewhere.

But even that would be useless. They would soon establish that he had been gone only moments. They would deduce that he could not have gone more than a few yards. A search would soon find him, and, what was worse, they would know that he had regained consciousness and General Mok would start the interrogation.

Yuan hunted around in desperation. He had to find somewhere to hide. Somewhere further away. In the few moments remaining before the alarm was raised, he launched himself into the darkness, scuttling over the dust and debris like a crab.

He glanced back fearfully over his shoulder, expecting the cry, and at that moment tumbled headlong into a man. There was a grunt as the two of them collided. Yuan clenched his fists, summoning the remnants of his strength for one final struggle. He reared up on to his knees to gain height and found himself staring wildly up into the cold bemused eyes of Captain Daniel Smith.

14

Sitting on his horse, Caspasian knew why he had once declined an offer to join the cavalry. High off the ground, his visibility might have been improved but he felt horribly vulnerable. He was certain he could be seen for miles around and would far rather have been down in the scrub with the infantry, secreted in cover, for he knew the devastation that a well-sited machine-gun could cause. Lead was no respecter of flesh, neither a horse's nor a man's. It would chew through both with equal indifference, so at that moment Caspasian felt that a shell scrape or a foxhole would have been preferable to the saddle. However, for the next few hours speed would be the prime requirement. Rapid transit around the battlefield.

The day had dawned grey and overcast. The clouds hung low in the sky, as if sagging on moorings that were about to give way. In the distance Caspasian could see files of rain sweeping across the landscape and from the wind direction he judged that he himself was in for a soaking before the day was much older.

To right and left of him lines of mounted men waited, similarly restive and eager for the fight to begin. Caspasian had sited them in a grassy depression. On the lip of ground to their front, a scout lay on his belly keeping watch for the approach of General Mok's advance guard. Word had already been received that the entire force was once again on the march and Caspasian was suffering that private torment that afflicts every commander, at whatever level, as he waits to see how long his carefully laid plans will survive contact with a real enemy.

Caspasian's horse fidgeted. It could either sense his own disquiet or else the coming rain storm. Caspasian leaned forward and patted its powerful neck, trying to soothe the animal. Its head tossed in response, swinging up and down like an axe.

Something was wrong. Caspasian could feel it. Since first light he had felt a knot in his gut and for him that meant only one thing. All was not as it should be. Somewhere, one of the pieces was refusing to fit, but he was damned if he knew what. Again and again he had run through the battle in his own mind. Sure enough, his plans would be sorely tested once the first fire was exchanged. But he had nevertheless been confident on the previous day that he had done everything he could to ensure victory, as far as anyone ever could.

He had parted from Lilin during the night, leading his screen force out of the main camp, as she herself prepared to go with the remainder to see them all into position. As they had gone their separate ways, Caspasian had glanced back and found her watching him go. He had smiled. When she had returned it Caspasian had felt an electric shock through his body. At that moment the full significance of failure had struck Caspasian. The plan had to work. It had to. But then dawn had come up, grim and threatening. Somehow, it seemed to Caspasian that it was the sort of morning on which nothing good could happen. And with that came the unsettling disquiet.

The scout suddenly looked back and signalled frantically. Beside Caspasian, a mounted soldier, one of Yuan's officers, turned to him and said, 'It is time.'

Caspasian looked up at the sky. The rain would be upon them shortly but it was too early to say which side the bad weather would favour. Reduced visibility would impede his machine-guns and artillery, but then it would also help to cover his own withdrawal as he pulled the screen force back through the killing ground, luring

Mok's men into the trap.

With a confident glance along the lines of soldiers, Caspasian spurred his horse forward and up the slope leading out of the depression. He had armed his men with sabres wherever possible, and had ensured they had all been resupplied with ammunition and small arms captured from the Dragon. As he crested the rise the foremost elements of Mok's army came into view. Mok had chosen to push a dismounted column out in front. A mounted officer trotted formally at their head, as if leading them on to a parade ground. At the sight of Caspasian's attacking cavalry the infantry column froze. To Caspasian's surprise, instead of forming ranks and preparing to return fire, the soldiers broke in a mad panic and ran back the way they had come.

'Shit,' Caspasian muttered blackly. Clearly he was going to have his work cut out if he wanted to draw the enemy forward. An aggressive advance seemed to be the last thing on their minds. He could hardly signal a withdrawal of his own now that the enemy had chosen to run away. It would telegraph his intentions to General Mok as clearly as if he had sent him a typed dispatch outlining his entire plan.

Reluctantly Caspasian waved his men

forward. As one, they advanced in extended line, accelerating first to a trot and then a canter. The important thing now, Caspasian knew, would be to maintain control. All the men had been carefully briefed to keep glancing in to him, to watch for his signals. The worst thing would be for them to get over confident. If cohesion was lost, then so would the screen force and, with it, any chance of leading Mok into the trap whose final preparations Caspasian imagined Lilin was laying at that very moment.

He almost missed the movement from far off to his right flank. Almost, but not quite. Caspasian stared hard and saw the glint of metal once again. Then another and another until he realised what was happening. A broad sardonic smile spread across his face.

'Nice try, General Mok,' he said to himself.

He chuckled as he understood that Mok had just tried to do exactly the same as he himself. The fleeing infantry was a ruse intended to convince Caspasian's men that it was safe to pursue. Knowing that a horseman likes nothing so much as a foot soldier running away, Mok had attempted a similar ploy of his own. The outflanking manoeuvre had worked for him once, against Yuan. Clearly his tactical repertoire was so limited that he could only repeat a past success. He was unable to experiment, improvise and adapt. Mok was too confident and had acted hastily as a consequence. He had not waited for Caspasian's force to become fully engaged in a fight. Had he done so, he would have caught Caspasian's force at their moment of greatest weakness, committed to one fight, control lost in the heat of battle, and then suddenly faced with a second, fresh force attacking them from a flank.

Caspasian's hand shot up and he reined his horse to a shuddering halt. The animal bucked and reared, dancing on the spot as the rest of the mounted soldiers on either side of him stared at their English leader in consternation. Nevertheless, they followed his lead. Some of them cursed, watching the exposed backs of General Mok's hated infantry making good their escape, unpursued. However, as more and more of them noticed the same signs that had alerted Caspasian to the approaching danger, they wheeled their horses around in readiness for a withdrawal, their respect for their new leader greatly enhanced.

Sure enough, the moment their change of direction was noted by the fleeing soldiers, volleys of fire erupted from unseen infantry who had remained concealed until then, lying in wait for Caspasian's force. Fired in exasperation at the missed opportunity for slaughter, the bullets fell short, out of range. As Caspasian led his men back the way they had come, he checked behind him and saw that not only had the fleeing infantry started to regroup for a fresh advance, but that a second mounted force had emerged from wooded cover and was riding at full speed after him.

'The chase is on,' he called to those nearest him. The men grinned back, excitement having conquered fear, at least for the moment. With Caspasian at their head they felt more than capable of taking on General Mok. Their Englishman had just proved himself correct. Surely under his guidance they must succeed?

Caspasian himself found it difficult to resist the enthusiasm. He was in the middle of an armed force of several score mounted soldiers, flying across the countryside with an enemy in hot pursuit. In front of him lay the safety of prepared defensive positions and a further force much greater in numbers, lying in wait with a powerful array of weaponry. He smiled to himself as he felt the onrush of air in his face and, in it, the first drops of rain.

During the course of the next two hours the flight continued. Twice Caspasian drew his men to a halt, ordered them to dismount and hastily establish a fire line. On both occasions General Mok's pursuing cavalry ran headlong into them. Each time the enemy suffered heavy casualties, until Caspasian started to fear that his men might be doing too good a job of delaying the advance of Mok's army. The last thing he wanted was to make his enemy so wary that the advance should grind to a halt.

So, after the second successful ambush, he ordered his force to remount and led them away from the scene at a canter, resolved to make no further halts until the enemy was securely inside the middle of the nominated killing ground, and he and his men were back amongst their comrades, machine-guns and artillery ready to take over the fight.

Stretching out before Caspasian, the broad gently undulating plain lay invitingly open. At the head of his force, he cantered in the lead, giving his horse its head, exulting in the speed and onrush of rain-flecked air as he felt the animal surge into a gallop, streaking across the firm ground, racing the other beasts on either side of it. Caspasian glanced to one side at the horseman nearest him and grinned. But the man was staring ahead, his face creased into a frown. Caspasian felt a cold pang. In the successes of the past hours he had forgotten his earlier sense of unease.

Now it flooded back into him.

He followed the direction of his neighbour's attention and recoiled in horror. In the distance, stretching across the line of their retreat, rank upon rank of infantry was advancing steadily towards them. Caspasian drew his horse to a stop, his men gathering about him in a confused mass, all of them talking, calling to him, asking what was happening.

Caspasian shouted for quiet. He called for his officers and, while they were getting control of their men, took a pair of binoculars from his saddle bag and studied the advancing troops.

'Are they General Mok's?' asked one of the officers beside him.

'How ever could they have got right around us?' another said in horror. 'They can't have done. There wasn't time!'

Caspasian's expression hardened as he focused the eyepieces and scanned the approaching force from end to end.

'They're not Mok's,' he said at last. 'They're ours.' His voice was expressionless, but in his mind a torrent of questions raced.

'I don't believe it,' the officer beside him said. 'They'll ruin the whole plan. They're not supposed to attack until the enemy's been hit by our guns.'

'Look for yourself.' Caspasian handed the binoculars to him and waited as the man studied the infantry, his jaw moving soundlessly as he struggled for something to say.

From behind him Caspasian heard someone say, 'Such an important task should never have been given to a woman.'

'Lilin has let us down,' another said.

Caspasian was quick to respond. 'Shut up! We don't know what's happened.'

'Yes, but . . . the infantry? She knew the signals to launch the advance.' The man waved a hand miserably in the direction they had just come. 'The enemy's not even in the killing zone yet. They'll see it's a trap. We're finished.'

'Don't jump to conclusions,' Caspasian barked.

'Caspasian's right,' another of the officers said. 'Let's wait and see.'

'We don't have time to wait and see,' Caspasian said, glancing over his shoulder. There was no sign yet of Mok's pursuing army, but he knew they could not be far behind. Something had gone desperately wrong. He had to find out what had happened. More importantly, he had to keep his men under control. He could sense the mounting panic. It was up to him to keep a cool head and try to salvage something from the whole appalling mess.

He looked around and spotted a wood off to the flank. Turning to the senior officer present he ordered, 'Take the men into those trees and conceal yourselves until I get back, do you understand?'

The man blinked at him, still wondering whether his best chance might be to fly from the battlefield altogether.

Caspasian drew his horse close alongside and fixed the man with a cold stare. 'Listen to me. We can still win this fight. Now do as I say.'

'Where are you going?' the man answered, clearly terrified at the responsibility being placed upon him.

'To find out who ordered our men to advance.' Caspasian forced a confident smile. He raised his voice so as many as possible could hear him. 'Come on, lads. You've done a great job so far this morning. We can still win the day. Believe me.'

Most of those nearest Caspasian rallied, drawing strength from him. They turned to follow the officer into the cover of the wood, the rest of the force tagging along behind.

When the last of them had ridden past him, Caspasian spurred his horse towards the nearest of the infantry. As he approached, he was struck by their dress. In contrast to

General Mok's army, Yuan's men had barely two uniforms matching. The ranks were ragged by comparison, but Caspasian was relieved to note that at least weaponry had been greatly improved since the destruction of the Dragon and the salvage of the armaments from the wreck. In a straight face-to-face contest with General Mok's men they would nevertheless be no match. Not yet. However, that had never been his intention. Their advance should have been against a disorganised force already decimated by fire. Somehow the situation had to be reversed if tragedy was to be avoided.

Cantering up a grassy slope, Caspasian came to the first of Yuan's men. He hunted around for an officer but could not see one. He shouted to one of the men for an explanation, but his enquiry was met with a puzzled shrug. He rode further along the line of the front rank until he came to an officer.

'What the devil are you doing?' Caspasian called out to him.

The officer stared back, mystified, as if it was obvious. 'Advancing. What does it look like?'

'Who ordered you to? Was it Lilin?'

'No. Of course not. She's been relieved of command?'

Caspasian felt his blood run cold. 'Who by?'

Another officer stepped forward, smiling brightly. 'Haven't you heard? It's fantastic news!'

'What is?' Caspasian called back, fighting to control his horse who whirled on the spot, startled by the ranks of advancing foot soldiers bearing down upon it.

'Why, General Yuan, of course. He's alive. He's back with us. He's taken command again. He's in control now.'

The words almost knocked the breath out of Caspasian. 'How? When?' he stammered.

'Barely an hour ago. He arrived back in the gun line, behind the trees,' the man said, indicating the treeline out of which they had just advanced, and behind which the artillery was waiting, ready to pour its fire into the killing zone on the plain.

'But Lilin,' Caspasian stammered, 'didn't she explain the plan to him? Surely she . . .'

The officer laughed, waving aside Caspasian's question as being of no consequence now that their leader had returned safely. 'She was still siting the machine-guns. A rider has been sent to give her the good news.'

'But surely General Yuan didn't simply order you to advance without knowing the complete picture?'

'Oh, he understands all right,' the man reassured Caspasian patronisingly. 'The other Englishman is there to help him.'

Caspasian stared, dumbfounded. Speechless.

'Captain Smith,' the officer continued, as if explaining to an idiot. 'He helped General Yuan to escape. He's switched sides.' He smiled. 'You see? Everything's going to be all right now. Mok's lost his advisor. Captain Smith is now in charge of us.'

'And General Yuan?' Caspasian shouted back.

The man frowned, concerned. 'He's not very well. He's resting. But he told us to obey Captain Smith. After all, the man saved his life.'

Caspasian felt the rage building inside him. 'You fools! You complete bloody idiots! Don't you see what's happened?'

The officers stared back, their faces reddening.

'He's fooled you too. Smith hasn't changed sides at all.'

The men blinked, wondering. 'But he must have done. General Yuan said he saw Smith kill at least two of Mok's men in the course of the escape. He himself was fired upon. He's on our side now.'

'I don't care how many men Smith killed.

It means nothing to him. He'd kill his own mother if he felt it would advance his cause.' A chilling thought suddenly occurred to Caspasian. 'Is Smith still at the gun line?'

'Possibly. When we left he was preparing to move forward to join the observers in the trees.'

Caspasian whirled towards the distant trees from which the infantry had recently emerged. He could imagine Smith lying there at that very moment, watching, like a big fat cat waiting for the unsuspecting sparrow to hop right into its path. He stared back at the plain. Yuan's infantry had already entered their own killing zone and far in the distance he could see the lead elements of General Mok's army only now approaching the battlefield.

'Oh, my God,' he muttered. 'Dear God, no.'

At that moment he heard the telltale crump of an artillery gun firing from behind the woods. It was followed immediately by another and then another. The shells were in the air. Instinctively he gazed up at the cloudy sky. The rain had started to fall, heavy and persistent. He had only seconds to act.

'Get your men down! All of you!' he screamed.

The officers looked at one another. 'But our orders . . . ?'

'Do as I say! Take cover! Don't you see what's happening?'

But it was too late. With a sickening whine the first shell came screaming in, the shrill whistle growing in pitch to a demonic howl as it raced earthwards and slammed into the sodden ground just yards in front of the leading rank. Huge clods of mud spewed skywards, white-hot metal fragments of shell casing splintering in all directions. Caspasian's horse reared in terror, almost throwing him from the saddle. The infantry stared in horror, their step faltering.

A second shell drove deep into the ground and exploded in a fountain of earth, the wet clumps of soil raining down on Caspasian. A jagged shell splinter tore the lower arm from one of the soldiers. The man studied it, stupefied, blood pumping over his trousers, pink ends of bone protruding from the torn cloth and flesh.

At last the infantry broke. Some hurled themselves to the ground, hugging the wet grass and willing themselves to be invisible. Most scattered, running in all directions. Far away, behind the trees, Yuan's gunners were bending diligently to their work, feeding shell after shell into the breeches of their smoking guns, their fire directed by the commands issuing from Captain Daniel Smith forward in his observation post in the trees, their own visibility of the carnage obscured by the woods. They were completely ignorant of the destruction they were wreaking on their comrades.

Still fighting to control his horse, Caspasian took in the destruction and murder all around him. There was nothing he could do. Seeing what was happening, General Mok would wait until Yuan's artillery had further decimated his own men, and then advance to complete the slaughter. It would be a total defeat. Yuan's men were now beyond rallying. Every man was fighting for his own survival. Nor did Caspasian have any way of knowing what Lilin might be doing. For all he knew, Smith might have got hold of her too.

He looked back towards the wood where he had ordered his mounted screen force to take cover. They were the only men he could rely on for the moment. They were his last reserve. He had just one chance. There was one last ploy that just might turn the tide of the disastrous battle and save the day. Swinging his horse towards the distant hideout, Caspasian dug his heels savagely into the flanks of his terrified beast and set off across the plain. Shells were exploding on all sides now. Smith had got the range and was wreaking havoc. As if in collusion, the clouds opened and rain poured on to the plain, churning up the battlefield where Yuan's men were dying. Caspasian leaned forward in his saddle and streaked away, struggling to keep a clear head. For greater than the instinctive fear for his own safety was his concern for Lilin. He had no idea where she was. Nevertheless he had to push all thoughts of her aside. For now he had to reach his horsemen. He had to turn the tide. And there was only one way he could think of doing it.

★ ★ ★

General Mok could hardly believe his eyes. Seated comfortably on horseback in the middle of his army, he stared across the plain at the slaughter of his enemy's soldiers by their own guns.

He turned to one of his officers and pointed across the plain. 'What's going on?'

The man shrugged. 'Smith?' he ventured.

General Mok scowled. Nothing had been heard of Captain Daniel Smith since the previous evening. The man had apparently deserted. What was worse, it seemed that he had taken the prisoner Yuan with him. At first General Mok had not believed it. He had been told shortly before first light and had rushed to see the body of the guard that had been found outside the farm building where Yuan had been imprisoned. A pursuit had been launched, in the course of which another man had been killed. The awful truth that his military advisor had defected to the other side had been a bitter pill to swallow.

However, looking across the undulating grassland and watching the distant puffs of dirty grey smoke, punctured here and there with sudden spasms of flame and gouts of wet earth, hearing the muffled crumps of the exploding shells and enjoying the spectacle of tiny figures darting and dying in the heart of the maelstrom, Mok felt a flooding return of faith in his tame Englishman. What he could not fathom, assuming his suspicions were correct and that Smith was indeed behind this latest deception, was why the man had not taken him into his confidence. Why ever had he kept it a secret from his employer. Mok decided that he would have to discipline his advisor once they met up again. He could not have any man under his command simply running off and carrying out plans of their own without at least informing him. Even so, if Smith had single-handedly engineered the defeat of his enemy, General Mok would heap rewards upon him. He would give him the pick of the women. After he himself had chosen, of course.

There was a cough at his elbow and he turned to see a cluster of officers beside him. All eyes were upon him, waiting expectantly for orders. Deprived of Smith, General Mok groped for the appropriate command.

'We advance,' he said at last. It was all he could think of, having exhausted his stock of tactical alternatives with the use of the previous outflanking manoeuvre earlier in the day. It had gone badly wrong, the timing completely askew and he had watched in frustration as the mounted force of Yuan had escaped, slipping from his clutches unscathed. Now however he had the enemy where he wanted them. They lay open before him, disorganised, their numbers depleted by their own artillery fire, fit and deserving for slaughter.

With a blast of trumpets his army lurched forward. His cavalry, having received a bloody nose up until then from the retreating screen force of Yuan, had retired to lick their wounds in the rear. They would not fight again that day. They had made that clear. Well, let them sulk, General Mok mused as he allowed his own horse to lumber forward in the heart of his infantry. I'll manage without them. With the enemy so utterly routed he expected little resistance to his attack. He would advance across the plain, straight into the teeth of the enemy troops. Looking at the artillery fire, he only hoped there would be some of them left alive for his men to use their bayonets upon.

The spectacle was magnificent. This was what he lived for, General Mok reflected. He stood in the stirrups and gazed admiringly over the heads of his soldiers. Three battalions were marching in line abreast, rifles carried in the shoulder. He could hardly wait until they closed with the enemy, and for the moment when he would give the command to fix bayonets. He could almost see the forest of steel glistening into place, almost hear the rasping of blades from scabbards. The lethal points would be lowered to present the surviving enemy with a wall of steel. And then would come the slaughter. Mok himself would keep well to the rear, until such time as it was safe for him to venture forwards and perhaps indulge in a spot of cut and thrust himself.

His men knew the drill to perfection. Once all serious opposition had been silenced, a handful of near-helpless captives would be presented for their General's pleasure. A pretence of resistance would be made, but in truth it would merely be sabre practice for the General. That way he could convince himself that he had played more than a spectator's role in the engagement.

The wind played with the feathers of the plume on General Mok's new hat. To shield himself from the worst of the rain he slid inside an immense canvas cape that fastened round his neck and hung down the flanks of his horse. He thought it a shame that it hid the magnificence of his uniform and his array of medals, but decided it was better to be snug and dry inside. From a distance, the plumed *képi* protruding from the teepee-shaped cone draped across both rider and horse, presented an extraordinary sight. Mok was the only one amongst his troops so dressed. He liked that. It made him even more visible to his men. He stood out a mile.

★ ★ ★

At first Lilin had been overjoyed as she listened to the news brought by an exhausted horseman telling her of her father's escape and his arrival back in the lines. She had been with the machine-guns, siting them as Caspasian had directed. Each gun had its location that Caspasian himself had checked and marked. Lilin was meticulous in enforcing his will.

The news spread amongst the soldiers

manning the machine-guns who broke away from the task of digging pits for the guns, to dance around and slap each other on the back. Lilin fought back tears as she drank in the news. However, the moment the rider went on to tell her about the defection of Captain Daniel Smith, she almost choked. What on earth could be happening? She wished desperately for Caspasian, longing for him to tell her what to do. It might well be true that Smith had switched sides, but something deep inside her urged caution. When the rider added that Smith had asked the whereabouts of Caspasian, and had also requested Lilin's immediate presence back at the artillery position, her caution turned to alarm. She had asked why the order had not come from her father. Apparently, the rider said, he was too weakened by his ordeal to take command. Nevertheless, he had told his officers that he had every faith in Smith and had ordered them to obey Smith's every command.

There was something wrong. Lilin was sure of it. The moment she had been hailed by one of the machine-gun crews and had run across to be shown the lines of troops advancing out of the positions in which she, on Caspasian's instructions, had hidden them, she knew that her suspicions were correct. They were being double-crossed. They had been fooled by Smith.

She had watched powerless as a tiny figure on horseback had appeared over the horizon and knew without reference to binoculars who it was. She could imagine Caspasian's horror, equal to her own, at the turn of events.

Then the artillery fire had started. She had despatched the rider back to the gun line with orders to the gunners to stop firing immediately. But she had little hope that he would succeed. Smith was undoubtedly far too clever to allow that. She even tried to recall the fellow, realising that Smith would probably kill him before he could deliver her message. It was too late. In his eagerness to save his comrades, the rider had already left, riding full tilt back the way he had come. Riding to his death.

At that point Lilin had snatched up a pair of binoculars and sought out the figure of Caspasian. Hunting through the plumes of smoke and fire, she found him eventually and with immense relief saw him make good his escape. But where was he going? He knew the location of the machine-guns, where she was. Why had he not made his way there? Lilin racked her brains for an answer. Perhaps he suspected that Smith had arranged a trap to catch him there. Just as Smith was using the artillery to destroy her father's small army, so too might Caspasian think he had organised some ploy whereby he might also bring the machine-guns into play. Lilin was appalled lest Caspasian think she had somehow let him down.

She paced up and down, searching for something she could do to stop the slaughter. Perhaps she should go herself, taking her own men with her. But how could she be sure her father's men would back her? After all, she was a woman. If they had heard her father order them to obey Smith's commands, was it not likely that they would do just that? What was more, from their position they were unable to see the carnage their own guns were producing.

No, it was better that she remain where she was. At least that way she and Caspasian remained in control of the machine-guns. At least they had some firepower at their command. With her father's meagre forces already dangerously split into several groups, the largest of which was being cut down before her eyes, she and Caspasian would need all the resources they could get.

Then she realised. The screen force. Caspasian had been alone when she had seen him a moment ago. He had left them somewhere, in a position of safety. He would be going to fetch them. But to what purpose? Surely not for an assault on their own guns? No. To do that he would have to lead them through the heart of the artillery fire. He would never attempt anything so stupid. But what then?

At that moment, General Mok's army had crept into view, row upon row of ant-like figures in the distance, advancing relentlessly across the plain. Lilin felt the panic rise inside her. She was completely on her own. All around her, the machine-gunners looked to her for a lead. She could see the fear on their faces. They knew something had gone terribly wrong, and they knew that Lilin did not know what to do about it. She could see the struggle seething inside them. To run or to stand? She had to do something. Anything.

'Man your machine-guns,' she ordered, aware that her voice was quavering.

No one moved.

'Didn't you hear what I said? Man your guns.' She paused. 'Now!'

One by one, the men returned to their fire positions. None of them knew what Lilin intended. Nor did she herself. It would be suicide to engage General Mok's army by themselves, divorced from the wider plan devised by Caspasian. Their part in the operation only made sense as part of a greater whole. Now, with the other pieces blown apart, her own task had become irrelevant, superseded by events. What on earth, she wondered, was she doing slavishly sticking to it? The moment she thought of the question, she knew the answer. She was trusting Caspasian.

If he had been told that she was with the machine-guns, she knew that he would trust her to stand fast. He would trust her not to lose her nerve and run. With at least one piece of the puzzle still secure, and with a mounted reserve somewhere in hiding, it was just possible that Caspasian might yet find a way of turning the battle around. Lilin had to believe that. She did believe that. She was trusting Caspasian, because she knew that he would be trusting her.

15

Racing headlong towards the wood where he had sent the men from his screen force, Caspasian was tormented all the way by the fear that they might have fled. If so, his last hope would have gone. He would then have to seek out Lilin and make good their escape. There would be nothing more he could do. Even Yuan would probably be beyond his help.

As he approached the foremost of the trees his fear mounted. There was no sign of anyone. He called out. There was no reply. Slowing, he urged his horse carefully through the trees, ducking underneath the low-hanging branches. He called again, peering hard into the darkening interior where the trees thickened into a dense, tangled mass. To his immense relief he heard a faint answering cry from deep within the wood, followed, a moment later, by the sound of hooves. He stopped, waiting for a lone horseman to emerge from the trees. It was the officer to whom he had entrusted the force during his absence.

Caspasian sent him to bring the rest of the

men. When he had returned, bringing everyone with him, Caspasian sought out a clearing and gathered them around him. They dismounted and closed in to hear what he had to say, listening sombrely as Caspasian recounted the story of betrayal and slaughter.

'Then General Yuan is alive?' someone asked.

'It seems so. But if Smith's got him he'll be dead the moment he's served his purpose.'

'You mean the moment our men have been defeated,' the officer said grimly.

Once again Caspasian felt all eyes upon him. 'That hasn't happened yet.'

'But what's to stop it? Our main force is being butchered and Mok's army has entered the field of battle. It's now just a matter of time. Mok's got us where he wants us.'

'Which is exactly why we'll take him by surprise.'

Everyone stared at Caspasian. Before they could erupt with protests, he quickly continued. 'This is the battlefield,' he said, reaching for a stick and drawing a large circle in the dirt at his feet. 'This is our main force and these are the guns.' He drew a smaller circle to represent the men now under fire, and a line signifying the position of the artillery.

'This is where we are,' he said, scratching a

small circle well off to one flank. 'And this will be Mok's line of advance,' he added, drawing a straight line through the centre of the battlefield.

'How do you know?' the officer asked.

'Because it's the shortest route to the slaughter,' Caspasian said. 'Mok is confident. He is thirsty for blood. He will take the quickest path to the butchery.'

Everyone pushed and jostled to get a better look at the diagram. The officer snorted in derision, thinking he could read what was on Caspasian's mind. The small circle of their hideout lay to one side of the line of Mok's advance.

'How can we possibly take them in the flank? Even if they still don't know we're here, and even if they don't send out a clearing patrol to check the wood's free of their enemies before they pass by, even if all of that goes in our favour, we'll be a force of ... what? ... barely more than a hundred attacking an army of several thousand. Sure, we would inflict casualties, but eventually they'd soak us up like a sponge. Their giant sponge to deal with our tiny puddle. Even if every single one of our shots counted, we haven't got enough bullets amongst the lot of us to kill them all.' He stood back, arms folded defiantly across his chest.

Caspasian smiled. 'We haven't got to kill them all. We've only got to kill one of them. Mok.' The moment he said it he knew he had their attention. 'In fact, we haven't even got to kill him. Just frighten him.' He grinned innocently. 'And how difficult do you think that can be?'

Some of the men laughed. Caspasian ignored the continuing doubt written for all to see on the senior officer's face.

'A very long time ago, there was a great warrior. A great commander. His name was Alexander. One day he found himself in a situation a bit like this. He found himself facing an army many, many times larger than his own. It was at a place called Gaugamela, thousands of miles to the west of here. But he gambled on two things. He gambled that Darius, the enemy commander, was unused to close combat and would panic if directly threatened, and he gambled that his own men were more courageous and committed than the enemy. In both instances he was right.'

'So what happened?' the officer asked, becoming interested.

'While Darius' army was occupied elsewhere, their attention fixed on other things happening around the battlefield, Alexander led his body of hand-picked cavalry, his Companions, in a charge straight at Darius and the men surrounding him. He ignored everything else. He had chosen Darius himself as the one weak point in a massive army, the link in the chain that was most likely to break. And it did. Had Darius stood his ground, it would have been a very different story. But Alexander's gamble paid off. When Darius saw Alexander and his cavalry coming straight at him, cutting their way through his bodyguard, he panicked, turned and fled.'

'But his army,' the officer asked. 'Surely if they were that big they could still have defeated this Alexander?'

'Not at all. Everything hinges on morale,' Caspasian answered. 'On the belief we all have in ourselves. When Darius' men saw their leader turn and run, their morale broke and they too began to run. First in twos and threes, and then in a flood. It was a tremendous victory for Alexander.' He paused, letting his message sink in, reading the effect on the faces about him. 'And we are going to do exactly the same.'

The officer studied the diagram on the ground thoughtfully and then said, 'But if Mok runs away, we'll just have to fight him another day. He'll regroup and come back. Maybe it'll take him a week, maybe a month, or a year.' He shrugged. 'Where's the victory in that? You'll be gone by then and there'll be no one to help us.'

Caspasian smiled. 'No. We're going to finish this today. Once and for all.' He looked around at the men gathered on all sides. 'You want your families to live in peace, don't you? You want to tend your farms and raise your children. For that you need stability. That's why, when we bear down on Mok, we're going to wait until he reaches here.' He stooped and drew a broad swathe in the dirt. 'There's a re-entrant here, on the far side of the plain. We'll wait until Mok's army is opposite the mouth of that, and then charge. The re-entrant will offer Mok a perfect line of escape. It will be too tempting to ignore.'

A light dawned on the officer's face and he beamed with sudden understanding. 'The machine-guns!' he said, impressed.

'Exactly. That is where I told Lilin to place the machine-guns. From the heights above the re-entrant they have excellent fields of fire right down it and across the plain. Anyone trying to move in that direction will be walking into the teeth of fire from all the Maxims and Vickers guns we captured from the Dragon.'

'But how can we be sure they're there and in position?' someone asked.

'Because Lilin will have seen to it,'

Caspasian said simply. His answer proved good enough for everyone.

Leaving the men to sort out their equipment and prepare their weapons, Caspasian made his way back to the edge of the wood. He fastened the reins of his horse to a branch and moved cautiously through the last of the bushes, ensuring he remained out of sight to anyone scanning the woods. He took out his binoculars and focused them on Mok's army. It was making rapid progress across the plain, haste thrusting aside caution. They were eager to close with their enemy and enjoy the slaughter. They could taste blood and feel the resistance of flesh on their bayonets.

The foremost ranks had already bypassed Caspasian's wood some five hundred yards distant, advancing in line abreast. Their rapid pace had messed up their parade-ground dressing and the ragged lines were becoming ever more disorganised with every passing minute. Behind the lead battalions, and roughly central, Caspasian could see General Mok and his immediate entourage. The plumed *képi* and beige-coloured cape made him stand out like a beacon.

To the rear, a further two battalions came on. There was no sight of any cavalry. Caspasian smiled with relief. He searched for them everywhere but they had clearly had enough earlier in the day. He knew that Mok would regret allowing them to retire and sit out the rest of the battle, licking their wounds. They were the one element capable of spoiling Caspasian's plan. With Mok's cavalry arm out of the fight, and with the infantry formations becoming ever more broken, the way straight to General Mok lay open.

Movement in the trees behind Caspasian told him that his men were ready. On either side, mounted soldiers moved up beside him, pushing through the boughs and branches. Sabres rasped from scabbards, the steel honed to a fine white edge. Pistols and revolvers were hefted, magazines and cylinders fully charged with bullets. Carbines were checked. The sights set, safety catches flicked off, ready for action. Hand grenades were prepared, the pins pinched tight for easy extraction, and then stowed in pockets, ready to blast a way through to the enemy leader.

The men were ready. Caspasian had fired their imaginations. He had given them a glimpse of hope like a patch of blue sky spotted through a break in the sombre clouds from which the rain still poured. The rain that would hide the sound of their approach until it was too late. The men were thinking of their families and of their farms. Somehow they had to save them from destruction. The old plan lay in ruins, shredded by Smith's murderous cunning. But Caspasian had fashioned it anew, reassembling the surviving parts into a new and even more devious and deadly shape.

Caspasian retrieved his horse, mounted and moved to the centre of the line. He waited a few minutes more, wiping the rain from his face. It was cold but refreshing. He could not remember when he had last slept, but now the rain awakened him. He felt alive and ready for anything. He could feel the energy coursing through his limbs. His heartbeat quickened and he deepened his breathing to control his excitement. Deep down he felt, as always before combat, the corrupting effects of fear, working away at his cool confidence like heat melting ice. But he knew that was as it should be. For the fear would promote caution and counter the recklessness. He had little use for blind courage or bravado. A cool nerve and a clear head had proved themselves superior time and time again. And so it would prove again. He knew it.

With a final check of his bridle, stirrups and holster, Caspasian gathered his reins in one fist, lightly kicked his horse's flanks with his heels and coaxed it forward, out of the wood. On either side, the lines of mounted soldiers mirrored him, the whole force emerging from the trees like a long, slender blade being unsheathed. The rain fell upon them and they narrowed their eyes into it, settling upon their distant target. Caspasian drew his sabre and motioned for his men to advance.

★ ★ ★

General Mok's men could hardly contain themselves. Even their officers had stopped urging them to keep in line, equally as eager as the men under their command to close with the helpless enemy upon whom they could still see the artillery fire falling. Now they were much closer, they could feel the ground reverberating with the crump and crash of the exploding shells. They could hear the whine and rush as the rounds shrieked out of the dark clouds like bolts of lightning hurled down by malevolent gods. It was spectacular. The more so because they had a grandstand view as they crossed the plain, stepping out with a lively gait, anxious to get there while there was still someone alive for their swords, bayonets and rifle butts.

General Mok himself even considered

riding on ahead but his innate, though unadmitted, cowardice held him behind the forward elements of his infantry. Throughout the army however, there was an almost palpable thirst for blood. Rushing headlong towards the shell-churned earth, they resembled an assembly of gluttons bearing down on a free lunch.

The grass was now sodden and on all sides men were slipping, boots and sandals scoring streaks of viscous mud. The noise of the bombardment was now loud enough to drown out almost everything else. It sent a thrill through General Mok and he shifted impatiently in his saddle, willing his foot soldiers forward. He scowled at them ferociously. Why did he not have his cavalry with him? They were as useless as the infantry. Everyone always let him down. He wished he could kill everyone.

The rain drummed on his cape but underneath he remained dry. Huge drops bounced off the taut canvas, coursing in rivulets down the beige fabric and on to the ground where his horse's hooves cavorted, each crashing step churning up fresh mud.

He reached up a hand through one of the slits in his cape and wiped the water from his eyes. He tossed his head, seeing a fine spray burst from his plume. Something caught his attention at the periphery of his vision. He turned towards it but a sudden flurry of rain struck him full in the face. Angrily he wiped it away, then cupped his hand to the peak of his *képi*, shielding his eyes to see more clearly.

'Excellent!' he boomed. He turned to an officer riding beside him and grinned delightedly. 'My cavalry! Now we can get a move on.'

The officer followed the direction of the General's pointing finger and stared. His face blanched. 'They're not ours.'

'Don't be stupid. Who else could they be?' General Mok said gruffly, turning to study the horsemen more closely, a tingle of concern running down his spine. He reined in his horse, gripping its flanks with his knees as the beast skidded on the slippery turf. By the time he was able to examine the approaching horde again he was startled to see how much ground they had covered. They were closing at full pelt. Because of the rain he found it difficult to identify their uniforms. Oddly, they did not even seem to be wearing the same dress as each other. Each one appeared to be different and generally quite ragged. Also, instead of riding in column as would cavalry who were coming to rejoin the main army, they were galloping in extended line as for a charge. In fact, as he looked closer, he saw that it was an arrowhead formation, the centre-most point protruding ahead of the rest like a flock of wild geese, and aimed straight for him. Leading it was a single horseman. Mok felt himself go cold as he recognised the tall figure, a blade glinting dangerously in his fist.

'Turn the men round!' he screamed at everyone and no one in particular. 'Get one of the battalions to face about. Get some fire down on them. Quick!'

His horse sensed his panic and gambolled and bucked. General Mok struggled for control, his arms getting tangled up in the voluminous cape. He drew the riding crop that was thrust under his saddle but when he tried to thrash the animal, the layers of canvas restricted his frantic swipes.

As Caspasian's cavalry assault closed, the right flank of the battalion closest to him began to wheel round to face this new and unexpected threat. In the wet grass and churning mud, the soldiers' feet slithered, some of them spinning to the ground. The battalion's left flank, on the other hand, never heard the order. The rain whipped away the words of command the second they were spoken and the troops marched merrily on, ignorant of the attack coming in from the side, and of the gap that their forward march was gradually opening in the middle of their formation, widening with every step that took them away from their comrades.

Watching anxiously with mounting panic, General Mok saw that Caspasian had noticed the breach and was heading straight for it, and behind him, the entire arrowhead formation wheeled smoothly into the slight change of direction.

'Stop, you idiots!' General Mok screamed as the vast bulk of his army marched on across the plain. 'About turn! About turn!'

He managed to free some of the buttons of his cape, struggling to get an arm free. A gust of wind leapt inside and the great sheet of wet canvas whipped and snapped, slapping him across the face and winding itself around his head. Letting go of the reins, he snatched at it, tugging it loose. Relieved to be free of its rider's irritating commands, his horse bolted, taking off across the plain, the blinded General Mok lurching wildly from side to side, his enraged screams muffled by the wet canvas gag.

Some of the soldiers nearest to him heard the commotion and turned to see what was going on. One glance took in the surging force of cavalry now just yards away from the breach in the disorganised battalion, and the mounted figure of General Mok, apparently fleeing in the opposite direction. Terror spread like a breeze through standing wheat. One or two of the officers, seeing what was happening, attempted to rally groups of men to face the new threat, but most of them absorbed the sight of charging cavalry and ran. Rifles were an encumbrance and soldiers hurled them aside, shrugging off packs and wriggling out of webbing straps and ammunition pouches, stripping themselves of anything that impeded their flight.

At the head of his cavalry, Caspasian hurtled through the gap in the infantry. Behind him, his men followed. At the outer edges of his formation, where the arrowhead was widest, galloping horsemen crashed headlong into foot soldiers, trampling them beneath their hooves and continuing on without faltering. Caspasian's eyes were fixed on one person. General Mok. He was barely a hundred yards away now. But while most of the General's men were fleeing, sufficient of them had regrouped and started to return fire to make the air around him crackle, alive with bullets. Caspasian ducked low, laying himself along his horse's foam-streaked neck. In his right fist, the sabre waited, tip down, inches off the ground, its blade honed and ready.

With a flurry of blows and punches, General Mok fought free of the encircling cape. The first thing he saw was Caspasian streaking towards him, the intervening ground alarmingly void of obstacles. With a shriek of terror, he gathered up his reins, drove his spurs into his horse's flanks and set off. Galloping along the rear ranks of his disintegrating battalions, he shot past his startled men, the furthest of whom had still not realised why their companions were running, nor why they themselves were taking off after them. Then they saw Caspasian and his men and understood.

Without time to think or consider his options, General Mok took the line of least resistance. This led him between two low hills. It was only after several minutes that he realised it was not a valley but a re-entrant that was getting ever narrower the further he rode into it. Not only was it shrinking in front of him, but the ground had also begun to slope upwards as if he was riding into a giant scoop. His horse pounded on, its hooves slipping every few paces on the wet grass. He had made good progress and, turning to look over his shoulder at his pursuers, was delighted to see that Caspasian had been delayed by a resolute band of infantry. He appeared to be hacking his way through them, but the delay had enabled Mok to pull ahead. He had not yet cleared the far side of his own army and, in front of him, he could see a large number of his men running up the slope towards the head of the re-entrant.

The next moment, tongues of flame sparkled along the lip of the high ground to his front and General Mok watched in horrified wonder as his men toppled and fell in droves before him. His horse stopped as if it had run into a barn door, rearing up on to its hind legs. General Mok clung to its neck but, soaked with rain and sweat, his efforts were pointless. His boots slipped out of the stirrups and he slid over the beast's rump and on to the churned grass. The moment it was free of its burden, the horse cantered out of reach. General Mok screamed after it, jogged a few steps, and then gave up with a stream of abuse. A burst of machine-gun fire brought him to his senses and he hurled himself to the ground, mud covering the front of his uniform and oozing across the array of medals. He pushed his *képi* back on his head and looked up the slope to his front.

'Attack! Attack!' he screamed at his men, waving them on.

Trapped between Caspasian's cavalry charge and the machine-gun fire, the army of General Mok seethed in a confused mass. The bullets from their own Maxims and Vickers, captured from the Dragon, tore through their shattered ranks, while at their backs Caspasian and his men cut and slashed and drove them on, herding them forward like cattle into the abattoir.

On the ridgeline, Lilin crouched behind one of the sand-bagged machine-gun positions and swept her binoculars across the battlefield. Extending to either side of her, the machine-guns were at work. Firing pins hammered frenetically at the belts of ammunition fed to them by the gun Number Twos. Behind each gun, the Number One sat or knelt, head and shoulders hunched forward, eyes squinting down the sights, peering through the cloud of gun smoke at the dancing figures several hundred yards away where the bullets peppered the earth.

On Caspasian's instructions, she had placed each of the guns about twenty yards apart, so the overall line of a dozen or so weapons extended nearly three hundred yards, virtually the full length of the ridgeline.

She had sited herself roughly in the centre to make control as easy as possible. At the very head of the re-entrant, she had the best view down to the plain below and, looking now through her binoculars, she could see Caspasian cutting his way through towards her. When he had first charged, she had been unable to see what was going on. The rain had just thickened and obscured her view of the far side of the plain. General Mok's army was passing below and she had been in a storm of indecision, whether to open fire and kill as many of them as possible before they could redeploy and destroy her and the guns, or whether to allow them to pass, perhaps leading her men on an escape to live and fight another day.

The first she knew of Caspasian's attack was when she saw those troops nearest to her break away from their battalions and head in her direction. For a moment she had thought that someone had spotted her and she had almost given the order to open fire then. It would have been disastrous as Mok's men would have received warning of the machine-gun positions early enough to allow them to choose an alternative withdrawal route.

Just then however, she had seen the panicked form of General Mok and, almost immediately afterwards, other mounted figures pursuing him. It had not taken her long to identify Caspasian and now that the machine-guns were thundering on either side of her, she sought him out again. His own men had caught up with him and seemed to be holding their own. Mok's men were fighting for their lives. They were no longer trying to defeat their enemy.

Lilin scanned the turmoil in the re-entrant and, at last, settled upon one small figure hugging the ground. General Mok.

She reached across and tapped the nearest gunner on the shoulder. 'There,' she shouted above the noise. She pointed, her arm rigidly indicating General Mok until she saw the gunner's mouth crease into a smile of understanding.

He swung the barrel of his gun round, shifting his backside behind it, steadying himself in the new position ready for the engagement. He sat upright, craning to ensure the barrel alignment was correct, and then bent to squint through the sights. When he was happy with the aim, he gripped the two wooden handles and his thumb pressed the firing button on the rear of the gun. The Vickers jumped into action, shuddering heavily on its tripod as it hammered out its lethal message.

The gun Number Two fed the cloth ammunition belt into the breech. On the far side of the gun, a steady stream of hot empty brass cases cascaded on to the pile that the earlier fire had already produced. The corrugated metal casing on the water-cooled barrel had grown so hot that rain falling on it hissed and steamed. From the fiery muzzle, shrouded in a cordite mist, the stream of lead was completely invisible. It was only at the far end of the gun's trajectory, where the bullets impacted on the ground, that the effects of the fire could be seen.

Lilin gripped her binoculars and stared hard at the point where she had seen General Mok. For a moment she was unable to find him again, but then she saw him. He was hugging the ground even tighter, as all around him the ground looked as if it was alive. Solid earth had become like water in heavy rain. Each of the hundreds of bullets produced its own tiny eruption, the whole mass combining to terrible effect. Yet somehow he survived. The man had a charmed life, clinging to it as desperately as he clung to the torn earth.

There was a cry from beside Lilin and she looked up to see the gun Number Two pointing in alarm. Caspasian's men had reached the mouth of the re-entrant and were in danger of running into the fire from their own machine-guns. Reluctantly Lilin ordered the gunner to switch his fire away from General Mok. Along the ridgeline, the other guns did likewise, swinging their barrels to fire on targets closer to them. The enemy was running in every direction now. As Lilin surveyed the slaughter, she prayed for an end.

★ ★ ★

Caspasian was hunting for Mok. The tide had been turned. He could sense it. He had been through enough battles to know the moment a force's morale breaks. They had almost reached the stage where there was no more point to the killing. But first he had to see to Mok.

The fleeing foot soldiers were no longer bothering to fire at Caspasian or his cavalry. They were too intent on escape. Caspasian's force had lost cohesion too. From a solid arrowhead they had fragmented into splinters once they had crashed through the infantry's broken screen. Now he could see them in twos and threes across the battlefield, wreaking the revenge they had longed for and expunging the last of the fear they had felt for months, working it out on the running enemy soldiers with sabre and gun.

Caspasian was halfway along the re-entrant when he heard the sound of someone ranting. He stood in the stirrups and hunted for the source. The mud-covered, tottering figure that caught his attention was barely recognisable as General Mok. He was raging. His hat was gone, and brown, dripping medals and braid hung from his torn jacket like parts of his own body. He seemed to be talking to himself, but as Caspasian approached he looked up and saw him. He blinked, not recognising the mounted figure at first. Caspasian wondered if the man's mind had gone. But then he saw recognition register on the General's face. He saw a hatred so intense it convulsed General Mok in a fresh torrent of abuse, the words spitting from his swollen, split and filthy lips with uncontrollable passion.

Caspasian nudged his horse forwards and as he did so Mok suddenly seemed to remember something. He fumbled with his holster, his fingers fighting through the mud encrusting the buckle fastening the flap.

'You!' he screamed, apoplectic. Rage had conquered fear. 'I'll kill you!'

Caspasian drew his own revolver. 'Don't, General Mok,' he commanded, his voice carrying easily across the intervening, body-strewn ground. 'Surrender and I'll let you live.'

It was as if he had not spoken. Either that or Mok had been deafened by the din of battle. But the gun in Caspasian's fist was plain enough to see, the barrel levelled at Mok's chest.

Instead Mok continued the struggle, finally managing to get the holster open, but almost dropping the pistol in the mud as he drew it.

'Mok!' Caspasian shouted, bringing his own revolver into the aim.

Mok's fists worried over the grip, his lips working all the time, uttering new obscenities. He swung the gun up and blazed off a wild shot, the bullet going wide of the mark.

Caspasian fired a shot of his own, a warning round that skimmed inches past Mok's right shoulder. He knew that Mok might not be capable of hitting him but it would only take one lucky shot, and Caspasian was not prepared to risk it. Not for Mok. Caspasian was too far away to try anything fancy. No time for wounding shots. The next one would have to count, and the only worthwhile point of aim for a handgun was the centre of the target's chest. Caspasian took aim.

Mok raised his pistol, firing as he did so. Three shots cracked, the first two Mok's, the third and last, Caspasian's. The bullet knocked Mok backwards off his feet. Caspasian nudged his horse towards him, holding his aim. Mok raised his head and looked at Caspasian with hatred. His right arm, still clutching the pistol, twitched and came up, the weapon waggling uncertainly. As Caspasian saw the General's finger tightening on the trigger for another shot, he fired his revolver. The bullet smashed a hole in Mok's forehead and the General fell back with a splash into the mud.

Caspasian felt every muscle in his body go limp. He slumped in the saddle, exhaustion rushing to embrace him. His eyelids suddenly felt like weights and he knew that he could sleep for a week. Sporadic bursts of gunfire brought him to his senses and reminded him that he was still in the middle of the enemy. Even a beaten opponent could fire a parting shot. It was no time to relax his guard.

He scanned the re-entrant. The machine-guns had mostly fallen silent. Only on the right flank, where the last of Mok's infantry was still visible disappearing across the plain, did a brace of Maxims chatter after them, snapping at their heels.

Suddenly someone was running at Caspasian. Alert, he swung round to see Lilin coming towards him. He swung his left leg over the horse's neck and slid to the ground as she ran the final yards and threw herself at him.

'Lilin,' he said quietly as she hugged him.

She pulled back to look at him, her arms still round his neck. There were tears in her eyes. 'You did it,' she said.

Caspasian smiled, tired to his bones. 'Your father,' he said. 'We must get to him.'

She shook her head, turning to beckon

forward a horseman. 'It's all right. He's safe.' She looked to the messenger. 'Tell him,' she said.

The man nodded. 'It's true. General Yuan's alive and well.'

'But Smith?' Caspasian asked doubtfully.

'Gone.' The man smiled. Seeing the question on Caspasian's lips he went on. 'The General recovered and found out what was happening to his men. He discovered the guns were firing on our own troops and he ordered them to stop. When the guns fell silent and Smith saw your attack on Mok, he fled.'

Caspasian's face tightened. 'How?'

The man reddened. 'He was directing the fire from the treeline. We were on the far side of the woods. General Yuan sent men forward to seize him. By the time they got there he had managed to give them the slip in the thick of the woods. We've got men out hunting for him now.'

'Double your efforts,' Caspasian ordered, although in his heart he knew that they had little or no chance of finding Smith. He would have made sure of his escape route. Caspasian knew that by now he would be far away, looking out for himself, just as he always had done.

Wearily, with one arm tightly around

Lilin's waist, he gathered up the reins of his horse and started away from the battlefield. There were numerous tasks to be done. The men had to regroup, the wounded had to be cared for, prisoners had to be guarded, arms and equipment gathered up, and a thousand and one other things. But for now he just wanted to be alone with Lilin. The battle was over. They were alive. The other tasks could wait.

16

In the days that followed, nothing more was heard of Captain Daniel Smith. Caspasian ensured that patrols were sent out to cover every stretch of ground. Pickets were positioned to watch every likely escape route and farmers were questioned and told to look out for the rogue Englishman. General Yuan offered a reward but it was all to no avail. Smith had vanished as if into thin air.

Someone suggested that perhaps he had been caught up in the chaos of the rout and had died. Caspasian thought otherwise. He could not help feeling that at some point their paths would cross again.

'I can't believe I fell for it,' General Yuan said from his sickbed.

Sitting beside him, Lilin placed her hand consolingly on his. 'Don't blame yourself, Father. You were very confused and weakened. You weren't to know.'

Yuan shook his head angrily. 'I should have done. I trusted him. I believed he really did want to help us.' He chuckled. 'I believed his word, given as an English gentleman.'

'That's the last thing Daniel Smith ever

was,' Caspasian said bitterly.

'Do you suppose General Mok was in on it too?' Lilin asked.

Caspasian shrugged. 'Who knows? I doubt it. Smith was probably hedging his bets, positioning himself so that he could jump either way. The destruction of the Dragon must have alarmed him. He probably realised that throwing in his lot with General Mok might not have been such a wise move after all. By seeming to rescue your father he was balancing between the two sides. Had Mok won, Smith could have said that it was due to his efforts. Had your father won, he would have claimed the credit for that too.'

'How? After the slaughter with the artillery?'

'Up until then, Smith had been playing it by ear. He didn't know our strengths. He only knew that we had managed to defeat Mok's armoured train, the General's prize possession. However, once he got your father back to the gun line and saw how weak we were in comparison to Mok's army, he made up his mind. You and I were both away, your father was in no state to take command, so Smith thought he saw a way of winning the battle for his old boss. Imagine Mok's gratitude if he had won! Smith would have had anything he wanted.'

From his bed General Yuan laughed. 'Well he'll be lucky to have a bowl of rice now. He's alone in the middle of China and he's on the run.'

'Where do you think he'll head for?' Lilin asked.

Caspasian walked across to the window and leaned on the sill. It was a bright sunny day and everywhere he looked people were starting to get their lives back to normal. 'Hong Kong maybe. Perhaps Shanghai. Who knows?'

'There'll be nowhere for him to hide,' Yuan said confidently.

Caspasian smiled. 'I'm afraid I don't agree. There'll be a hundred people ready to employ a man like that.'

Lilin stood up and joined Caspasian. 'Well, he's out of our lives, and that's all that matters,' she said brightly. She was about to place an arm around Caspasian's waist but stopped herself, aware of her father's eyes upon them.

General Yuan looked carefully at Caspasian before speaking. 'And what about yourself? What will you do now?'

Caspasian turned from the window, leaning back against the sill, folding his arms reluctantly across his chest when he would far rather have put them around Lilin who stood awkwardly at his side. She moved a step away, arms similarly folded.

'I'm not sure. I suppose I'll have to return to Shanghai.'

'That won't be easy,' Yuan said. 'You were sent here to make an ally of General Mok for the British. Instead you killed him and saved his enemy.'

Caspasian sighed and ran a hand through his hair. 'Yes, I did rather, didn't I?'

'What will they do to you?'

Caspasian thought. 'Chuck me out perhaps.' He smiled. 'There are worse fates.'

Lilin moved a pace away from him before saying, 'You could always stay here.' He tried to appear unconcerned.

General Yuan watched the two of them closely, his mouth set in a straight line. 'I don't think that would be a very good idea, do you, Captain Caspasian?' he said evenly.

Caspasian sunk his hands in his pockets. 'No.' He turned to Lilin. 'I'll have to go back at some point.'

'What for?' she protested.

'To explain why I acted as I did.'

'That's madness!'

General Yuan watched his daughter and did not like what he was seeing. 'The Captain's right, my dear,' he said. 'He has to clear his name. If he doesn't, the British will probably send someone to fetch him.' He looked at Caspasian and added firmly, 'Won't they?'

'Your father's right, Lilin,' Caspasian said. 'I've got to go.'

'When?' she asked miserably, fighting to keep her feelings hidden from her father.

Caspasian looked out of the window again. 'In a day or two.' In the courtyard below, a pile of captured weapons had been stacked. Half a dozen of Yuan's men were sorting them, separating the ones that were still serviceable from the ones that could only be cannibalised for spare parts. A large number of Mok's men had been taken prisoner and even more had surrendered in the days immediately after the battle. Their choices had been stark, either to wander the countryside and starve or fall victim to one of the numerous bandit gangs roaming the province, or else throw themselves on the mercy of the victor, offering their services to him as their replacement employer. These were now being drilled on the fields beyond the courtyard and Caspasian could hear the distant words of command echoing faintly off the walls of the surrounding farm buildings.

Strangely, the atmosphere was one of peace. With their enemy defeated, Yuan's men had gone quickly back to their old lives. They had crops and cattle to tend and the many tales of famine ravaging other parts of China were a spur to hard work. They would not let their children starve like so many others elsewhere. Caspasian had given them this chance and they were all seizing it with both hands.

'Will you excuse me, Father?' Lilin said, leaving the room quickly, a stiff smile hiding the turmoil inside her.

Yuan bowed his head slightly and watched her go. When the door had closed behind her he stared at Caspasian.

'I suppose, as the traditional Chinese father, I should be outraged,' he began. From his place by the window Caspasian tried to match Yuan's even gaze, knowing what was coming, but he could feel himself starting to squirm. To his immense relief the General abruptly changed his tack.

'But then my daughter has never been traditional, as you have gathered.' General Yuan sighed, unable to maintain the severity of his tone. 'Furthermore, I owe you a great debt of gratitude, both I myself and everyone under my care. It would be churlish to be angry with you. Worse than churlish. After all, you have saved us.' He held up his hands in a helpless gesture that made Caspasian feel worse than ever.

'General, I never meant any insult to . . . '

General Yuan instantly held up a hand for silence. 'I have also seen more of the world than most supposedly traditional Chinese patriarchs. I know that the values of an old order always change, however difficult those changes might be to handle.'

Caspasian writhed inwardly. Whether the General had intended it or not, he had succeeded in making Caspasian feel that he had abused his hospitality.

'I would ask only one thing,' the General continued. 'Please keep your relationship with my daughter discreet. If you have to be lovers, please do not flaunt it for everyone to see. Do not make me lose face.'

Caspasian blushed to the roots of his hair. 'General, what can I say?'

'Just say that you will exercise discretion.'

'Of course,' Caspasian stammered. 'Anything you say.'

General Yuan gently punched his pillows and eased himself down in his bed. 'And now, go. I am very tired.' He smiled. 'Besides, I think Lilin would like to see you.'

Caspasian went quickly from the room to look for Lilin but she had disappeared. He knocked lightly on her door but there was no answer. He turned the knob and went in. The room was empty. Outside in the courtyard he asked one of Yuan's soldiers whether he had seen her.

The man looked up from the pile of captured rifles he was working through. 'She was on horseback. That way,' he said, pointing out of the gate towards the road that led to the hills.

'Thank you.' Caspasian walked briskly to the stables, resisting the urge to run. He found his horse in its stall, the saddle and bridle hanging on pegs beside it. By the time he rode out of the gate he estimated that she must be at least a couple of miles away.

Heading in the direction the soldier had indicated, he rode hard and was surprised when, after only a couple of minutes, he saw Lilin a little way ahead of him. She was riding slowly, her horse walking alongside a small plantation of young silver birch saplings that had been planted only a few years before to act as a windbreak for one of the fields. Caspasian slowed as he approached her, drawing gently alongside. She glanced over at him and smiled.

'He knows about us,' Caspasian said.

'Of course he does. My father knows me too well for me to be able to hide anything from him. Especially something like this.'

'I'm sorry.'

'What for?'

'I don't want to cause any trouble between

you and your father,' Caspasian said.

'You haven't. I live my own life. I always have done and he knows that.'

They had reached a bend in the track. Lilin stopped and slid from her horse. 'Come with me. I've got something to show you.'

Caspasian dismounted and together they led their horses into the trees, Caspasian following Lilin as she sought out an almost imperceptible path. 'This way,' she said at last.

The path was heavily overgrown and as she went Lilin pushed aside the brightly coloured branches of the saplings. Behind the screen of birch were older trees, the tops so thick that only moss could grow on the ground between the stout trunks. The light that fought its way through was sparse, and the air warm and moist. The whispering sound of the silver birch seemed a long way away, replaced by an eerie stillness.

Suddenly Caspasian became aware of another sound. Water. A moment later they were standing beside a small stream, narrow but vigorous. The mossy banks overhung the sides, trailing green fingers in the clear water. Lilin fastened her horse's reins to a branch, and then took Caspasian's and did the same.

'It's just over here,' she said.

Caspasian was wondering what he was

417

about to be shown but remained silent. He felt that Lilin was about to entrust him with a secret.

They jumped across the stream and walked the last few yards around a small tree-covered knoll. Behind it were the tumbled ruins of a building. The stones were green with lichen and moss, and clearly it had not been occupied for a very long time. Lilin stood to one side and smiled.

'My castle,' she announced.

Caspasian laughed, understanding. He walked around it slowly, inspecting it. 'I had a place like this when I was a boy,' he said. 'Up on the bluff overlooking Yokohama. A place where no one else came. Just me.'

'I knew you'd understand,' Lilin said. She came to him and they held each other, Lilin's head against his chest. 'I found it many years ago. I used to come here whenever times were hard, or just when I wanted to be alone. I came here when my mother died.'

Caspasian stroked her hair. It was soft, warm after the ride in the light outside the trees. She put back her head and he kissed her on the mouth. He drew her gently to the ground, the spongy moss soft as a mattress. They knelt in front of each other and she watched him, amused, as he opened her blouse and slid it from her shoulders. He cupped her breasts in his hands and bent to kiss the nipples, one after the other. Lilin sighed deeply. She wriggled her knees from under her and lay back.

Caspasian gazed at her, mesmerised. The ancient building smelt strangely of wine, a ripe, rich heady scent that told a story of its own. It filled their nostrils, pungent and dark, as Caspasian stroked her body, feeling her move beneath his hands and lips. He wanted to caress every inch of her but impatience got the better of them both. They laughed as they felt it taking possession of them with the force of flood water, pressing at the river banks until fit to burst.

They lay together for a long time afterwards, the moss cool on their skin. Through the trees they could hear the horses, impatient, growing troubled by the absence of their riders. Bridles tinkled like wind-chimes and from further away the noise of the saplings sounded like a pebbled shore as the wind strengthened. In the older trees around the two still figures, boughs that had grown entangled creaked like sailing ships, wood scarring wood.

Caspasian eased on to his back, gathering Lilin to him to keep her warm. He could feel the goose bumps on her flesh as the breeze dried the perspiration coating her.

'We'd better go,' he said at last.

'Why?'

'I don't know,' he laughed. 'It seemed the right thing to say.'

Lilin ran her fingertips down his chest and stomach. Caspasian shivered. 'What are we going to do?' she asked.

'Your father wants me to leave.'

'But what do you want?'

Caspasian was silent, thinking, aware of the tension that had crept into Lilin's body.

'I could come with you,' she said.

He turned his face to her. 'I was hoping you would.'

'Then why didn't you ask me?'

'I don't know what's waiting for me when I get back. At the moment you're safe here. I don't want to put you at risk.'

Lilin laughed. 'Haven't I proved I can cope with risk?'

'You've more than proved it,' Caspasian answered. 'But Shanghai's just as dangerous as any battlefield. If anything, it's more so. Don't forget the Green Gang. Old Fatso will be waiting.'

'I know,' she said, her voice resolute.

'And that doesn't scare you?'

'Of course it does.'

'Thank God for that,' Caspasian said.

Lilin stroked back the hair from Caspasian's forehead. 'Do you think Smith will be waiting for you.'

Without pause Caspasian answered, 'That depends on whether he thinks he'll be able to destroy me or not.'

Lilin frowned, puzzled. 'Why does he hate you? And why do you hate him?'

Caspasian gazed up through the trees. Faintly, through the sounds of the wood, the stream, the impatient horses, he could hear other sounds. Remembered sounds. Lilin nuzzled closer to him, folding one leg across his. Waiting.

★ ★ ★

Redoubt Isis became visible at dawn like a ghost ship emerging from a thick sea mist. All that was missing was the fog horn, Caspasian thought, as he stood on the duck boards, slapping himself warm. He stamped his feet, small, fast steps like a Red Indian dance, and every time, liquid mud squelched up between the rotting wooden struts, adding to the foul coating already cloying his boots.

It had almost become meaningless to speak of Redoubt Isis when referring to the muddled patchwork of broken trenches, torn wire and shattered bunkers that had once been a cohesive defensive structure. Over the past days the redoubt had been subjected to one savage bombardment after another, each rolling into the next with only the briefest of pauses for the German gunners to dig their guns out of the mountains of empty shell cases that threatened to engulf them. But then, with fresh rounds carried to the gun lines by mule and porter, the bombardment would begin anew.

With all withdrawal routes out of the redoubt severed, the wounded were tended to the best of the ability of the exhausted medical officer and his overworked stretcher-bearers and orderlies. It was not long before even the most rudimentary medicines and field dressings ran out. That was when the madness began.

Caspasian had never seen it before and it terrified him. In every face he looked in, he could see the same expression. The faces of men who know they are marked for slaughter, and that there is nothing that any of them can do about it. It was beyond terror. It was a complete emptiness, like a living body robbed of its soul. Men became less than men. Less even than human. Caspasian felt as if he had been transported to live amongst a different species. As if he was existing among insects, creatures who communicated by emitting chemicals. Warmth, love, humanity were gone, blasted by the German guns into the same stinking mud into which Redoubt Isis was disintegrating.

On one of the last days before conversation had died, one of the soldiers had asked why anyone would think of such a stupid name for a redoubt. Caspasian had answered. 'Isis was one of the Egyptian gods. Together with her brother Osiris and the rest. Atum Ra gave birth to them by himself.'

'How the fuck did he do that?'

'Well,' Caspasian began awkwardly, 'it was a spontaneous act. He . . . '

Private Dobson helped him out of the tight corner. 'You could say he took himself in hand, my lad.'

The soldier guffawed. 'Well, I'll be blowed. I see now why the General chose the name. I always knew he was a wanker.'

Shortly after that the bombardment intensified and Caspasian found himself amongst an alien race. What most terrified him was that he saw the same expression when he looked in the small shaving mirror nailed to the wall of his dugout. He was losing himself, like everyone else around him. Everyone, that was, except Private Dobson.

Dobson was a walking miracle. Rather grandly, Caspasian liked to think of him as proof of Plato's theory of Ideal Forms, or what little he had understood of the theory when he had studied it as a youth. Dobson was proof that qualities such as courage, goodness, kindness, humility and the rest of them, had some kind of objective existence outside the human realm, in some unimaginable place of their own. Dobson was like a window linking the two places, the hell in which Caspasian now found himself, and somewhere better, untouchable, incorruptible, unsullied.

Of course, he knew full well that Dobson would not have had any idea what he was talking about, had he been stupid enough to broach the subject. The man would have laughed that laugh of his, and looked at Caspasian as if he was just another gawky young subaltern, still wet behind the ears, a look which was both humbling yet kind at the same time. The only other man Caspasian had known who was capable of the same gently appraising gaze had been his grandfather. It was not lost on him that perhaps this accounted for the liking he felt towards the old soldier.

But if Dobson was the window, Smith was a filthy smear right across it. Where Dobson exemplified a way of being, by his behaviour and personal example, Smith smudged the vision. In fact, he did his utmost to slam the window shut. It was as if he, like Caspasian, recognised something special in Dobson. But whereas Caspasian would have the window thrown open so Dobson's light could shine upon the surrounding misery, Smith spent his time hunting for rocks to hurl at the fragile glass. Smith would have seen it smashed. And eventually he did.

The mist was clearing. The morning was damp, chilling Caspasian to the bone. It seeped into everything, prising its way through whatever layers of lice-ridden clothing the soldiers managed to squeeze into. Caspasian was the officer of the watch with another thirty minutes of his stag to run. Smith was down below, his soft snores emanating from the dugout. The German guns had fallen silent the evening before. The occupants of Redoubt Isis had stood-to immediately, expecting infantry to assault. Hour after hour had passed and eventually they had been stood down. Clearly the Germans were just pausing once again to bring up fresh stocks of ammunition. The men had passed a peaceful night, the first in ages. Even the moans of the wounded had failed to keep them awake.

Next to Caspasian, Dobson was on sentry duty. He was exhausted and Caspasian had let the man sleep. Slumped on the fire step, Dobson slumbered softly. Caspasian, watchful of others approaching, stood ready to kick him awake lest his sleeping invite a charge under military regulations.

Caspasian was just blowing into his cupped hands when he caught the movement. Over the sandbagged lip of the trench, a hundred yards out in no-man's-land, the mist was parting, stirred by the morning breezes that always combed the scarred landscape at that hour. Through a rent in the mist he saw a single figure. It was an infantryman. He was moving at a fast walk, jogging a few paces and then, when encountering a difficult patch of ground, slowing to a walk again. But fast, methodical. Determined. The gap in the mist broadened and there were the rest of them. At least company strength. Each man carried a satchel around his shoulders. Stick bombs. And the coal scuttle helmets, patchwork pattern of their jackets, and — most of all — their professional fieldcraft evident in the way they advanced, identified them as stormtroopers. Everyone in the house was asleep. The murderers had come.

'Oh, Christ.' Caspasian kicked Dobson's foot. Then again when the older soldier failed to rouse. He felt the bile rise in his throat and swallowed it down, hard.

'What is it?' Dobson asked, creaking to his feet.

'Stormtroopers.'

Dobson was instantly awake. 'Good God, lad, don't whisper it. Scream it!' He brought his rifle butt into his shoulder, aimed and fired off a round.

Caspasian turned along the trench. 'Stand-to! Stand-to!' He dug in his holster for his revolver and found that his hands were shaking.

Soldiers tumbled out of the dugouts and ran to their fire positions. Shots started to crack the silent morning like smashing glass but it had taken too long. Instead of coming straight on, like ordinary infantry, the stormtroopers slipped with deadly ease into their drills. As one group put down withering covering fire, another group darted forward. Just far enough to gain ground and to reach some new point of tactical advantage closer to their objective. Then it was their turn. While they fired, their comrades jogged forward, passing them to a flank and pressing on, ready to repeat the process as, group by group, they leapfrogged all the way to their morning's grim business.

From the far side of the redoubt there was a sudden dull thud. Caspasian spun round in time to see a black smudge rising in the air.

'Stick grenade. They're in!' he said, his voice trembling.

'Fuck.'

It was the first time he had heard Dobson swear. For Caspasian its significance was greater than the grenade's.

Caspasian struggled to control his breathing. He had to sweep himself free of panic if he was to survive.

Suddenly Smith was beside him. His face was ashen, his eyes hollow. 'You were on duty, Dobson. Why didn't you see them?'

'He did,' Caspasian cut in sharply. 'It was the mist. It covered them all the way in.'

'Damn them,' Smith cursed. Caspasian noticed that the barrel of Smith's Webley was quivering in his hand. To his amazement he saw that his own was now rock solid. He was back in command of himself.

A handful of soldiers came round the far corner of the fire trench, bolting in the opposite direction. Caspasian barred their way, seizing the nearest by the scruff of his sodden jacket. 'Where the hell are you going?'

The man looked straight through him, his eyes crazed with fear. 'They're inside,' he jabbered, saliva foaming on his trembling lips. 'They killing everyone.'

As if to confirm it, there was a flurry of

grenade explosions, each a little closer than the last. The garrison had been reduced by the bombardment to the point where there were barely two platoons-worth of able-bodied men left to defend the place.

A muffled underground explosion shook the ground.

'Oh, God, they've bombed the Aid Post,' Dobson said. His face set hard. 'Come on, lads,' he said, including both Caspasian and Smith. 'Let's see if we can get the buggers out.' He started away, going in the direction of the small-arms fire now erupting on the far side of the redoubt.

Smith grabbed his arm. 'Just a minute. I'm the bloody officer here. Get back to your post. I say we stay here.'

'Dobson's right,' Caspasian said. 'Unless we clear them out they're going to kill everyone.'

Smith glared at Caspasian, terror vying with rage. 'Don't you dare countermand me in front of a private.'

Caspasian turned away, ignoring him. 'We haven't got time for this.' He grabbed three of the soldiers who had been fleeing and thrust them at Private Dobson. 'Dobson, they're under your command. I'll take the others. We'll advance as two groups, each supporting the other. Got any grenades?'

'Aye, lad.' Dobson pulled two Mills bombs from his pockets.

'And you?' Caspasian asked, gesturing to the others.

They fumbled amongst their equipment and produced a further half-dozen.

'Right then. Fix your bayonets, lads, and let's go. If we hit them hard enough we might just drive them out.'

As they jogged away, Caspasian and Dobson in the lead, Smith called after them, his voice plaintive and frightened. 'What about me?'

No one answered him. Their minds were already on the fight to come.

Caspasian's first sight of a stormtrooper was from the back. He rounded a corner, Dobson close behind him and there he was. He was a big man, stooping to pull a long-bladed knife from the stomach of one of the men he had just killed. Alerted by Caspasian's footsteps he spun, tugging the blade free of his victim who was still dying. Blood dripped from it as he brandished it at Caspasian and sank into a fighting stance ready to kill again.

Caspasian reacted without thinking. His foot shot out and kicked the German in the gut. The knife almost fell from his grasp but he snatched at it and swung for Caspasian's face. The tip of the blade hissed through the air in front of Caspasian's nose, an inch away. There was a deafening crack in his ear and smoke from the muzzle of Dobson's Lee-Enfield scorched his cheek. The German was flung backwards against the far wall of the trench, his face a mass of disrupted bone and pulp.

Dobson slammed back the rifle bolt, pushing a fresh round into the breech. Together they pressed on. Alerted by the rifle shot, a gang of three stormtroopers appeared over the top of the trench. Stick grenades cart-wheeled through the air and plopped innocently into the mud at Caspasian's feet.

'Shoot 'em, lad!' Dobson shouted at Caspasian. He blazed off one shot at the Germans to get their heads down and then dived after the grenades. He snatched up two and hurled them back over the trench wall. At Dobson's shout Caspasian had fired off two rounds from his revolver before going after the third grenade himself. It arched lazily back out into no-man's-land and all three exploded the next second. Mud and pieces of flesh and blood-soaked clothing rained down on them.

'We'd have felt that one,' Dobson said with a wink.

They went on, fighting their way from trench to trench. In places they encountered small pockets of British soldiers hanging on desperately to their positions. One by one they linked them together, slowly extending the area under their own control. It seemed that there was fighting right across the redoubt. Firing and grenade explosions sounded from all sides. In the confusion it was impossible to tell who was who, and which side held which sector of the redoubt. Caspasian realised that it was going to be a long, gruelling fight. The German stormtroopers were not the sort to give up quietly and withdraw. They would have to be killed, one by one, like rats.

He had just cleared a machine-gun emplacement, relieved to find it unoccupied, when he heard Dobson shouting for help. Caspasian had left him watching the rear approach to the emplacement on the other side of a trench wall. Instantly he darted down out of the emplacement and shot round the corner to find Dobson grappling with a German stormtrooper considerably larger than the old poacher himself. Dobson had his back to Caspasian and the German glanced up at the new arrival as he struggled. To Caspasian's surprise, instead of concentrating on the man in his grasp, Dobson was trying to crane back his head and look at him. He was saying something but the German had his hand across Dobson's mouth trying to force back his head.

Caspasian darted forward, his revolver searching for a clean shot, when, with one mighty effort, Dobson swung the German round, freeing his mouth in the same instant. It seemed to Caspasian that Dobson was using the German's body as a shield. He was puzzled. Why shield himself from Caspasian who was trying to help him?

Caspasian saw the look in Dobson's eyes and froze, his heart stopping. Everything suddenly stopped. Time ceased to move.

'There, lad, there!' Dobson screamed. Unable to point, his hands locked with his enemy, Dobson pointed with his eyes.

Caspasian turned to look. Every instinct from his training told him to dive. But he looked. There, its fuse fizzing, a stick grenade rolled to and fro on the floor of the trench, knocking rhythmically against the base of the sandbag fire step.

The revolver dropped from Caspasian's fist as his hands came up instinctively to shield his face. Instincts from training had been replaced by earlier ones. He was curling into a ball, turning away from the grenade when it exploded. The last thing he saw was Dobson propelling the body of the German past and beyond them both, one hand reaching out for

Caspasian. His face was contorted with the superhuman effort, throwing the German at the grenade. His eyes locked with Caspasian's. And then the window was slammed shut.

17

Above General Yuan's farmstead the night sky was clear. Caspasian stood at the window looking up at it. He had wrapped a sheet around his waist, knotting it at the side, but the air was sharp and his bare shoulders and chest were cold. Nevertheless, his mind was far from China and in a strange way the chill discomfort was soothing, like a cold compress applied to a burn.

Lilin stirred in the bed behind him. He turned to look at her and, as he did so, her eyes flickered open and blinked at him. She rubbed them, pushing herself upright when her sight cleared and she saw him across the room. The moon had risen and shone full into the room. Caspasian marvelled at the beauty of Lilin as she sat up in bed, her breasts and skin pale in the ghostly light. She looked like some ethereal creature from another world, something splendid and magical that had crept across the threshold to explore the human realm with benign curiosity.

'What are you thinking?' she asked. 'Is it Private Dobson?'

Caspasian smiled. 'Yes.' He had told her all about Redoubt Isis the previous day, on returning from the ruins in the wood, and about his recuperation afterwards, the news of the trial and execution of Dobson in his absence, and about his early suspicions of Smith.

Lilin stepped on to the floor and tiptoed silently to him. Caspasian gathered her naked body on to the sill beside him, unfastening his sheet and rearranging it around them both.

'You don't blame yourself, do you?'

'I didn't think I did,' he answered. 'But oddly enough, the more time goes by, the more I think I do.' He shook his head. 'I should have bloody well seen that grenade. I should have dived away from it, not just bloody well stood there, waiting, cringing like an idiot. If I had done, Dobson would have been alive today.'

'How?'

'Everything would have been different. We'd have been able to fight on together. Smith wouldn't have been able to contrive that obscene lie about his bravery and Dobson's cowardice, and . . . '

'You might well have been killed round the next corner,' Lilin cut in sharply. 'If you hadn't been unconscious, who knows what else might have happened to you? Don't you see? It's pointless to try and reconstruct the past. What has happened is fixed. Nothing can change that. However much you might want to.'

She reached up with one hand and stroked his face. 'This Dobson must have been a very special person.'

'He was.'

'Very brave.'

Caspasian thought about it for a moment. 'Yes. But it was something more than that. I think it was compassion. He understood the suffering he saw around him.' Lilin felt Caspasian shivering against her. She hugged him tighter as he continued.

'It took me a long time to realise what it was I'd seen on all those young faces. It was terrified incomprehension. A sense that the world in which they had always trusted had enacted the most profound betrayal. The earth itself, stuffed with mines, leapt and altered itself in the most violent and unpredictable way. The air they had always breathed, as unconsciously as fish inhale water, was suddenly poisonous and lung-defiling. The space they occupied was riven with bullet and livid shell splinter, flesh-tearing, bone-severing, life-negating. Everything they had known and accepted as necessary for their existence was turned

437

upside down in a mad, cacophonous fury. And in that incomprehensible extreme they were reduced to beaten children, terrified, uncomprehending, and they screamed for their mothers.'

He closed his eyes. Lilin could hear his teeth grinding as he remembered. Then he spoke again. 'The number of times I heard that word. Mother. Some clung to their sanity. They clenched their senses tight about them and wailed inwardly, silent and unseen. To those about them they were the heroes, storing up their terror for later when it would emerge in other forms. Twitches, withdrawn silence, moodiness, attempts at suicide even. Only the inhuman escaped unscathed. Men like Smith. But I even wonder about him now, whether he would have been as he is now had it not been for Flanders.'

Lilin gazed out of the window. 'I saw the same thing once. That terrified incomprehension you speak of. It was on the face of a baby. It was the child of one of my father's labourers. We suspected it was being mistreated. Eventually someone caught the father beating it. It was only weeks old. My father turned the man off the farm. We took the child and it was given to a good neighbour to raise. But that was exactly the expression on its face. Too young to understand anything.

And terrified.' She shuddered and laid her face against Caspasian. 'It was a terrible thing to see and I hope I never have to see it again.'

A breeze gusted into the room, plucking at their sheet and filling the room with a scent like dry hay.

'Come on,' Caspasian said suddenly, breaking away from the window sill and taking Lilin back to the bed. They wriggled under the blankets, pulling them up to their chins. 'That's enough of France. It was more than ten years ago. We've got more immediate problems.' They lay on their sides facing each other. 'I've been thinking about your father and about what we've got to do.'

'What can we do?'

'Grasp the nettle, just as I said before the battle,' Caspasian answered. 'The British saw an ally in General Mok. Well, why can't they have an ally in your father?'

'Because it's only worth having an ally to offset the power of Chiang Kai-shek if the ally's powerful. General Mok was, my father isn't.'

Caspasian grinned. 'Yes, but who won the fight? Your father. So how powerful was General Mok in the end? It was a fiction. Hundreds of Mok's men have now defected to your father, added to which he's got all of Mok's weaponry that's still of any use.

General Mok is dead. Long live General Yuan!'

Lilin bit her lip, thinking. 'My father is no soldier though.'

'Neither was Mok, when it came down to it. He was just another bandit. There's more of the soldier in your father than there ever was in Mok. Believe me.'

'Maybe, but he doesn't want to fight Chiang. That would be madness. He just wants to look after his people and be left alone.'

Caspasian sighed. He reached up and stroked her shoulder. 'I can understand that. But sometimes we don't have a choice.' He brightened. 'In any case, Chiang might not come this far north. The last I heard before I left the city, he had swung east along the Yangtze and was heading for Shanghai and the coast. But whatever happens, we've got to get your father accepted by the British and the other western powers. If we can accomplish that, Chiang might not dare attack him. It'll be more in his interest to make an alliance with him. That way we all get what we want. Chiang finds a new friend and moves on with this province secure. Your father is bypassed by the war and left in peace. The British get an ally to replace Mok, and I . . . '

'What do you get?' Lilin asked, cautious.

'I get the girl!' He kissed Lilin on the nose. She pushed him away. 'Be serious.'

'OK, then. If I'm lucky I get my old job back instead of being court-martialled for killing a valued British ally, murderous old bastard though he was.'

Lilin smiled. She placed a hand on Caspasian's chest, pushed him gently on to his back and slipped on top of him. 'So tell me more about getting the girl.'

★ ★ ★

The broad brown surface of the Yangtze writhed like a nest of snakes as the various currents conflicted, one against the other. Standing in the prow of the junk, General Yuan stared down at the hypnotic patterns as the junk scythed through the water. The vessel was in full sail, the huge bat-winged expanse of crimson arching overhead, the bamboo struts flapping as each gust of wind buffeted them.

A burst of laughter caused him to glance back to the wheelhouse. Caspasian and Lilin were leaning against it, enjoying a private joke. The General sighed. While still at the farm Caspasian had heeded his request to keep his relationship with Lilin discreet, but even then the General could tell it had been difficult for the two young people, trying to hide feelings that any fool could see were almost overpowering them. Here on the junk, however, prying eyes were few, and he was glad that his daughter was able to relax with the man she so obviously loved.

And Caspasian, the General wondered? What did he feel for Lilin? It was clear that he was enjoying her company, just as it was clear that he was enjoying her body. The General noticed how the two of them would suddenly disappear below deck, reemerging some while later, conspicuously one at a time, and employed upon some errand that would send them to opposite ends of the junk until, unable to bear the separation, they would gradually work their way back together again, and the quiet conversation would resume, continuing until the next trip below.

General Yuan smiled. He was not so old that he had forgotten his own youth and passions. His love for his daughter was such that it allowed room for her own happiness, whatever form that took. He found Caspasian an intriguing character. In a strange way, he was a bit like the Yangtze. There were many currents beneath the surface in violent conflict. Yuan suspected that the man himself was unsure of his feelings for Lilin. He had no doubt that he felt very strongly for her. He would probably do the decent thing, as it was called, should their exercise result in a child. Yuan suspected that Caspasian would do it willingly. But there was some indefinable quality in the man, something so unreachable, that Yuan could not shake off the final conviction that in the end Caspasian would leave, and leave alone. Somehow Yuan could not see Caspasian as the father of his grandchildren, although he would have been happy had it been so. But maybe he was wrong. Yuan hoped so. For Lilin's sake he desperately hoped so.

The decision to make the trip had been taken surprisingly quickly. Yuan had been thinking along the same lines as Caspasian, so when the subject had been broached, agreement had been reached quickly. The only area of dispute had concerned which of them should go. Obviously Caspasian had to return to Shanghai to make his peace, as best he could, with his political and military masters. However, he had wanted to go alone, intending to propose General Yuan as a replacement ally for Mok, setting in place the new alliance himself.

General Yuan had argued successfully that Caspasian's case would be much stronger if he himself were present. That way the British could reassure themselves of his good intentions, as well as vetting their new friend to ensure he was not another psychopath, not that that had worried them in the past. It was then only a short step to Lilin persuading them both that she too should go. She knew Shanghai better then either of them, added to which, she simply refused to be left behind. And that was that. The only concession she was prepared to make was that she agreed with Caspasian that both she and her father should travel incognito, and remain hidden in Shanghai until Caspasian had sounded out his superiors and they had convinced him that they were willing to view the proposal positively and with open minds. At that stage General Yuan and Lilin could be brought before them. If, on the other hand, the British received the idea with scorn, rejecting it outright, Yuan and Lilin could return home in secret and make whatever alternative plans might secure their future.

Although Caspasian had placed his own apartment at the General's disposal, it had been more out of courtesy. Both of them quickly agreed that it would be the first place the authorities would search if they learned that Yuan was in Shanghai. Fortunately, General Yuan had contacts of his own. A distant relation owned a house on Henderson

Road. Although the relation himself lived in Nanking with his wife and children, he was sufficiently wealthy to maintain the Shanghai household in a state of perpetual readiness for the few occasions when he travelled there on business. A housekeeper and other essential staff lived there throughout the year, awaiting the arrival of their master. Yuan said that he would simply turn up and invite himself in.

By the time the news reached his relation in Nanking, his business with the British would have been concluded and he and Lilin would have departed. His relation would probably not mind in any case, but he was not renowned for his discretion and on this mission, secrecy was vital. Caspasian agreed the plan, but as they neared Shanghai he found himself regretting the coming separation from Lilin. He had grown used to her and was not looking forward to having to part. He also discovered that his feelings for her went far deeper than he had realised. For the first time since the war, he dared to hope that his soul was recovering. He was able to feel again. And this woman with whom he spent every possible part of his days and nights was the one person he most wanted to be with.

They smelt Shanghai long before they arrived there. While still some way upriver faint aromas, carried on the air coming up from the city and from the sea beyond, told them that their river voyage was nearing an end. Closer still, raw sewage floated past on both sides of the junk. The river traffic thickened, with junks, sampans, barges and steam boats veering in every direction. Finally they spied the first substantial buildings, still well clear of the famous Bund and the International Settlement.

General Yuan directed his crew to seek out a mooring near the Chinese City. Teeming with people, it would be a relatively easy task for the three of them to slip ashore unnoticed and make their way to Yuan's chosen hideout. The junk and its crew would wait at the quayside for as long as Yuan's mission took.

After the countryside, the city hit Caspasian's senses like a physical blow. The noises, smells and sights all vied for the prize of most horrific experience. Beggars, whores and ragged children thronged the waterfront, darting between rickshaw-pullers and porters. Caspasian wore a broad-brimmed hat and kept it pulled low at the front. He felt like a criminal and wondered, to his dismay, whether perhaps he was. Time would soon tell.

They had brought only a few items of luggage with them. Nonetheless, Caspasian had ensured that the bags contained several pistols and revolvers, as well as half a dozen hand grenades captured from General Mok. For himself he had selected a Webley which he kept readily to hand in his right-hand jacket pocket, a box of cartridges in the left.

Lilin had dressed in a dark cotton cheong-sam, a plain design in an equally modest colour adorning the front. At Caspasian's insistence she had also put on a hat, adding a dark gauze veil to shield her face. Disdaining the rickshaws that materialised on all sides, shrieking for a fare, the three of them fought their way across the crowded street where Caspasian managed to hail a taxi.

'Henderson Road,' General Yuan shouted through the half-closed partition separating the driver.

'What number?' the man snapped back over his shoulder.

'I'll show you when we get there,' Yuan replied.

The taxi lurched forward and the three passengers sat back and looked at one another. Trepidation showed on every face.

'Here we go then,' Caspasian said as merrily as he could. In normal circumstances, had he been alone or just with Yuan, his present predicament would not have bothered him. However, he was unsettled by the presence of Lilin. Or rather, by his attachment to her. If dangers appeared he would not be able to face them with a calm, unruffled mind. In effect, she had given him an Achilles heel where one had not existed before. It set him off balance. He would be like a fencer parrying sabre cuts, suddenly having to defend a target area twice the usual size. But he only had to think of having Lilin near him to know that he would not have it any other way.

The house in Henderson Road was a mock-Tudor affair like so many in Shanghai. It stood behind a high brick wall, two stone pillars flanking the twin wooden entrance gates. A small door was set in one of the gates to admit pedestrians, and a bell-pull hung at the left-hand side for attracting the attention of whoever waited on the inside to undo the lock.

The taxi drew up outside the house and the passengers got out. Yuan paid the driver who sneered openly at the modest size of the tip. To Caspasian's relief there were few passers-by and no one seemed to pay them any attention. Yuan pulled at the bell and they waited. Eventually, a small rectangular hatch slid open in the door and furtive eyes inspected them, darting from one to the other. Yuan explained who he was but it was only after the gatekeeper had scampered away and referred the matter to someone else that they heard a series of bolts and locks being unfastened on the other side of the door.

'Your relative's a wealthy man,' Caspasian frowned.

'Reasonably. But then this is Shanghai. Anyone who doesn't have this level of security is asking for trouble.'

They were admitted into a small courtyard, just large enough to manoeuvre a single automobile. An ominous-looking kennel lay to one side and a vast dog shot out of it as if propelled by slingshot, its chain almost tearing its head off as the links snapped taut inches from Caspasian's leg. The dog's hind quarters were catapulted round and, as the new arrivals edged their way cautiously past the electrified animal, its jaws sawed at the air, working from left to right as if eating a cob of corn.

The attendant giggled with embarrassment and gestured at Caspasian. 'Englishman?' he crooned.

'Yes.'

The man shrugged as if that should be explanation enough for the dog's red-eyed hatred.

The housekeeper was waiting for them in

the vestibule and recognised General Yuan from a previous visit some years ago. She listened politely as he explained that he was in Shanghai for a couple of days and was in need of lodgings. He pretended to her that he was surprised to find his relative away and made to leave. The housekeeper protested, as intended, and, after a flurry of activity amongst the servants, during which the three new arrivals stood innocently to one side, they were shown to three large bedrooms on the second of the house's three floors. Caspasian had decided against returning to his own apartment for the night. The afternoon was well advanced and it would be best to wait for the following day to visit the British Consulate. He did not want to be seen until then and a return to his own flat in Cherry Tree Apartments on Rue Lafayette simply increased the risk of compromise.

The cook produced a reasonable meal for them that evening and after dinner they sat together in the drawing room. General Yuan found a chess set and, while he and Lilin played, Caspasian leafed through a book he had picked from one of the shelves. Its subject was botany and he thought it was one of the dullest books he had ever inspected. He had positioned himself so that he was facing Lilin. Eased back in the chair, legs crossed, he tried desperately not to glance her way between every four or five words.

General Yuan, sitting with his back to Caspasian, was initially surprised at the ease with which he robbed his daughter of her chess pieces, until he noticed that her eyes were hardly on the board at all. With a deep sigh he suggested that they all retire for the night. The following day was to be very important for all of them. Lilin and Caspasian agreed earnestly.

Caspasian bade them both goodnight, went to his room, sat on the bed and waited. The minutes passed with agonising slowness, but when at last he judged it reasonable to assume the General would be asleep, he tiptoed back to the door and cracked it open. The corridor lay in darkness. Fortunately, the General had been placed at one end of the corridor, Lilin at the other, and Caspasian in the middle. Easing out on to the bare floorboards, Caspasian crept stealthily to Lilin's door and knocked as softly as he could. He waited a moment and then hissed her name through the lock.

The door swung open and General Yuan stared out at him, smiling sweetly. 'Can I help you?'

Caspasian jumped backwards. 'General? I . . .'

'My own mattress was far too soft,' the General explained. 'Fortunately that's the way Lilin likes it. But I expect you know that?'

From the sudden heat Caspasian knew that he had turned scarlet.

'Apart from which, I do not want my relative's house to be sullied by any impropriety of ours. We are here as his guests. I know you will respect his hospitality. Even if it has been given unknowingly.'

Caspasian bowed his head in acknowledgement and returned to his room. As he reached his door he heard Lilin's creak open. From the opposite end of the corridor General Yuan's voice called out, 'And goodnight to you too, Lilin, my dear. I will see you both in the morning at breakfast.'

18

On his way to the British Consulate the next morning, Caspasian was struck again by the tense mood in the air. In many respects it was just another Monday morning. British, American, French and other western bankers and businessmen, smartly turned out as ever, left their mansions and luxury apartments and drove to work along the Bund or to their well-appointed offices in the broad boulevards leading off it. Left to their own devices at home, their wives would prepare for another arduous week of coffee mornings and afternoon tea in the smart hotels, and shopping expeditions to check the latest fashions and accessories that had arrived in the Sincere and Wing On department stores.

Behind it all however there was something else. As Caspasian directed his taxi along Nanking Road, he noticed first one and then another group of young Chinese. There seemed to be a very great many of them, no one group large enough to attract the attention of the Shanghai Municipal Police, but nonetheless numbering anything up to twenty fit young men each. There was something unwholesome about them. They were the sort of youths encountered on the waterfront, labour for quick and uncomplicated hire. Muscle.

None of them appeared to be armed, although a number carried sticks that were a little more stout than necessary simply for walking. However, as the major port city in China, Shanghai was a magnet to such men in search of work, and with the progress of Chiang Kai-shek's army through the south and the inexorable spread of fighting along the Yangtze, it was natural enough that the numbers of such men would grow, driven from the countryside, fleeing conscription by the various local warlords. Caspasian also supposed that it probably explained the high profile being taken by the Shanghai Volunteer Force who had obviously been mobilised in his absence. Numbering a thousand men, he had already seen four of their ten armoured cars deployed on street corners, their Vickers, Lewis and Browning machine-guns polished to a gleam, and the ruddy faced young subalterns enjoying a break from office life and their more usual clerical duties to show off instead in front of the admiring passers-by.

As he saw the façade of the consulate rear up in front of him, Caspasian felt a tightening in the pit of his stomach. He tried to quell the butterflies that were dancing a polka in his gut, but the roasting that he expected the moment he confronted his boss had let them loose to create whatever internal mayhem they wanted. He felt as if he was knowingly walking straight into an ambush, and yet there was no alternative. He had to explain his actions if General Yuan and Lilin were to have any chance of survival. Only with western backing would they be able to stand up to the inexorable spread of Chiang Kai-shek's influence, and they would only receive that support if Caspasian was able to convince his superiors that they were a better bet than the late General Mok had ever been. It was not going to be easy.

He was somewhat taken back therefore when he entered the building and ran into Colonel Preston who greeted him almost cordially.

'Well, well, well. The prodigal son. And about as prodigal as they blasted well get!' the Colonel bellowed across the entrance hall. But there was a twinkle in his eye and he waved cheerily as he swept on up the stairs. 'See you in my office when you're ready,' he called genially over his shoulder.

Caspasian was thunderstruck. The butterflies found an open window and disappeared.

Even the smell from the river seemed suddenly less pungent. He made his way up the stairs and went first of all to his own office. Strangely most of the other offices were either empty or else the occupants were working behind closed doors. Still, Caspasian had unexpectedly been given reason to hope, and the burst of bright light blotted out everything else, suffusing the whole morning with a balmy sense of promise.

After gathering his wits, he made his way to Colonel Preston's office, straightened his tie and then knocked on the door.

'Come!' For all his earlier confidence Caspasian nonetheless recoiled at the muted bark from within. Somehow it recalled countless summonses to the headmaster's study in days long gone.

He opened the door and marched smartly in, squaring his shoulders and halting in the middle of the carpet. His arms rigidly to attention at his sides, he reported himself for duty.

Colonel Preston sat slumped back in his chair, eyeing Caspasian with interest. Behind the huge oak desk, he reminded Caspasian of a machine-gunner boredly passing the minutes before inflicting further slaughter. The Colonel's left hand rubbed his chin thoughtfully, while his right hand drummed fingers on the green leather desk top.

'What are we going to do with you, Caspasian?'

'Sir?'

'Oh, for God's sake, at ease man.'

Caspasian wondered whether this extended to having a seat but decided it did not. He suddenly became aware that they were not alone in the room and turned quickly to see another figure seated in a high-backed chair behind the door.

'I believe you've met Chief Inspector Ewan Cameron before?' the Colonel said.

Caspasian stared in surprise. Cameron nodded, his expression somewhere between inscrutable and rude. 'Good morning, Captain,' he said, his eyes boring into Caspasian.

Caspasian's earlier optimism vanished, replaced by suspicion. He had been about to launch into an explanation of his actions but decided instead to let the Colonel speak first.

Colonel Preston leaned forward, elbows on the desk and fingers steepled beneath his chin. 'I believe you've killed one of our allies?' he asked pleasantly.

Caspasian glanced at Cameron, wondering whether he had been the source of Preston's intelligence.

Preston read Caspasian's expression and answered. 'Chief Inspector Cameron, among

457

his many other duties, has responsibility for anti-smuggling operations. In that capacity he hears things faster than anyone else in the city.' He paused, awaiting Caspasian's response. 'Well?'

Caspasian glanced uneasily at Cameron, shifting his position so he was not quite so trapped between the two men. 'Naturally, I've got a great deal to report, Colonel, but . . . '

Seeing Caspasian's concern Preston said, 'You can speak freely in front of the Chief Inspector.'

Caspasian was astonished. 'But Colonel, my report concerns Military Intelligence. With all due respect, what's that got to do the Shanghai Municipal Police?'

'Right now, everything. The military situation in the countryside is inextricably linked to the security picture here in the city, and that's where the Chief Inspector comes in.'

Cameron stood up, enjoying the slight height advantage he had over Caspasian. He placed his hands behind his back and paced across to the window where he stood with his back to the river. With the sun coming in through the window behind him, he was consciously forcing Caspasian to squint. Even then, he knew his features would remain largely obscured. 'Listen, Caspasian, things have moved on a wee bit since you left Shanghai. Yes, I heard all about your liaison visit with General Mok.' The heavy tone of sarcasm was not lost on Caspasian. 'Not a great success was it, laddie?'

Caspasian could feel his irritation mounting. 'That depends how you look at it.'

Colonel Preston tried to reclaim the interview. 'And just how do you look at it, Caspasian?'

'General Mok was a psychopath, Colonel,' Caspasian began. 'Now I know that doesn't disqualify him from being an ally of His Majesty's government . . . '

'Don't be cheeky!'

' . . . but he was also incompetent,' Caspasian continued quickly. 'Yes, he was reasonably well armed and equipped, but he had no idea how to use his army.'

'As evidenced by the ease with which you assisted one of his enemies to defeat him?' the Colonel retorted, unable completely to suppress his admiration.

'I'd hardly use the word ease, Colonel. A lot of men died.'

'Of course, of course,' the Colonel said with a dismissive wave of the hand. 'War's a messy business. We all know that. My point is, the news of Mok's defeat and death, brought to me by the Chief Inspector here, who heard of it through his own sources, has given me a problem. By destroying the only organised force in that province you've created a power vacuum that Chiang Kai-shek will slip straight into.'

'No I haven't, Colonel,' Caspasian went on.

'You're going to tell me that this other General Yuan will have an army equal to the one you helped him to defeat?'

Caspasian stared, not altogether surprised now that Cameron's part in the scheme of things had unfolded. 'You know of Yuan already?'

Preston and Cameron swapped glances. 'Of course I do,' Preston said.

'General Yuan is everything that Mok was not,' Caspasian said. 'Firstly he is a man of honour, an ally we can be proud of, instead of having to excuse. Secondly, he is courageous. His army badly needs weapons and training, but with a man like Yuan leading it, it has the potential to be far superior to any force ever fielded by that murderous idiot, Mok.'

Colonel Preston held up his hand. 'All right, all right. He's clearly done a good selling job on you. But you must understand my position. I can't allow the British government to change horses in mid-stream with quite such apparent speed. It would send exactly the wrong message to all our other allies in China and throughout the region.'

'Which is why I've brought Yuan with me so you can interview him yourself, Colonel. You and the Consul, of course.'

Preston stared wide-eyed. 'General Yuan? Here in Shanghai?' He looked past Caspasian as if expecting the General to march in through the door. 'Where is he?'

Caspasian started to speak but something in Cameron's manner stopped him. Silhouetted against the light from the window, Cameron gave the impression of a predator. However irrational, Caspasian did not like it. 'He's in hiding,' he said at last.

'What the devil do you mean?' Preston said, blanching, though whether from anger, guilt or something else Caspasian was unable to tell.

'Not unnaturally he fears for his safety,' Caspasian explained, improvising as he went along. 'He's a long way from his power base and Shanghai's hardly a safe haven of law and order.' He turned to Cameron. 'With all due respects to the Chief Inspector.'

For the first time Cameron laughed. 'No offence taken, laddie. If I were him, I'd be watching my back as well.'

Preston was less conciliatory. 'Well, tell me

where he is. I can have a guard arranged. The Chief Inspector and I can guarantee his safety.'

'He's already quite safe at the moment, thank you, Colonel.'

'Look, man. I'm giving you a direct order. Tell me where . . . '

Cameron stepped away from the window, smiling at Caspasian as if the two of them were old friends. 'Don't press the young man, Colonel. I admire principle when I see it, and I don't see it very often in a place like this. Caspasian's right. General Yuan's probably fine where he is.' He turned to Caspasian. 'We will need to arrange a meeting between him and the Consul though.'

'I know that,' Caspasian replied. 'Which is why I'm here.'

Preston muttered something under his breath and scowled at Caspasian. Aloud he said, 'When will you deign to allow the Consul to meet the General?'

'Tomorrow?' Caspasian suggested. To his surprise, the other two glanced at each other uneasily.

'Can we not make it this afternoon?' the Colonel tried.

Once again, Caspasian felt uncomfortable. However, he kept his face impassive. 'I'm afraid it will have to be tomorrow, Colonel.'

'Why?' Preston asked, fighting back his temper.

Cameron leaned across the desk and whispered something to him. Preston sighed. 'All right then. Tomorrow.' He glared at Caspasian. 'Is noon convenient for you?' he asked sarcastically.

'Noon should be fine, sir.'

'Noon it is then,' Cameron said. He clapped a big hand on Caspasian's shoulder. 'I probably shouldn't say so, but good work, laddie. You've pulled off quite a coup.'

Caspasian noticed that Preston looked at Cameron as if mystified, but nevertheless followed his lead. 'Yes, we can probably salvage something from this unholy mess after all. If Yuan proves to be the man you say he is.' He thought a moment. 'So we can leave it to you to get the message to Yuan, can we?'

'Yes, sir,' Caspasian said.

'Right, then. Until tomorrow,' he concluded, dismissing Caspasian from the office.

'Until tomorrow, sir,' Caspasian said, He got up and left, resisting the temptation to exit the office as if all the hounds of hell were after him. Something was wrong. Something was terribly wrong, and he had to find out what. It had all been too easy. They had known all about Mok's death and had

463

anticipated Caspasian's proposal of General Yuan as the replacement. That could be explained by Cameron's slick intelligence network amongst the Yangtze smugglers. So far so good.

But of greater difficulty was the fact that during the whole course of the interview, no one had asked him anything about Yuan's military strength. If he was to be considered as an ally, surely they would have wanted details of his artillery, cavalry, and infantry strengths? How many machine-guns he had. His stocks, his reserves, his dispositions. All right, so they could ask Yuan himself tomorrow, but surely a report from their own man, Caspasian, would have been required, so they could brief themselves before the crucial meeting? Furthermore, no one had so much as mentioned Captain Daniel Smith. Yet, in Caspasian's mind at least, the hated name had hung in the air between the three of them throughout the meeting, unspoken, but stinking like an evil presence.

With every alarm bell in his head ringing, Caspasian left the building, knowing that the very last place he could now go would be back to Yuan and Lilin in Henderson Road. Yet that was the one place that every fibre of his being made him long to run to, for he realised that they were in appalling danger, although he did not yet know why and from whom. However, first he would have to identify the tail that he knew would have been placed on him, and in the teeming streets surrounding the Bund that could take quite some time.

★   ★   ★

A little over half an hour after Caspasian had left the consulate, Chief Inspector Cameron himself marched briskly out, putting on his peaked cap and searching around for his car as he did so. He saw the black limousine waiting for him on the opposite side of the road, and dodged between the traffic towards it. As he approached, the rear door swung open in readiness.

He climbed in and tapped the driver on the shoulder. 'Get going. Quickly! I told you to wait out of sight.'

'I told him to park there,' the car's other occupant said.

Cameron turned to Daniel Smith. 'Well, you shouldn't have done. I can't afford to have my position compromised.'

Smith chuckled. 'Don't worry. It's almost over.'

'That's all very well for you to say. You've got absolutely nothing to lose. You're practically a dead man already.'

'Now, now. Don't be so unappreciative, Chief Inspector. After all I've done for you.'

Cameron glared at him but bit his lip rather than rise to the taunt.

'That's better,' Smith whined. His jaw set hard. 'I saw him coming out,' he said, his voice as cold as ice. 'So high and bloody mighty. The great John Caspasian. Marching through the crowds like a fucking prophet.'

Now it was Cameron's turn to goad. He smiled, enjoying Smith's jealousy and hatred. 'He gave you a licking, though, didn't he? Twice by the sound of it.'

Smith forced himself to smile, a mirthless grimace that twisted the corners of his mouth, leaving his eyes as dead as stone. 'Well, we'll see who's left standing when the bell sounds at the end, shall we? I don't suppose he told you anything?'

'About Yuan?'

'And the girl,' Smith prompted hungrily.

'No, of course not. I didn't think he would, although that idiot Preston seemed to think he might.' He laughed. 'In a curious way I feel sorry for Caspasian having to serve under cretins like that. It's too bad. I could use a man of his calibre.'

'No, you couldn't, and you know it,' Smith said. 'He's too bloody pure. He wouldn't touch you or your little schemes with a barge pole. Indian Army. Gurkhas, don't you know,' Smith sneered. 'Too bloody good for the likes of you and me.'

Cameron eyed Smith dangerously. 'You speak for yourself, laddie.' He stared out at the crowd, regretting having to deal with a man like Smith. 'Anyway. The tail will get him.'

Smith laughed bitterly. 'Do you really think our Caspasian will fall for that little ploy?'

Cameron smiled, shrugging. 'Maybe he will, maybe he won't. It doesn't matter really. That's not the only iron in the fire. There's always Wu Yun.'

Smith brightened, happy for the first time since Cameron had got into the car. 'Yes,' he enthused. 'Good old Wu Yun. Is everything set?'

'Just about,' Cameron said, sinking back into the seat and closing his eyes. 'Just about. Only a miracle can save Caspasian. And who ever heard of a miracle in Shanghai?'

★ ★ ★

Unable to identify the tail, Caspasian decided to do a spot of shopping. Heading for the Wing On department store at 551 Nanking Road he jogged nimbly up the steps and made his way through one department after another, veering past every mirror and reflective window he could find, checking his back frantically for the tail. The clock was running and he was desperate to get back to Yuan and Lilin to warn them of the danger.

As he walked, he ran over the meeting with Preston and Cameron at the consulate. He wondered if he was over-reacting. After all, perhaps it was natural for the two of them to want to know the General's whereabouts. Maybe they were telling the truth, and their only interest was Yuan's safety. But every instinct in Caspasian told him that there was more to it. If only because they had given up too easily. They, on the other hand, seemed almost nonchalant about it, but not because they were unconcerned. On the contrary, Caspasian got the distinct feeling that Yuan's whereabouts were of great importance to them, but for some reason they were hiding from him.

But there was more. Shanghai, as a whole, was out of kilter. On the walk from the consulate he saw yet more of the Chinese gangs and, what was more alarming, in some strange way the police seemed to be in collusion with them. On at least two occasions, Caspasian saw a group of policemen veer away from a gang. Not out of fear, but as if by agreement. The police were allowing them to roam the streets, provided they remained in gangs small enough to avoid notice.

Then there were the armoured cars of the Shanghai Volunteer Force. At one street corner, Caspasian stopped beside one of them and smiled innocently up at the young subaltern hanging importantly out of the turret.

'What's going on?' he called up.

The youngster grinned back. 'Nothing to be alarmed about, sir. Just an exercise.'

'Not much of an exercise,' Caspasian answered. 'Can't be much fun just sitting there. Have you been on the ranges?'

'Oh, yes,' the subaltern said, eager to impress. 'Guns have been zeroed and we're all bombed up.'

'Really? What for?'

'Just a mobilisation exercise. Flying the flag. That sort of thing. A show of strength to show you civvie chaps the International Settlement's quite safe.' He grinned, checking no superior officer was near to rebuke him. 'No matter what happens in the Chinese quarter.'

Caspasian's blood ran cold. To the subaltern he nodded as if impressed. 'Jolly good work. Keep it up.'

469

What the devil was going on? Suddenly he remembered Swinton. If anyone knew what was going on, he would. Not wanting to lead a tail to Swinton's apartment, Caspasian made for a public telephone and dialled Swinton's number. It rang and rang. Whatever was happening, Swinton was obviously at work on a story. With a sudden bolt of alarm he realised he did not know the phone number for the house where Yuan was staying.

Still unable to identify the tail, Caspasian decided to go back to his own apartment. The tail could damn well follow him there. His address was known to the consulate, so he had nothing to hide. Hailing a taxi, he jumped in and set off. When he arrived at the block, he paid the driver and made his way up to his rooms. It was good to be home, although he could hardly enjoy it, knowing that Lilin and her father were waiting for him and wondering where he was.

He went through to the kitchen and made himself some lunch. However, he had just started to eat, sitting in the drawing room and wondering what to do next, when there was a knock at the front door. Caspasian put aside the tray of food and went across to his desk. The drawer was open and he pulled out a pocket .38 Webley revolver. Steeling himself, he made his way out to the hall and opened the door a crack. Jack Swinton fell through it, gasping. His clothes were dishevelled and he looked as if he had not slept for a week.

'Caspasian! Thank the Lord!' He pushed himself inside, snatching the door from Caspasian and slamming it shut. He grabbed the bolts and shot them across. He stared at the Webley. 'Good old Caspasian. Well prepared as ever.'

'I tried to ring you,' Caspasian said. 'Jack, what the hell's going on?'

Instead of answering the question, Swinton said, 'Have you been to the consulate?'

'Yes, of course. I work there.'

Swinton cursed. His eyes were everywhere, as if expecting an ambush.

Caspasian took him by the arm. 'Come and sit down.' Swinton allowed himself to be steered through to the sitting room. His gaze fell on the tray of food.

'Can I?'

'Of course,' Caspasian answered.

Swinton attacked the food, stuffing it into his mouth.

'Drink?' Caspasian asked.

'Whisky.'

As he retrieved the bottle and a couple of glasses, Caspasian calmed himself. Swinton might be close to breaking point, but it was obvious that he knew something and was probably going to be able to shed some light on what was happening in the city.

Out of the blue Swinton said, 'He's here. Chiang Kai-shek. The Generalissimo himself.'

Caspasian stared at him. Swinton shrugged and carried on eating. 'At least he was. I saw him. Tailed him to Rue Molière where he had some kind of meeting.'

Trying to digest the information, Caspasian asked, 'Do you know who the meeting was with?'

Swinton grinned. 'Hey? What kind of reporter do you think I am? Of course I fucking know.'

'And?'

Swinton paused, as if gauging whether or not he could trust his old friend. At last he said, 'There was a whole collection of them. Think of every big name in the Shanghai Chinese business and banking world. That's who was there.'

Caspasian poured himself a stiff Scotch and sat down opposite Swinton. He felt numb. 'Why? I mean, Chiang's the arch Satan as far as they're concerned. The Red Menace.'

Swinton chuckled. 'Sure. *Pravda* writes of him in heroic terms, so does that German Commie rag, *Rote Fahne*, not to mention the

Frenchies' goddamned *L'Humanité.*' He shook his head in wonder. 'Stalin's even publicly praised him in speeches in Moscow. That's the whole beauty of it. And no one's seen it coming.' He grinned. 'Except old Jackie boy here.'

Caspasian slid the gun into his pocket.

'I'd keep that to hand, if I were you, buddy. Things are going to hot up around here very soon.'

'I guessed as much. I've seen the armoured cars. But what about the rest of the story? Why the meeting? What's Chiang up to? If he's meeting with anyone, why isn't it the Communists?'

Jack smiled sourly. 'The Reds don't even know he's here. His own supposed allies. Isn't that great?'

Caspasian was amazed. 'But how can he meet the arch capitalists that hate him?'

'It's simple, old buddy. Like any business-man who's in a tight corner, he's re-financing his operation.'

'He's what?'

'Chiang's in bed with the Communists, right? So much so, everyone's assumed he was one. Moscow bankrolls him. But the guy's not stupid. Chiang realises that in the long term the Communists are a bigger threat to him than the westerners in their fat little concessions, and the capitalist Chinese. Hell, the Chinese were capitalists before anyone in the west thought of the word!'

He leaned forward, bits of food on his lips. 'He's replacing Moscow's money with money from right here in Shanghai. He's already got pledges for a three million dollar loan. Then there's to be a further loan of another seven million dollars and, best of all, plans for another one of fifty million to set up a new capital in Nanking. And it's all on one condition. That he breaks with Moscow and the Commies.' Swinton laughed. 'The stupid fools think they can control him! The bankers think Chiang's the man of tomorrow, and Chiang knows that the Communists are a bigger enemy to him than anyone else.'

With his food gone, Swinton slumped back on the sofa, taking a deep swig from his tumbler. 'So there you have it. Game, set, and, with effect from tomorrow morning, match. The most traitorous volte-face of our times.'

But one question was uppermost in Caspasian's mind. 'Why tomorrow morning? What's so special about that?'

Swinton grinned. 'Well, you don't just think the Communists would take it all lying down, do you? At least Chiang doesn't think so. So he's going to go for them. The whole fucking lot. They've been planning a rising here in the city for months. You and I've known that for ages. But get this,' he said leaning forward, 'they've given their complete plans to Chiang, assuming he's going to help them.' He fell back again, enjoying the irony of it all. 'Help them? He's going to slaughter them!' His fingers formed an imaginary gun which he pointed at Caspasian. 'Bang, you're dead.'

'But, the armoured cars? You mean the British, Americans, French, and all the rest know about it?'

'Know about it? They're in there as thick as the best of them! That's the pity of it. I've just about got the whole story, risked my life every hour of every day to get it, and it's not going to excite anyone to action, 'cos they're all in on it.'

Everything fell into place. Of course there was a complete lack of interest from Preston in General Yuan. The British had only needed him as an ally against Chiang Kai-shek. If they were suddenly allied to the great Generalissimo himself, then of what possible use could Yuan be? None at all. The smallest of small fry.

For a moment Caspasian felt a wave of relief. Surely, with Chiang an ally and Yuan reduced in importance, Yuan and Lilin would be safe to return home. However, the next second he realised that the last thing Chiang would accept would be possible rivals, however small and seemingly insignificant. It was the oldest game in the book. Once you secure your throne, you eliminate all other possible rival claimants. With the British now Chiang's friends, they and the other western powers would be anxious to prove themselves loyal to their powerful new ally. They would be anxious to hand over anyone like Yuan to Chiang's murderers.

As if reading his mind, Swinton said, 'And I heard all about your escapades upriver. Quite a show. All quite irrelevant now, of course, but damn impressive nonetheless.'

Caspasian got up and paced the room. He had to get out. He had to get to Yuan and Lilin. 'Sure, all irrelevant now.' He turned quickly. 'Look, Jack. I've got an idea. I've got to get out of here. I've got to get to General Yuan.'

Swinton stared at him. 'He's here?'

'Yes.'

'Jesus, Caspasian. He's dead meat.' He pointed at Caspasian. 'And anyone connected with him.'

'I need your help. I need you to cover my exit from here. I can slip out, but you've got to make it look like I'm still here.'

Swinton grinned. 'You mean, my Caspasian-like silhouette moving casually in front of the curtains?' He bellowed with laughter. 'Come on, John. Give me a break! No one'll buy that.'

'The old ones are sometimes the best.'

Swinton thought about it. 'And where are you going?'

'Henderson Road. Number 43. Yuan's there in some old relation's house. Well? Will you do it?'

Swinton got up and moved across to the window and looked out. 'On one condition.'

'What?'

'Leave me the keys to your drinks cabinet. That's one hell of a Single Malt you've got there.'

Caspasian smiled, moving across to his old friend and shaking him warmly by the hand. 'Thanks, Jack.'

Caspasian rushed through to the bedroom to gather up some things. If he was going to help Yuan escape, he was going to be acting against Preston and the consulate. He was going to be on the run himself. He found a holdall and hurriedly stuffed some clothes into it. He snatched a razor, soap, a towel and comb from the bathroom and zipped the bag closed.

When he was ready, he ran back through

the apartment and into the drawing room. The blow from the cosh caught him behind the ear. The room spun. Caspasian went down on hands and knees.

'I told you he was one tough fucker,' Swinton said, speaking to the Chinese policeman who had clubbed Caspasian from behind the doorway.

Through a thickening haze Caspasian raised his head, pounding fit to burst. Swinton stood by the window. Through the open doorway on the far side of the room, Caspasian could see the apartment outer door standing open into the hall. Framed in it, Chief Inspector Cameron walked towards him.

'You took your time, Swinton,' Cameron said. 'I thought you were never going to give us the signal.'

'Slowly, slowly, catch you monkey, Ewan,' Swinton said. 'I couldn't just ask him for the goddamned address.'

Caspasian struggled towards him. 'You bastard!' His hand reached for the gun in his pocket. The pocket was empty.

Swinton looked across at him. He held up his hand, dangling Caspasian's .38 by the trigger guard. 'I'm sorry, John. Really I am. I didn't have a choice.'

Cameron sneered. 'That's true enough.

Money never gives a greedy man a choice.' He came towards Caspasian, flanked by two policemen. 'So?' he said to Swinton.

'43 Henderson Road,' Swinton said, turning quickly away to look out of the window, avoiding Caspasian's eyes.

'I'm much obliged,' Cameron said, peering down at Caspasian. 'And so will someone else be, Captain Caspasian. There's someone else who is looking forward to seeing you. An old friend of yours.'

And with a nod, he ordered the policeman to club Caspasian unconscious.

19

The first thing Caspasian saw when he came round was a face peering inquisitively into his own.

'He's back,' it said, speaking without taking its eyes from Caspasian's.

'Smith,' Caspasian croaked. As he spoke, a fist punched him hard in the midriff. The air went out of his lungs and he gasped.

'Did I say you could speak?' Smith said, smiling.

Vision clearing, Caspasian found himself seated on a bench, leaning back against a wall. The brickwork was damp. In fact, everything was. There was a fetid smell in the place and, from the mixture of sewage and rotting fish and vegetation, Caspasian guessed he was somewhere on the waterfront. His wrists were securely tied behind his back. His ankles were tied with cord. Without appearing to, he tested the knots, exerting gentle pressure on them. They did not budge.

Smith pulled up a wicker-topped stool and sat down in front of his prisoner, contemplating him. 'Well, this is a turn up for the books, isn't it?' When Caspasian remained silent,

Smith sarcastically indicated he could reply.

'What do you want?' Caspasian asked.

Smith looked surprised. 'Why, nothing. Absolutely nothing. You see, I've got you. You're all I want.'

Caspasian chuckled. 'And I suppose I now die, is that it?'

Smith turned to the men behind him. 'He's a smart one this, eh?' The smile froze into an ugly leer as he punched Caspasian on the jaw. Caspasian tasted blood.

'Big man, Smith. Aren't you?'

'Don't give me that stuff. If you think I'm going to untie you and have fisticuffs by Queensberry Rules, you're even more of a fool than I thought. I know what you can do. No, I'm happy with you where you are.' And he punched him again, half rising from the stool to give it extra force.

Looking past Smith, Caspasian noticed there were three other men, all Chinese. One of them was wearing the uniform of the Shanghai Police. He was examining his revolver. There was something about him that Caspasian thought was familiar but he could not place it.

Smith caught his glance and smiled. 'Surprised to see the police here? Chief Inspector Cameron and I are old friends. Not as long-standing as you and me, of course.

We're more business partners.'

Caspasian frowned. Then he understood. The smell, he knew there was something else about it. And then the policeman looked up and smiled grimly with his one good eye. An empty socket gaped where the other should have been.

'Opium,' Caspasian said, shaking his head, cross with himself for not realising it before. The policeman had been Cameron's supposed prisoner on the junk which Commander Hewson had intercepted on his way up the Yangtze. The same man Caspasian had fought. The man saw Caspasian's recognition and grinned at him malevolently.

'Yes,' Smith said. 'Opium. You've really mucked up what was a very nice little operation. Not so little, actually. It was a nice little earner for General Mok and me. Shipped it through Shanghai, Cameron got a rake off for seeing it got through without any questions being asked.' He nodded at the policeman. 'Cameron and a few of his most trusted coppers, that is.'

Smith frowned. 'Then along comes John fucking Caspasian, knight in shining bloody armour, and blows the whole show out of the water by killing my erstwhile employer.' He punched Caspasian again. 'But now it's pay back time.' And he punched Caspasian again.

'Untie him,' he said. 'Just his ankles. And watch out for his feet. Don't give him room to use them.'

Two of the others came forward and hoisted Caspasian upright. His legs felt like jelly but he forced his strength into them and balanced precariously. One of the men pulled out a knife and severed the cords.

'Where are you taking me?' Caspasian asked.

'You're going for a swim,' Smith answered, obviously enjoying every minute of their encounter. 'I'd like to finish you off here, but Cameron's a bit twitchy about murdering a serving British officer. He wants it to look like an accident. Sort of.'

The canals, Caspasian thought. A blow on the head and then in I go. Nice. Not a very convincing accident perhaps, he reflected, but Preston was not the sort to ask too many questions.

They manhandled him up some steps to the exit door where they draped a jacket round his shoulders to hide the fact his wrists were tied. Then, with one man holding him under each arm, and the policeman and Smith leading the way, they went out into the street.

Night had fallen. Caspasian looked about him and saw that he had been right. It was the waterfront area, a network of alleyways, canals and dark and dingy backstreets. They passed a couple of whores leaning against a wall, one Chinese the other Russian. Both looked as ancient as hags but were probably only in their thirties. Caspasian noticed that while the Chinese spoke in Mandarin, the other answered in Russian. It was hard to tell if they understood each other but neither seemed to care.

'So who's going to do it?' Caspasian called out to Smith, goading him. 'Have you got the guts, or will it be one of your henchmen here?'

'Oh, no, I'll do it. Can't wait,' Smith called back cheerily. 'I've got the guts all right. You'll see.'

'Like you had guts when you took the credit for what Dobson did at the redoubt, and then had him shot to cover up the truth of your cowardice?'

Smith stopped in his tracks and whirled, his eyes vicious.

'What I'd like to know,' Caspasian persisted, 'is how you got the other men to keep quiet. How did you browbeat them? Threats? Promises? Did you fix it so they could have a nice long leave back at home?'

'Shut up,' Smith hissed.

That's good, Caspasian thought. Lose

control. Go on. Do it.

'What's it like being scared, Smith? Did you wet yourself when the stormtroopers came over the top?'

'I said shut up!'

'Did you crap in your pants? Did you . . .'

Smith screamed and rushed at him. It was the moment Caspasian had been waiting for. Holding back until the last instant, Caspasian drove all his weight into the man on his right, swinging himself and his two escorts around so that they were side on to the charging Smith. Unable to stop himself, Smith ran headlong into Caspasian's escort. For one second both were winded.

Beyond Smith, the one-eyed policeman saw what was happening and went for his revolver. Caspasian saw the holster flap opening and knew he had to act now or never. With his escorts winded he was able to break away from them. The jacket fell from his shoulders. His legs were free and at last he had the space to move. His right foot came up and knocked aside the revolver as the policeman pulled it clear of the holster. The gun was attached by a lanyard fixed to the pommel, hanging it round the policeman's neck. It flew out of his fist but swung there, still dangerously within reach.

Balanced on his left leg, Caspasian pulled

back his right foot, pivoted at the hips, and drove the edge of his right shoe hard into the policeman's throat in a jodan yoko-geri side kick. The man's single eye bulged. The cartilage crunched under the force of the blow and blood spouted from his lips as he sank to the ground, gasping for breath, dying.

With his arms still securely pinioned behind his back, Caspasian staggered but managed to remain upright. Smith and the others were recovering. He set off up the alleyway, expecting to feel the smack of a bullet in the back at any moment. Ducking round the corner, Caspasian found himself in a narrow street. There were bars along either side, and outside one of them the comatose form of a drunk lay in the gutter, vomit pooling away from his face. Judging from the relative quiet, Caspasian guessed it was now the early hours of the morning.

He hurled himself up the street, hearing the sound of running footsteps behind him. He turned to glance back over his shoulder and saw Smith and the other two round the corner. There was a gun in Smith's hand. Ahead of Caspasian the street lay open and empty. He knew there was no way he could outrun his pursuers.

With one last spurt of effort he tried to lengthen his stride and ran headlong into a group of half a dozen sailors that stepped out suddenly from one of the bars. They were fairly far gone with drink, the smell of stale beer rising from their soiled white uniforms.

'Where the fuck do you think you're going?' one of them drawled, his voice threatening.

Caspasian looked up, fighting for breath, knowing he could not possibly take them all on as well.

'Mr Caspasian, sir?' a voice said.

Caspasian turned and found himself staring at Watts and Jones, the sailors from the gunboat that had taken him up the Yangtze.

'Jones!' Caspasian said in amazement. But Smith was there, shoving his way rudely through the press of bodies towards him. Quick as a flash Caspasian shouted. 'Coppers! Lend me a hand, lads!'

There was a cry of outrage from the sailors as Smith and the two Chinese tried to lay hands on Caspasian.

''Ere, leave him alone,' one of the sailors shouted.

'Do you know 'im, Alf?' another one cried.

'Sure I do,' Jones replied blearily. 'He's a mate of ours, ain't he, Wattsy?'

In an instant the sailors' mood switched. Smith brought up his revolver only to have it knocked out of his hand by a knuckled fist covered in tattoos. 'Watch 'im! He's got a gun!' someone shouted.

'Get the fucker!'

Incensed, the sailors waded in, fists and boots swinging. Under the rain of blows, the two Chinese and Smith were thrown back, huddling together, shielding themselves as best they could from the violent assault.

Jones and Watts snatched at Caspasian and dragged him out of harm's way.

'My wrists, lads. Cut the rope!' Caspasian said.

A blade flashed and the rope fell away. Caspasian searched over the tops of the heads for Smith and saw him down on his hands and knees, scrabbling after the revolver again. He was only a foot away from it. Fighting his desire to finish it once and for all, Caspasian turned away from the fight.

'Go on, sir. Run for it,' Jones shouted. 'We'll take care of the coppers.'

Caspasian clapped a hand on his shoulder. 'I won't forget this,' he said, and darted away up the street, running as hard as he could.

As he ran he rubbed the life back into his wrists, the numbness from the ropes slowly easing. His fingers tingled as the blood rushed back into them. Eventually he slowed to a walk. The streets were all unfamiliar to him but he guessed that he was somewhere in the Nantao district, east of the Chinese City. Sure enough, he finally turned into Chung Hwa Road and his bearings fell into place.

'Right,' he said quietly. Now he knew where he was, he knew where he had to go.

★   ★   ★

Swinton was fast asleep when the bedroom door crashed inwards. Before his eyes were fully open, he was being hoisted bodily off the mattress, the covers torn aside, and rushed headlong through his apartment towards the bathroom. That door too, split asunder with a single ferocious kick. As Swinton found his head being thrust into the lavatory he finally put two and two together and realised he was in the unforgiving grip of John Caspasian.

'Where are they?'

'Who?' Swinton answered, his voice echoing strangely off the surrounding porcelain.

Instead of receiving an answer, Swinton's face was thrust into the tepid lavatory water. He had forgotten to flush it after urinating there before tumbling into bed. He gagged.

The next second he was being pulled free, but held an inch above the stinking surface. Caspasian had his right arm doubled up behind his back. Swinton's hand was up between his shoulder blades and he could feel the ligaments straining and at the point of giving way.

'Where have they taken Yuan and the girl?'

'I don't know. I swear it,' Swinton gasped, choking.

Caspasian was silent for a moment. 'Why?' he said eventually.

'You mean why don't I know?'

'Don't be so fucking stupid. Why did you do it? Are you in on the opium deal like the rest of them?'

Swinton's shoulders heaved as he gave a bitter chuckle. 'No such luck. They're making thousands out of it. You don't think they'd let just anyone in, do you?' he said.

'And that means you, of course?' Caspasian said mockingly. 'So if not the opium, then what?'

'I told you. I discovered Chiang was here in Shanghai.'

'Go on.'

Swinton spat the tainted water from his mouth. 'Look, can we discuss this somewhere else, old buddy?'

'No, this suits me fine, thank you' Caspasian said. He thrust Swinton's face into the urine again, held it there for a few seconds and then pulled it out. 'And I'm not your old buddy, OK? Now talk.'

Swinton spat and shook his face. 'Christ, Caspasian. Let me up and I'll tell you what I know.'

After a moment, Caspasian lifted the American out of the lavatory and dropped him on to the tiled floor beside the bowl. He stood over him, out of range of Swinton's feet. Swinton used the edge of his pyjamas jacket to wipe his face and mouth, spitting in disgust. 'Jesus, Caspasian. That was hardly called for.'

Caspasian's foot shot forwards and kicked Swinton in the chest. Swinton grunted, his sternum fit to burst.

'Talk!'

'OK, OK,' Swinton gasped, choking. 'They discovered I'd found out about the deal with Chiang and were afraid I'd spill the beans before everything was in place.'

'Then why didn't they just kill you?'

Swinton chuckled. 'Slitting the throat of some Chinaman is one thing. An American citizen is quite another. In any case, Chiang needs the US as an ally. He doesn't trust the Brits or the French.'

Caspasian remembered Cameron's words. A greedy man. 'So he bribed you?' Caspasian said.

Swinton smirked. 'Don't look so high and mighty. It was more cash than I'd ever be able to make from pen-pushing. So what if I agreed to keep my mouth shut until it was all over? What's the big deal?'

Caspasian reached up to the lump behind his ear. 'This is.'

For the first time Swinton looked scared. 'Yeah, well, I'm sorry about that. But I didn't have a choice. It was that bastard, Cameron. They were holding me on ice, just in case the money wasn't enough to keep me silent. He dragged me out of the cell and told me that unless I helped him get the address out of you I could forget any pay-off.' He looked up at Caspasian, hoping for mercy. 'Hell, John, I need that money. The younger guys are getting all the breaks on the paper. My reporting days are over. This is my nest egg.'

Caspasian glared at him with loathing. 'I trusted you, Jack. We were friends. Do you realise what you've done? You've killed those two people, as surely as if you put the gun to their heads yourself. And all for your fucking nest egg. How does that feel?'

'OK, Caspasian, don't rub it in. I'm a shit. I admit it.'

'You're going to do more than admit it. You're coming with me to find them.'

Swinton looked up, fear in his eyes. 'You've got to be kidding?' He saw from Caspasian's face that he was in deadly earnest. 'It's too late. They'll already have taken them.'

'Cameron's men?'

'The Green Gang. They're helping Chiang. They control the whole underworld in Shanghai. Chiang's going to use them to weed out the Communists. You've seen the gangs in the International Settlement? The police have been sheltering them. When it all starts, they're going to enter the Chinese quarter and then it all begins.'

'The arrests?'

Swinton laughed. 'The massacre. The police are going to hand over anyone found in the International Settlement or the French Concession. That's why they wanted Yuan's address. They'll all be taken into the Chinese quarter and killed.'

'When does it start?'

In perfect answer, from across the city came the unmistakable sound of a single machine-gun. A single, long burst of fire. Then silence. Caspasian glanced at the wall clock. It was four o'clock in the morning, Tuesday 12th April.

'I guess it's started,' Swinton said unnecessarily.

Caspasian grabbed him by the lapels and hauled him to his feet. 'Come on.'

Swinton protested all the way to the bedroom. Caspasian slung him on the bed, ripped a shirt and trousers from the back of the chair where Swinton had flung them earlier that night, and threw them in Swinton's face. 'Get dressed.'

'You don't want me,' he pleaded. 'I'd just get in the way.'

Caspasian saw his own .38 Webley on the dressing table. He picked it up and checked the cylinder. It was full. Swinton had even taken the box of cartridges. Caspasian stuffed the box in his pocket and pointed the gun at Swinton. 'You either come, or else I shoot you here.'

Swinton knew the man well enough to know that he was not bluffing. 'But what for, John?' he asked miserably as he started to change into the dishevelled clothes.

'What good can I be?'

'Good bloody question, but I'll think of something.'

When Swinton was ready, the two men slipped out of the apartment block. Since the opening burst of machine-gun fire there had been others, and now, from all across Shanghai, gunfire was erupting. Here and there, lines of tracer spun up into the sky, as bullets ricochetted off the brickwork against which anyone believed to be a Communist had been placed and shot.

Caspasian was desperate to get to General

Yuan and Lilin. He had only been gone from them for less than one day but in that time the whole situation in China had changed. The balance of power had shifted. Chiang Kai-shek was now allied to the western powers and to the capitalists in Shanghai and other big cities. He had split from his old friends the Communists and had now set in motion the bloodiest of purges.

The journey back to Henderson Road took longer than it should have done. Gangs now roamed the dark streets, no longer hiding their weapons but brandishing them openly. On one street, Caspasian and Swinton came upon a crowd of armed youths who had taken several prisoners. As the two westerners slipped past on the opposite side of the street, keeping to the shadows, they saw the prisoners being forced to kneel. One after the other, each of them was beheaded with a Chinese broadsword. The thud of each of the falling heads hitting the pavement was followed by an enthusiastic cheer from the gang.

At last Caspasian turned into the road, but as he approached No. 43, he felt a shiver of apprehension run down his spine. The small door set in the gates stood open. He stepped inside. Across the yard, a chain extended from the dog kennel, and on the end of it lay the dead body of the guard dog, its skull cut in two.

'Jesus Christ,' Swinton muttered.

Caspasian thrust him towards the house and hammered on the door. It swung open on its hinges. They stepped inside.

'Lilin!' Caspasian called. His voice echoed round the building. From the back room he heard the sound of shuffling feet and a moment later the small housekeeper peered out at him.

'Go away! Leave us! You have brought enough trouble already.'

'Please, tell me where they've gone,' Caspasian tried.

'I don't know. Now go.'

She turned and started to shuffle towards the kitchen but in three strides Caspasian had caught her. From behind him Swinton said, 'Are you going to try and beat it out of her too? Maybe there's a lavatory you can stick her head down.'

'Shut up,' Caspasian snapped. To the woman he said, 'I have to know, please think. I might be able to save them.'

The woman glared at him. 'Why should I care? They are nothing to me. Nor are you. Now get out,' she shrieked, trying to pull away from him.

Caspasian pulled the Webley from his

pocket and held the muzzle against her temple. Swinton shouted. 'Christ, man. Don't do it!'

Through gritted teeth, Caspasian said, 'I love that girl. Now where did they take her and the General?'

Terrified, the woman looked first at Swinton, seeing the welts bruising his face, and then at Caspasian. In his eyes she saw the desperation and knew he would pull the trigger.

'I heard one of them say they were taking them to Manchu Park. They will be executed there.'

Caspasian pushed her away, snatched Swinton and strode towards the door. As they got there Swinton tugged him back. 'Hang on a minute, Caspasian. What the hell can you do? There'll be a whole bunch of them and what have you got? A .38 pocket revolver.'

'You're right. This way,' Caspasian said, and pulled him back into the house and up to the room he had occupied just the day before. Furniture had been overturned and the doors to the bedrooms had all been broken down. But the Green Gang had been after people. They had not been there to plunder. Stuffed under his bed where he had left it Caspasian found the satchel. Unzipping it he pulled out two more handguns and the bag of grenades.

From behind him, Swinton whistled. 'I might have guessed. Can I have one?'

'You must be bloody joking.'

'Look, I'll help you. I said I was sorry. You and I are friends. Give me a gun.'

'Fuck off.' Caspasian kicked Swinton back into the corridor and down the stairs.

Back in the street they turned in the direction of Manchu Park. Gangs of youths roamed now on all sides. Seeing the westerners, they cheered and brandished their weapons and broadswords. Some of them waved severed heads at them, congealed blood matting the hair, the lifeless eyes glazed and half shut.

Gunfire echoed from every street. Somewhere a building was on fire, a vast plume of black acrid smoke spiralling into the sky that was starting to lighten as dawn approached. Caspasian looked up at the sky. Time was fast running out, if it had not already done so.

As they raced through the streets, he could think of only one thing. Lilin. In the house he had just left he had caught a smell of the perfume she had used on the Sunday evening when they had arrived and had dinner together. His stomach churned to think of her in the hands of the Green Gang. He had to get to her. The hand grenades would help but even they would not be enough. And what if he did manage to rescue Lilin and her father? They would then have to make their way out of the city, being pursued and hunted every step of the way. Somehow he had to increase his firepower and find a way of making a fast escape. And he had to find it now.

Glancing at Caspasian out of the corner of his eye, Swinton saw the tight lips, the fixed, desperate stare from the narrowed eyes, and he trembled. The men now holding General Yuan and Lilin might be superior in numbers, but Swinton knew Caspasian all too well. He knew that in his present frame of mind Caspasian was capable of absolutely anything.

★   ★   ★

Wu Yun had enjoyed the night. Gathering his men together shortly after midnight, they had made their way first of all to the Chapei district in the north, waiting for the appointed hour. When 0400 hours had come, they had moved in, like hundreds of other gangsters and soldiers loyal to Chiang Kai-shek, elsewhere throughout the city.

Breaking into houses, they dragged Communists, trade union leaders and workers sympathetic to the Communist cause from their beds and murdered them, either on the spot, or else herded them into the streets for a more public execution.

Within half an hour, heads had been strung up on lampposts throughout Shanghai, and even in the International Settlement and the French Concession. Anyone who tried to escape by seeking refuge in the International Settlement was arrested by members of the Shanghai Municipal Police and handed over. The whole operation was turning out to be a brilliant success. Nevertheless, Wu Yun knew that it would take several days to complete the massacre. Once the initial burst of activity was over, they would consolidate. Then the detailed hunt would begin, searching from house to house. They were determined to winkle out every leftist sympathiser in the city. In return the Green Gang would be left by Chiang to run the criminal underworld in Shanghai. Indeed, Wu reflected, it was hard to see where the underworld ended and the supposedly legal world began. Rather, the two were entwined in a cesspit of lucrative affairs, all of them producing money, whether banking and trade, or prostitution and drugs. And the money earned from all of these went to pretty much the same people.

Throughout Nantao, Woosoong and in the Pootung district across the river, the sounds of the massacre hung over the city like the pall of smoke rising from the burning buildings. They had broken into the General Labour Union Headquarters in the Huchow Guild in Chapei. The word was that the Communists and trade union leaders would make a final stand at the big Commercial Press building on Paoshan Road. Wu did not expect it to fall until sometime later that day. When it did, there would undoubtedly be hundreds more deaths as it was stormed.

Moving from task to pre-planned task, Wu and his thugs worked methodically until their arms ached from wielding their broadswords. He had just arrived at Manchu Park to oversee the execution of a number of Communist sympathisers when one of his men came running up to him.

'There is a prisoner here,' the man gabbled.

Wu yawned. It would be light soon. He was growing tired and was considering taking a nap somewhere before continuing the work later that morning. 'So what?'

'We were asked to pick him up by Cameron.'

Wu's ears pricked up. 'Cameron?'

'Yes.'

Wu often had dealings with Chief Inspector Cameron over the opium traffic. The man had become more greedy in recent weeks and demanded ever greater payments for his assistance. Presumably this was someone the Chief Inspector wanted out of the way.

'He is a warlord.'

Now he had Wu's attention. 'He says his name is General Yuan.'

Wu stood up and sauntered past the rows of prisoners awaiting execution. All had been forced to kneel, hands tied behind their backs. The men carrying out the beheadings were taking a break.

He came to the man indicated by his follower. 'This is him.'

The man looked up. Wu stared at him with interest. 'Who are you?'

'My name is General Yuan,' Yuan said. 'There has been a mistake. I am not a Communist. I demand you release me.'

Wu laughed. 'You're in no position to demand anything.' He glanced the length of the line. 'In any case, we're taking care of more than just the Communists. You could say we're doing a bit of spring cleaning. If the British authorities want you dead it is because Chiang Kai-shek wants it. Who am I to disobey?'

Yuan hung his head. He had been beaten when the house was raided and he could hardly keep his back straight. But he became aware that Wu was no longer listening to him. His attention had wandered. Yuan looked up and saw Wu staring fixedly at Lilin kneeling at his side. Yuan's heart went cold.

'Look up,' Wu commanded, addressing Lilin.

Lilin did not move. She had seen who it was and she was fighting back her fear.

Wu stooped and took a fistful of her hair, yanking back her head. He stared into her face. 'You!' he hissed. He was suddenly fully awake. He took her by the shoulders and hoisted her to her feet. Delight flooded through him, mixed with a growing rage. 'My little song bird. It is truly wonderful to see you again.'

Yuan staggered forward. 'Leave her alone. She is my daughter.'

Wu's foot shot out and Yuan toppled over backwards, spitting blood from his broken lips. Lilin tried to go to him but Wu held her tightly. From the ground Yuan said, 'I can give you money if you let us go. Both of us. Let us go and you will be well rewarded.'

Wu grinned, his eyes on Lilin. 'Oh, but I have all the reward I want right here,' he said. 'I can't think of anything more I would rather have.'

He pulled her roughly away. Lilin screamed, looking back at her father. Two of Wu's men dragged Yuan back on to his knees but held him firmly in place.

Dragging Lilin towards the executioners, he called out, 'Get up you idle pigs. Time to work again. I've got a special one for you here.'

Yuan cried out but was cuffed into silence.

The executioners had taken up station beside a concrete drainage ditch. As each prisoner had been executed, both body and head were tumbled over the top and a substantial pile had already grown beneath them. Wu dragged Lilin the last few yards and flung her at their feet.

'Do it then,' he commanded.

The executioners looked at one another, mystified. Even in her dishevelled state it was obvious to anyone that she was beautiful. 'Don't you want to have her first?' one of them said.

Wu glared at her disdainfully. 'No, but don't let me stop you.'

The men grinned, laying aside their broadswords again. They scanned around for a suitable spot, eventually selecting the large square top of a drainage cover. Gripped with the urgency of it, they pushed and pulled her across it, each vying to be first.

'Get on with it,' Wu called, leaning back against a tree to watch. Some of his men gathered beside him to enjoy the spectacle of this unexpected diversion from murder.

Lilin kicked and struggled, until one of the executioners managed to grab her ankles. Wu's men howled with laughter at the sight.

The sound of a motor caused Wu to glance over his shoulder. Making its way across the park was an armoured car of the Shanghai Volunteer Force. Wu frowned, puzzled.

'Those bloody idiots,' he muttered. One of his men turned to see. 'They live in Shanghai and even then they get lost,' Wu joked. 'Doesn't he know he's outside the International Settlement?'

He turned back to the struggle, starting to regret having turned down the chance of raping the girl. His men had now got her across the drainage cover and the senior executioner was stooping over her, fumbling excitedly with her clothes.

Wu glanced back at the armoured car. Executions were one thing, but he did not really want some western bank clerk and part-time soldier to see the rape. He might try to intervene and do something stupidly British and chivalrous.

'Go and see what he wants,' he said dismissively to the man beside him. 'Tell him how to get out of the park.'

The man jogged away and Wu turned back to his men. They had started to clap in unison, cheering on their friend who had pulled out a knife to cut the buttons his fingers had been unable to cope with.

The burst from a machine-gun stopped them in their tracks. Wu spun round, his mouth opening like a fish, and saw his man tottering backwards as bullets from the Vickers cut through him. On top of the armoured car, the turret was turning in his direction. The vehicle was looming menacingly closer, the hatch closed.

Sighting on the gang of men, Caspasian squinted through the gun turret's firing slit. In the driving seat beneath and in front of him, Jack Swinton obeyed his every instruction, knowing that to do otherwise would invite instant death. Caspasian had found his quarry. Now he was out for blood.

20

Through the gun sight, the gang of men grouped around the drainage ditch made an easy target, and Caspasian was sorely tempted to give them a whole belt of ammunition, tracking from left to right. But he knew he had to be careful. He was not particularly fussed if some of the Communists got in his line of fire, but if the old housekeeper had been correct, then Lilin and General Yuan were somewhere amongst them.

Firing short, controlled bursts, he worked through the men, directing his fire at everyone he could identify in the early dawn light as a Green Gang thug. He caught sight of the bodies in the ditch and swung the gun round to rake with bullets four men he saw running away carrying broadswords.

Through the driver's eye slit Swinton whooped, calling out, 'What's it like being on the receiving end, guys?'

The driver's seat was in front and below the gunner's, and Swinton could feel Caspasian's knees pressing against his shoulders. Both he and Caspasian were too tall for the cramped conditions inside the armoured car, but that had not stopped Caspasian commandeering this one. It had been standing idly at a road junction. Caspasian had pulled himself up on to it and banged on the turret. The young subaltern had stupidly opened it and popped his head out to see who it was. Before he could protest, Caspasian had grabbed him under the armpits and lifted him out.

Swinton could not help smiling when he remembered it. The poor young fellow had started remonstrating at that stage, but Caspasian had simply placed his hand in the man's chest and shoved him clean off the top of the car. The driver had been next, dragged out and tossed aside like a sack of rice. After that, Swinton and Caspasian had torn through the city streets, ignoring traffic signals, junctions, the lot. Swinton had thought it terrific and had started to regret his earlier betrayal of his friend. Nevertheless, money was money.

The car was still heading for the centre of the group when Caspasian caught sight of a figure struggling off the ground beside a drainage ditch cover. Even at that range he recognised Lilin. He could see by her movements that she was dazed. He kicked Swinton in the kidneys and barked out directions. As the car swung towards Lilin, Caspasian raked the rest of the gang members, most of them now fleeing for their lives. Several of them darted behind trees for cover but the .303 bullets of the Vickers simply chewed through bark and wood, finding them on the other side.

With a final burst of fire, Caspasian ordered Swinton to halt. The car skidded to a stop and Caspasian flung open the turret. The heavy iron lid crashed down on the turret, Caspasian jumped down to the ground and ran to Lilin. She looked at him, shaking. Her clothes were torn and she was in shock.

'My father,' she murmured, pointing to the line of bound prisoners.

Leaving her by the armoured car, Caspasian ran across to General Yuan. He pulled a knife from his pocket and cut the rope binding his wrists. All around them, the other prisoners were getting to their feet and running away through the park, disappearing back into the city before the men from the Green Gang could recover and hunt them down.

A hatch in the front of the car slammed open and Swinton's head appeared. 'We've got problems,' he said, and pointed to the far side of the park. Lumbering through the trees, two more armoured cars of the

Shanghai Volunteer Force were heading for them. Hanging on to one of them, the subaltern who Caspasian had ejected. His arm was waving frantically in Caspasian's direction, indicating the target for the two cars' machine-guns.

'Get in!' Caspasian shouted.

General Yuan clambered up on to the car and reached down for Lilin as Caspasian helped her up.

'It'll be a bit of a squeeze but you'll be better off inside,' Caspasian said.

By throwing out the equipment belonging to the previous crew members, and getting rid of several large boxes of rations, they were able to make enough space.

'It was him,' Lilin said, trembling. 'Wu Yun. The bull.'

Caspasian looked up sharply, but before he could say anything Lilin added, 'He got away. I saw him.'

'Let's get out of here,' Caspasian said gently, helping Lilin into the turret. When she was safely inside he slipped back into his seat and kicked Swinton.

'Now I know how a goddamned horse feels,' Swinton said as he rammed the car into gear and shot off, turning sharply to head away from the pursuing cars at best speed.

Inside, the armoured car was like a cocktail

shaker. Swinton ground his way ferociously through the gears, pushing the engine to its limits, tearing through the Chinese quarter of Shanghai, heading away from the park as fast as he could.

'Where are we going?' General Yuan shouted, clinging to the sides. 'The International Settlement?'

Caspasian glanced down from the machine-gun sight. They had outstripped the pursuing cars and the road both ahead and behind was clear. 'No, it's not safe. If they caught us they'd hand you and Lilin over again.'

'Well, you'd better think of something soon, boss,' Swinton called back. 'I'm going to need some directions.'

'Our junk on the waterfront,' Lilin said. 'Why not go there?'

Caspasian shook his head. 'Too dangerous. The police'll know about it by now. Especially now they're cooperating with the Green Gang.'

'But can't we pick up another vessel?' Yuan said, feeling ever more desperate by the minute. He was concerned for Lilin's safety. 'Surely there must be someone who will take us back upriver?'

Again Caspasian disagreed. 'I'm sorry. I think the river's out. Cameron probably controls everything that moves on it. We can't take the risk. Once he hears you've escaped, the river's exactly where he'll be looking for you.' The next second, Caspasian realised the significance of what he had just said. 'Of course! The river!'

Lilin and General Yuan looked at him. 'What?'

'Everyone will be guarding the river, expecting you to try and make your way back to Changsha.' He grinned at them. 'So we'll go in the opposite direction. Tientsin, north along the coast.'

'Of course! A port.' General Yuan said, considering.

'Exactly. We'll find a ship. You can then get out of China altogether or, if you want, head down the coast to Hong Kong and either lay up there until all this has blown over, or make your way home overland.'

'We'd be going through Chiang's heartland,' Yuan said. 'It would be safer to remain in Hong Kong. I have relatives there. They will shelter us.'

Struggling to control the top-heavy armoured car that rolled dangerously every time it swerved round a corner, Swinton shouted over his shoulder. 'It's more than five hundred miles to Tientsin. You're mad, Caspasian, stark staring mad!'

'We're not going to drive there, you idiot. We'll take the overnight train.'

Swinton laughed. 'And how do you plan to get through the station? Don't you think Cameron will be having it watched? Not to mention old Fatso and his boys? If they're trying to sweep up all the Communists, they'll be checking every possible escape route out of the city.'

'We'll make it,' Caspasian assured them all, not fully clear himself how he was going to manage it.

'I hate to be the one who fucks up the plan,' Swinton shouted again, 'but as the train doesn't leave until this evening, where are we going to lie up for the rest of the day? I take it you don't intend to drive around in this tin can until dark? Both your apartment and mine are out of the question. Too goddamned obvious.'

Caspasian racked his brains. 'You're a member of the American Club, aren't you?' he said to Swinton.

'Yes. So what?'

'So you'll book in to a room there.'

'We can't just waltz in looking like this,' he replied. Caspasian had to agree. They were all dishevelled and bloodied. It would hardly go unnoticed.

'You're the most respectable of the lot of

us,' he said to Swinton. 'You check into the room. We'll come in through the back. You can let us in through the service entrance.'

Swinton grinned, suspicious. 'That's all very well, but how do you know you can trust me? If I go in by myself, how do you know I won't call Cameron, or do a runner?'

'Because I would hunt you down and kill you, so help me God. And you know it.'

'Yeah,' Swinton said miserably. 'I sure do.' He was already paying for double-crossing Caspasian and he knew he was lucky to be alive. He did not want to risk it a second time. He knew no police cell could hold the Englishman and he knew that, the moment he was free, Caspasian would carry out his threat without a second thought. Especially if the girl had suffered as a result of a second betrayal by Swinton.

'OK,' he said. 'Let's do it.'

They parked the armoured car in an alleyway off Foochow Road, selecting a place some distance from the American Club so that their destination was not obvious, and walked briskly the rest of the way. While Swinton went inside, Caspasian, Lilin and Yuan went round to the service entrance at the back. It was a full twenty minutes before the door was unlocked and Swinton ushered them inside.

'The service elevator's this way,' he said, leading them through a dark corridor lined with wheeled baskets brimming with dirty laundry. He had taken a room on the top floor at the end of the corridor and next to a fire escape. 'I thought old Hawkeye here would like a second exit,' he said, nodding at Caspasian.

Lilin scowled at him. She had learned of his betrayal and hated having to entrust him with their safety.

Once they were inside and had the door locked, Caspasian took stock.

'We're going to need new clothes,' he said. He had brought revolvers for himself, Lilin and General Yuan, and a couple of hand grenades. More than that would be difficult to hide when going through the station and boarding the train later that evening. For cash they had the money Swinton had been given to keep silent. It was more than enough to get them to Tientsin and out of China. 'I'll do the shopping,' he continued. 'Lilin, you and your father watch Swinton.'

Swinton started to protest.

'Getting the room is one thing,' Caspasian said. 'But I wouldn't want to test your newfound resolve too far by letting you loose in the city, and with your own cash in your pocket. You might not betray us, but you sure as hell wouldn't come back.'

When he had cleaned himself up as best he could, Caspasian left the others in the room and went out of the club, walking boldly out through the reception area as if a long-standing guest. The show of confidence worked and no one gave him a second glance.

First stop was the Wing On department store where he bought a couple of holdalls which he then filled with clothes for himself and the General, as well as a fresh change of clothes for Swinton. In the distance he could hear firing from outside the International Settlement. In the streets around him, however, business was being conducted as usual.

The purchase of clothes for Lilin presented him with more of a problem because in the rush, he had not asked her for her sizes. Making his best guess, he made a selection and went to pay, enjoying the use of one of the rolls of Swinton's bank notes.

His next stop was Bubbling Well Road and the railway office to purchase tickets and make reservations for two sleeper compartments on the Shanghai-Tientsin overnight express later that day. He was not surprised to find that it was already heavily booked with people anxious at the sudden violence and trying to leave the city. Nevertheless, he managed to get the sleepers with the aid of another of Swinton's bank rolls as a bribe.

Checking his back, he made his way once again to the American Club, picking up some food on the way. They would need supplies for the journey, even though the overnight train was equipped with a dining car.

Back at the club he went quickly up to the room and knocked on the door. To his immense relief they were all there, safe. With the best part of the day still to run, they settled down. Caspasian and General Yuan took turns to keep an eye on Swinton, while Lilin curled up on one of the beds and slept. It was going to be a busy night and Caspasian knew that the most dangerous part was still to come.

★ ★ ★

In his office at Police Headquarters Cameron was fuming. Standing before him, Wu Yun refused to be cowed.

'I am not one of your men, so don't treat me like one,' he snarled. He turned to Smith who leaned by the window. 'If you hadn't let this Caspasian slip through your fingers this would never have happened. Yuan and the girl would be dead and that would be that.'

'What the hell does it matter?' Smith

answered testily. He gingerly fingered his swollen cheek where the sailors had punched him repeatedly. 'They're just small fry in the middle of the whole wider business.' Outside from across the city, gunfire echoed. 'Hundreds of Commies are being dealt with out there. What do three people matter?'

Cameron leaned across his desk on clenched fists. 'I'll tell you why it matters, Smith,' he said, spitting out the name as though it was grit between his teeth. 'Caspasian's a British officer with Military Intelligence and General Yuan is a warlord who could, just could, become influential unless he's eradicated. Now how do you think the new man in town, Chiang Kai-shek, is going to thank us when he learns that we let him get away? What's more, Caspasian now knows about our little trading arrangements up and down the river. You don't think he's going to keep that to himself, do you?'

Smith shook his head resolutely. 'Caspasian doesn't matter,' he said. 'His own people have disowned him. They won't believe a word he says. He was supposed to bring Yuan in. Instead he's on the run. He helped him escape. Caspasian's finished. As good as dead.'

'Don't be so sure,' Cameron answered, holding his anger in check with difficulty. 'I've seen that young man and frankly I wouldn't like to be in your shoes when he catches up with you. And he will. It's just a matter of time.'

Wu Yun spat in disgust. 'I've got a score to settle with Caspasian.' He glared at Smith, realising that they were going to be reluctant allies until Caspasian was dead. 'No one can be allowed to cross the Green Gang like he has and get away with it.' He turned back to Cameron. 'I will find him and deal with him. And the General and the girl. And when we find them they won't escape again.'

Cameron stood back and smiled at them, arms folded. 'And just how do you expect to do that?'

'I've got men watching every exit from Shanghai,' Wu Yun said. 'The moment I get word of their location, I'm going to deal with them myself.' He glanced at Smith. 'And he's coming too.'

'So what do you want of me?' Cameron asked.

'Put out descriptions of them to all your officers across the city. Together we will close off every gap through which the rats can run.'

'And if my men see them? I handed them over to you before and look what happened,' Cameron said.

'If your men see them order them to do

absolutely nothing. Under no circumstances must the fugitives be alerted to the fact that we are on to them.' Wu Yun grinned. 'This is between me and Caspasian now. I am going to enjoy it. There will be no more escapes.'

Cameron looked at Smith. 'That should suit you nicely. Once again you've got someone else to do the dirty work for you. I suppose you'll make sure you're there to watch?'

'I wouldn't miss this for the world,' Smith answered.

★ ★ ★

Shanghai station was awash with people trying to get out of the city. The packed crowds were ideal for Caspasian's purposes. General Yuan had agreed to be disguised as Caspasian's manservant, while Lilin passed herself off as Caspasian's wife, complete with a babe in arms. However, wrapped in the bundle was her revolver and the two hand grenades, heavily swaddled in blankets and shawl.

Swinton was ordered to stay close by Caspasian's side. As Caspasian had all his money, he hoped this would be sufficient coercion for Swinton to remain there. In case it was not, his Webley was within easy reach in his pocket and he had told Swinton he would use it.

In the chaos of the station concourse, Caspasian was relieved to note that the few policemen present were concentrating their attention on the Chinese passengers. When he presented himself at the barrier leading on to the relevant platform, the constable gave him little more than a cursory glance before waving him on. He was about to search Yuan when Caspasian barked that he was his manservant and they were in a frightful rush to locate their compartments. Lilin suddenly made a great fuss over her bundle, shrieking that the child was ill and the police constable shoved Yuan roughly past the barrier, turning quickly to the next in line.

Their carriage stood halfway along the platform and as they walked along the side of the train, Caspasian glanced in the other windows to see, as far as he could, whether there was anyone on board who might recognise him.

The sleeper compartments were next door to one another and as Caspasian and Lilin were masquerading as husband and wife, they took one compartment while General Yuan and Swinton took the other. Lilin had discarded the baby charade as soon as she was through the barrier. On the train it would have been impossible to maintain the act without arousing the suspicions of the carriage attendants. Instead, she slipped the bundle into one of the holdalls carried by Caspasian.

Secure in their compartments, they settled down to wait for the train to depart. All of them were tense, even Swinton who was beginning to wonder whether he was now safer with Caspasian than if he had been left behind. After all, he had assisted in the rescue of Yuan and Lilin. The Green Gang were not the sort of people to listen sympathetically to his excuse of having done it under duress. More likely they would kill him out of hand.

Keeping away from the window, Caspasian and Lilin sank on to the seat. Lilin leaned against him and closed her eyes. 'Are we really going to get away from here?' she asked.

Caspasian stroked her hair. 'Yes. And then a ship to Hong Kong or wherever we can manage. We'll have to see what's available in Tientsin.'

She opened her eyes and looked at him. 'And what about us? What are you and I going to do?'

'I don't know,' he answered truthfully. 'I want to stay with you, but I'm not sure that's the best.'

'The best for who?'

'For you and your father. It'll be hard enough for your father to persuade his relatives to take the two of you in, without having me along as well.'

'Then you and I can go somewhere else,' Lilin said.

'Lilin,' he said gently. 'I'm going to be a fugitive after this.'

'Surely you can find someone to explain everything to? Someone higher up than your boss in the consulate?'

'I'm not so sure. The army takes a pretty dim view of someone who disobeys orders. Your father's escape could cause my government some embarrassment with Chiang Kai-shek. And I'm responsible for it.'

'Well, you shouldn't be. The whole affair stinks. The newspapers should be told. It should be made public.'

Caspasian shrugged. 'Maybe. But in a way that would make it even more difficult for me to fit back in. If I publicised the whole affair, they'd hardly thank me for it.'

Lilin brightened. 'Then if you're going to be a fugitive, we'll be fugitives together!'

Caspasian thought about it. 'It wouldn't be much of a life for you.' But she had planted a seed in his mind. He wondered. He could return to Yokohama. His grandfather was dead and the business sold, but he still had contacts there. Perhaps he could make a go of it.

'Well?' Lilin asked eagerly.

'I'll think about it. We'll have to discuss it with your father, of course.'

'Oh, Caspasian!' She threw her arms around his neck and hugged him. 'Think of it. The two of us, living somewhere with no warlords, no Green Gang, right away from the whole wretched lot of them. Just you and me.'

Caspasian did think of it, and the more he did so, the more he warmed to the prospect. Perhaps it was possible to make a complete break with the past. Perhaps he could finally leave behind him the stench of Flanders, the curse of Redoubt Isis and all the many other shell holes he had cringed in for cover. Perhaps he could forget Smith and the institutionalised murder of Private Dobson. Perhaps a man could come back from the dead. Him, John Caspasian.

As the carriage shuddered and the train moved off, Caspasian laid his head back against the seat cushion and dreamed about the future. He slept. But as he slept, other images invaded his dreams. He was convalescing in southern England, but the Home Counties rehabilitation centre was a strange mix of many other places. As he sat in a wheelchair in the green of the ample gardens, he looked across to the mountains of the North West Frontier. Amongst the nurses were Indian orderlies wearing turbans, and Chinese porters in long silk coats and rope-soled shoes.

His wounds from the grenade splinters were healing well, a doctor informed him, but the news of Dobson's execution was like a fresh gash opening. He had written numerous letters but they had all been too late. The deed had been done. The hierarchy was concerned with the latest offensive and the stream of casualties coming back from the front daily. Dobson was yesterday's briefing paper on some minor staff officer's desk. Smith had disappeared, and the other survivors of the redoubt battle had been returned to their units across the length and breadth of the entire British Expeditionary Force. Dobson had saved Caspasian's life, but somehow Smith had convinced the chain of command that he had done it, and that he had rallied the men and held the redoubt until the relief force had broken through the following day. It was one tiny incident in the larger war. No one was interested in it and Caspasian was left to rage in isolation.

Smith. Daniel Smith. Captain Daniel Smith.

The train powered north out of Shanghai, leaving the massacres behind it and steaming on through the countryside and into the deepening night.

21

'Are you sure they're on the train?'

'Of course they are,' Wu Yun snapped. He was getting sick of Smith's presence, hovering at his shoulder like a bad smell. They were standing in the corridor of the rear carriage of the Shanghai-Tientsin overnight express. Behind Wu, a further four of his men loitered, gripping the rail every time the train ran over points, rocking violently from side to side. They had only just made it in time, swinging aboard seconds before departure. The call had come through from Cameron's man on the barrier who had recognised Caspasian and the others but, in line with instructions, had let them pass uninterrupted. Wu and Smith had torn through the streets in Wu's car, one thing on both their minds. Caspasian's death.

They now awaited the return of the attendant in charge of the sleeper compartments. Faced with a threat from one of the most powerful members of the Green Gang, the man had shot away in terror to carry out the task given to him by Wu. To identify the compartments occupied by Caspasian and his companions, and to report back. The moment he returned with the information, Wu would consider how best to proceed. He was not going to underestimate Caspasian a second time. He would plan this assault properly.

They had come equipped for the job. All six of them carried revolvers inside their jackets, and two of Wu's men had Thompson sub-machine-guns as well, bundled into holdalls, each with a fully charged drum magazine attached. Chicago pianos, as they were affectionately known. Wu intended to overwhelm Caspasian with firepower. There would be no escape for him this time.

Wu reached inside his jacket and fingered the grip of his revolver. He was getting impatient. He was just about to send one of his men to check on the carriage attendant when the man appeared at the far end of the corridor and balanced his way towards them, bouncing off the walls as the train hurtled along.

'I've found them,' he said, his voice quavering. He pulled a grubby handkerchief out of his pocket and mopped his brow. His eyes caught sight of the revolver strapped to Wu's chest and he swallowed hard. 'Please,' he mumbled, 'Don't let anyone know it was me who told you.'

Wu fixed him with a pitiless stare. 'You haven't told me anything yet,' he said coldly.

'Carriage H. Compartments ten and eleven.'

'You're sure you did nothing to alert them?' Smith asked, speaking over Wu's shoulder.

'Nothing. I promise you. I checked the records and . . .'

'And you're sure they're in the compartments now?'

'I'm sure. I heard their voices.'

'You didn't look, though?'

'I didn't have to. One of the doors was ajar. I could see they were inside.'

Smith and Wu looked at one another. In spite of himself, Wu could not suppress a smile. He had them. He really had them. He turned to his men. 'You know what you've got to do?'

They nodded, faces blank as slate.

'Let's go then.'

The carriage attendant stood to one side but Wu grabbed him by the scruff of his lapel and propelled him forwards. 'You lead the way. There aren't going to be any mistakes.'

'Please, I . . .'

'Move!'

With the attendant in front, Wu's party moved resolutely through the train. Working through the carriages, they tried to look as inconspicuous as possible. The train was crowded and, although Wu did not care whether any of the other passengers were killed in the cross-fire, he did not want to cause any unnecessary alarm before he reached Caspasian lest it create a mass panic and people get in his way.

They rounded a corner and stepped across the junction plates linking two more carriages. A metal plate on the side wall bore a large green capital H.

'Just along there,' the attendant said, pointing along the corridor and flattening himself against the carriage wall.

Wu stepped past him. 'You stay here,' he commanded gruffly. 'You two,' he said, indicating the men with the holdalls. 'Do it.'

The two men unzipped their bags and pulled out the sub-machine-guns. Metal rasped on metal as the cocking handles were snapped back, loading rounds into the guns' breeches. Safety catches clicked off, fingers were on triggers.

'One carriage each,' Wu commanded.

His men stepped forward, one man to each of the two compartments. They braced their backs against the corridor wall, the muzzles of their Thompsons levelled at the door of the compartment opposite them. The remaining two men took post beside each of the doors, flattening themselves against the compartment's wall. Keeping well out of their comrades' line of fire, they both reached a hand towards the door handles. They looked at Wu, awaiting the signal. He drew his revolver, hearing Smith do the same, and then nodded, a single, almost imperceptible movement of the chin.

The doors were ripped open, revealing the compartments' interiors. Fingers squeezed tight and the guns burst into life. Smoke from the guns quickly filled the narrow confine of the corridor. Wu and Smith recoiled instinctively from the deafening noise and cordite blasting into the two compartments. Each of the firers blazed an entire drum magazine, raking the compartments from left to right and back again, hosing the squat, snub-nosed .45 calibre bullets into every corner of the sleepers. Empty brass cases cascaded in a jangling stream on to the wooden floor and only when the last of them had tumbled smoking from the scorching hot guns and the breech blocks had slammed to rest on empty chambers, smoke from cordite and gun oil billowing from the baking weapons, did Wu and Smith lunge forward to feast their eyes on the handiwork. Revolvers at the ready, they jumped into the doorways, hungry to view the slaughter.

Seats were torn as if clawed by frenzied tigers. Windows and mirrors were smashed into tiny splinters. The walnut panelling was shredded into matchwood. Apart from that, the compartments were empty.

The cry from Wu Yun rose from deep inside him, exploding with ferocious intensity. He turned on the carriage attendant, his revolver hand coming up in the same movement. The muzzle jammed against the attendant's forehead and Wu fired.

★ ★ ★

Taking their seats in the dining car two carriages further along the train, Caspasian held Lilin's chair for her. Across the table from them, Swinton was already studying a menu, running his finger down the list of hors d'oeuvres.

'Just what the doctor ordered,' he mused contentedly. 'Caspasian, old buddy, will you ask the waiter for the wine lis . . .'

The sound of the gunfire, muffled by the distance and the noise of the train, was nevertheless unmistakable. They froze. Swinton's eyes came up to Caspasian's.

'My father!' Lilin said, her knuckles white on the arms of her chair.

General Yuan had paused on the way to the dining car to relieve himself in the lavatory one carriage distant. Without answering her, Caspasian grabbed her by the elbow, snatched up the holdall at his feet and barked at Swinton to go in front of them.

'Where?'

'Along the train, you idiot. Move!'

Lilin held back. 'But my father?'

'He'll have heard it to. He'll be right behind us.'

'But . . . '

'Come on!' He pushed her on. Elsewhere around the dining car, people were looking up from their meals. To them, the sound of the gunfire was less obvious. Only one or two of the men realised that it was not some new noise thundering from the train itself.

Before any panic could set in and block their avenue of escape, Caspasian herded Lilin and Swinton before him down the car, heading for the door at the far end. The maitre d' stood before them at the end of the aisle, a quizzical look on his face.

'Is anything the matter, sir?'

'Nothing at all,' Caspasian answered politely, forcing a relaxed smile. 'Keep our table please. We'll be back in just a moment.'

'Of course, sir,' the man answered, bowing from the waist, head cocked to one side. He stepped neatly out of their way and the three diners swept past him and out of the car, heading for the engine several carriages in front.

Lilin kept turning back to see if her father was following but the pressure on her arm from Caspasian's grip was unrelenting. 'Keep moving,' he hissed.

Hurrying at the head of them, Swinton called back, 'Just where do you think we're going to hide? If you think I'm going to play Douglas Fairbanks and climb up on the roof you've got another think coming.'

'Won't be necessary,' Caspasian snapped. 'We're going to Tientsin. Where the rest of the train is headed is not my concern.'

Several carriages further on, they arrived at the freight carriage, beyond which only the guard's wagon separated them from the engine itself. Coming to the junction point, Caspasian stopped.

'Hold it there,' he called to Swinton. 'Come and give me a hand.' Thrusting Lilin ahead into the freight carriage, he crouched down and tore up the single sheet of linoleum covering the metal floor plate that covered the coupling. 'Grab the other end,' he said to Swinton, tucking his fingers under the edge and heaving. Swinton helped him and together they lifted the plate. It swung to one side on hinges and clanked against the ribbed, heavy-duty canvas curtains separating the join of the two carriages from the outside air. Beneath him, Caspasian saw the coupling and the electricity cables and water pipes linking the carriages. Underneath them, far below in the darkness, the ground shot past in a deafening blur.

The coupling was of iron and fastened in place with immovable bolts.

'Nice try,' Swinton said looking at the bolts, rusted fast. 'What's Plan B?'

'To complete Plan A,' Caspasian answered. He tore open the holdall and dug inside, rummaging around until his hand came out clutching first one and then the other of the two grenades. 'Somehow I just knew these would come in handy.'

'Lilin, your stockings please.'

Lilin stared at him, agog.

'I don't have time to explain . . . '

Turning away from Swinton's smiling gaze, she leaned against a pile of suitcases, lifted her skirt and unfastened the suspenders. As each silk stocking rolled off her leg, she tossed it to Caspasian.

Taking the first stocking, Caspasian made a small hole halfway along it near the knee. Then, he slipped one of the hand grenades into the open top, working it down until it reached the hole. Working the lever and pin through the hole, he made sure that the body of the grenade remained secure inside the tight silk tube. He then repeated the procedure using the second grenade and stocking as Swinton and Lilin watched absorbed.

Lying on his stomach, Caspasian reached down and placed the first grenade on one side of the coupling, holding it firmly in place while he used the two ends of the stocking to wind around both coupling, pipe and cables. Pulling them tight, he tied them in a secure knot. He then did the same with the other grenade, fastening it on the opposite side. With both of them he ensured that the levers and pins were left facing upwards.

'Swinton, give me your belt,' he said. He saw Swinton's mouth open. 'Don't argue!'

Swinton obeyed, stripping his belt from the waist band loops and handing it down. A yard below Caspasian's face, the ground hurtled past. Taking the pointed end of the belt, he slipped it through first one of the grenade pins, and then through the second pin, before passing it back through its own buckle and fastening it, thereby making a strong loop or handle that was threaded through both grenade pins.

He pinched each of the two splayed ends of

the pins flat, easing them half out of their grenade fuses. He tested the whole assembly by pulling very gently upwards on the belt. As he did so, it began to pull the pins clear of the grenades. Protruding from the holes he had made in the stockings, the two levers stood ready to spring clear, igniting the fuses lying in the explosive's core, and detonating the grenades.

'Steady on!' Swinton shouted, whipping up one arm instinctively to shield his face as he saw the pins jerk half out of their sockets.

Caspasian beamed up at him, hefting the belt loop in his fist. 'Makes a fine trigger.' He shuffled back from the opening between the carriages and got to his feet. 'Now we just need something to extend the range, so we can detonate the grenades remotely from behind a wall of luggage.'

They found a large brown leather trunk that the owner had secured with a lashing of cord. Caspasian pulled out a lock-knife from his pocket, cut the cord close by the knot, and pulled it from the trunk. He tied one end round Swinton's belt and laid the cord along the floor of the freight car, leading back to a wall of cases and trunks that Swinton and Lilin were heaping.

'Now all we need is the General,' he said, looking anxiously back down the corridor on the far side of the breach between the carriages. He knew that whoever had fired the shots would proceed methodically along the train to ensure they did not bypass their quarry. Every compartment would have to be checked and while this would take only a second or two each, it had nevertheless given Caspasian, Lilin and Swinton time to pull back and for Caspasian to prepare the grenades. However, he judged their time had almost run out and yet there was still no sign of General Yuan.

'I'm going back for him,' he said abruptly.

Swinton made a grab for his elbow. 'Hang on a minute, buddy. Who's going to detonate that thing?' he said pointing at the coupling linking the two parts of the train.

'Not you for a start. You'd cut the train the moment I'd gone if it was left to you.'

Caspasian handed the end of the rope trigger to Lilin. 'Keep down behind cover.' He eyed Swinton suspiciously. 'Got your gun?' he said to Lilin.

She followed his gaze and understood. 'Yes. Don't worry about him. We'll wait for you.'

'Hey, guys,' Swinton said, insulted. 'What do you think I am?'

'I don't have time to tell you right now. But touch that rope and you're dead,' Caspasian said. And with that, he had gone.

Three carriages from the grenade device, he heard the sound of firing. Sub-machine-guns blasted, followed by the intermittent snaps of a revolver. General Yuan was in trouble. What was more of a problem, Caspasian could hear the screams of the other passengers. If people stampeded away from the gunfire they would swarm towards the freight car and the engine, crossing the grenade device and fouling the severing of the train in two. They had to be driven the other way, even if it meant herding them past the Green Gang or whoever was doing the firing.

Caspasian barged into one of the sleeper compartments and found it empty, the occupants having gone to the dining car. Ripping two woollen blankets from the beds, he stuffed them in the sink and turned on the water taps as full as they would go.

He then searched frantically through the assorted belongings scattered about the compartment until he came upon a cigarette lighter and a container of spare fuel.

Back in the corridor, he rushed back up the carriage in the direction of the engine, and at the join between two carriages, smashed the bottle of fuel against the canvas sides and then lit them. Flames leaped up the canvas, engulfing the corridor.

When he saw that the fire had taken hold

sufficiently to keep people from passing, he headed once again towards the sound of the firing. As he passed each compartment he pounded on the door shouting that there was a fire on the train. Heads poked out of sleeping compartments further along and, seeing the smoke and flame, people rushed headlong back towards the rear of the train.

Advancing behind them like a shepherd driving along his flock, Caspasian kept his right hand in his jacket pocket, the fingers tightly grasping the butt of his revolver.

It was in the dining car that Wu Yun, Smith and the others had caught up with the fleeing General Yuan. Yuan had just been exiting from one end as Wu Yun and his men had entered at the other. A fusillade of shots had blasted into the woodwork and glass around the General who had dived to the floor and pulled out his revolver to return fire. Diners screamed and ducked beneath their tables as the bullets snapped close overhead, smashing wine glasses, plates, punching through seat backs and bursting the ceiling lights.

General Yuan tried to reach the door but whenever he moved out of cover, bullets snapped ever closer. He was just searching frantically for a way out when the door behind him burst open and a stream of panic-stricken passengers poured into the carriage screaming that the train was on fire. Gripped by terror, their minds fixed on escape from the flames, they swept straight past him and were halfway down the carriage before they realised that they had stepped into the middle of something even more dangerous.

Fresh screams erupted, but as people tried to turn round and go back the way they had come, others were still pouring into the carriage from behind, forcing them forward in an irresistible tidal wall of bodies that coursed along the aisle of the dining car and flowed over the crouching figures of Wu Yun, Smith and their men.

'Get out of the way!' Wu Yun screamed hysterically, catching sight of Caspasian over the top of the milling crowd. He raised his revolver over the heads of the fleeing passengers and fired, but Caspasian ducked easily out of sight, hunting around for Yuan.

He found him under one of the tables, grabbed his clothing and pulled. 'Come on. This way,' he shouted.

'But the fire?'

'I've taken care of it.'

Wriggling backwards out of his cover, Yuan and Caspasian crawled towards the door and slipped through it as the passengers streamed out of the far end towards the rear of the train, knocking aside the guns of Wu's men who stared at him helplessly, awaiting instructions as to how they should tackle this wholly unforeseen situation. Beside Wu, Smith was apoplectic with rage, trying to push past the crush of bodies to get a clean shot at his hated enemy whom he knew was escaping.

Once out of the dining car, Caspasian and General Yuan had a clear route all the way back to the fire. As they approached the blaze, Caspasian darted into the compartment where he had left the blankets soaking in the water and pulled them from the sink, water pouring from the saturated wool.

'Here, drape this over yourself,' he said, throwing one of the blankets at General Yuan.

The flames had engulfed the ribbed canvas screens linking the two carriages but had not yet taken hold of the woodwork itself. Caspasian had judged the timing just right. The distance spanned by the fire was no more than a couple of yards deep, enough to present the aspect of a fearsome blaze but not so much as to make it impassable by people suitably covered with improvised protective clothing.

He guided Yuan to the edge of the fire and then, when he saw that he was ready, thrust him through it. With a cry the General disappeared from view.

Next, Caspasian gathered himself, pulled the blanket tight around his face, and leapt into the flames, bounding across the fiery chasm where the two carriages joined. As he did so, bullets spat and hissed at his feet and elbows, signalling the arrival of his pursuers. He had seen who they were and, in spite of his desire to see Smith dead, he had no great wish to confront the bull and his henchmen.

With three carriages to go, Caspasian hoped the fire would delay the Green Gang team. Together with Yuan, he shed his blanket and ran shakily down the length of the first carriage, rebounding off the train's sides as the engine driver, oblivious of the happenings on the train, powered on through the night.

They reached the end of the carriage, ran through the next one, and entered the third and final carriage. At the far end, the corridor turned sharp left, obscuring the grenade device rigged to the iron couplings.

'Almost there,' Caspasian said, one hand between Yuan's shoulders shoving him forward. 'It's . . . '

The explosion at the far end of the carriage tore the insubstantial wooden panelling asunder. Caspasian and Yuan were flung to the ground by the blast of debris that funnelled down the length of the carriage.

'What the . . . ?' Caspasian looked up through the clearing smoke. A sudden rush of cold air told him that the sides of the carriages had been breached. The slim walls that had hidden the couplings from sight had vanished and he could see straight across the gap between his carriage and the luggage car where Swinton and Lilin were hiding behind a wall of cases. The grenades had been detonated. The couplings were severed.

'Come on!' Caspasian shouted. He grabbed his dazed companion by the scruff of the neck and hauled him to his feet, dragging him behind him. Ahead of him, he could see the gap between the two carriages widening, the luggage car starting to pull away from the rest of the train which was now being carried along by nothing more than its own momentum.

They were almost at the breach when shots rang out from behind them. Yuan instinctively veered towards cover but Caspasian snatched him and thrust him forward. He knew there was no time now to hide. If they failed to cross the breach before the engine pulled clear then they would be dead anyway. It was all or nothing.

A voice cried out from in front of them and Caspasian looked up to see Lilin struggling with Swinton. She slapped him across the face and for a second he reeled backwards, losing balance as the train sped on. Caspasian reached the widening gap and without pausing pushed Yuan across. The General leapt, hands grappling for the far side. He landed, stumbled and fell. But he was across.

'He snatched the rope from me,' Lilin screamed at Caspasian. 'Jump!'

Caspasian launched himself across the intervening space between the carriages. The grenades, prematurely detonated by Swinton, had done their job exactly as Caspasian had intended. Pins tugged free by the rope and belt assembly, they had exploded in unison, each one smashing asunder the iron coupling, and ripping apart the pipes and cables.

He landed badly, going down hard on his knees. But he was up in a second, his temper flaring, eyes searching for Swinton. He saw him, moving in fast, Lilin's revolver in his fist. The barrel was coming into an aim, Swinton's finger tightening on the trigger.

'Behind you!' The warning shout from General Yuan was all that was needed. While Swinton glanced up at the figures of Wu Yun and Smith looming in the far doorway on the other side of the breach, Caspasian acted. He shot forward, knocking aside Swinton's gun as he closed in and seized him by the shoulders of his jacket. With one convulsive movement, he swung the big American round, clasping him tightly and presenting his back to his new assailants as a shield. Bullets from the guns of Smith and Wu Yun slammed into Swinton's back. Caspasian felt them hammering home. Swinton's eyes widened and he looked for all the world as if he was smiling. His mouth opened to speak.

'Sorry, old buddy. Heard the shots. Didn't think you'd make it. Couldn't risk . . . '

A trickle of blood burst across his tongue and down his chin. His eyes rolled up into his head and he slumped in Caspasian's grasp, dead.

There was a blur of movement and the next moment someone powered into Caspasian, knocking him and Swinton's lifeless body to the floor. Before Caspasian could recover a fist slammed into the side of his head. He could hear laboured breath. There was a smell of cordite, and he realised that the bull had joined him on his side of the breach.

He twisted round, pushing Swinton to one side and brought up his right arm in a block as he did so. It caught a second punch in mid-stream, sweeping it aside. Behind the incoming fist Caspasian saw the blazing eyes of Wu Yun, boring into him with hatred. As Wu bore down onto him, Caspasian rolled on to his back, drew his knees up to his chest and kicked out. Wu grunted as the air was knocked from his lungs. Over Wu's shoulder, Caspasian saw another figure leap through the doorway. Only just making it across the breach, Smith grabbed hold of the handles flanking the luggage car's entrance and pulled himself to safety. Behind him, as the main body of the train began to slow, the gap had finally reached the point where no one else would be able to follow. Wu's men tottered uncertainly in the far doorway, the muzzles of their guns seeking a clear shot at their enemies. One of the men pushed forward, attempting to leap. Jostled from behind, he mistimed it and fell screaming on to the rails below. His comrades pulled back from the abyss. It would now be up to their boss and the Englishman Smith to deal with the fugitives on their own.

Caspasian rolled away from the bull and sprang to his feet. In jumping, the bull had lost his gun. Smith took a step forward but General Yuan and Lilin closed on him and the three of them went down in a mess of flailing fists and feet. Caspasian had to fight the temptation to help Lilin. He knew that he could not even afford to glance in her direction. The bull was in front of him and death was in his eyes.

Wu surged forward with a flurry of attacking blows, seeking to overwhelm Caspasian with the sheer force of his assault. Backing against the wall of cases, Caspasian responded with lightning blocks and parries, all of them coming automatically. They had been drummed into him since his boyhood training in the gym in Yokohama all those years ago. As on many previous occasions, they saved his life.

Struggling against the violent rocking motion of the carriage, neither man dared risk a kick. Each of them had locked their leg muscles, welding them to the floor in the firmest stance possible. With knees slightly bent, Caspasian tensed his abdomen, imagining himself as part of the carriage, moving with it while his upper body weaved this way and that, dodging and blocking Wu's punches.

Wu was fighting to keep his breath steady. He was amazed that nothing he threw at the Englishman was managing to get through. It was as though he was trying to snatch at an apparition, or grasp trickling sand. His only consolation was that his blows were keeping his opponent fully occupied and therefore unable to retaliate in kind, although he knew he would be unable to keep it up forever. He could already feel his arms tiring.

In an effort to break the deadlock Wu took a step backwards, seeking a new opening. The very moment he did it he realised he had made a mistake. In pausing, if only for a fraction of a second, he had offered Caspasian an opportunity for attack and before he knew what was happening, the tall Englishman was sweeping forward. It was as if Caspasian was on castors. His feet glided smoothly across the rocking floor of the carriage, hips and legs locked into a firm but mobile stance. His fists powered into Wu in a devastating series of tsuki punches, each one so fast it was all Wu could manage to deflect them. Finally Caspasian feinted to Wu's chin, and then fired in a lethal yubi hasami blow, the web of his right hand between thumb and forefinger finding the bull's windpipe. Caspasian felt the bull's Adam's apple buckle. But Wu was unbelievably fast and even as the blow was making contact, Wu was twisting out of range.

Nevertheless, the jab had made his eyes stream with water and given Caspasian the gap he needed. He had the bull on the defensive now and he was not going to let the opportunity slip away. He punched gedan, low down at belt level, then, with the other fist, jodan, high at the bull's face, and other blows ranged at every point in between. His hands opened and closed between blows, now firing in as a solid seiken fist and now as an open shuto knife-hand cut, a tettsui hammer blow, a nukite finger-tip thrust. He aimed at the bull's abdomen, at his solar plexus, his sternum, throat, collar bone and eyes. Then, with one ferocious kiai shout straight in Wu's face, Caspasian launched himself bodily forward, dropping down and to the left side, sliding in beneath a counter punch from Wu, and attacking with a powerful empi elbow strike to the ribcage. It connected, and with Caspasian's full force as he twisted his hips and locked his upper body into the strike. Wu grunted, and beyond that, Caspasian felt the telltale crack of ribs. He had him.

As Wu struggled to regain his stance, focusing all his efforts on blocking yet more attacks from Caspasian's fists, he missed the footsweep. It slammed into his ankle and he felt himself going down. Knowing what would come next, the drop punch to the face, Wu tried to roll away from it. But Caspasian was on top of him, blows raining down. In desperation Wu brought his arms up in front of him trying to shield himself from the continuous assault.

Seeing his chance, Caspasian went for the kill. Ignoring Wu's well-protected torso, he punched him low in the groin. As anticipated,

Wu doubled, hands shooting down instinctively to cover himself. Caspasian, positioned in readiness above him, drew back his fist to strike.

'Hold it!'

The sound of Smith's voice froze Caspasian on the spot.

'One move and your girl dies.'

Caspasian raised his eyes. Smith was standing with his back to the open doorway. General Yuan lay at his feet, barely moving, on the brink of unconsciousness. Clasped in Smith's grasp, Lilin struggled for breath. Smith's forearm was across her throat, choking her. In his other fist, a revolver pressed against her temple.

'Move away from the Chinaman,' Smith commanded. His breathing was coming in gasps. Winded from the struggle he had to lean against the doorframe. Behind him, the open countryside was a churning black blur. The wind tore through the opening, deafening and wild.

Caspasian slowly straightened up, stepping away from the bull who groaned with pain. Smith looked down at him, face blank.

Wu struggled to sit up, easing on to his side, hands on the floor and pushing himself to his feet. 'Leave him to me,' he spat through bloodied lips, his eyes livid with pain and hatred. He turned to Caspasian. 'He's mine. I'll kill . . . '

The shot from Smith's gun roared in the confined space of the carriage. The bull staggered. His hands clutched at his chest and he stared at Smith in wonderment as the gun fired again. The second bullet hit him in the face. He spun away from Caspasian, dead.

Caspasian stared at Smith as he swung the smoking muzzle to point directly at Caspasian's chest. 'You don't think I'd let anyone kill you but me, do you? Besides, he'd served his purpose. It's you I want.'

Caspasian looked at Lilin. She was choking but he knew that Smith would not let her die so long as he needed her as a shield. He gauged the distance between himself and Smith. It was too far. If he had felt there was the slightest chance of reaching Smith before he could discharge the gun in his fist, Caspasian would have tried it. He would do anything to save Lilin. But he knew it would be impossible. The expanse of floorboard between himself and Smith might as well have been a hundred yards. In the face of the smoking gun on the far side of the carriage, all of Caspasian's skill evaporated, leaving him completely at the mercy of Smith.

'OK then, Smith. What do you want? Me?

Here I am. Let the girl and her father go.'

Smith smiled, his eyes pure evil. 'If you only knew how I've longed for this moment. The great John Caspasian at my mercy. You can't really believe I'd let the girl go, can you?' He tightened his forearm across her throat. Caspasian took a step forward as Lilin gasped. The second he moved, the muzzle was pressed against Lilin's temple.

'Go on,' Smith taunted. 'Try me. I can blow her brains out and still have bullets enough for you.'

'Are you sure about that?' Caspasian said.

There was a flash of doubt across Smith's face. 'Nice try. But I know you won't risk her life.'

And Caspasian knew he was right. Even if there was only one bullet left in the gun he would do nothing to risk it being fired at Lilin.

'You know what I hate most about you, Caspasian?' Smith said. 'You think you're so goddamned perfect.'

'No. What you hate most is yourself Smith,' Caspasian answered evenly. 'You can't accept the fact that you betrayed everyone in Redoubt Isis by your cowardice, and then framed Dobson for it and had him shot. You hate yourself for that. But no one can live with that kind of hatred. So you go around throwing your hate at everyone you come across. Making everyone else suffer for your failings except the person who should. You.'

'Shut up!' Smith screamed. 'Do you hear me? Shut up!'

As he had been speaking, Caspasian had seen Lilin looking at him. She looked into his eyes. In spite of the arm pressing against her windpipe, she smiled at him. Caspasian was puzzled. Then, as Smith screamed at him, and raised his gun hand, removing the muzzle from Lilin's temple and aiming it instead at Caspasian, with a bolt of sheer terror, Caspasian realised why he had been unsettled by Lilin's smile. She had been saying goodbye.

As Smith squeezed the trigger, his gun aimed straight at Caspasian's heart, Lilin drove herself backwards into her captor, projecting the two of them back through the gaping doorway and out into the rocketing night.

The second he had realised what she intended, Caspasian had started towards her, one hand reaching out. Although everything happened with appalling slowness there was a terrible inevitability about it. Caspasian shouted to her, his words lost in the blast of air through the approaching doorway. Smith's expression turned from hatred to alarm as he was thrown backwards off balance. The gun fired, but the bullet slashed harmlessly past Caspasian's face. Smith's expression was still turning into something else as he disappeared into the black void, something beyond mere alarm, beyond fear, something that reminded Caspasian of Redoubt Isis, all those years ago.

'Lilin!' Caspasian shot towards the doorway, almost going out of it himself. With one hand he grabbed hold of the railings flanking the door frame. The other he thrust into black space, the taut fingers wide and grasping, to snatch Lilin back from the abyss. Caspasian's hand locked around hers, crushing it in a grip that only death or success would make him release. His shoulder muscles screamed for mercy as Lilin swung below him. He felt as if he was wrestling with the night itself, embodying some invisible and malevolent force of nature that sought to tear Lilin away from him.

At Caspasian's feet, General Yuan crawled towards the edge and stretched out his hand. With all his concentration, Caspasian focused his strength into his arm, contracting the muscles and slowly drawing Lilin back towards him, reclaiming her. As she neared the carriage door, her father lunged at her and caught her other hand. Together,

Caspasian and General Yuan pulled Lilin inch by painful inch back into the freight car until all three of them lay exhausted on the floor.

Unable to speak, Caspasian clutched Lilin to him. He looked out beyond her, staring into the churning darkness into which Daniel Smith had disappeared. He felt as if something long unfinished had finally been completed. A circle had been closed. A debt repaid. A wrong avenged.

Epilogue

Tientsin was like a wasp's nest that had been poked with a stick. With Chiang Kai-shek's army progressing ever further north, people had flocked there from Peking, a hundred or more miles away, as well as from other cities throughout northern China to try and secure a passage out of the war-torn country. Shipping lines and booking agents were doing a roaring trade, offering berths at hugely inflated prices to anyone desperate enough and rich enough to pay.

'Are you sure this is going to work?' General Yuan asked as they made their way through the throng of people outside the station. 'We've got Swinton's money but I doubt if even that will be enough.'

'It will where I'm going,' Caspasian answered, his broad shoulders clearing a path for the three of them. Several minutes later they turned down an alley and found themselves standing outside a door above which a notice board read, 'Wah Fu Shipping: Freight and Passenger Bookings'.

General Yuan and Lilin looked doubtfully at one another. Caspasian smiled and went in. All three were still accustoming themselves to the gloom when they heard the sound of shuffling feet. A curtain shutting off the back of the office flicked aside and a small Chinese man peered suspiciously out at them.

He opened his mouth to speak but froze. He peered again more closely at Caspasian and his face slowly opened into a broad smile.

'It isn't? Young master John.' He chuckled merrily as he came forward and shook Caspasian's hand in both of his.

'Hello, old friend,' Caspasian said, clapping him on the back with his free hand. 'It's been a long time.'

'What, it must be all of fifteen years,' the old Chinaman marvelled. He turned to General Yuan and eyed him shrewdly. Then Lilin. He looked back at Caspasian, serious. 'I was so sorry to hear of your grandfather's death. Our transactions over the years were business but I flatter myself that he thought of me as more than just a business associate.'

'It's not flattery at all, Mr Wah. My grandfather always said you were his most trustworthy contact.'

Mr Wah laughed, obviously delighted. He wagged a finger. 'He still drove a hard bargain, mind.' He sighed, remembering. 'Ah, it was all so long ago. We were still ruled by an imperial dynasty in those days. Since then . . . ' he shrugged, leaving the noise of the chaos outside to tell the rest of the story for him.

Brightening, he said, 'But how can I help the grandson of my old friend?' Once again he looked at Caspasian's companions, nodding his head knowingly. 'Can it be that you need to get out of the country?'

Caspasian nodded. 'Can you help us?'

Mr Wah went across to some ledgers. Beside them, hanging on a notice board suspended from the wall, a chart listed the handwritten names of several vessels. He considered it carefully. 'I have nothing going to Yokohama I'm afraid, but . . . '

'What about Hong Kong?' General Yuan cut in.

'Yes. There is one vessel,' Mr Wah said, running his finger down the list until he reached the name he was looking for. 'The *Ocean Pride*. Out of Macao. It is leaving tomorrow morning.' He shook his head doubtfully. 'I will do my best but . . . '

'Whatever you can do, Mr Wah,' Lilin pleaded.

'How many berths will you be needing?'

'Three,' Caspasian said.

Lilin moved beside him and placed her hand on his arm. Mr Wah looked at them and smiled. 'I will see what I can do. I know the Captain. He owes me a favour.'

They took rooms at the Imperial Hotel for the night. Mr Wah had agreed to deliver the tickets to them in person at first light the following morning. Sitting together at dinner in the restaurant that evening, Caspasian, General Yuan and Lilin looked at the other guests. The restaurant was full of people like themselves, all in search of a way out. There were families, young couples and old people, but all sharing the same haggard look of those on the threshold of exile. Before all of them the future waited full of uncertainties.

In subdued mood, they retired to their rooms after supper. General Yuan went quickly, saying a brief goodnight, no longer interested whether his daughter spend the night alone or with Caspasian. Too much had happened for such niceties any longer to hold relevance for him. Instead, he smiled wearily and walked away along the corridor.

However, recognising that Lilin too was exhausted Caspasian led her to her room and, after opening the door for her, kissed her goodnight, saying that he would see her in the morning. She paused, reluctant to let him go, but a huge yawn escaped from her and they both laughed.

'There'll be plenty of time on the ship,' Caspasian said.

'And in Hong Kong,' Lilin added. With one more kiss, she slipped into her room and the door closed.

Caspasian slept a deep and dreamless sleep. For once there were no images of redoubts or trenches, and he awoke feeling more relaxed and refreshed than he could remember doing for a very long time.

He lay there staring up at the ceiling, hardly caring to stir. It was only the sound of Mr Wah's familiar shuffling steps in the corridor outside and the gentle knock on his door that took Caspasian reluctantly from his bed. The dawn had barely broken and only the greyest of lights could be glimpsed through the curtains. He opened the door. 'Mr Wah, you're even earlier than . . . '

When he later thought back to that moment, Caspasian would still be baffled why he had failed to hear the other noises that must have accompanied the military police escort that crowded around Colonel Preston and Chief Inspector Cameron, revolvers drawn and levelled at his bare chest.

'Get dressed, Caspasian,' Preston snapped, his eyes wary for attack. 'And don't try anything stupid. You might once have been a British officer but frankly, right now you'd be better off dead. It would cause us all a lot less embarrassment that way.'

Caspasian caught his breath. His heart was pounding and his one thought was for Lilin.

Preston read his mind. 'The girl and her father have gone.'

At this Caspasian took a step forward. Instantly half a dozen hammers clicked back, fingers poised on triggers. Preston moved deftly out of the line of fire.

'Now then, laddie,' Cameron said, trying to calm the situation. 'It's not what you think. They've not been harmed. Yet.'

Caspasian stared at him coldly. 'No thanks to you, I dare say.'

'I've got nothing against the old man.'

'Then why did you hand him over to the Green Gang to be murdered?'

'That was in Shanghai,' Cameron answered, his voice smooth as silk. Caspasian wanted nothing more than to kill him, but he had to find out what had happened to Lilin. 'Different rules apply here,' Cameron continued. 'Chiang Kai-shek will have forgotten about him in a few weeks time, if he even bothered about him before. Things move on very quickly in China. Chiang's getting enough blood and severed heads even for him at the moment. General Yuan's barely even big enough to be small fry.'

'So where is he?' Caspasian asked, trying to mask his desperation.

'Exactly where you planned for him to be. Right now he and his daughter are on the *Ocean Pride* bound for Hong Kong.'

For the first time Caspasian stared past the big westerners to where Mr Wah stood miserably under close guard behind them. His eyes met Caspasian's. He was weeping. 'Forgive me, Master John. They came in the night and took me. They had . . . '

Cameron silenced the small Chinaman with contempt. 'Your friend knew nothing of all this. We tracked you to the hotel last night and found out about your meeting with Mr Wah.'

'But the ship?'

'It sailed early on my orders,' Colonel Preston said. 'General Yuan and his daughter were removed two hours ago under close arrest.'

Caspasian was thunderstruck. 'You're lying. If you've killed them I'll . . . '

'You'll what?' Colonel Preston laughed, his expression lacking the confidence he was trying hard to muster. 'In any case, General Yuan will be more use to us in Hong Kong. You never know when a tame warlord might come in handy.'

Now it was Caspasian's turn to laugh.

'Haven't you learned anything, Preston? The General's a man of principle. He won't be used by you or any of your lickspittles in Hong Kong.'

Colonel Preston smiled. 'Oh, won't he? Not even to save all the people under his control who are still stuck in China?' His smile broadened into a grin of the purest self-satisfaction. 'You're wrong, Caspasian, but for exactly the reason you yourself have cited. General Yuan will indeed serve the interests of my lickspittles, as you term His Majesty's servants, and exactly because he is a man of principle.'

He paused for effect, none of which was lost on Caspasian. 'And so will his daughter.'

Caspasian blinked. He felt as if he had been punched in the midriff. The effect was doubly hard to withstand because he knew that Preston was one hundred per cent correct. If Preston had made promises and given guarantees that Yuan's province and everyone living there would be left intact so long as Yuan himself stayed in Hong Kong under British protection, Yuan would be forced to accept, however unwillingly. And Lilin would subjugate her own longings for the same noble end.

'How can you guarantee anything?' Caspasian said, his head reeling. 'Chiang could murder every one of Yuan's men and their families tomorrow and there's not a damned thing you or this corrupt copper could do about it.'

'True, but now he's come in from the revolutionary cold, Chiang needs western support. Meanwhile, we will keep Yuan on ice, our own tame warlord in case there is ever a need to field an alternative to Chiang. He might not be in Chiang's league, but from little acorns, we could always try to grow an oak.'

Caspasian had moved back into his room. He slumped down on to the bed. All sense of relaxation had gone. He suddenly felt very tired. The military police moved in after him, standing in a half circle, revolvers still poised.

'All right, Preston. So you've got Yuan and the girl. Let me join them.'

At this Preston laughed out loud. 'You must be joking! You, Captain Caspasian, will be lucky to escape a prison sentence. If you think I'm simply going to let you get on the next ship to Hong Kong and cause chaos and confusion there too, you've got another think coming.'

'What then?' Caspasian asked sarcastically. 'A court-martial? That would be interesting, wouldn't it? I wonder how the court would react to the story of opium smuggling by an officer of the Shanghai Municipal Police.'

'I know nothing about that,' Preston snapped.

'And he couldn't prove a thing in any case,' Cameron said to him.

'What exactly am I supposed to have done?'

Preston gaped at him amazed. 'What have you . . . ?' he stammered.

Caspasian straightened his back and planted his fists defiantly on his knees. 'Yes, come on. Tell me.'

'Where the fuck would you like me to start?'

'Well the way I see it, I overthrow an ally who was rotten to the core, but produced a much more viable alternative. In most peoples' books that would be called using one's initiative.'

'And is it using your initiative to commandeer an armoured car, cause mayhem throughout Shanghai, blow up a perfectly good train and disobey order after order after order? And I haven't even started on the trail of bodies you've strewn in your wake across the length and breadth of China!'

Caspasian rose to his feet, ignoring the warning revolver muzzles. 'Cameron delivered Yuan and his daughter to be murdered by the Green Gang, for God's sake! What was I supposed to do?'

'You were supposed to fucking well act like a British officer and obey orders!' Preston bawled.

'Let them be killed?' Caspasian shouted back.

'Yes! If that's what it takes. We're all just small parts of a much greater whole. If you can't see that then you don't deserve to be an officer. You might not always like what you have to do, but if every little cog in the machine started to think for itself, then the whole damned edifice would come tumbling down!'

'And not a moment too soon, if it means abandoning a man of honour and a girl to the likes of the Green Gang murderers!'

For a few moments, Preston and Caspasian faced each other, the military police standing like Dobermans on a leash.

'We're wasting time,' Preston said eventually. 'I don't have to justify myself to you or to anyone else. It's not going near a court-martial or any other kind of court. I was acting under orders. Any accusations you have against Chief Inspector Cameron are your own affair.' He glanced at Cameron who stood smiling easily in the doorway. 'Although frankly, I wouldn't advise you to try it. I don't fancy your chances.'

'So what now?' Caspasian asked.

Preston waved a hand at Mr Wah who came forward and offered him an envelope.

'There is another vessel leaving in three hours' time. You're going to be on it.' He stared at Caspasian. 'And don't even dream of going anywhere near Hong Kong. If you do you will be arrested the moment you set foot on land. In any case, General Yuan and his daughter will be living at an undisclosed address.'

Caspasian laughed. 'Do you really think you can keep me away from them?'

Preston opened the envelope and took out a ticket. He studied it and smiled. 'I'm not going to have to. Someone else is going to have that pleasure.'

He handed over the ticket. Caspasian looked at it. It was for a tramp steamer called the *Bonne Ideé*, and it was bound for Marseilles.

'We have come to an arrangement with our French allies. You will remain under close arrest until the ship sails, and when it does, you will spend the voyage in the brig.' He smiled, enjoying the moment.

Caspasian sneered. 'So what's it to be? The Foreign Legion? That's a bit theatrical, don't you think?'

'Don't tempt me, Caspasian. I'd love nothing more. En route to Marseilles you will disembark at Port Said.' He grinned maliciously. 'They've got a little job for you in Cairo. Cairo or thereabouts. Bon voyage.'

* * *

The Chinese peasant farmer came across the body of the westerner halfway through the morning. Instantly he was terrified. In times such as these it was likely someone would accuse him of the murder. He straightened up and scanned the horizon warily. There was no one to be seen. Reassured, he stooped again to inspect his discovery, parting the tall bulrushes that filled the deep ditches on either side of the Shanghai to Tientsin railway tracks. With his fear temporarily abated, the thought of plunder crept in at its heels like a rat from the sewers.

The corpse's face was bruised but the markings seemed largely to have been inflicted at some earlier period because they were partially healed. There was a lot of blood around the back of the skull but the farmer did not like to probe too deeply lest he soil his hands with the fellow's brains. He could not see any but he suspected that if he were to roll the body over they would spill out. He had seen it happen before and once was enough.

Instead, he slipped a hand inside the body's jacket. With a surge of hope and greed, his fingers touched leather. His hand closed upon it. It was a wallet. And fat, by the feel of it.

Pulling it out, he opened it and his eyes bulged in his head at the sight of so much money. He had never seen so many bank notes in his life. Stuffing it hurriedly in his pocket, he returned to his search. There was a good watch and the farmer unfastened the leather strap, shook it until he heard the mechanism working, and placed that in his pocket too.

Working methodically across the corpse, he produced further treasures. There were some papers that he was unable to read, a handful of loose change, a bunch of five keys and a couple of boiled sweets. To his consternation, in one of the trouser pockets he found three bullets, small and snub-nosed. In terror he tossed them away, hearing them plop harmlessly in the water pooling in the bottom of the ditch.

When he was satisfied that he had taken everything the body's clothing possessed, he moved aside and sat down with his back to the poor unfortunate man, and set about contemplating his finds. The wallet held his greatest interest and he fingered through the notes again and again, chuckling at his good fortune.

He was so rapt with his windfall that he completely failed to notice the movement at his back. The first thing to catch his attention was the foul-smelling breath at his shoulder. The farmer spun round, his whole body shaking with terror. The dead man was standing over him. One eye was almost closed from bruising, and a fresh flow of blood from the unseen head wound mingled with the dried crusts matting his hair.

'I think you'll find that's mine,' a voice said, as if issuing from the grave.

The farmer shot to his feet but in his haste, entangled his feet in the rushes and fell face down. As he tried to rise, the man was upon him, one knee in the middle of the farmer's back, hands clasping beneath his chin. With disinterested slowness, the man pulled back the farmer's head until the neck snapped and broke.

As the farmer crumpled lifeless, the westerner sat down beside him, retrieving his belongings one by one. He unwrapped one of the boiled sweets and popped it in his mouth. It was strawberry flavour and the sugar sent a bolt of fresh energy to his aching, bruised and battered limbs.

When he felt able, he eased himself into an upright position and tested himself for balance. He was hardly going to do the hundred yard sprint, but he could just about walk. Like the farmer, he decided not to explore the head wound too closely for fear of what he might find. Best get to civilisation before tackling that.

Civilisation. The man smiled bitterly. That was a joke. There was no such thing anywhere in the whole godforsaken country of China. It was time for him to be moving on. There would always be plenty of places for a man of his talents. But one thing was for certain. Wherever he went he had a debt to settle. Along with the consciousness, had come a return of hatred and loathing. Oddly, he remembered his enemy's name before his own. Caspasian. That was the bastard he was going to get.

With this one driving thought in his mind, Daniel Smith set off along the tracks, walking shakily in the direction of Tientsin.

★ ★ ★

It was a fortnight before Caspasian was allowed up on deck. With the guards at his side, he emerged into the daylight, screwing his eyelids tight against the unaccustomed

572

glare of the sun. He walked unsteadily to the rails and gripped them with both hands. With head back, he drew in the salt air, rinsing his lungs of the stench of the cell. As his vision cleared, he glanced at his guards. They were slobs. In a second he could have had them both over the side. But to what purpose? In front of him, the Indian Ocean stretched into the curve of the distant horizon, the seam joining sea and sky blurred in the harsh light. Already the Strait of Malacca and the South China Sea lay far behind him, and with them, Hong Kong and China. Lilin had been taken from him. But, if Preston and Cameron had told the truth, at least she was alive. And if she was alive, then Caspasian could find her. One day. For now, he had to survive.

He had had plenty of time to reflect on what Preston had said. They had spoken further, while Caspasian was waiting for the French ship to get up steam. Caspasian was an embarrassment to His Majesty's government. He was to be silenced. He did not doubt that Cameron had proposed a more permanent solution to the problem, but, whether due to Preston's intervention or to other factors beyond Caspasian's knowledge, he had been spared a bullet in the back of the head or a knife thrust between the ribs.

Caspasian had racked his brains, trying to

think of someone to whom he might appeal for help. Even the few names he could produce were inaccessible to him in his present state. They would remain so for some time to come, assuming he continued on his present course. But even if any of them were able to secure his release, what then? Preston had said what awaited him if he were to make his way to Hong Kong. Even if he managed to evade capture and enter the colony in secret, and even if he were able to track down Lilin when he got there, what would the two of them be able to do? Preston had said that her father's followers were to be held hostage. Their continued safety within a China dominated by the new regime was to be dependent on General Yuan's continued cooperation with the British authorities. Lilin was an integral part of that cooperation. Caspasian knew how she would choose. Though it would tear her apart, and though she would suffer as much as he was now suffering, he knew that Lilin would elect to remain with her father, for the sake of his followers in China. What was more, Caspasian realised that it would be wrong of him to face her with such a choice.

He leaned his elbows on the railings and buried his face in his hands. He had not been allowed to shave for three days and the stubble on his cheeks pricked the flesh of his palms. He rubbed the balls of his eyes with his thumbs until stars jumped in the darkness before him. The sound of the waves filled his head and beneath his feet he could feel the gentle rise and fall of the ocean, as if he was standing on the breast of a slumbering colossus. It reminded him of when he was a boy, sailing the seas in his grandfather's service. He had felt it then, the same deeply breathing giant. Far from unsettling him, it was an image of the world that had comforted the young Caspasian. Its forces, no longer the blind collision of atoms, had become spirits. And whether destructive or gentle, such a world was not indifferent to his passing. To a youth on the brink of adult life that had been important.

Now, standing on the deck of the *Bonne Idée*, surging westwards across the Indian Ocean, Caspasian was surprised to find himself recalling the feel of that hopeful expectation. Heavily abraded by the years, it was nevertheless present and it heartened him. Eyes closed, he raised his face and let the salt wind drum on his skin. He felt like a crusader returned to a bankrupt estate, discovering in the deepest cellar, a single remaining treasure, the wherewithal to rebuild his fortunes and seek a new course.

For Caspasian, the remnants of his old hopeful expectation would be his seed corn.

He opened his eyes and turned to his guards. They regarded him warily, hands resting on the pistols stuffed in their belts. Caspasian smiled. An open, powerful smile. For the briefest of moments he considered vaulting over the railings and diving down into the sea. It would be interesting to see whether the captain would bother to stop the ship for him. And if not, what then? To the north lay Ceylon with its jungle green hills. In his present frame of mind Caspasian reckoned that he might just be able to make it.

One of the guards, alert to his sudden mood of defiance, jerked his head in the direction of the cell. Caspasian drew in one more breath, deep and bracing, his eyes sparkling with mischief, his mind poised on the cusp of decision.

He let it out, let it go. For now.